Praise for M...
Pigs ...

"*Pigs Don't Fly* is another beautiful novel. . . . It is compelling; I got caught reading it late at night, and lost sleep, because it did what fiction seldom does: held my attention beyond sleep."   —**Piers Anthony**

"Funny, moving and always unpredictable, Brown's (*The Unlikely Ones*) incredible journey . . . is a find."
—*Publishers Weekly*

"It's about friends and love and seeing things as they really are and what makes a person valuable. And Brown manages it without being preachy. . . . *Pigs Don't Fly* is a humorous, romantic, suspenseful novel."   —*Starlog*

". . . a deliciously unconventional quest story. . . ."
—Faren Miller, *Locus*

"This is a captivating fantasy, with a lovable cast of characters traveling through a richly described medieval countryside. Girls, especially, will enjoy Summer and the animals using their wits and courage to overcome every obstacle. . . ."   —*VOYA*

"Brown has written a delightful light novel. . . . Readers will enjoy the various mishaps the group deals with, the humor Brown has instilled, and the satisfactory conclusion."   —*Kliatt*

". . . the long-awaited second fantasy adventure by Mary Brown. . . . Don't miss this brilliantly conceived, superbly crafted and eminently beguiling fantasy foray."
—Melinda Helfer, *Romantic Times*

Books in this Series

MASTER OF MANY TREASURES

MARY BROWN

MASTER OF MANY TREASURES

A Baen Books Original

Baen Publishing Enterprises
P.O. Box 1403
Riverdale, N.Y. 10471

ISBN: 0-671-87693-7

Cover art by Darrell K. Sweet

First printing, November 1995

Distributed by SIMON & SCHUSTER
1230 Avenue of the Americas
New York, N.Y. 10020

Printed in the United States of America

For my husband
Peter
with my love.
Thanks for
everything!

Acknowledgements

My thanks to the Baen team—
especially Jim, my editor Toni,
and Hank—for their many
extra kindnesses.
Thanks again to Barry and
Margaret Shaw for helping us
with Christopher.
Special thanks to my friend
Ingrid von Essen for her expert
research—and for the beer-
bottle label!
Sam: I know how you hate all
pens, paper, typewriters and
word processors, so I'll try
and rearrange my schedule
next time! Love you . . .

PROLOGUE

It was a difficult journey.

Once in the air he had thought the flight would be easy; after all, he would be flying higher than all but the largest raptors. The thermals, currents of air, clouds, and winds provided his highways, hills and vales, and the skyscape freed him from the pedestrian pace of those on the earth beneath. In that other skin he had once worn ten or fifteen miles a day had been enough, but now he could easily manage a hundred in one stint, though he usually cut this by half. After all, there was no hurry.

No problems with the route, either. Like all of his kind the ways of the air were etched into his brain as a birthright, a primitive race memory he shared with birds, fishes and some of the foraging mammals.

At first the wind aided him on his way and the sun shone kindly at dawning and dusk, for he preferred to return to land during the day for food and rest, ready for the guidance of the stars at night. The sleeping earth rolled away beneath his claws, and his reptilian hide adapted to the cold better than he had expected, not slowing him down with his reduced heartbeat as he had feared.

Rivers glinted in serpentine curves beneath the moon, hills reared jagged teeth, tiny pinpoints of light showed where those wealthy enough burned candles and tapers

1

in castle or church, and he grew complacent, so much so
that when the Change came, he wasn't ready for it.

It was that comfortable time between moondown and
sunrise and he was cruising at about a thousand feet,
ready to do a long glide down in search of breakfast,
when he suddenly became aware that something was terribly wrong. Although his wings were beating at the same
rate, he was losing height rapidly and feeling increasingly cold.

Glancing from side to side, he was horrified to see that
his wings were almost transparent, were shrinking; his
heartbeats were quickening, his legs stretching in an
agony of tendons and muscles, his clawed forefeet turning
into . . . hands?

Then he remembered.

She had kissed him, not once but three times, and so
as part of those accepted Laws—Laws that until now he
had dismissed as mere myth, though he had jokingly told
her of them as truth—he would now have to spend part
of his life as a human, earthbound as any mortal.

All right, all right, so he was going to be a man for a
minute, two, five, but why no sort of warning? He was
falling faster and faster, but all he could think about was
there should be some way of delaying the Change, or of
controlling it—

He landed plump in the middle of a village rubbish
dump, all the breath knocked out of him but otherwise
unhurt. For a moment he lay dazed and winded, then
the stench was enough to make him stumble to his feet
and stagger drunkenly down the main (and only) street,
shedding leaves, stalks, bones and worse. Halfway down
he realized he was not alone.

A small boy, perhaps five years old, clad only in a
tattered shirt, was watching him with solemn brown eyes
in the growing dawnlight. By his side was a smaller child,
perhaps his two- or three-year-old sister, in a smock far
too short for her, thumb stuck firmly in her mouth.

He thrust his hands out in a useless gesture of friendship.

"Sorry, children: didn't mean to scare you. Just passing through. . . ."

Fiercely he concentrated on his real self—though what was real anymore?—and to his relief he began the awkward pain of changing back. In the midst of his discomfort he became aware of the children still watching him, their eyes growing rounder and rounder with amazement, and the humor of the situation struck him even as he took a running leap into the air, as clumsy as any heavy water fowl.

"Good-bye," he called, but it sounded just like the rumble of thunder, and he could see now the terrified children beneath him rush for the nearest hut and safety. Never mind, they would have a tale to tell that would keep the village buzzing for months.

After that the weather became more hostile, and not only was he battling against his "changes," which took time to recognize and regularize, but also strong easterlies, snow, and sleet, so it was well after the turn of the year before he saw in the distance his objective, four thousand miles from the Place of Stones of his transformation: a small conical hill set proud on a plain, a hill that shone softly blue against the encircling mountains. . . .

PART ONE

CHAPTER ONE

Venice stank. For the loveliest city in the world (so I had been told), center of Western trade, Queen of the Adriatic, she certainly needed a bath. One would have thought with all that water around the smells would have been washed away, but the reverse was true: it made it worse. The waters in the canals were moved only by the water traffic, which stirred but did not dissipate, and all the slops and garbage merely settled a few feet further on.

The city was certainly busy with trade and teeming with merchants and dripping with gold, but she was only beautiful at a discreet distance. Pinch one's nose and one could admire the tall towers, fine buildings, richly dressed gentry; one could feel the sun-warmed stone, listen to the sweet dissonance of bells and the calls of the gondoliers; watch the bustle at the quays as the laden barques and caravels were rowed in the last few yards . . . but keep one's nostrils closed.

I moved restlessly from bed to window and back again: three paces and then another three. It was hot and stuffy in this little attic room, but when I had opened the window some time back the stench had made me gag, so it stayed shuttered. Consequently it was not only stifling but also dark: I had trodden on my dog twice, but couldn't keep still.

Mind you, I was lucky to have a room to myself. Apart

7

from Master Adolpho, the trading captain, all the others—horse master, interpreter, accountant, guards, cooks
and servants—had to share. And why was I so privileged?
Because I bore papers that proved I was under the personal protection of the wealthy merchant who had
financed the expedition, Master Matthew Spicer.

And I was the only one who knew the papers were
forged. By me.

I had a couple of other secrets, too, and secrets they
must remain, else this whole journey would be jeopard-
ized, and that mustn't happen. I had left too much
behind, risked too much, hurt too many people to fail
now. This was the most important journey of my life,
and to justify what I had done, it must succeed.

A bad conscience and a real fear of pursuit had kept
me glancing over my shoulder during our journeying the
last couple of months, but at least then we had been
moving, whereas for the last two weeks we had been
stuck in this stinking city. No wonder I couldn't keep
still. I—

Feet on the stairs, a thumping on the ill-fitting door.

"Hey, boy! Wake up there. . . . Cargo's in, we're going
down to the quay. Coming?"

Action at last! Telling my dog, Growch, to "stay," I
jammed my cap on my head, grabbed my tally sticks and
clattered down three flights of wooden stairs to the street
below. Outside it was scarcely less hot than my room,
but at least there was shade and a faint breeze off the
sea. Master Alphonso, the interpreter, and half a dozen
others were milling around, but as soon as I appeared
we set off for the quay, through the twists and turns of
narrow streets, across the elegant curves of bridges,
through the busy thoroughfares, all the while having to
contend with the purposeful and the loiterers; carts, wagons, riders, pedestrians, children, dogs and cats impeded
our progress. Watch out for the overhead slops—forbidden, but who was to see?—and be careful not to trip
over that heap of rags, a sudden thin hand snatching at

your sleeve for alms. Keep your hand on your purse and your feet from skidding in the ordure. . . .

Matthew's ship was already being unladen. Because of the press of the sea traffic she was anchored some way out, rowing boats busy ferrying the cargo ashore. A couple of our guards stood over the deepening piles of bales on the quayside, and our accountant started setting out paper, pens and ink on his portable writing desk, ready to itemize the cargo.

I tugged at Master Alphonso's sleeve. "How soon before it is all unladen? When can we go aboard? When do we sail?"

He twitched his sleeve away impatiently. "How many times do you have to be told, boy? When all the cargo is on dry land and checked by description against the captain's listings, then it is taken to a warehouse, opened and itemized, piece by piece. Then, and only then, will it be distributed as Master Spicer wishes. In the meantime the ship will take on a fresh crew and fresh supplies, the new cargo will be listed and loaded aboard. Then if the weather is fair, the ship sets sail. If not, it waits. Satisfied? I shan't tell you again."

I nodded, but inside I was in turmoil. Just how long would all this take? A week, at least . . . I turned away, but he stopped me.

"Just where do you think you're going? You may be Master Spicer's protegé, but that doesn't mean you skip out every time there's work to be done. You're here to learn the business, that's what your papers say, so stop farting around and go help the accountant."

So I spent a long, hot afternoon working my tally sticks at top speed against the accountant's vastly superior abacus, then helped load the cargo for the warehouse. All my own fault; when I had forged Matthew's signature on the carefully prepared papers, I had represented myself as a privileged apprentice, to learn a merchant's trade from the bottom up. This was obviously the bottom. Up till now I had been a supernumerary; now it appeared I was about to earn my keep.

Snatching a meat pie and a mug of watered wine from a stall, I followed the cargo to a warehouse on the outskirts of the city. There the bales were off-loaded, recounted against the existing lists and at last opened to check the contents.

This was the exciting bit. Although Matthew was principally a spice merchant, and some eighty percent of the cargo was just this—mainly pepper, cloves, nutmeg, and mace—he also traded in whatever was out-of-the-way and unusual, sometimes to special order. Thus the rich, black furs would be auctioned off in Venice, the jewelry entrusted to another outlet; some rather phallic statues were a special order, as were certain seeds of exotic plants. This left drawings and sketches of strange animals, two curiously-shaped musical instruments, and several maps. These last were earmarked for Matthew himself, together with a couple of rolls of silk so fine it ran through one's fingers like water.

And who was in charge of these sortings and decisions? A tall thin man with a hawk nose, conservatively dressed, who Master Alphonso whispered to me was Matthew's agent in Venice, responsible not only for distribution and collection of cargo, but also for hiring and firing.

It happened that he and I were the only ones left later: he because he was arranging for warehouse guards, I because I was going back over one of my calculations which did not tally. By now I was almost cross-eyed with fatigue, so was only too grateful when the soft-spoken Signor Falcone came over and in a couple of minutes traced my mistake and amended it.

"Only one error: tenths are important, youngster. Still, well done." His fingers were long and well manicured. "You are Master Summer, I believe?"

I nodded. Relief at having finished without too much blame made my tongue careless and impudent. "Matthew must have great trust in you. I wouldn't—" and I stopped, blushing to the roots of my hair.

"Trust someone so greatly without supervision? Of course you should not, unless you know him well." He regarded me gravely. "But then, you see, I owe him and his friend not only my livelihood, but my education. And also my life."

"Your life?"

He hesitated.

"I'm sorry," I said. "I shouldn't be so inquisitive."

"No matter. At your age I was the same." He hesitated again. "It is not a tale I recount easily. Still . . ." His eyes were bright and dark as sloe berries. He took a bundle of keys from his belt and, beckoning me to follow, locked up the warehouse, nodded to a couple of armed men lounging nearby, and started back towards the center of the city. "Come, we shall walk together. . . ."

It was a strange enough tale, and I forgot my weariness as I listened.

"When I was eight years old I was sold into slavery by a parent burdened by too many children. It was in a country far from here, and I was pretty enough to be auctioned as a bum-boy—you understand what I mean?—but I was lucky. A stranger stopped to watch the bidding and among those who fancied me was an old enemy of the stranger. So, to teach this man a lesson, the stranger bid for me too, and in the course of time he won himself a boy he had no use for. The stranger's name was Suleiman, on his way to visit his old friend Matthew Spicer—I see that first name means something to you?"

I wasn't conscious of having betrayed myself, but I nodded. "I met him while I was at Master Spicer's." I didn't add that it was the gifted Suleiman whose doctoring had saved the life of my blind knight, the man I had once fancied myself in love with.

"Then you will know that he is both wise and kind. He left me with his friend, to care for and educate, to learn to read, write and calculate. There I also learned French, Italian and Latin, for my own language was Arabic. At about the same age as yourself I was sent abroad to learn the ways of trade, and after some years Matthew appointed me his agent here. I have never regretted it, nor, I believe, has he. His is a generous and trusting nature, and such a man's trust is not easily abused. Nor should it be: remember that."

How could I not? For in my own way I had betrayed his trust in worse ways than Signor Falcone could imagine.

We had reached the end of the street where I lodged.

"Your journey starts in a day or two. I do not think you have the slightest idea how far it will take you, nor are you mentally prepared as you should be. About that I can do little, but at least I can see you are physically ready. Do not forget you will be representing Master Spicer, and you need a new outfit for that." He fished in his purse and brought out a handful of coin. He saw my eyes widen with surprise at the gold, and allowed himself a wry grimace. "Call this the Special Fund. For emergencies—and youngsters who need smartening up. Choose good materials, and something neat but not gaudy." He put a couple of coins in my hand. "You will also need travelling gear: leather breeches and jacket; a thick cloak; good, strong boots; riding gloves." Another couple of coins in my hand. "It can be cold at nights where you are going, so a woollen cap, underwear and hose." A last coin. "And a good, sharp dagger. Go to Signor Ermani in the Via Orsini and say I sent you." And he swung away across the square. "And get your hair cut! At the moment you look like a girl!"

It was so late by now that the pie shop around the corner was closing as I went past, but I managed to grab some leftovers and broken pieces for my dog, who was almost crossing his back legs in an effort not to relieve himself by the time I reached my room. So pressured was he that he forwent his supper until he had christened every post and arch within a considerable distance. I trailed after him without fear of marauders, for he had a piercing bark, an aggressive manner, and extremely sharp teeth.

And, after all, when one has bitten a dragon and got away with it, what else has a dog to fear?

That evening, what was left of it, I brought my journal up to date. This was Part Two of my life. Part One was already finished the day I left Matthew's for the second time. It was a bulky volume, bound with a wooden cover, and as I weighed it in my hands I realized how much of an extra burden it would be to carry it any further. It would be better to leave it with someone I could trust.

Part Two was far less bulky. I had already devised a form of shortened words and wrote smaller, so could justify taking it with me. Pen and inks would have to go with me as part of my job, and a couple of extra rolls or so of vellum were neither here nor there.

Next morning I went out in search of new clothes. Neat but not gaudy, Signor Falcone had said, but although hose, breeches and boots were easy enough in shades of brown, the jacket was an entirely different matter. Finding a good, plain one was practically impossible. They all seemed to be embroidered with vine leaves, pomegranates, artichokes, red and white flowers and even stars and moons, but then Venice catered mainly to the rich and fickle. The materials, too—silks and satins—were too fine for prolonged wear, but at least after a search I tracked down a fawn-colored jerkin with the minimum of decoration, and a green surcoat of fine wool, without the usual scallops, fringes and frills.

The afternoon I spent in mending my existing hose and underwear, a chore I detested, but just as I had decided it was candle time, there was a rush of feet on the stair and a hammering at the door.

"Master Summer? You there?"

"Yes . . ." I was practically naked, so the door stayed shut.

"Master Alphonso says you're to be ready at dawn."

"So soon?"

"Outbreak of plague reported in the south. Report to the quayside at first light." The feet stumbled back down the stairs.

Plague? Perhaps the greatest fear man had, far more threatening than battle or siege. Against a human enemy there were weapons, but the plague recognized no armies but—deadlier than sword, spear or arrowhead, unseen, unheard, unfelt—could decimate the largest army in the world within days. Either great pustules broke out on the skin and the victim died screaming, else it was the drowning sickness, when the chest filled with phlegm and a choking death came in less than a day—

I shivered in spite of the heat, fear closing my throat and opening my pores. No time to waste. I must call down for water to wash in, then collect my cloak from the laundry down the road. Once my father's, then my mother's, it was practically indestructible, being of a particularly fine and thick weave, though light and soft, with a deep hood. Much mended and much worn, it was nevertheless better than many new ones I had seen, but I had thought to have the mire and mud of the journey to Venice dispersed by a good soak.

So, that to collect, a good scrub for myself—and the dog, if possible—then everything to be packed as tight as could be. Something to eat, and lastly a safe place to leave Part One of my journal.

I hurried as well as I could, but the last streaks of gold and crimson were staining the skies to the west when I knocked at Signor Falcone's door, praying that he had not gone out to dine.

I was shown by a liveried servant to an upstairs room and gasped in wonder at the fine furniture, glowing tapestries, delicate glass and silken drapes. My host smiled at my expression.

"Without Suleiman and Matthew a mere slave could never have afforded all this. . . . What do you want of me, youngster?"

I started to explain about the plague and our early departure, but he cut me short.

"I know all this. We have worked throughout the day to get everything loaded and ready. What is that package under your arm?"

Straight to the point, Signor Falcone! I had rehearsed my story on the way.

"It contains a journal I have been keeping. Before I—before Master Spicer sponsored me I had some amusing adventures, which I have written down plain. If—if anything should happen to me on my travels I should wish Master Spicer to have it. A sort of thanks . . . It might also explain some of my actions more clearly." I was floundering, and I knew it. "Besides, it is too heavy to carry. Please?"

"So, if anything should happen to you on the way—Allah forbid!—this is to be forwarded to Matthew? Otherwise I hold it until your return; is that it? Very well. The package if you please." Going over to his ornate desk he extracted sealing wax and, rolling the stick in a candle flame, dropped the pungent-smelling stuff onto the knots in my package. He motioned to quill and ink. "Write Master Spicer's name there clearly. So. Now come with me."

Taking up a candle I followed him down a short passage into a small locked back room, windowless, full of shelves and nose-tickly with dust. Boxes, scrolls, books, small paintings and other packages lined the shelves, all neatly labelled. He placed my parcel high up on the nearest shelf.

"There, it will be safe till you return. And, should anything happen to me, my servants' orders are to forward everything in here to the name on the label. And now, if there is nothing else you wish to tell me, I think I shall take to my bed, and I would advise you to do the same." Ushering me downstairs, he opened the door on a night of stars, with a thin veil of mist creeping up from the east. "Hmmm. Don't like the look of the weather."

"There's no moon, no land breeze either, but the sky is clear enough."

"Exactly. Moon change and a sea mist. Still . . . off you go, sleep well." He turned to re-enter, then turned back. "I thought I told you to get your hair cut!"

Dear Lord, I had completely forgotten! Surely it would be too late at night now. Taverns, brothels, gaming houses, eating places would be open for business, but barbers . . . Collecting Growch from some odorous rubbish bin, I set out to look.

I was lucky, although it looked very expensive.

A gilded sign above the door hung motionless, announcing to those who could read that Signor Leporello was hairdresser and barber to the greatest in the land. On the door was tacked a list of prices; a trim didn't look too expensive. Telling Growch to wait, I lifted the latch and peered within. A little bell on a string gave a melodious tinkle.

"Hallo? Anyone there?" A couple of candles burned on a side table, otherwise the room was empty. I called again.

A moment's pause, then a bead curtain swung back and a creature teeter-tottered forward on those ghastly wooden-platformed shoes that the fashionable all seemed to be wearing these days. This man—if it was a man—had mismatched hose, red and blue, slashed sleeves and a surcoat flapping with pink and gold embroidery. Topping it all off was a huge green turban with a large purple stone set in the center. Probably real, which made it all worse. Gaudy, but not neat . . .

A waft of oil of violets, the glint of rings as he lit a couple more candles. "And what have we here? A late customer, I do believe. Come in dear boy, come in! A shave perhaps? No, not a shave, definitely not. A trim?

Yes, a trim I think. A trim and a wash. Pretty hair like yours should always be clean and dust-free. . . ."

"Pretty hair?" I squeaked. This was obviously the sort of place and proprietor young boys were warned about. "I'm sorry, there is some mistake: I have no money, and—"

"Nonsense! You need a trim and I am in a good mood. Come, it shall be on the house," and before I knew what was happening he had plonked me down on a tall stool, and swiftly plucked a few hairs from my head, holding them to the candlelight. "See these? All different colors. Two shades of red, two of brown, blonde and black." It was true. "All together they are individually responsive to light and shade, like those clear eyes of yours. Now, bend over that basin and we'll begin!"

If there was to be a dangerous moment, this would be it, but my worries soon vanished as he washed, rinsed, rubbed, combed, brushed and clipped. At last he brought me a mirror, and even with its uncertain depths and the flicker of candles I was gazing at a different me. Gone was the tangle of jagged ends and unruly curls. The hair was layered and waved neatly to my head—

"Is he someone I would know? How long ago did you run away from your family—or the convent, perhaps? Come, I've seen all this before, many times. A young girl imprisoned against the unsuitability of her beloved, dresses as a boy, runs away to find him. . . ."

"A—girl!" I stammered, and I must have been as red as fire.

"Why, yes! Oh come!" and he leant forward and lightly brushed his fingers across my chest. "I have been leaning over you for near an hour . . . I happen to have some stretch webbing that will hide those breasts much more discreetly, young lady, and only a silver piece a yard. . . ."

CHAPTER TWO

The morning was gray, dull, misty, chill. A sulky red sun lurked behind the mist and I was shivering, both from cold and anticipation. Strange to think the Shortest Day was but a week past: it felt more like November.

Dirty water slap-slapped against the piles of the Piazetta as the rowboats came and went, ferrying the last of the cargo aboard. Behind us the square was deserted, or so I thought, but at the last moment a figure came scurrying across carrying a tray of freshly baked rolls and pasties. They were delicious, the meat sending little pipes of steam into the air from the crumbling pastry. The baker was an enterprising fellow baking so early—but then his prices were enterprising too, as I discovered after Growch and I had burnt our tongues.

"Feel better?" asked a familiar voice. I turned to see Signor Falcone, well wrapped against the cold.

"Much!"

"Well try and keep it down. I still don't like the look of the weather; red sky at morning, sailor's warning . . . Still you're safer away from the plague, and the captain has done this run many times."

"Aren't you afraid of catching the sickness?"

He smiled. "It is as Allah wills. If it comes too close I have a small villa in the hills to the north. I usually spend August there anyway: it is pleasantly cool, and Matthew curtails his trade during the hottest months. In

19

fact, the stuffs now in the warehouse are the last but one Master Alphonso will escort back till fall."

I glanced over to where the trade captain was talking to his accountant. "But—but I thought they were coming with us.... With me." I should be alone, no one to ask questions of, to depend on. A little fist of panic curled up in my stomach, and I could taste the pasties a second time around.

Falcone patted my shoulder. "Stop worrying. Master Scipio takes over on the other side, and he is a competent man, one of the best. You'll be safe enough with him. Matthew's papers and listings are on board, and mention has been made of you.... Have I said how much better you look with your hair cut?" He smiled. "Now, I must bid you farewell, but first I have a commission to execute." He pulled a small, tightly wrapped package from an inner pocket. "This arrived some time back, but I had to be sure it was going to the right person."

I took the package and turned it over. No name, no superscription. "Who's it from? How do you know it's for me?"

"The sender is a mutual friend. And how do I know it is for you? Just answer me one question: what is the name of your dog?"

"My *dog*? Why, Growch . . ."

"Exactly! That was the password, just in case I was not convinced by my own observations. You make a handsome enough lad, but I'm sure the woman underneath is even more attractive." He laughed a little at my stricken face. "Your secret is safe. Our—friend—believes he knows the purpose of your journey and its destination. You are a brave lass: may Allah be with you. Now go: you don't want to miss the boat."

As the rowers pulled away from the quay, my mind was in turmoil. Disguising myself as a boy had seemed a good idea at the time, but in less than twenty-four hours two men had discovered at least one of my secrets. Did anyone else suspect? I felt as though my face was burning as I tried to flatten my chest, pull my long legs in under my surcoat.

Of course even twelve months ago it would have been impossible to think of posing as a boy. At that time I had still been decidedly plump, decidedly female. It had been that last, impossible journey back to the haven of Matthew's home that had fined me down to the weight I now carried, that and the pain of losing the one love I could never replace, the love I had found too late by the Place of Stones. . . .

I had tried, of course I had, to be satisfied with a substitute, but even the kindest of men—and Matthew was certainly that—could not compensate for that searing moment when I discovered what true love really meant.

And that was why I was here, in this rackety little rowboat, heading for—for what? Even I wasn't sure. All I knew was that somehow I must find my love again, see him just once more, for the touch that had fired my blood with an indescribable hunger could never be satisfied by another.

Perhaps I would never find him, perhaps if I did he would spurn me, or be so changed I would matter less than a leaf on a tree but at least I had to *try*! Nothing else in the world mattered.

The rowboat bumped against the towering hull above, a rope ladder dangling just out of reach. Only the most agile of monkeys could have scaled that, what with the overhang and the sluggish dip and sway of the ship, but luckily there was one more bale to be hauled up by hand, and Growch and I went the undignified way, bumped and banged against the ship's sides on what felt like a bed of nails.

If I had expected a fanfare of trumpets to greet me once on board I was to be disappointed. In fact no one took the slightest notice of us at all. We were tipped unceremoniously off the bale, which was then lashed to others on the deck. The whole ship was boiling with activity, and gradually we were pushed into an obscure corner as sailors scurried around getting us ready for sea. Up came the anchor, down came the sails, two men unlashed the tiller and swung it across, and everyone seemed to be shouting commands and countercommands. What with that and the creak of chain, snap of sail, hiss of rope and scream of the gulls overhead, I doubt if anyone would have noticed if I had set fire to myself.

But all this frantic activity didn't seem to be getting us anywhere at all. The ship wallowed uneasily from side to side, the sails flapped listlessly, everything creaked, but we weren't moving. After half an hour or so, a flag was run up on the forward mast, and eventually a rowing barge came astern, took a line and ponderously towed us, tail first, outside of the shipping roads and into clear water.

Peering over the side, I could see how, even here, the contamination of the city behind us reached its dirty fingers into the main. The water was still brown and scummy and I could see flotsam from the sewers float past, plus a broken packing case and the bloated carcass of a goat. I glanced back at the city and now, at last, she resembled the lady I had heard about. She looked to float well above the water, the pale sun gilding her towers and cupolas till she seemed crowned like any queen.

The sails above me filled at last, the tiller was pushed over to starboard, and at first slowly, then with gathering speed, we headed northeast into the open sea. Immediately I had to grab at the side to keep myself from slipping: it was probably only a cant of a foot or so, but it was most disconcerting for me and worse for Growch, for his claws slipped and he slithered straight into the scuppers. We would have to find a place to call our own.

The ship was quieter now, although everyone seemed to have a job to do: trimming sails, coiling rope, swilling down the deck, and I could see an extremely large lady was shaking out bedding and punching energetically at what seemed to be a feather mattress. Probably the captain's wife: I had heard they often accompanied their husbands to sea. I had correctly identified the captain as the man who shouted the loudest and longest, and decided now was the time to introduce myself. He was a self-important looking man, stout and short, with a bristling beard and lots of hair in his ears. He stared at me as I approached.

"Who's this, then?"

I introduced myself, but had to explain who and what I was before his brow cleared and he nodded his head. Yes, yes, he'd heard I was coming aboard, but it had slipped his mind, and now he was too busy to deal with me personally. I would have to see the mate, find myself quarters, settle myself in. And keep that blasted dog from under everyone's feet. . . .

The mate, when I found him, had even less time for me. I was handed over to one of the crew, who showed me round in a desultory manner, and had me peering down the bilges—sick-making—and trying to climb in and out of a string bag he called a hammock; needless to say I fell out either one side or the other immediately. Apparently all the crew slept in these because a) they took up little space and b) they always stayed level, however the ship swayed. I went down into the hold, where everything was stacked away neatly, and into the galley, where it wasn't. Pots and pans, jugs, bottles, a side of ham, bags of flour, jars of oil, dried beans, strings of onions and garlic, sultanas and raisins, boxes of eggs, all hugger-mugger on shelves and floor. Outside, a couple of barrels rolled from side to side, and a couple of crates of scrawny chickens were stacked next to a bleating nanny goat. The cook was snoring it off in a corner.

But where was I to sleep? There were eighteen crew, split into three watches, so that at any one time there would be six on duty, six asleep and six relaxing, and I wasn't going to fall out of hammocks all day and night. Besides, there was no locker in which to stow my gear. I asked if there was any other space, but apparently not.

The captain and his wife had quarters aft, the mate a tiny cubicle next to the rope locker and the cook slept in the galley.

The sailor had one useful suggestion. I could either doss down in the hold, although the hatchway was normally battened down, or find myself a niche topside, among the deck cargo.

I didn't fancy being shut away, so I inspected the bales on deck and, sure enough, they were so stacked that there was a cozy sort of cave to one side, which I thought would do. Even with my gear dragged in as well, there was room to lie down or sit up quite comfortably, and the smell of tarred string and sea salt was far pleasanter than bilge water.

I had about got myself settled down when bells rang for noon and food. I never quite got the hang of those bells; I knew they signalled change of watches, time passing, but the number of chimes never seemed to fit the hours, striking as they did in couples.

By the time I had unpacked my wooden bowl and horn mug I was almost too late; there was only a scrape of gristly stew left and a heel of yesterday's bread, plus some watered wine, but I wasn't particularly hungry so Growch benefitted. The bread and wine sloshed around uncomfortably in my stomach, for the ship was definitely rolling more heavily now. Before long, too, there came the pressing need to relieve myself. I had watched at first with embarrassment, then in increasing awareness of my own problems, as the crew relieved themselves when necessary over the side, and had seen the captain's wife empty a couple of chamber pots the same way. I couldn't do the first and hadn't got the second. Then I remembered there were some buckets and line in the rope locker. I pinched the smallest of the former and fastened it to a length of rope long enough to drop over the side and rinse in the seawater as I had seen the crew do when they needed water for swilling anything down.

Temporarily more comfortable, I slid my knife under

the seals and string of the packet Signor Falcone had
given me and drew out a letter. I might have known: it
was from Suleiman.

"I believe this will reach you before you sail. Do not
fear pursuit for there will be none. Matthew was most
distressed to find you gone, and hopes for your return,
but I know better, I think. Something changed you
before you came back to us; I have seen that restless
hunger in other eyes. So, go find your dragon-man—yes,
you talked a great deal in your delirium, but I was the
one who nursed you, so it is our secret. In case you did
not copy all the right maps before you left, I enclose one
that is the farthest east that I have.

"Use the gold wisely: you will need as much as you
can, the way you go. May all the gods be with you, and
may you find your dream."

There were tears in my eyes as I unfolded the map and
found the gold coins he had enclosed. His understanding
touched me deeply.

Sitting back I recalled the time Suleiman had taken
the handful of coins my father had left me and arranged
them across a map of the trade routes, showing how each
one—copper, silver or gold—led inexorably towards the
east and the unknown, the very way a certain dragon had
gone, that night when he had left the Place of Stones—

And me.

Towards evening the weather steadily worsened. The
wind blew in gusts, first from one quarter, then another,
the lulls leaving the ship rolling uneasily on an increasingly oily swell. Dusk came down early, showing the thin-
nest crescent moon slicing in and out of the clouds; the
cheese I had for supper was causing me great discomfort.
At last it and I just had to part company, and I rushed
for the rail, only to be jerked back at the last moment
by the brawny arm of the mate.

"No puking into the wind!" he hissed. "Else you'll

spend all night swilling down both the decks and yourself!"

I made it to leeward just in time, and spent the rest of that miserable night rushing back and forth to the rail. Sometime in the small hours all hands were called to shorten sail, and now I was pushed and cursed at and stumbled over, until in the end someone tied a rope around my waist and wrapped the other end round the after mast, leaving just enough room and no more for me to move between the rail and my improvised quarters.

In the end there was nothing more to come up and I curled up miserably in my cloak, dry-retching every now and again, a sympathetic Growch curled against my hip. In the morning I was no better; I staggered along the now alarmingly tilted deck to fetch food—cheese once more—but it was for my dog. I took a sip or two of wine, but up it came again, and as I was leaning over the rail a huge wave came aboard, near dragging me away back with it, and soaking me to the skin.

Somehow I just couldn't get dry again; rain came lashing down, and the ship was running bare-masted before a wind that had decided to blow us as far off course as possible. The whole vessel creaked and groaned under the onslaught of the waves, and it took three men to hold the ship steady, the tiller threatening to wrest itself from their grasp. I lay half in, half out of my shelter, too weak now to move either way, conscious of Growch's urgent bark in my ears, but lost in a lethargy of cold and darkness of soul and body. Soaked by the rain, tossed to and fro by the motion of the ship, stomach, ribs and shoulders sore and aching, I slipped into a sort of unconsciousness, aware only that I was probably dying. And the worst of it was, I didn't care, even though the ring on my finger was stabbing like a needle.

Suddenly an extra lurch of the ship rolled me right into the scuppers. This is it, I thought. Good-bye world. I'm sorry—

Someone grabbed me by the scruff of my neck, hauled

me to my feet and shook me like the drowned rat I so
nearly was. A couple of discarded chamber pots skittered
past my feet and a voice boomed in my ears in a language
I couldn't understand. I shook my head helplessly, muttered something in my own tongue and tried to be sick
again.

"Ah, it is so? You come with me . . ." and I was tossed
over a brawny shoulder and carried off in a crabwise
slant across the deck. A foot shoved hard, a door crashed
open and I was spilled onto the floor of a room full of
fug, wildly dancing lantern light and blessed warmth.

Dimly I realized that the stout boots and swishing
skirts that now stood over me were those of the captain's
lady, and that it was her strong arms and broad shoulders
that had brought me to the haven of their quarters.
Squinting a little through the salt water that still stung
my eyes, I saw the captain and mate seated at a center
table screwed to the floor, studying what looked to be
maps. They had obviously been discussing how far we
had been blown off course, but the captain's wife
wasn't interested.

I was hauled to my feet again.

"What is this poor boy doing out there? Who is he?
Where he come from?" She was speaking my language,
although with a strong guttural accent.

The captain rose to his feet. "Ah—an apprentice, my
dear, to be delivered to Master Scipio—"

"Then what he do dying out there in storm? No good
to deliver dead boy! What you thinking? Get out, both
of you! I take charge now—"

"But my dear, we were just—"

"Out! This is now sick bay. Find elsewhere. I take care
now. You go sail ship, storm slack soon."

There was a scuffle of feet, a door opened to let in a
gust of tempest, shriek of wind. "And you find chamber
pots and bring back clean. . . ." The door shut.

I was picked up again, more gently this time, and

placed on a bunk in the corner. A large hand felt my
forehead, brushed the salt-sticky hair from my brow.

"There, poor boy! You stay still and Helga will care
for you, make you well again. Now, out of those wet
things and we give wash ..." and fingers were at the
fastenings of my clothes.

I tried to sit up, to protest, but my voice was gone, my
hands too feeble to pull my jacket tight across my chest.

"Now, boy, no modestness! I have born and raised six
strong boys, and know what bodies is like! Lie still! Once
I have ... Ahhh!" There was a moment's pause. "What
do we have here, then?" Rapidly the rest of my clothes
were peeled off and I lay naked and exposed, in agonies
of shame.

I think I expected almost anything but what I got: a
great roar of laughter.

"This is what you call a joke, yes? I feel sorry for
skinny lad, and what do I get? A young lady instead ..."
But the voice wasn't unkind, and even as I tried to
explain in my cracked voice I was enveloped in a bone-
breaking hug. "No talking, that come later. We get you
warm and dry first."

A knock at the door. "You wait...." Hastily she flung
a blanket over me. "What is it?"

Apparently the return of the chamber pots. "Good.
Now you fetch two buckets fresh water. Where are your
things?" to me. I whispered. "And boy's things in bales
on deck. He stay here. Hurry! What devil is *this*?"

"This" was Growch, a small, wet, filthy bundle that
hurled itself across the cabin and onto my bunk, sitting
on my chest and growling at everyone and everything,
teeth bared.

I found my voice. "My dog. Very devoted. Please don't
throw him out. He and I are alone in the world." Weak
tears filled my eyes.

"Poor little orphans!" Another hug, for us both this
time. "He can stay, but on the floor. Is *filthy!*"

As usual.

The water arrived plus my cloak and bundle. Ten minutes later I was in cold water, being scrubbed clean, my dirty clothes were handed out for washing, and then I was rubbed warm and dry, donned someone's clean shirt and drawers, and was thrust back into bed. A moment later and Growch was in the tub as well, too shocked to protest, and five minutes later he was shaking himself dry in a corner, thoroughly huffy.

Out went the dirty water, in came food, a sort of broth and some real bread. I went green at the thought of anything to eat, but the captain's wife insisted.

"If you going to be sick, better you be sick with something to be sick on. Dip bread into soup, suck juices, nibble bread. Count to ten tens—you can count?—then do again. And again. Try . . ."

I did, and it worked. After a few queasy moments I kept the first two pieces of bread down, and the rest was easy. The last few pieces of bread and broth I indicated were for Growch.

A hammering on the door again, and that loud-voiced martinet who strode the deck of his ship like a small but determined Colossus and ruled his crew with the threat of a rope's end, was heard asking his wife in the meekest way possible if he might have some more maps?

"Take them and be quick about it! Take also a blanket and your eating things. You will bunk with the mate. Now, be off with you! I have work to do. . . ."

I suppose my mouth must have been hanging open, because as he left she turned and winked at me. "Never let them get away with nothing, my chick," she said comfortably. "Out there—" she gestured to the sea, the storm, the tossing deck, "—he is boss. In here, I am, and he don't forget it."

I looked around the cabin. Comfortable, yes, but not luxurious. Not the sort of place one could call home.

"Do you sail with him all the time? I mean, haven't you got a place ashore? And aren't you ever afraid?"

She laughed. "No, yes, and yes. I sail when I want a

change, go to new places. I have a home far from here, near youngest son, not yet married. Afraid? Of course. But this not bad storm, only little Levante who blow us off course forty-fifty mile. Rest of voyage routine. My man know this: he only want maps to make him look important." She bustled about, tidying the already tidy. "Now you get some rest. Tell me all about yourself when you wake up." She held up one of the chamber pots. "You or dog want pee-pee?"

I slept all through the rest of that day and the night, and when I awoke at last the storm was off away somewhere else, my sickness had gone, I was hungry for the first time in days and all I had to do was concoct a romantic enough story to satisfy my indulgent hostess. It wasn't too difficult: I remembered my beautiful blind knight, invented parents who didn't understand my love, relived parts of my earlier journeys, including a near rape, and finally sent my betrothed off on a pilgrimage from which he had not yet returned, thus my escapade.

Tears of sympathy poured from her eyes. She sighed, she sobbed as my tears—of hunger: where was my breakfast?—mingled with hers.

"My dearest chick! How often I wish for a daughter! Now my prayers will all be with you. . . ." She dried her eyes, glanced at me. "You are sure you are set on this knight of yours? My youngest son, he is not the brightest boy in the world, but . . ."

I was almost sorry to disappoint her.

One fine evening we sailed between two jaws of land into the mouth of a bay made bloodred by the setting sun. Climbing the hill behind was a beautiful city, with gold cupolas, pierced minarets, palaces and tree-lined streets. Even as we nudged in towards the quay, lights appeared in windows, along streets, moving with carriages or hand-held, until the whole city resembled a rosy hive alive with sparkling bees.

Matthew's ships had a permanently allotted landing stage, so we were rowed in and tied up right on the quayside. Immediately aboard was the Master Scipio I was waiting to meet. Of medium height, with a forked beard, he exuded authority. After a brief courtesy to myself, he took Falcone's papers from the captain and started the unloading with his own team, disregarding the swarm of itinerants who crowded the quay touting for work.

The cargo was checked by myself, now fully recovered, and Master Scipio's assistant, a dark man called Justus, then it was borne away to a warehouse for storage. It was well into the night by the time we finished and we ate where we stood, highly flavored meats on skewers with a sort of pancake bread. At last we went back to the ship for what remained of the night. It was strange to lie down and not be rocked from side to side, and it took a while, tired as I was, to get to sleep.

Added to the lack of motion there was the noise from ashore. Used as I was to the creaking of the ship, the noise of wind and sea, my ears were now assailed by the sounds of humanity at large, determined to wine and carouse the night away. The ship was moored right up against the "entertainment" part of the harbor, and the night was alive with singing, wailing and shouting, wheels, hooves, and musical instruments. I learned later that the captain's wife had stood guard for the rest of the night on the gangplank, armed with an ancient sword, turning back not only those members of the crew who wished to creep ashore, but also any enterprising whore who attempted to board.

Before we went ashore finally she drew me aside and pressed a small packet into my hand.

"Is a nothings," she said. "But pretty enough perhaps. You take it for present. My husband he bring it back as gift when he sail alone. Say it come from wise man down on his luck. . . ." She laughed. "Only truth is, I get gift means he has another woman somewhere. Guilty conscience. Better you have it for dowry," and she gave me another of her bear hugs, which almost had my eyes popping out. "Take care, chick; I so hope you find your man!"

On shore Master Scipio was waiting with his second-in-command, half a dozen guards and a horse master. After briefly introducing me, we went off for breakfast at a small tavern some half-mile from the port. We ate a thick fish stew, more of the pancakelike bread, olives, a bland cheese, and drank the local wine. A street and a half further on were our lodgings; a three-story house in a narrow twisting alley, that almost touched its neighbor across the street at roof level.

Our rooms were little more than cubicles, overlooking a central courtyard where a small fountain tinkled pleasantly amid vine-covered walls. I was lucky enough to have a small space to myself: a clean pallet and a stool, and it was relatively cool.

Master Scipio spoke to us from the stairs. "I have things to arrange. We shall meet again tonight at the same tavern. To those of you who are new to the city, a word or two of advice. Don't venture far and keep your hand on your purse. Don't get involved in arguments on religion or over women, because I won't bail you out. Watch both the food and the drink; if you are ill you are left behind. One last thing: do not discuss our cargo or our destination."

"How long are we here for?" asked one of the guards.

"We start out at dawn tomorrow. Anyone not packed and ready will be left behind," and off he clattered down the stairs. Not a gentle man, but at least one knew where one was with him.

Two of the guards set off almost immediately, to "see the sights," as they put it, but the others lingered. Eventually one, a local man, went off to visit some relative or other, and the others decided to go out sightseeing.

"You coming, youngster?"

I would dearly have loved to explore the city, but after

last night's sleeplessness the pallet was more inviting. I took off my jacket and lay back, promising myself a good wash later. My eyes closed. . . .

At the foot of the pallet Growch made a great to-do of hoofing out his ears and nipping busily for fleas.

"Can't you do that on the floor?" I asked sleepily.

"More comfortable up 'ere." He was quiet for a moment or two, and I began to drift off. " 'Ow long you goin' to kip, then?"

"An hour or so. Why?"

"I'm 'ungry!"

"You're always hungry. . . ."

"Can you remember the last thing I ate? No, and neither can I."

"Just give me an hour," I said between my teeth. "One hour . . ."

CHAPTER THREE

Actually he let me sleep for two and I woke gently and naturally, lying back in a luxury of lassitude. I could hear him out on the landing, snapping at flies. He was quite good at it, usually; having such short legs he tried to compensate in other ways, and quickness of paw, mouth, and eye were three of them.

And of course it was Growch who had alerted me to the other of my secrets: the power of the ring I wore on my right hand. One could hardly guess it was there, I thought, lifting my finger to gaze at it. As thin as a piece of skin it nestled on my middle finger as if it were a part of it. I couldn't remove it, either. According to what I had heard, the ring chose its wearer and stayed there, until either the wearer had no further use for it or grew unworthy to wear it.

This latter must have been what happened to my father, who had left the ring, some coins and his cloak as the only legacies to my mother and myself. He had been hunted down and killed on a false accusation before I had ever been born, but my mother—who was the village whore and no worse for it either—had kept the few pieces he left as mementos. She had worn the cloak I now possessed, had spent all the current moneys he had left, but was unable to change the curious coins I inherited, that had so fitted the maps Suleiman and I

had studied. Coincidence perhaps, but intuition told me
my father had once come this way, too. A good omen.

As to the ring I had slipped on my finger so thought-
lessly the night my mother died, it had been the most
magical thing in my life. According to Growch, the first
creature I had met after fleeing the village where I was
born, it was a precious sliver of horn from the head of
a fabulous Unicorn, and as such enabled me to communicate with other creatures and also, as I discovered later,
warned of impending danger.

I wondered what sin my father had committed for it
to leave his finger; my mother had not been able to fit
it to hers either, whereas it had slipped onto mine like
bear grease and stuck like glue.

I couldn't have managed without it. Nor, I thought
with a wry smile, would I have once encumbered myself
with not only a blind knight, but also a dog, Mistral the
horse, Traveler the pigeon, Basher the tortoise, and my
beloved little pig. . . . No, I mustn't think about the pig.

Be that as it may, the ring had completely changed
my life. My mother had had ambitions for me. With the
help of her "clients," I had been educated far beyond a
village girl's station. I could read, write, figure, cook, sew,
carpenter, cure, fish, hunt, brew, farm, spin and weave.
She had plans for me to become the sort of woman who
could choose her own husband and take a place in society, but the queer paradox had been that she couldn't
bear to part with me, so had, knowingly or not, fed me
with sweet cakes and honeyed fruits until I was the fat-
test, most unattractive girl in the province and no one
would have me. I hadn't realized it until after she died,
and it took a while to become reconciled to her duplicity,
conscious or not.

But, as I said, the ring had changed all that. By the
time I had learned to communicate properly with all the
creatures I met and who needed my help, the original
intent of seeking the first husband I could find had disappeared under other considerations.

Not that understanding the animals had been easy. Only one-tenth of animal speech is in sound—barks, neighs, bleats, etc.—and another three-tenths are in body movement, position of head, legs, ears, and feel of coat and fur. The other, and greater part, is thought-talk. This last was the most difficult for me, even with the help of the Unicorn's ring. Animals think in sorts of pictures, colored only by their own thoughts and seen from their own angles, so a bird didn't send back the same images as, say, a dog or a horse. Eventually, though, it became easier, and Growch and I spoke to each other almost entirely by thought.

Dear dog: all he had wanted in the beginning was a real home, a warm fire to curl up by in the winter, regular food and a pat or two, but he had left all that behind to follow me into an uncertain future. He had pretended that his real reason was to find more of those "fluffy bum" bitches he had fallen for in our earlier travels, pampered creatures from Cathay with legs as short as his and no morals whatsoever, but I knew better. He had decided that his real role in life was to keep an eye on me: he was convinced I couldn't manage on my own.

He trotted in now, one ear up, one down, as usual.

"Awake now, are we? 'Ow's about some food, then?"

We assembled in a small square behind our lodgings in shivering dawn. The sun would soon rise above the rearing mountains, but now the sky was a pale greenish-blue, and the mist lay knee-high in the streets. Breakfast was pancake bread and honey, and as the church bells called out six and a muezzin sang from his tower, the convoy got under way.

A string of heavily laden mules, two wagons, eight mounted guards and horses for Master Scipio, interpreter Justus, horse master Antonius and our guide, a skinny fellow called Ibrahim. Nothing for me: Master Scipio explained that I either walked or hitched a lift in one of the wagons.

"Do you good, boy," he said robustly. "Half day walk, half ride. And you can alternate the wagons. One driver doubles as the cook—you can give him a hand, he'll teach you what foods are best for travelling. T'other wagon is driven by the farrier: knows all there is to know about horses. Right?"

So we were off, all yawning, for we had none of us had much sleep at the lodgings. The guards had straggled back at all hours, full of the local wine and boasting of their winnings and/or conquests.

I reached up to pull at Master Scipio's sleeve.

"Where are we bound?"

"For the trading town of Küm."

"How long will it take?"

"Over the trails we follow, four or five days."

So long! Now that we were finally on our way proper I was eager to complete my journey east as fast as I could. It seemed I would have to be patient.

Our way lay to the northeast, and once we left the city behind the travelling was frustratingly slow. We twisted and turned along trails that followed the lowest contours of the land; the tracks had been there for time immemorial, the easiest for man and beast, and for the most part were within easy reach of water, but were also rutted and broken by the years of travel.

At first the surrounding countryside was relatively well wooded and we were hemmed by low hills, but the further we travelled the wilder became the terrain. The hills grew higher and crowded closer, the trees gave way to low scrub and the sun burned us in the breezeless valleys. It was cooler at night, but we always built a fire, both to cook the evening meal and to deter any wild animal; every evening we heard mountain dogs howling at the moon, sometimes near, sometimes far.

We had brought our own provisions with us, to avoid paying high prices in the small villages we passed through, and this proved our undoing.

On the third night the cook prepared a stew, and in

order to disguise the (by now) high smell and taste of the meat, threw some very pungent herbs and spices into the pot. I watched him take various packets from his pockets, but after asking the names of a few, all unknown to me, I lost interest; besides, he said my watching him made him feel nervous. He was a taciturn man at best, and poor company if I rode in his wagon. He wasn't a very good cook, either.

I took a portion of the stew over to Growch and sat down beside him to eat mine, but two very disconcerting things happened. One, my precious ring gave a little warning stab, and two, Growch took one sniff and flatly refused to eat any.

Now, my dog doesn't refuse food. Ever. He can devour stuff that turns my stomach even to look at.

"What's the matter? It smells all right. A little spicy, perhaps, but you've eaten worse." I lifted my spoon to my mouth but his tail got in the way, and at the same time my ring prickled again.

"Don' touch it! S'not good to eat. Don' know why, but somethin' in there ain't right."

"Are you suggesting it's poisoned?" I tried to laugh it off. I was hungry.

"Not poison. Told you, don' know what's wrong; all I know is, I'm not havin' any, and you shouldn' neither."

The ring stabbed again. "All right," I said crossly, as much to it as to Growch. "Cheese and dates."

"Skip the dates. . . ."

As I went to return our untouched food to the stew pot, I noticed others doing the same. Not all, by any means. About half the men were eating heartily, others were just picking. If I had needed any confirmation that it wasn't entirely palatable, I would have had it in the fact that the cook himself wasn't eating his own food: he had just handed the guide Ibrahim a plate of dried fruit and cut himself a heel of cheese, although he scowled when I asked for the same.

It wasn't until we had been on the road for a couple of

hours the next day that the wisdom of avoiding the stew became apparent. One by one men groaned, clutched their stomachs and disappeared into the brush to be violently ill. By noon about half were incapacitated, unable to ride, and had to be hauled up onto the wagons, their horses tied behind.

Master Scipio called me over, his face gray and sweating.

"Here, boy: take my horse. I'm going to rest for a while," and off he disappeared into the bushes, to reemerge some moments later to help me up on the horse and then climb himself onto the nearest wagon.

At first it was just fine to be riding up so high, feeling well and fit while all around were groaning and moaning, but Growch was grumbling that he was wearing his legs down to their stumps trying to keep up with me as I rode from one end of the line to the other, as Master Scipio did, and after a while the high wooden saddle began to chafe and the bottom of my spine felt bruised. I checked up and down once more: half the mule drivers and half the guards were riding the wagons and the guide, Ibrahim, was driving the farrier's cart.

I brought the horse to an amble beside Master Scipio.

"Like to ride again? Or shall we halt and have a rest, water the horses?"

He looked better, but not much.

"Not yet. We won't stop, because if we do we'll never get going again. Keep riding; there's a good camping place a few miles further on. We'll stop there overnight."

The trouble was, we had had to travel so slowly with the overladen wagons that we had made very little progress by the time the sun slid behind the hills and the valley we travelled became gloomy and full of shadows. Once again I implored Master Scipio to take to his horse but once again he refused.

"A mile or so more, that's all, then we can rest, I promise. Ride up to the head of the line and see if you can hurry up those mules. . . ."

I was so sorry for myself and my saddle sores as I rode to the front, noting the weariness of the animals as they plodded on, heads hanging, puffing and blowing, that it wasn't for a moment or two that the growing noise behind me made any sense. It seemed that the hubbub and the prickling of my ring coincided, which meant danger, so I wheeled the horse as quickly as I could (not easy because the track had narrowed to a defile) and pushed him back towards the wagons and Master Scipio.

Our whole caravan stretched back now over a quarter-mile or thereabouts, because of the growing dusk, general weariness, lack of Scipio's incisive leadership and, most of all, the narrowness of the trail. As I kicked my reluctant jade to a faster pace, Growch panting at our heels, the noise—shouts, yells, neighing of horses, clash of swords—made no sense, until I rounded a curve and saw the horde of ragged men armed with spears, swords, clubs, and knives that were creeping out of the bush and attacking the wagons.

Ambush!

My heart gave a *thump* of terror, and the hand that fumbled at my belt for the dagger I kept there was slick with the sweat of fear. My horse had caught the scent of blood and reared suddenly, so that I lost the reins and had to hang on to his mane with both hands as he turned away from the battle. I tried my damnedest to pull his head round, find the reins again, but all of a sudden a figure leapt from the undergrowth, a knife between his teeth, a spear in his hand.

The ring was burning on my finger but I could do nothing but freeze in horror as the spear was lifted in my direction and the man's mouth opened in a howl of exultation. Death stared at me, and I couldn't even pray—

There was a growl, a yelp, a cry of pain, and the spear missed me by a fraction and struck my horse's rump. It reared with a scream of pain, its flailing hooves downed my would-be attacker, luckily missing Growch, then it plunged off again down the track and away from the fighting.

Once more it was all I could do to hang on as I was bounced and jounced like a sack of meal on that horrid hard saddle. I bumped both nose and chin on the high pommel, banged my leg on a rock as the horse swerved at the last moment, and scratched my arm on some branch or scrub that scraped our sides.

Tears of pain squeezed past my closed eyelids: would this never stop? We must have galloped at least—

The animal came to an abrupt halt, forelegs quivering, and the sudden lack of motion did what the flight couldn't. I fell off onto the ground and lay there with my head spinning and everything else hurting, while the wretched animal cropped the grass next to my ear with a sound like tearing linen.

I'm dead, I thought. I must be. No one could have survived that headlong gallop. I'll just lie here and wait for the golden trumpets. . . . Washed in the blood of the Lamb—

Nothing so sacred. I was being washed, but by a sloppy, anxious dog. I sat up gingerly.

"Go away, Growch! I'm all right. . . ."

"Then get up and tell 'em! 'Bout the ambush!"

I opened my eyes. We were in a clearing full of people running towards us. Over to one side a huge fire was flickering. For a desperate moment I thought I had stumbled into the ambushers' camp, but a closer look showed these were respectable travellers. In a moment I was surrounded and a babel of tongues was flinging questions at me till my head hurt worse than ever. I explained in my own tongue, market Latin, a little Italian and a couple of words of Arabic I had picked up (I think these last were profanities, remembering where I had heard them, but no one seemed to mind) and a moment or two later armed men were clattering away back the way I had come.

Someone led me over to the fire and smeared an

evil-smelling grease on the more obvious bumps and
bruises, and gave me a mug of spiced wine which I
downed gratefully. I accepted another and a bowl of rice
and chicken. Something nudged my arm, and half the
contents of the bowl were on the ground.

"Ta!" said Growch pleasantly, licking up the last grains.
"That was fun, wasn' it? That fella din' 'alf yell when I
nipped 'im! Quite a battle . . ."

Of course! I remembered now. He had doubtless saved
my life when he bit my attacker's ankle, though I didn't
know whether he realized it. I tipped the rest of the rice
out.

"Here: I'm not hungry. . . . Thanks."

"Nothing to it. 'Ere: why don't you ask for another
bowlful?"

It appeared the ambush had been well planned. The
stew had been dosed with a powerful emetic, and both
the guide Ibrahim and the cook had made good their
escape. We had lost two guards and a mule driver and
there were several wounded, including Master Scipio,
who finally rode in with his arm in a sling. But I was
hailed as a hero for riding to seek help and feted with
choice titbits and a handful of hastily gathered coin, a
whip-round from the survivors.

I felt a trifle guilty as I accepted the coins and blushed
when they called me a hero, but as Growch remarked,
now was not the time to tell them my horse had bolted
from a superficial spear wound and heroism had nothing
to do with it.

Master Scipio accepted the offer of our new friends
to travel under the protection of their bigger caravan—
a friendship cemented in gold I noticed—as far as the
trading city. Being a larger party, and with wounded to
care for, our progress was of necessity slow, so it was on
the third afternoon after our rescue that we topped the
final ridge and I gazed down on the city of Küm.

CHAPTER FOUR

"But that's not a town," I said, bitterly disappointed. "It's just—just a collection of tents!"

Scipio drew his horse alongside the wagon I was riding in.

"Tents maybe, but still the largest trading center for hundreds of miles." He gestured below. "A plain some three miles wide, the same long, with a river to the east. Mountains all around, yes, but with age-old trails that lead in from Cathay, India, the Middle Sea, the Baltic, the Western Isles . . ." He leant back, let the reins lie slack, as we waited for the wagon ahead to start the narrow trail down. "Looks fine now, doesn't it? But in the autumn when the rains come the river down there is a raging torrent; in the winter the bitter winds blow in from the north, the river freezes over and the sands below are as sharp as hailstones as they whirl across the plain. In the spring the rain and the melting snows from the hills flood the plateau, but when the waters recede and the sun comes out, the grass and flowers grow thick and fast. Then the advance parties come, those who cut and dry the grasses for forage; after them come the men with tents for hire, the cooks, the laundrymen, the farriers, and the men who dig the cesspits. Local villagers bring in fresh fruit, vegetables, chickens, sheep, and goats, and there is a committee of those concerned who ensure everything runs smoothly for when the first of the traders arrive in mid-June. From then until mid-September the place is seething. I truly believe one can find anything in the world down there if needed. . . ." And off he spurred down the hill.

I turned to Nod, my driver. "Have you been this way before?"

"Oh, aye: wouldn't miss it for the world. Just as Master Scipio says: the world and his mate meet here. Nice rest for us too. We can just sit back and enjoy ourselves while the bosses natter and bicker and blather and dicker over every blessed piece of barter." He was chewing on a root of liquorice and spat a brown stream over the edge of the wagon as we began the descent. "I seen stuff there as you couldn't imagine: furs, silks, wools, dyes, carpets, rugs, 'broideries; copper pots, clay pots, glass, china; daggers, swords, spears; paintings and manuscripts, pens and brushes; all the spices you could think of and dried herbs; wines, dried fruits, rice, and tea. There's even bars of gold and silver, precious jewels, children's toys— Whoa, there!" He was silent for a moment or two as we negotiated a difficult turn. He spat out more juice. "Then there's the animals. . . ."

"Lions and tigers?"

"Sometimes. They're mostly to special order. I seen a panther and a spotted cat with jewelled collars, tame as you please, and even once, a helefant, with a nose longer than its tail. . . . No, mostly they's more portable. Monkeys, 'xotic birds, snakes as thick as your arm, queer little dogs . . ."

Oh, no! I thought. Not Growch's "fluffy bums"; keeping an eye on him in that place would be difficult.

"Then there's the slaves. Mostly men, 'cos women and children don't travel well, but you see the occasional two or three. All colors, too: mostly black or brown, but there's some yellows and near-whites. Dwarfs, sometimes, they fetch a good price." He spoke as indifferently as if they were bales of cloth.

We were on easier ground now, and the town beneath

seemed to be taking on a pattern. The tents appeared to be arranged in rows rather than haphazardly, and although the number of people running around made it seem chaotic, there also seemed to be a purpose in all they did.

Nod pointed out the various vantage points with his whip.

"To the right there, by the river, is the laundries, below 'em the cesspits, above stables and forage. In the center the living accommodation, to the left the cooking areas. Below us are the money-changers. Top left the brothels. Clear space in the middle, the market, held daily. Doubles up for special entertainment at night."

"What sort of special entertainment?"

"Oh, dancing girls, snake charmers, acrobats—whatever's going. One year there were those belly dancers from Afriky: sight for sore eyes they were. . . ."

It seemed Master Scipio was right: everyone was catered for.

Rent-a-tent came first. We hired four. Scipio, interpreter Justus, horse master Antonius and I shared one, the remaining guards and mule drivers another, larger, and our goods took up the last two.

The sleeping tents were circular, those for the goods rectangular. The poles were bamboo, the canvas thin and light, for no rain was expected at this time of year. Other traders had brought their own, more luxurious, with hangings to divide the interiors into smaller sections for sleeping or entertaining. Some had oriental rugs and silken cushions to sit upon, small brass or inlaid wooden tables, oil lamps and fine crockery, but we had grass matting, stools and wood-frame beds strung with rope, which were highly uncomfortable. I stated my intention of sleeping on the floor, but Scipio pointed silently to a double column of ants, in one side of the tent, out of the other. He then handed me some small clay cups.

"Fill these with water, then put the feet of the beds

in them, otherwise we'll have all sorts climbing up. Bad enough with the mosquitoes."

He wasn't joking; I spent a most uncomfortable night, listening with dread for the sudden silence which meant they had found their target. The next night I was given a jar of evil-smelling grease, which helped, but that first day I was as spotty as any adolescent lad.

Even without the mosquitoes, that first night would have kept me wakeful. I had not yet learnt how to fold my blanket so as to even out the rope sling I was suspended upon, the moon shone with relentless brightness through the thin walls of the tent, and the night was full of unaccustomed noise. There were snores from my companions, barking from scores of dogs—including Growch, who was absent without leave—the flap-flap of canvas as it responded to the night breeze, shouts and yells in the distance, and somewhere someone was singing what sounded like an endless dirge full of quarter tones that scraped at my sensibilities like the squeaks of an unoiled axle.

That first day—and many afterwards—was spent visiting tent after tent with the attendant interminable bargaining that seemed so much a part of any sort of trade out here. No price was ever fixed, not even for the food we ate, and even less so for the goods we bought and sold. A great deal of exchange and barter took the place of coin: we exchanged all our wool, for instance, for what seemed to me a minute quantity of saffron and some lily bulbs, but Scipio was more than satisfied.

I had to attend as it was part of my (supposed) training, and if it hadn't been for the endless hospitality—sherbet, yoghurt or mint tea, small sweet cakes or wafers—I should have dropped off long before the sun was high. Nearly everything had to be done through our interpreter, Justus, and one had to go through all the politenesses of enquiry about travel, friends, relatives, weather and health long before one revealed one's true objectives. It seemed such a waste of time, but Master

Scipio was insistent that I realize it was the only way to get things done, and was less than sympathetic when I begged off the last visit with an ill-concealed yawn.

"I'm sorry: I didn't sleep very well last night. I'll be better tomorrow, I promise."

"And so you better had; you're here to work, to learn, to become a trader, and a night or two's lost sleep is neither here nor there. A young lad like you should party the night away and then be fresh as new milk in the morning. I don't know what the world is coming to: why at your age . . ." and so on.

They went off on their last visit, I smeared myself with grease, fell on the bed and must have slept for hours, for when I awoke, hungry and refreshed, they were all abed and snoring and it must have been around an hour past midnight. It was Growch's cold nose that had woken me: he was hungry too.

As he had been absent most of the day I wasn't sympathetic, would probably have turned over and tried to sleep again, except that my own stomach was grumbling likewise. I was also sweaty and sticky and needed a good wash. By the sounds outside, the food stalls would probably still be open, so I swung my legs off the bed and we crept out through the tent flap into the moony night.

It was as near light as day, and there was no problem in finding our way towards the cooking stalls. I found one of our guards seated on a long bench by a large barbecue and he invited me to join him in a dish of chicken, lentils and herbs. I sneaked some to Growch, then repaid the guard by buying the wine. While we travelled food and lodgings were paid for out of the travelling purse, so at a place like this we were given a food allowance every day, the same for all. The guards and drivers were either paid their wages at the end of the journey or re-engaged to be paid at the other end on their return, which was the case with our guards and drivers, so they would have little enough to spare. I left him a couple of coins for more wine, then strolled in the

direction of the river, hoping it would be deserted
enough for a wash.

It seemed, though, that some people worked throughout the night. The forage-and-horse lines were relatively
quiet, but the launderers were hard at work, washing and
rinsing, beating out the dirt on great flat stones and drap-
ing the clothes out on rocks to catch the early sun. Here
the river was scummy with dirt, which flowed on down
towards the cesspits, where I could hear the noise of
digging.

I turned north, past the great tumps of hay and straw
to where the land grew rockier and the river flowed
faster, and was lucky enough to find a tiny sandy bay
which curved round a pool where the water was quieter.

I gazed about me but could see no one, and all the
activity seemed to be away south.

"Keep watch," I said to Growch. "I fancy a quick
dip—"

"You're mad!" he snorted. "Wouldn' catch me bathin'
in that! Un'ealthy, all this washin' . . ."

I stripped right down and plunged into the water, stifling a yell as the freezing mountain water all but
numbed me. Summer it might be, but the water didn't
know that. After the first shock, however, I luxuriated in
the fast-flowing water as it washed away the stinks and
grime of the last few days. Even my bruises from the
bolting horse had started to fade, I noted. My underwear
and shirt joined me in the water: they could dry out on
my body, for the night seemed positively hot after the
icy water.

My last act before getting clothed again was to pick
up a furious, scratching, nipping Growch, and dump him
in the deepest pool I could find. . . .

He cursed for a full fluid minute without repeating
himself when he reached dry land, but I had a couple
of raisin biscuits in my pouch which mollified him somewhat, though he did treat me to an exhibition of the

hollow cough he had suddenly picked up, and shivered most convincingly.

"Don' ever do that again! 'Nough to give me my death, that was!"

I suggested a walk, to dry us both off.

"Quickest way to the food tents is straight across," he said, so that was the way we went, though I doubted they would still be serving. Luckily for him we found a couple of stalls still open and I bargained for some skewers of meat, which we chewed as we wandered back towards the sleeping tents.

Growch stopped in midstride. "Listen . . ."

At first I could hear nothing, then the wind picked up the sound. A soft whimpering, moaning, keening, like the sound a child will make when it has been punished and sent to bed, but dare not make too much noise unless it invites more punishment. The breeze changed direction and the noise died away, then I heard it again.

Growch's nose was working overtime. "Back there," he said tersely. His nose was pointing way beyond the rest of the encampment. "Not nice . . ."

My ring was warm on my finger, so there was no danger, and there was something in the sound that called out to me, like the despair of a trapped animal. Almost without conscious thought I started to walk towards the crying. At first, in spite of the moonlight, I could see nothing unusual, but as I rounded an outcrop of rock I saw what looked like a huge cage, or series of cages, like those in which they kept the exotic animals on offer.

But animals didn't sound like this, or smell like this either.

I wrinkled my nose with distaste and beside me Growch was growling, not in anger but rather in a mixture of bewilderment and disgust, as if this was a situation he did not know how to cope with. I moved closer till the moonlight threw the shadow of the bars across me like cold fingers, and I could see the full horror of what lay behind them.

The cages were crowded with human beings, men, women and children, all shackled, and all standing, sitting, or lying in their own foulnesses. Even in the stews of large towns I had smelt nothing like this, and it was not only the excrement but a sort of miasma of despair and fear that came from the unwashed captives that made me recoil in disgust.

Hands were stretched out between the bars towards me, the keening rose in volume and now there were words I could not understand, except that they were pleas for help. Against my will I moved closer and now the chains were clanking, the babble of words grew louder and fingers clutched at my sleeve with a strength I would not have thought possible.

"I can't do anything," I said urgently, although I knew they would not understand. "Let me go. . . ."

But their seeking hands found more and more of me, until there was a prickle from my ring and almost at once a shout and running feet. At once I was released and, looking back, I saw a couple of men with lanterns bobbing in their hands running towards the cages.

"C'mon," barked Growch urgently. "We don't want to be caught by that lot. They'll think we've been tryin' to help 'em escape. . . ."

Dodging in and out of whatever shadow I could find, I ran back to the safety of the lines of tents, my heart beating uncomfortably fast, my mind churning. It was not that I didn't know slavery existed—why, in the very village in which I had grown up, we were less than animals to the lord of the manor, who held the power of life and death, imprisonment or mutilation, as he chose. But there at least we had known the rules and abided by them, and life was comfortable enough if we paid our dues. Besides we knew no other existence; those poor captives back there had been snatched away from homes and families against their will—and what sort of future could they expect?

That they would be exploited there was no doubt. If

you paid for something you expected your money's worth. Physical labor, prostitution, degradation, these were the least they could look forward to. Perhaps I should not have minded so much if I hadn't remembered Signor Falcone's far kinder fate—but where were the Suleimans of this world to rescue this batch? And the thousands of others, both now and in the future? How many of these would still be alive in, say, a year's time?

I was saddened and frustrated, and said extra prayers for those poor creatures before seeking what I thought would be a sleepless bed, but I must have been more exhausted than I thought, for I slept like a child.

The following days were spent in more trading. It seemed that you could exchange what you had for something of equal value, and the next day swap that for something you considered to be more valuable, sell half that, find a customer for the rest, use the money for another purchase and so on. In this way our tents of goods were emptied and filled at least three times to my knowledge. Master Scipio did not appear to lose by these deals for he went about with less than his usual degree of taciturnity, though whether this had anything to do with the nightly entertainments he went to, I do not know. Sufficient to note that he, Justus and Antonius seldom came to bed before the small hours.

The pattern of barter and trade soon became easier for me to follow, although I still found the whole process tedious and realized I would never have either the patience of Matthew nor the acumen of Suleiman. But this apprenticeship was the only way to my goal, so I tried my hardest to learn and even earned compliments from Scipio for my diligence. Of course there were still the language barriers, but I was picking up a word or phrase or two of Arabic every day and could refer to our interpreter, Justus, if I had need.

On the fifth day I asked Scipio how much longer we

should be at Küm, to receive the answer that we awaited one particular trader to conclude our business.

"We shall do no more trading until he arrives," continued Scipio, "so why don't you take the afternoon off and see the sights? Here, go buy yourself a trinket or two," and he tossed me a couple of coins.

Glad enough not to be shut up in a stuffy tent for hours, Growch and I wandered off into the sunshine. For many this was the afternoon time, which meant we could roam at will without being trampled underfoot, so we stopped for sherbet and barbecued meat on sticks, then watched a basket weaver for a few minutes. Growch decided he was going to investigate what sounded like one of the interminable dogfights that went on day and night, so I just walked where my feet took me, refusing a sweet seller here, a rug seller there, until I found myself at the western end of the camp, beyond the tents.

Here on the edge of the encampment lived those too poor to hire tents, or nomads who preferred to wander the fringes with their flocks, sleeping under the stars. Among the former were the fearsome men from the far north who had brought their shaggy ponies laden with furs, carvings of wood and bone and metal ornaments in the shape of dragons and strange sea creatures. I had learned from the horse master, Antonius, that they found no trouble in disposing of their wares, exchanging them for salt, dried fruits, linen and presents for their women: combs, polished metal mirrors, needles and colored threads, but that as it was all strictly barter they were always short of cash for food and amusements, and often went to unorthodox methods to obtain it. Of course they could go straight home once the goods were exchanged, but it seemed they stayed as long as they could, loath to return to their cold and barren lands.

They were wild enough to look at, these northerners. Dressed in their outlandish gear of iron skullcaps (some with horns affixed), fur capes and short leather trews, their faces scarred with ritual knife cuts and adorned with straggling moustaches, they would have been fearsome enough even without the assortment of knives and axes they stuck in their belts.

If truth would have it though, they were probably no more fearsome than the adolescent town louts of any large town, swaggering the streets with boasts of their conquests on the field and in bed, swearing that they could drink anyone under the bench. All mouth and cock, as my mother used to say.

They appeared to have arranged some sort of wrestling match and had shouted up a reasonable audience for it, one man busy taking bets on the outcome. It was to be a no-holds-barred free-for-all, with kicking, gouging, biting, hair-pulling and balls-grabbing part of the fun, as a bystander explained to me; he seemed to think all the fights were fixed, but watching the first, in which the loser ended up with half an ear torn off and his face ground into the dirt till he lost consciousness, I wasn't convinced.

Someone came round with an upended skullcap and I tossed in the smallest coin I could find. Another bout was just starting—promising, from the look of the combatants, to be even bloodier than the first—but by now more people, siesta over, had arrived to watch, and being slighter and smaller than most I found myself elbowed out to the fringes, where I could see but little. I had just decided to look for amusement elsewhere when there was a nudge on the back of my leg and Growch, absent till now, said quietly: "Look at that feller over there; pickin' their purses, he is. . . ."

Nearby was a stack of bales, ready for loading onto the shaggy ponies when these warriors decided enough was enough and I moved behind it to watch the thief unobserved. He was younger than most—around seventeen I should guess—and slim, stealthy and quick. I could not help but admire the way he circled the back of the crowd, picking his next victim, then holding back till the people surged forward at a particularly vicious

moment in the wrestling to yell encouragement to one
or other contestant, then taking advantage of the press
of bodies to lift a purse to his hand, weigh its possibili-
ties—I saw him reject two in this way—and then use his
sharp knife to detach pouch and contents from its owner.
Judging from the bulge at the back of his trews he had
been busy for quite a while.

I was so busy admiring his expertise that it wasn't until
he had lifted three more purses that I realized that I
should do something about it. But what? Shout "Stop
thief!"? Thieving was a sin, but did I owe the gullible
crowd anything? Besides he was an artist, in his own way,
and nearly everyone would steal if the need was great—
Stop it, Summer! I told myself severely. Never mind the
ethics, just prevent him from further robbery.

I had a word with Growch, then stepped from behind
my hiding place and tapped the young man on the shoulder. He jumped about a foot in the air and was about
to bolt, but Growch's teeth were now fixed lovingly in
his right ankle, and he had no alternative than to follow
me to my hiding place behind the bales.

Perspiration was pouring off his forehead and I could
smell the acrid sweat of fear. We knew not a word of
each other's language but I mimed my disgust at his
actions and threatened to trumpet his thefts to all
within earshot.

He crumpled at my feet; purses and bags came tum-
bling from his trews. One by one he offered them to me,
his hands shaking, but this was not what I had meant at
all. He was obviously terrified, so the purpose of my
intervention had worked: there would probably be no
more stealing today.

I shook my head vigorously at the pile of purses at my
feet and backed away, but he must have thought I
wanted more, something special, for he offered me a
blue amulet that hung round his neck, then an iron ring
set with a red stone, and the more I shook my head,
waved him away, the worse he got. I suddenly realized

the reason for his fear; thieves could be hung, or at the least their hands cut off—

Something was thrust into my hands, a hard object wrapped in soft leather, and from the look of the thief's face it was his prize possession, the ultimate gift. I unwrapped it, curiously, but all it was was a piece of stone or rock or metal pointed at one end, about two fingers long and one wide. There was a small groove around the middle and wound round this was a piece of gut with a loop at the end so that it could be hung from one's finger. What was it? A weapon? A child's toy?

My puzzlement must have shown, for the thief took it from my hand, gestured to the north and held the stone so that it pointed in that direction. He looked at me, then turned the pointed end to the south, let it go—and it swung back to the north again. He handed it back to me and it worked once again. Sure that there was some trickery I twisted the gut round and round and let the stone twirl—still it ended up pointing north. Light dawned: this was a fabulous navigating instrument that would work even if the sun was hidden or the night without stars. Just think how wonderful it would be at sea, with no landmarks to steer by!

But apparently this stone had other properties, for he held out the iron ring on his finger and the stone swung towards it, then to his iron dagger and it did the same. He shook his head, indicating that it would only work away from iron.

As the sounds of the fight—which I had completely forgotten—rose to a real hubbub of yells and counter-yells, I tried the stone myself on an iron spear, a discarded buckle, then back to the north again, thinking with wonderment as I did so that there must be the biggest mountain of iron in the whole world up there in the frozen wastes—

" 'E's orf!" barked Growch. "Want me to chase 'im?"

I shook my head. The thief was gone with his gains,

but he had left behind something far more precious to me: a magic stone!

When I returned to our tent and showed it to the others, I could not miss the look of envy on their faces.

"That there is a Waystone," said Antonius at last. "Heard of 'em but never seen one before."

"Look after it well, boy," said Scipio. "It could fetch a penny or two. Want to sell it?"

I shook my head.

"Where did you get it?" asked Justus.

I decided to tell them half the truth: the rest was too complicated. "I had it from one of the northerners. He wanted cash to spend before he left for home."

Luckily they didn't ask me how much I had spent, but apparently they, too, had a surprise for me. Sayid ben Hassan, the trader they had been expecting, had turned up at last, and we were to go to his tent at sundown for the usual courtesies.

"So, spruce yourself, boy; put on something more appropriate. And we don't take dogs."

Obeying Master Scipio's instructions I scared up a clean shirt and the clothes I had bought in Venice, sending the rest down to the laundry via one of the guards. Buying a bucket of water from one of the water sellers I made myself look as presentable as I could, and bribed Growch to be good in my absence with a pie from the stall nearest the tents.

Sayid ben Hassan's tent was at the end of a line. He had obviously brought his own, although the three next to it, full of goods, were hired. It was huge, to my eyes, easily rivalling any others I had seen. Fashioned of some dark-blue material, thicker than the usual canvas, it was layered like some extravagant fancy, the lowest being a sort of corridor, then the next, rising higher, compartmented into small rooms and the third and highest a spacious circle full of rugs, small tables and embroidered cushions.

Incense smoked on one of the tables—a sickly sort of

smell, like powder—and water was bubbling in a little burner. A servant came in and made mint tea and remained to serve small dishes of nuts and raisins. Elaborate courtesies followed, meaning nothing but essential to Eastern hospitality. Then out came the cargo manifests from both sides and the haggling began. For once I didn't mind, for there was plenty to look at.

Sayid himself was a tall, slim Arab with a large hooked nose and piercing black eyes. He was dressed simply enough in white robes, but on his wrists were several gold bangles and the dagger at his belt had a jewelled hilt. The servant and the guards outside were all young, handsome men, dressed in short blue jackets and voluminous baggy trews; and the rugs, hangings, cushions, shawls, tables, lanterns and pottery were of the highest quality. I wouldn't mind living in such sybaritic luxury, I thought, but there was something perhaps a little too soft, too cloying, for it to be enjoyed forever.

I dragged my mind back to the haggling and Justus' whispered translations. It seemed that we had raw ivory from Africa and cotton from the same source and he had a mix of spices and silk carpeting of an incredible lightness and color. I let my mind drift again, only to be brought up short by the mention of my name.

"Master Scipio just said that you will be travelling with Sayid to—"

"With him? Why not with you?" I interrupted. Surely I wasn't going to be shuffled off to someone strange yet again?

"I thought you understood that," said Scipio. "We all go only so far, you know. We each have our own territory and our own contacts. I go no further than this." He saw me open my mouth and snapped: "Don't argue! As an apprentice you do as you are told! If you don't wish to continue your journey now you may come back with me for the winter but you will have to start over again next year. Or, if you wish, you can surrender your papers right now and cancel your apprenticeship. It's up to you."

Out of the corner of my eye I could see Sayid listening
to what was said, and from the expression on his face I
believed he understood much more than people imagined. For some reason I began to blush, and I thought
I saw a spark of amusement in the Arab's eyes. He murmured something to Scipio, who looked annoyed.

"What did he say?" I whispered to Justus.

"He said ... He said he didn't know Master Scipio
was in the habit of hiring children to do a man's job!"

All of a sudden I hated this supercilious Arab with his
fine tent and expensive accoutrements and would have
given anything not to be travelling with him. But what
choice did I have? I had come this far in pursuit of a
dream, far, far further than I had ever been before. How
big was this world of ours, anyway? If I went back now
I would be wasting all I had planned and saved for. And
it would all be worth it in the end, it had to be!

"I shall be honored to travel with you," I said and
bowed to Sayid.

"Good, good," said Scipio. "And now, if the business
is concluded I believe Sayid wishes to visit the slave
market?"

The Arab nodded.

"Then we shall join you. Come along, boy: it should
be an interesting experience for you."

CHAPTER FIVE

We made our way to the open marketplace, cleared now of stalls and lit with flares and torches. A temporary platform had been erected in the middle and there, huddled together as if for mutual protection, were the captives I had seen in the cages.

They had all been washed down, for there was less smell, and now the shackles had been removed and they were roped loosely between the ankles. They looked reasonably well fed; most were dark-skinned, but one or two were lighter. An overseer stood on the platform with them, running the thongs of a whip through his fingers.

Many of those crowded round had merely come to watch, but there was a scattering of genuine traders like Sayid, who had their servants clear a way close to the platform.

The slave master, a fat Arab wearing rich robes, had a thin, drooping moustache and great dark pouches under his eyes. He waited until he reckoned all prospective buyers had arrived, then stepped up onto the platform and the sale began.

But first he had to extol the worth of his wares, the exotic locations they had come from, the distances travelled, the hardships he had had in transporting them, all to bump up the price as master Justus explained as he translated for me. "He doesn't say how many he lost on the way, though," he added.

I shivered, although it was a warm night.

One by one the slaves were paraded around the platform. Bids were called in a leisurely fashion, and betweentimes would-be buyers went up on the platform and examined the slaves as casually as they would choose fruit in a market. Mouths were wrenched open for teeth to be counted, heads inspected for ringworm or lice, joints tapped, eyelids lifted and—embarrassing to me at least—genitals were scrutinized for disease and, in the case of the men, testicles weighed in cupped hands.

"Estimating whether they will be good breeders," said Scipio. "Bit of a hit-and-miss way to do it, I should have thought. I remember . . ."

He turned to Antonius and I missed the rest.

The slave master could have earned his living on the stage. He had a rather high-pitched, whiny voice, but he wiggled and postured across the platform in spite of his bulk, all the while beseeching, cajoling, exhorting. He begged for bids, he pretended horror at their paucity and near wept with gratitude when his price was reached.

Sayid ben Hassan went up to examine four men of much the same height and age. He bid for three and settled for two, having them led off by four of his guards. Once again Justus explained to me.

"He had an order for two good-looking blacks for a widow in Persia. Got fancy tastes, apparently. Told to look for sweet breath and large, er, you-know-whats."

"Why didn't he bid for the fourth one?"

"Foul teeth and a leery left eye."

We were coming to the end; now there were only some four or five scrawny children left. These were going at much lower prices.

"Might survive, might not," said Scipio. "Not everyone wants to take a chance on a child. The next one, though, he's different: fetch the highest price of the night, I shouldn't wonder," and he pointed to a slight, exceptionally beautiful black boy of perhaps twelve or thirteen with huge, lustrous eyes.

"Why?"

He gave me a quick, almost contemptuous glance. "Where've you been, lad? Maybe you missed out on all that, but he's ripe for it. Bum-boys like that will be pampered pets for years, then go to train others. Wait for the bidding. . . ."

And indeed the boy fetched an astronomical sum, sold after brisk bidding to a thin Arab with long slim fingers that could not forbear from caressing his purchase even as he led him away. Another two children went for small sums, and now there was only one figure left. At first I thought it must be a dwarf, so much smaller and squatter he was than the rest. The other boys had been either brown or black, this one was a sort of yellowish color. His hair was as black as the others had been, but unlike theirs it was straight as a pony's tail, hanging over his eyes in a ragged fringe. His body was muscular enough, but his legs were slightly bandy and he scowled horribly.

For the first time the auctioneer seemed less than confident.

"What does he say?" I asked Justus.

"He says the boy is special. He comes from the east, was captured by brigands, nearly drowned trying to escape, was sold to someone or other who lost him in a game of chance. He speaks an unknown tongue, but is fit and healthy and good with horses." He yawned. "That's as may be, but the lad looks like trouble to me. Probably a pickpocket and thief—Ah!"

This exclamation was prompted by the said small boy suddenly bending down and freeing himself from the ropes around his ankles, butting the overseer in the stomach and jumping off the platform into the crowd. Although he seemed as slippery as an eel as he successfully eluded one pursuer after another, he really had no chance in that audience, and was finally hauled back onto the platform, kicking and biting. The overseer grabbed him by his hair, lifted him off the ground and hit him so hard across the face that he at last hung limp and shuddering.

My ring was suddenly warm on my finger, throbbing with my heartbeat.

The auctioneer stepped forward and spoke, but his words were lost in a howl of derision from the crowd.

"He says all the boy wants is a bit of correction and lot of understanding," translated Justus, without me asking. He snorted. "The only thing that child would understand is a rope's end. . . ."

The slavemaster made a last appeal; the overseer lowered the boy to his feet and gave him a shake. The boy turned his head and spat, accurately.

The audience clapped and jeered, but in a good-natured way, the overseer lifted his hand to administer another blow—and the ring on my finger throbbed harder than ever.

Without quite realizing what was happening, I found I was on my feet.

"I offer—ten silver pieces," I called out, astounded to hear my own voice. Now why on earth had I done that? I sat down again in confusion, conscious of the incredulous looks of those around me. Never mind: perhaps the auctioneer hadn't understood, for I was speaking in my own tongue.

But slave-trading auctioneers don't get rich without learning more than one language. He understood all right. He gesticulated, cupped his ear, pretended he had misheard my paltry bid. Then came the histrionics. The very idea that anyone could have the gall, the impertinence to offer a mere ten pieces of silver for this treasure of a boy! High spirited he might be, yes, but with a little judicious discipline . . .

He appealed to the audience: he would be generous. As a great favor he wouldn't ask for twenty-five silver pieces, though even that was a mockery: just this once he would settle for fifteen, although that in itself was sheer robbery . . . the bargain of the day! Now, what about it?

The audience laughed, they jeered, they clapped their hands together, they pointed at me.

"What are they saying?"

"That yours is the best offer he will get!"

As if to underline this the boy tried to kick the overseer where it would hurt the most and almost succeeded, to be rewarded by another blow to the head. My ring throbbed again and I leapt to my feet.

"Stop that! I said I offer ten silver pieces—"

Scipio reached up to pull me down. "Steady on, boy: if you're not careful you really will buy him, and you don't want ..."

But I was pushing myself to the front. I stepped up on the platform, fumbled in my purse and took out the ten coins.

"My final offer! Take it or leave it!"

The slave trader stared at me. "Twelve?"

I knew enough Arabic to count and shook my head.

Behind us the audience were whistling and jeering. The auctioneer must have realized he was making an idiot of himself by trying to force up the price, because his face darkened and he snatched the coins from my hand, grabbed the boy and thrust him towards me.

"Take the son of Shaitan then," he hissed between his teeth in a sort of market-Latin. "And may Allah deliver me from such again. You deserve each other!"

The boy had sunk to the ground. I touched him on the shoulder and he flinched. Reaching for his hand, I pulled him to his feet.

"Come with me. There's nothing to fear."

I knew he would not understand, but hoped the tone of my voice was enough. The ring on my finger had quietened down, so I was obviously doing the right thing. Not according to Scipio, Justus and Antonius. They were loud in condemnation.

"Complete waste of time and money ... be off as soon as you look away ... watch your purse, etc. ..."

Luckily Sayid ben Hassan had already left, so I didn't

have to undergo his scorn as well. As it was I felt like a mother who has been left with her newborn for the first time: I hadn't a clue what to do next.

I needn't have worried. "What you goin' to do with that?"

Him as well! But that was the spur I needed. "We're going to feed him, wash him and clothe him, Growch: in that order. And you can come along to see he doesn't run off. Right?"

"Right!" If I hadn't named our chores in that particular order he probably wouldn't have been so cooperative.

Keeping a firm hold on the boy's hand we made our way over to the food. I let him choose. He pointed to rice, curd cheese, and yoghurt, mixing it together in the bowl and eating hungrily with his fingers, while Growch and I chose something more palatable. I let him have a second helping, then dragged him towards the river.

All at once he twisted away and was gone, running across the sand like a young deer.

"Growch . . ." But he was already in pursuit, his short legs a blur of determination. They both disappeared behind some rocks, there was a yell, a cry and then Growch's bark.

"Come and get 'im!"

When I reached them the boy was sitting on the ground rubbing his left ankle, where a neat row of dents, already turning blue, showed how my dog had floored him.

I knelt by his side and mimed a slap, upon which he immediately cowered, but I shook my head. "No," I said slowly. "But you must be good," and I made soothing gestures. "And now—" I mimed again "—down to the river to wash . . ."

Half an hour later we were all soaked, for it was obvious the boy and water were virtual strangers, but at least he didn't smell anymore. We found the tailors and menders next to the launderers, which should have been obvious. Now what clothes to fit him with? I looked at his naked body and could see faint marks which were paler than the rest. It seemed that once he had worn short trews of some sort and a sleeveless jacket. I asked the tailor in market-Latin and sign language for what I wanted, adding underdrawers and a short smock, remembering what Signor Falcone had said about the cold to come. We bargained, the tailor fetched a relative to help with the sewing, and the clothes were promised within the hour.

What next? I looked at the scowling little face: I could hardly see his eyes. At the barbers he panicked again once he saw the knives and shears, but this time I had a firmer grip. Patiently I mimed and he consented to sit on a stool, his eyes tight shut, shivering like a cold monkey as the barber snipped and cut his hair into a basin cut, so that at least his eyes, ears, and nape of the neck were free of the wild tangle that had obscured them before.

The barber brushed away the cut hair from the boy's face, neck, and shoulders, then proffered a polished silver mirror. The boy stared at his reflection, his narrow eyes slowly widening, until at last he flung the mirror away before bolting again.

"Probably never seen hisself afore," said Growch resignedly, before taking off in pursuit. This time he didn't get so far, and I led him back to the tailor's. The clothes were ready, and now, washed, barbered and decently dressed, he really looked quite presentable.

But how to keep him from running off? He looked quite capable of taking care of himself, but supposing another slave trader found him? Or if he was caught stealing and had his hands chopped off? Or starved to death because of not knowing the routes? No, I had bought him and he was my responsibility.

But how to convince him of that? How to explain that he would travel with us until he was near enough to his home and people to travel alone? How had things been explained to me as a child, when words were not enough?

Of course! I led him back out beyond the tents until I found a smooth stretch of sand. I motioned him to sit beside me, then pointed at myself, repeating my name slowly and clearly, Then I pointed at him and raised my eyebrows in enquiry. He just grinned as if it were some sort of entertainment, but at least it was the first time I had seen him smile. I tried again.

"Summer. Summer. Summer . . ."

A grunt, then "Umma . . ."

"Good, very good!" I clapped my hands. Did I have one of those salted nuts left in my pouch? I did, and popped it in his mouth.

"Summer. Summer . . ."

"Zumma. Summa . . ."

I clapped my hands again, gave him another nut, then pointed to him. He said nothing, so I cupped one ear as if I was listening and jabbed him in the chest.

A slow smile spread over his face, making his eyes crease up more than ever. He pointed to himself and out came a string of clicks and whines and grunts that sounded something like: "Xytilckhihijyckntug." I tried it out—hopeless! His black eyes crinkled up more than ever. He repeated the word more slowly and again I made a fool of myself, waving my hands in frustration. Again. And again. The only bit I could remember was the last syllable: tug.

I pointed to him. "Tug?"

He grinned again, then nodded. He pointed to me. "Summa" then to himself "Tug," clapped his hands as I had done and held his out for a nut.

So far so good, but now he had become withdrawn again, the scowl was back, and he kept glancing from side to side as if gauging his chances of escape.

Right, if words wouldn't do, it would have to be pictures. I smoothed out the sand, took out my dagger and drew a circle in the sand. The rising moon cast our images long across the ground, so I moved round until what I drew was clear of shadows. Inside the circle I drew a rudimentary tent, then pointed back at the encampment. Then came two little stick figures. I pointed to him and to me and the tent. He nodded his head. Now came the tricky bit. Moving a little way to the west I drew another circle, another tent, another stick figure, then pointed to myself. Then I "walked" my fingers slowly to the first circle. And stopped, pointing at him and then to the east. He took the dagger slowly from my hand, and I had a moment's panic, then he moved away to the path of the rising moon and drew a wavery circle. A tent inside the circle, a line with a little head atop, and his fingers walked back to the first circle the way mine had done. But had he understood so far? I hoped so, for the next bit was the important one.

Taking his hand, dagger safely back in my belt, I walked our fingers to the west, to my circle, then shook my head, making sure he was watching. Back in the center circle I pointed first to him then to me and used our fingers to reach his circle. I looked at him; his brow was creased in thought. At last he took my hand and we went through the same performance, only this time he did the finger-walking and it was he who shook his head at my circle. When we came to his he nodded his head vigorously, pointed at both of us and clapped his hands. I shared out the last of the nuts.

" 'E's got it," said Growch wearily. "The thickest pup in the world wouldn' 'ave taken that long. . . . Now do the bit about you 'avin' the cash an' buyin' the food and all that. . . ."

That night Tug slept at the foot of my bed, ants or no ants, with a watchful Growch stretched across the tent flap in case he did a runner.

The next morning Scipio and company were keen to be on their way. They were travelling back with another trader for extra safety, and I spent most of the day helping them load up, after making a careful inventory of the goods they carried. They set off midafternoon, with just enough time to make their first scheduled camp stop. Tug had stayed near my side all day, helping with the loading and carrying. He was even more anxious than I was to be on our way, and every now and again he would pull at my sleeve and point towards the east. I had no idea how much longer Sayid wished to stay, so I pointed at the sun, mimed it rising and setting twice, and luckily for Tug's faith in me, was exactly right.

That night I had presented myself at Sayid's tent, and one of the guards pointed me in the direction of the tents packed with goods, which suited us fine. It seemed we were not invited to eat with the rest of them, and I felt a little anxious about this, as food and lodging were normally included, but reasoned that once we were on the road things would be different. So we made pigs of ourselves on chicken and rice and slept comfortably on the bales of wool in the tent.

Tucked inside my jacket were my apprentice papers and a note from Master Scipio to the merchant at our next destination; they had been entrusted to me rather than to Sayid, and for this I was both apprehensive and grateful; apprehensive because it seemed that Scipio trusted Sayid about as much as I did, grateful because it meant that even if I was abandoned I had the means, and the money—for Scipio had given me an advance— to make my own way.

The next day, and the next, Sayid did more trading, we slept in the same tent and bought our own food. On the third morning, however, things were different. At dawn the tent was pulled down around our ears, a string of men carried the goods away and we found ourselves on the edge of the camp, shivering in the cool morning air, while a half-dozen grumbling, spitting camels and the same amount of mules were loaded up.

It was the first time I had been near one of these fabled camels, with the floppy humps, long legs and disagreeable manners. Growch had warned me about them: apparently he had been near enough to just escape being badly bitten. From what I had heard, however, they were the ideal beasts of burden over long journeys, being strong, swift, and needing little water: every three days was enough, Antonius had said.

Water: I had seen two or three large containers being loaded onto one camel. Did that mean we should bring our own? I turned tail and ran back to the water carriers, purchased two flasks and a fill from the yawning vendor. Why didn't anyone tell me? As I arrived back I saw my pack being loaded onto an already overloaded mule; hastily I strapped on my flasks.

It seemed we were ready. The camels were loaded, so were the mules, on two of which perched the cook and Sayid's personal servant. The two slaves the Arab had purchased were manacled in the space between camels and mules. The guards and Sayid were mounted on magnificent Arabs, but where was our transportation?

It seemed we were to walk. (Later it transpired that we were to share the mules, but it was an uneven swap: the servant and the cook were loath to set foot on the ground.)

Tug had given a moan of terror when he saw the chained slaves, but I quieted him. During the last couple of days I had spent an hour or two teaching him simple words and phrases, and he had responded remarkably well. Now was the time for another lesson.

I pointed to the manacled slaves. "Tug bad, chains. Tug good, no chains . . ."

"Tug good," he said perfectly clearly, and held out his hand for a reward.

CHAPTER SIX

Thus began the most arduous part of my journey so far. Our destination, a town called Beleth, was some three hundred miles away, and it took four weeks to reach it. Of those three hundred miles, I reckon Tug, Growch and I must have walked two-thirds. Growch I carried when he was too exhausted to go further. Tug's feet were tough and horny, but after the first day my soft leather boots were the worse for wear and my feet were killing me.

At the first village we stopped at, Tug—yes, Tug of all people!—persuaded me with signs and a few words to buy a pair of the ubiquitous sandals worn there, and after that it became easier. It was Tug, too, who made the first contact with the rest of the caravan that eventually made our presence more welcome. Every night he helped with unloading the camels and mules, assisted with setting up Sayid's tent, brought wood for the cook and led the horses down to drink. He was a marvel with the horses, and before long the guards allowed him to ride their mounts for an hour or two each day. He was even allowed to groom Sayid's own mount, a magnificent white Arab, whose mane and tail nearly reached the ground.

Thus it was we found ourselves welcome in the big tent at night, albeit in the outer corridor with the slaves, and shared the somewhat monotonous food: couscous or rice with whatever meat or vegetables the cook had been able to buy.

We travelled a well-worn trail from village to village, though there were days when we camped out at night. A large fire was always built and the guards would spend the evenings in wrestling with each other or playing endless games of chance. I took these opportunities to teach Tug more of my language; in the meantime he was also picking up a good deal of Arabic. One day I noticed he wore a brand-new knife at his belt; I decided not to ask him where he got it, although I suspected he could gamble with the best.

For the most part the weather was fair, although it became progressively colder, not only because the nights were drawing in, but also because we were climbing, gradually but surely, into the foothills of the mountains that loomed ever nearer. Those nearest were green with thick vegetation; behind, some fifty miles farther away, they assumed a more jagged and unfriendly look, while those on the farthest horizon reared so high they seemed to touch the very sky, their sides white with snow.

Was it there, among those unimaginable heights, that my love, my dragon-man, had his home?

The terrain around us changed in character, too. From sun-baked earth, scrub, and tumbled rocks, with scant water trickling down deep canyons, we then travelled grass-covered slopes, with herdsmen tending their goats along the trail, and through deciduous woods and wind-swept valleys. As we trekked even higher we were among pines and spruce, seemingly brushed by the wings of great eagles soaring on the thermals that sometimes took them beneath us, to dive on some prey unseen. It seemed the less we saw other human beings, the more vigilant Sayid became, and the guards closed up every time we traversed any place likely for ambush, and were doubled at night.

As there were now four guards around the campfires at night, that meant Tug, Growch, and I moved into one

of the smaller cubicles that led off the main room of the
tent. It was so nippy after dark that I wished I had more
blankets, and I envied Sayid the brazier that burned so
warm in his inner sanctum. I envied, too, those guards
he chose to share his luxury: a sort of reward, I supposed,
for their devotion. Sometimes it was one, sometimes two
or three. His method of choosing was always the same;
he would tap the privileged one on the shoulder and
offer him a sweetmeat, upon which they would disappear
to the cosiness of cushions and warmth, and the silken
drapes would be drawn to.

One night I, too, had my chance to sleep soft.

I had rolled myself up in my blanket and was drifting
off to sleep when there was a touch on my head, more
of a stroke really, and I opened my eyes to see Sayid
squatting by my side. As I sat up, struggling free of the
blanket, he popped a sugared fruit in my mouth and
then another. Taking my hand he pulled me to my feet,
nodding towards the inner tent as he did so.

I had taken no more than one step forward when there
was a sudden commotion and somehow or other there
was a fierce little Tug standing between us, knife in hand.
Shoving me back he hissed: "No! No! Bad . . ." and then
followed some words in Arabic I didn't understand.

But Sayid obviously did, for he backed away, a scowl
on his face, after a moment choosing one of his guards
to accompany him, who gave me a big grin and an
obscene gesture before following his master.

"What in the world . . . ?" I turned furiously to Tug.
"Why did you do that?"

"I shouldn't ask, I really shouldn't," said Growch.

But Tug was not inhibited, and after a minute or two
of a few words and plenty of bodily gestures I realized
what I had escaped.

"Yes, yes, thanks!" I said, to save further embarrassment. "Very good, Tug!"

I learned later that it was common practice among the
Arabs to seek out their own sex for relaxation when away

from women for any length of time and no one thought twice about it but, unprepared as I was at the time, I was both scared and disgusted. Luckily there was also a small bubble of amusement lurking around: whatever would have happened if Sayid had found out I was a girl? It would almost have been worth it to see his face. . . .

After that he was very cool towards me, and I also earned the derision of the guards, so it was perhaps just as well that we had our first sight of the city of Beleth less than a week later.

It lay like a child's toy extravaganza at the foot of a steep valley, probably some three thousand feet straight down from us. I could make out what looked like a large square with streets radiating from it, a palace, big and small buildings, twisty alleys and the smoke of a myriad house fires. I wanted to run down the track straightaway, but Sayid camped where we were for the night and I saw why in the daylight, for it took half a day to bring us all down safe, the precipitous trail winding like the coils of a snake in order to use the safest ground.

Everyone had spruced themselves up that morning, and there was a lot of combing, plucking and twisting of hair, oiling of skin and use of a blackened stick to enhance the eyes, but I decided to leave well alone, except for a clean shirt and the donning of my boots once again.

At noon, or a little past, we clattered across the wooden bridge that spanned the narrow river flowing to the west of the city. We had already passed through neat and obviously fertile fields, the soil dark and friable. At the town side of the bridge we passed under a splendid carved arch set in battlemented walls, and onto a broad street, paved with river cobbles, that led after a half-mile to the large square that dominated the center of the city. All the way along the route we were flanked by laughing children and saluted by well-dressed citizens. It seemed

a well organized, wealthy city, and my spirits rose. A
proper bed—

"A proper meal," said Growch.

And no more walking, at least for a while.

Everyone dismounted, and I was glad enough to squat
down and rest in the sunshine as the unloading began
and men rushed in all directions, presumably to herald
our arrival. The square must have been a quarter-mile
across; at the moment it was full of market stalls, but
these looked about ready to pack up for the day. Tall
houses, many set back in courtyards, ringed the perimeter, and facing us was the imposing facade of the palace,
with—as I learned later—one hundred marble steps
leading up to the columned portico, built in the Greek
style. Some twenty or thirty soldiers lounged on the
steps, and others were tossing a ball about in a corner
of the square. All very relaxed and comforting: obviously
they were more for show than use.

I glanced up at the houses. They were in different
styles, although most were white with flat roofs, and the
windows were either tightly shuttered or barred with a
fancy fretwork. Smoke rose lazily into the air and there
were tantalizing snatches of music, pipes and strings and
a tabor. Growch's nose lifted.

"Food . . ." he said.

Just then one of Sayid's guards returned, accompanied
by a fat, waddling creature in purple silks and a large
turban. He was perspiring freely and mopping his brow
with a long scarf, whose color matched his red leather
shoes with curved toes. He and Sayid embraced conven-
tionally and exchanged courtesies, then Sayid produced
papers, the fat man did the same; another thin man in
white started checking the bales and porters appeared
from nowhere and started to carry off the items as soon
as they were unloaded and checked on both manifests.
In no time at all it seemed all that was left to be dealt
with were two loaded mules, three loaded camels, the
slaves, and ourselves.

Sayid signed to his guards and drivers and the animals were led away. He assigned two guards to the slaves and these also were led away, but in a different direction. Sayid remounted and swung his horse in a long curvette before bowing his farewells to the fat man.

"Hey! What about us?" I ran forward to clutch at his bridle.

He spat on the ground just in front of my boots.

"You go with him," and he nodded in the direction of the fat man, who had sat down on one of the bales, mopping his brow again. He shouted something which sounded nasty, indicated us, then reared his stallion so sharply the bridle was snatched from my hand and I tumbled back in the dirt, then rode away out of the square.

I got up, dusted myself down, and walked over to the fat man who had relinquished the last bale to one of his porters.

I looked at him, he looked at me.

I bowed, he did the same. We spoke together.

"My name is Master . . ."

"And whom do I have . . ."

He had a sense of humor, this fat man, because he grinned when I did. I handed him the sheaf of papers Master Scipio had given me and introduced myself. He read through the scrolls rapidly, then handed them back to me, and bowed again.

"Welcome, Master Summer. I am Karim Bey, accredited agent to Master Spicer, and have been these past fifteen years." He bowed again. "I am happy to welcome you to our city, and hope to make your stay as pleasant as possible."

He spoke my tongue very well, albeit in a slightly archaic manner.

"I am happy to be here," I said. "Tell me, what did Sayid say to you about us?"

"Something to the effect that I had inherited excess baggage . . . Do not mind him. He is a very proud man, he likes his own way. But he is trustworthy, and guards his goods well. And now, if you and—your friends—would please to follow me?"

He led us to a pleasant house down a side street, set in a courtyard draped with bougainvillea and with a fountain tinkling away in the center. He indicated a stone bench covered with a Persian rug. Tug and Growch perched themselves on either side of me. Karim Bey looked at me interrogatively.

"My friend Tug," I said, indicating the boy. "I rescued him from a slave market and am trying to find his people. The dog's name is Growch, and he has been with me on all my travels."

"Where does the boy come from?"

"I don't rightly know. He speaks a language no one seems to understand."

"From his looks he comes from farther north and east. Let me have a word. . . ." He tried various dialects, but Tug shook his head, speaking in his strange clicks and hisses. Karim shook his head, too. "No, the language is unfamiliar to me, and he does not appear to understand any Italian, French, Spanish, Arabic, Turkish, Hindi, or Persian, all languages familiar to me. I will make further enquiries." He clapped his hands. "And now I think we shall eat."

Five minutes later we were tucking into kebabs of meat and red peppers, boiled and fried rice, pastry cases full of beans, peas and bamboo shoots, with a dessert of stuffed dates, peaches, cheese, and yoghurt. There was a chilled red wine, sherbet or goat's milk to quench our thirst.

After dining we were invited to bathe and rest, while Karim Bey made arrangements for our lodgings. We were led to a room in which stood two tubs of warm, scented water, towels, and various oils. Tug needed persuading to the water, but not the ointments: he smelt like a bunch of mixed out-of-season flowers when he had finished. In the next room there were pallets for our

siesta, and I persuaded him to take a nap so I could
bathe in private, unafraid my true sex would be discovered. I luxuriated in the chance to have a proper soak
and wash my hair, the first time since I couldn't remember when.

Around dusk Karim sent one of his servants to wake
us up, and announced that we were to lodge with another
of his "regulars"—whatever that meant—and that the
servant would escort us. He added that he would be
seeking my help the next day in the warehouses. More
tallying, I thought dismally.

The servant shouldered my pack with ease and led us
through a maze of streets and alleys until we arrived at
a thick double gate. We found ourselves in a courtyard
with a well in the center, stables to the left, living quarters to the right, and a low arch, on either side of which
was a washhouse and a kitchen, leading through into
what looked like a vegetable garden. Stone steps led up
to a galleried upper floor, with half a dozen closed doors.

The servant put down my pack, saluted and left, just
as a man emerged from the downstairs living quarters
and hurried towards us. He was dark-skinned, black-
haired, small and thin, clad in a white jacket, cap and a
sort of skirt looped between his legs and tucked into his
belt. On his fingers were many rings and a jewel dangled
from one ear, though both metal and gems looked too
large for real worth.

He was already gabbling as he came towards us, and
his speech was the most amazing I had ever heard. He
used words from every language I had ever heard, and
some I hadn't, though when he found where I came
from it settled into a mixture of Arabic, French, Italian,
market-Latin, Greek and what I learned later was his
native tongue, Hindi. Whatever it was, his sentences had
a quaintness that kept me constantly amused.

"Velly welcome, isn't it? Chippi Patel at your service,
young sir! Jolly damn glad see you. Room you are taking.
Up this, pliss," and he led the way up to the verandah.

Stopping at one of the doors he flung it open and ushered us into a small whitewashed room containing two pallets, two stools, two wooden chests, a grass mat, a row of hooks on the wall and a small, shuttered window at the back.

"Habitation of other young sir, Ricardus, happy to share. Boy sleep on mat. Dog too, yes?"

"You are most kind, Master Patel, but—"

"No, no, no! My name Chippi! Mix marriage, Daddy name Chippi, Mummy Patel. Many Patel, few Chippis."

"Very well, Master Chippi—"

"No mater-pater here! Just Chippi . . ."

"Well then, Chippi, my name is Summer, and—"

He took my arm and clasped it fervently, then clapped me on the back. "Happy you meet, Zuma! You happy here. Nice room, nice mate to share . . ."

"No, Chippi," I said firmly, disengaging myself from his clasp (he did smell awfully garlicky) and knowing that if I did not stop this garrulous little man right now I never should get my own way. "We need another. Just for us. For me, my friend Tug, my friend Growch." I indicated us in turn.

"Not friend with dirty pi-dog . . . ?"

"Not pi-dog . . ." I found to my exasperation that I was speaking just like him. "Dog is good friend for many miles. Long pedigree: much money. Not see another like him."

He looked askance at my filthy, tatty animal.

"You right there . . . Now, this room most commodious, and—"

"Karim Bey assured me we should have our own room," I said mendaciously.

That did it. At the mention of the agent's name Chippi scuttled away down the verandah and showed us into another room two doors down, the twin of the first. He had an injured air, but I learned later it was common practice to try to make newcomers share and collect for two separate rooms. Corruption became more rife the farther east we came, but it was all good-humored, played as a sort of game: you won some, you lost some, and within a minute or two Chippi was all smiles again, showing us the washhouse and taking away our dirty laundry, to be returned spotless within hours.

For the next few days I worked busily for Karim, first in the warehouses where I assisted his tally man as goods moved day by day; one morning we would exchange silks from Cathay for pottery from Greece, and in the afternoon check in rice or rugs or rich tapestries. Perishables were usually targeted to the market, but in the main office, full of scrolls, clerks and comings and goings, the rest of the goods were assigned to various caravans, north, south, east or west; orders were taken, part consignments made up, other traders contacted for out-of-the-way requirements. Karim also had an army of scouts distributed throughout the town and outlying villages, ready to report the unusual, and if he thought it worth his while he would send an expert to bargain for whatever it was. He also did his own trading, short journeys only, mainly in small goods and local pottery.

Besides the warehouses, and the office, I was also sent to the market to oversee the trading in the perishables, and by the end of that first week I earned a commendation for my hard work.

"And now we must concentrate on the language. Master Ricardus, he must be much of an age with you, and he was fluent in basic Arabic within weeks, could add and subtract faster than most and bargain with the best. An old head on young shoulders."

"And where is this young paragon now?" I asked, masking my irritation with a smile. I could just imagine this pompous, unbearable young man strutting around dispensing wisdom I didn't want at all hours of the day and night.

"He has accompanied a small caravan some seventy miles south, to act as my agent. It is the second such journey he has undertaken; he made me a good profit the last time. I expect him back within a couple of days."

But in fact he came back that very afternoon. When I returned to our room at sunset, after making a couple of deliveries of orders for ribbons and sewing materials to some small shops down the alleys, Chippi met me at the gate to the courtyard with a conspiratorial smile on his lips.

"Your new friend is back being with us. He has just had a big bath. . . ." He indicated the bathhouse. "At suppertime you will see."

I hurried up the steps, Tug and Growch close behind. I had better have a wash myself, find a clean shirt and comb my hair before I met Wonder Boy. But there was someone in my room already, bending over the wooden chest at the foot of my bed, just about to lift the lid.

"What the hell . . . !"

He straightened up guiltily, then just stared and stared.

"When I heard the name . . . You've come a long way, haven't you, *Mistress* Summer!"

The recognition was mutual.

"My God!" I said, "You . . ."

CHAPTER SEVEN

Instantly my mind was whirled back to a stretch of forest in a country hundreds of miles away. It must have been some eighteen months ago but it seemed like a hundred years. So much had happened in between that I didn't even feel like the same girl. Now the scene came back with sudden clarity, and I could see the dirty-faced stable lad who had helped me and my previous friends escape imprisonment and torture, been well paid for his trouble—and then robbed me of the rest of my moneys.

Even then I had somewhat admired his cheek and, remembering he was only stealing to help his widowed mother and sisters, I had told him to seek out Master Spicer, feeling sure that the kind man would give him a better-paid job in his own stables. I recalled Matthew had said the lad had been sent somewhere for "training," but until this moment had thought no more about it.

But the young man standing in front of me now, with his freshly coiffed hair, fine clothes and added inches of height—he must be at least as tall as I—bore little resemblance to the scruffy boy I had thought to be only about fourteen. Amazing what good food and an easier life could do; he must be about seventeen, I guessed, and the only familiar features were the thatch of fair hair—still untidy in spite of the fashionable basin cut with the curled fringe—the intensely blue eyes with their look of sharp intelligence, and the rather greedy mouth.

"What in the world are you doing here, Dickon?"

"Not Dickon anymore: Ricardus. I'm working for Matthew Spicer as a trainee trader and have done pretty well for myself—"

"So I've heard . . ."

"—and Dickon is a common, peasant name. Latinized it sounds far more impressive, don't you think?"

To me he was still Dickon. "How are your mother and sisters?"

A hint of a scowl. "Well enough. Master Spicer secretly sends them a part of my wages. My eldest sister has got married. . . . But what about you? Why are you here? And why dressed as a lad? What happened to the rest of the ragtag you carted round with you?"

"Part of it is still here," I said, pointing to Growch, who was growling softly. "Quiet, boy; you've met him before." I nodded at Tug. "He travels with us to find his people; he was stolen as a slave sometime back." Tug was scowling. "Friend, Tug. Ricardus. Say it . . ." But he wouldn't, and, still scowling, spat over his shoulder, which is neither easy nor a sign of approval.

"Looks a bit of a dimwit to me," commented Dickon. "What of the others?"

"The knight went back to his lady—"

"Thought you were sweet on him?"

"—and the mare, the tortoise and the pigeon found their own kind."

"What about the pig? The one I saw fly. What of him?"

"Nothing," I said defensively. I still didn't want to think about him. "He—went back to his beginnings." Which was true enough, but light on the full details.

"Thought you might have got some money out of it by selling him to a freak show. Pigs don't fly." His eyes were too sharp, too inquisitive.

"His wings were only temporary things. . . ."

"Oh, fell off did they? You should have sewed them on more firmly. . . . Still haven't told me why you're here, though. Must say you've got nice long legs, Mistress Summer!"

I pulled my jerkin down. "*Master* Summer, if you please!" I had had just about enough time to think. "I'm here for the same reason you are: to learn the business. Matthew—Master Spicer—thought I would be safer dressed this way." Why was I blushing?

He grinned, winked. "Way he talked about you, took me in without question on your word, thought he was keen on you. . . . Fact remains, dressed as a lad or not, this is no job for a female. Surprised he let you come."

"It wasn't a question of letting me—" I stopped. Better not tell him too much. Somehow I didn't feel I could trust him. Apart from that brief meeting a year and a half ago, what else did I know about him except that he was a thief, made the most of his opportunities and had become a bit of a snob?

His eyes were narrowed, considering me. "And no one knows of this change of sex, 'cept me?"

"Apart from Matthew, Suleiman—and Signor Falcone in Venice." Two of the three, anyway.

He seemed satisfied. "Must admit you don't look too bad. Bet you don't walk right, though; women walk from the hips, men from the knee."

"You haven't seen me walk," I objected.

"Not yet, but I'll bet you . . ."

"Just wait and see," I snapped. "At least I don't suppose you have ever been propositioned as a bum-boy!"

His eyes widened. "My, you have been living it up! How did you get out of that one?"

I shrugged. "A knife and a few words, carefully chosen . . ."

"I still can't believe Master Spicer sent you all the way out here just to learn the business." He narrowed his eyes again. "Are you sure you weren't sent out on a special mission? As a spy, perhaps?"

"Don't be ridiculous. I just wanted to see a bit of the world, that's all. I haven't the money to travel as a pampered female and I—we—thought this was a good way to do it." What had he been searching for in the wooden chest? Why was he afraid of someone spying? After all, he hadn't known I would turn up until he saw me.

Chippi came bustling up the stairs to announce that the evening meal was ready.

"Ah, the great friends they have met! Two such pretty young fellows, by damn! Much good pals will be. Wife has prepared special dish. Coming down for same, isn't it?"

Tables were set out in the courtyard as usual, but tonight Chippi deigned to sit with us at the table of honor nearest the kitchen. Mistress Chippi wouldn't join us, of course: women were generally of lower status than the menfolk out here. As dark as her husband, but much fatter, she bustled about setting out delicacies for starters: crisply fried savory biscuits, bean shoots, meat balls. Then came the special dish, a steaming heap of meat and vegetables on a bed of boiled rice. I watched how Dickon would cope; he took up one of the soft pancakes Chippi called chapatis, folded it round a mouthful of food, conveyed it to his mouth without so much as spilling a grain of rice and chewed appreciatively.

"Excellent!" He spoke with his mouth full: he hadn't learned everything yet.

It looked easy enough, and I managed quite nicely but, as I leant forward to scoop up another mouthful, a terrible delayed reaction set in.

My tongue, my mouth, my throat, my stomach—they were all on fire! I had been poisoned! My eyes were streaming, I couldn't breathe. . . . Struggling to my feet, choking and gasping, I signalled frantically for a drink— water, wine, sherbet, anything!

Slurping down whatever was offered—it could have been anything for all the effect it had on the terrible taste in my mouth—I could feel a gradual lessening of the burning heat. Perhaps I hadn't been poisoned after all.

At last I could breathe normally again. I mopped my streaming eyes and looked across at Dickon and Chippi—they were doubled over with laughter!

"It's not funny! What on earth was it?"

"Oh, dearie, dearie me!" Chippi blew his nose on his sleeve. "We are larks having, isn't it . . . First time you eat curry, yes?"

"What?"

"Curry. Very hot being. Wife cook it good, yes, Ricardus?"

"Very good," said the objectionable Dickon, tucking in heartily. "You'll soon get used to it, *Master* Summer."

"I will not!" And I kept my word.

For the next few days Dickon initiated me further into the mysteries of merchanting, and I took care not to show him how bored I became, trying to appear interested and attentive. He of course knew nothing of my true reason for taking on the guise of apprentice; my only worry was Tug, who was growing increasingly restless at being confined to the town.

I had a word with Karim Bey on the subject of moving on as soon as possible, pretending eagerness to travel further. He looked shocked.

"But it is entirely the wrong time of year to venture further, Master Summer; everything closes down shortly because the higher routes will soon become impassable. I had thought you would be content to over-winter here, and learn as much as possible for the spring journeys." He must have seen the disappointment on my face. "I myself shall not be sending out any more caravans. However, as you seem so keen, I will try and get you a place with an eastbound trader, if I can find one. You may well find that you end up at the back of beyond, forced to stay until the snow melts, and find it difficult to return. However, that is up to you."

And with that I had to be content. I told Tug we were

waiting for a special trader to take us further east, and I think he believed me.

Our daily work had to finish sometime, and in the evenings after supper Dickon, Tug, Growch, and I took to wandering down the myriad side streets and alleys that radiated from the square right through to the edges of town, as haphazardly as the tiny veins on the inside of one's elbow.

Here lay the real life of the city, a place where the great and wealthy never came. During the day one might see town officials bustling about in the city proper, respectable citizens about their business, soldiers exercising, merchants fingering the goods on offer in the market, discreetly veiled ladies taking the air, either on foot or in gilded palanquins, and all around were the workers, those who catered to their whims: servants, both male and female, stall holders, farriers, cooks, children running errands, water carriers, weavers, tailors, hairdressers, beauticians, fortune-tellers, launderers, beggars, refuse gatherers, cleaners, night-soil collectors, rope makers, jewellers, wine sellers, oil vendors—in fact all those unregarded people without whom the city could not function at all.

At night, though, it was as if a soft blanket came down on all this bustle and the little side streets and alleys came into their own, for this was where the workers lived. Here they had their homes; here they were born, grew up, loved, hated, became ill, died. Here was all manner of meaner housing; tenements, small one-roomed hovels, stables, tents, holes in the ground or in the walls, shacks and even the bare ground.

Here also were the little family restaurants, minor businesses, brothels, stalls that sold items not available in the open market: strange drugs, stolen goods, information; here there was trade in quack medicines and human beings; much gossip and entertainment; and lastly were the stalls that sold those small, largely useless objects that might just fetch enough to buy the daily bowl of rice.

These alleyways were only dimly lit and the town guard generally gave them a wide berth. It was not wise for a stranger to walk there alone, but I had always felt safe with Tug and Growch, though we didn't go far. However when Dickon heard of our expeditions he insisted on accompanying us, ostensibly as guard, but I suspected he had never dared go alone before and we were merely an excuse. As it was he strutted and postured like a young lord, especially when there was a pretty girl about. He was trying to grow a moustache, none too successfully, and he fancied himself as a lady-killer. In fact on the third evening he thoroughly embarrased me, suggesting a visit to one of the many little brothels.

"I'm not going to one of those! How could I?"

"You're dressed as a lad. You don't have to—participate. You can just watch, can't you?"

"Certainly not! You can do what you like, but I'm staying outside."

"Suit yourself! Just don't get lost: I may be some time. . . ."

Which left the rest of us wandering up and down the street, pretending to examine the goods at one or another of the stalls, fending off too persistent vendors and generally feeling conspicuous. I had almost made up my mind to trust Growch's sense of direction to get us back to our lodgings, when Dickon reappeared with a smirk on his face and ostentatiously adjusting his clothing.

"I hope it was worth it," I said nastily.

"Of course. I always ensure that I get value for money. Pity in some ways you ain't a lad: I could show you a thing or two in this town."

"If I were, I doubt if I'd take advantage of your offer. I wouldn't want to risk catching something nasty."

"I know what I'm doing—"

"Good for you. Can we go now?"

He didn't repeat the experiment, if that was what it was. After all he certainly hadn't been in there more than a quarter hour, however long it had seemed outside. But perhaps that was the way they did things in those places. I wasn't going to ask.

Two nights later something very strange happened.

We had wandered farther than usual and came at last to a narrow street that twisted and turned like a snake almost under the tall battlements that protected the city. Here were more stalls than usual, some set out on the ground on scraps of cloth, others displayed on stools or tables, yet more in tiny cupboardlike niches in the walls. There was less noise than usual and those who passed by seemed to do so as if in a dream. Even the bargaining sounded muted, the examination of objects slow and unhurried. At one corner the street seemed as light as a fairground, at another full of shadows, much as a candleflame in a draught will flare one moment and be down to a mere flicker the next.

I found myself infected with the same strange lethargy, yet my mind seemed as sharp as a needle. I found I, too, was taking my time at each stall, examining everything minutely, yet no one was pressing me to buy. I looked at small prayer mats, embroidery silks, combs and brushes, painted scarves, brooches and bangles; I picked up a length of silk here, a phial of perfume there. I waved a fly whisk, tried on a pair of felt slippers, tapped a brass tray, turned over some table mats, flicked my finger at a tray of pearls that rolled about like a handful of dry white peas; I bought and ate a couple of sticky, green sweetmeats, passed by painting brushes, colored inks, charcoal, dyes, spices, pellets of opium. . . .

Between a hole in the wall occupied by a man selling sachets of sweet-smelling dried flowers and a conventional stall laden with pots and pans, an old man squatted behind a small folding table on which was displayed a heterogenous collection of what looked like secondhand curios. I bent down to see a small, blue brush jar with a chip, a dented brass bowl, a piece of dirty amber, a paperweight dull with use, some scraps of embroidery, a yellowed piece of carved ivory. . . .

I straightened up, ready to pass on, when the old man lifted his head and looked straight into my eyes. He was nearly bald, what was left of his hair hanging white on either side of his face to mingle with a wispy beard. There were laugh lines at the corners of his eyes, and his whole expression radiated a warmth and good humor, although if you asked me to describe him feature by feature I could not have done so.

He nodded at me as if we were old friends, said something I didn't understand, then indicated the tray in front of him. Obviously an invitation to look closer. I glanced around for the others. Tug was bargaining for some sweetmeats in sign language with some coins I had given him. Growch was flushing out imaginary rats from some rubbish heap, Dickon was chatting up the girl selling rice wine in tiny cups.

Why not indulge the old man while I waited for the others? He seemed pleasant enough, although I had seen nothing that attracted me on the tray, except perhaps that little ivory carving—

Strange. The goods looked different. A pearl, discolored; a chipped blue and white cup; a carved bamboo flute the worse for wear; an old inkpot—surely those had not been there before? Ah, there was something I recognized: the little ivory figure. I couldn't quite make out what it was meant to represent. The old man said something, and as I looked up he nodded, wreathed in smiles.

I smiled back and squatted down in front of the tray.

Now the tray was full, and every object, cracked, chipped, dented, worn or just old, all were carved or decorated with representations of living things. The blue brush jar had a lively dragon wrapped around its base, the brass bowl had raised figures of mice chasing each other's tails; inside the amber, carved as a fish's mouth, a tiny fly awaited its fate. Embroidery covered with lotus blossoms, a paperweight with a grasshopper for a handle, a carved bee on the side of the flute looking alive enough to fly away, a pearl etched with chrysanthemums, a blue and white cup painted with butterflies, and an inkpot decorated with a flock of small birds: broken they all might be, but these objects had an exquisite living grace. And around them all, lively as a kitten, cavorted the ivory carving.

Some part of me, the sensible part, told me there was something very amiss here. Half a dozen pieces, less than interesting, then others, and now both lots together, and all worth a second look. But the sensible side of Summer stayed quiet and the credulous Summer just accepted what she saw.

Or thought she saw . . .

The old man stretched out his right hand and took mine; in his left he held a green bowl of water that danced its reflections in the lamplight as the ring on my finger tingled, but not unpleasantly. He nodded at me again, indicating that I should look into the liquid. I leaned forward and found myself gazing into a swirl of colors. Figures passed through the water; I saw a white horse with a horn on its forehead, a frog or toad, a cat, a black bird, a fish. . . . Then something I thought I recognized: another horse galloping across the sands, a scrabbling tortoise, a pink pigeon, a small elongated dog with short legs, a pig . . . Ah, the pig!

A pig with wings. A pig I had kissed three times. A pig that turned into a dragon.

And the girl in the picture kissed the pig-that-was-a-dark-dragon for the third time, and he turned into a man. A dark man called Jasper, Master of Many Treasures, and my heart broke as he turned back into a dragon again and flew away from the Place of Stones—

Leaping to my feet, I dashed the bowl from the old man's hands. I could feel the stupid tears welling up.

"How could you know? Dickon?" I called over my

shoulder. "Come and translate for me, please. I want to
ask this old man a couple of questions."

He, too, had risen to his feet, although he still had
hold of my hand. He was speaking again, but thanks to
Dickon who must have been standing behind me, I now
had a translation.

"I mean no harm, young traveller."

"The pictures in the bowl . . ." I stopped. I didn't want
Dickon to know what I had seen.

"Before you there was another who wore a ring," said
the old man, and now the translation was almost simulta-
neous. "Many, many years ago. She, too, adventured with
animals she was wise enough to call her friends. The rest
you saw was what you wanted to see."

"No! I never wanted . . ."

"Then the head denies the heart it would seem. You
travel far, girl, to find what you do not want, then?"
There was a gentle, teasing quality in his voice, which I
now seemed to hear clearer than Dickon's. "It will be a
long journey for the seven of you. . . ."

"Seven? Three, you mean." Me, Tug and Growch.

"Three is a lucky number, I agree, but seven is better.
She who first wore the ring knew that."

"It's just three," I repeated firmly.

"Life does not always turn out the way you want it. I
think you will need help with your journey, extra help."

"You—know where we are bound?"

"I know everything." He picked up the bowl again,
and miraculously it was still full of colored water. "Look
again. Closer . . ."

Forgetting Dickon, I gazed once more into the bowl.
The colors paled, faded, and now there was just a milky
haze. The haze steadied, snow was falling and I was in
it, flying like a bird between high mountain peaks. But
the snow started to drag at my wings, at the same time
destroying my perspective of the land beneath, the familiar landscape I should know so well. Mountain after
mountain, peak after peak, they all looked alike. The

snow grew heavier and now I was weary, blinking away
the flakes of snow that threatened to blind me. Each
beat of my wings seemed to wrench them from their
sockets; if I couldn't find what I was looking for soon I
should have to land, but it was unlikely I would find
shelter in unknown terrain.

Then, suddenly, I saw it.

A momentary lessening in the blur of snow, and the
three fangs of the Mighty One, gateway to my goal,
loomed up ahead. A turn to the left and I steered
between the first two of the three rock teeth that were
so steep that even now they gloomed blackly in the snow
that could not rest against their sides.

Over at last and down, down, down into the valley
beyond. There was the monastery on its hill, where the
saffron-robed monks rang their gongs, sounded their
queer, cracked bells and said their prayers to an endlessly
smiling, fat god. Finally a switch to the right, away from
the Hill of Constant Prayer and the village beneath, and
a long slow glide to the Blue Mountain and the cave
entrance hidden on the northern face.

Wearily I braked back, my leathern wings as clumsy
as the landing gear of a youngling. Wobbling a little, I
shoved forward my dragon claws and—

"Jasper!" I cried out, and smashed the green bowl into
a thousand pieces. "Jasper! *I* was *him*!"

The old man stooped down and picked up one of the
tiny shards of glass. One piece? No, for now all the others
seemed to fly into his hand and the bowl was whole
again. He tucked it away in his robe.

"And so you now know the way to go," he said. "It is
always the last part of the journey that is the hardest."

My mind was in such turmoil that I could think of
nothing to say—except thank him.

He bowed. "It is nothing; a breath of wind across a
sleeping face, bringing with it a dream of the poppies
over which it has travelled. . . . And now, young traveller,

you were thinking of bearing something away from my tray."

I was? Yes, perhaps I was. That must be why I was bending over the tray again, and now all the creatures and flowers were real, alive. A butterfly perched on my finger, then flew to the old man's beard; a tiny fly cleaned its wings of the amber that had imprisoned it; a fish swam in the brass bowl that the old man tucked away in his robe; a string of mice disappeared up his sleeve; a tiny blue dragon flew to his shoulder then vanished down his collar; a grasshopper leapt to his head, a flock of tiny birds circled the stall and a bee, heavy with pollen, rested for a moment on my sleeve, before crawling up a fold of the old man's robe, whose lap now held a mass of flowers. . . .

Now all that was left on the tray was the little ivory figure. It was still difficult to make out exactly what it was meant to represent—he looked like a mixture of dog, horse, dragon, deer—but he did have a very intelligent expression.

"How much?"

"He is not for sale. He goes where he wishes." He spoke as though the creature had a will of its own, but then nothing would have surprised me now.

"May I pick him up?"

"If he will let you . . ."

What did he do then? Bite? Disappear in a puff of smoke?

Gingerly I bent forward, picked him up between finger and thumb and put him on my palm. Exquisitely carved, he had the body of a deer, hooves of a horse, a water buffalo's tail with a huge plume on the end, a stubby little face with a minihorn in his forehead and what looked like fine filaments or antennae sweeping back from his mouth. Funny that I hadn't been able to see him clearly before, especially as he was the only perfect piece. He sat quite comfortably on my hand.

"What is it—he?"

"That is for him to tell you. If he wishes."

I waited for something to happen, but nothing did, so with a strange reluctance I put him back on the tray. My ring was warm on my finger.

"Are you coming? The young lass over there says her dad has an eating house round the corner." Dickon spoke over my shoulder. "I'm hungry even if you're not."

All the lights were suddenly brighter, and I could smell sewers.

He nudged my arm impatiently. "You've been staring at that tray for hours. Looks like a lot of junk to me."

I looked down. An old man squatted in front of a tray of secondhand objects, none of which I had seen before. The ivory figure I thought I remembered seeing wasn't there.

I shook my head, as much to clear it as a form of negation. "I can't see anything I want," I said slowly. "Thanks for translating just the same." I bowed to the old man, and we moved away down the street. I felt all jangled inside as if someone had jumped me out of a dream too soon.

We were finishing off an indifferent dish of vegetables and rice when Dickon said suddenly: "What did you mean: 'thanks for translating'? I wasn't anywhere near you."

"Yes you were! I called you over because I couldn't understand what the old man was saying. You were just behind me."

"Was never!"

"You're kidding. . . ."

"I'm not!"

And the more I insisted, the more adamant he became. Had I imagined it all, then? The whole episode was becoming less clear by the minute, but still I clung to an image, a feeling: a dragon—me, him?—flying in the face of a storm to the Blue Mountain.

Jasper . . . lover-dragon, dragon-lover.

He was what this journey was all about, of course.

Once upon a time I had rescued a little pig with vestigial wings from a cruel showman. The pig had grown and grown until one day when we found the place where he had hatched out, the pig's skin had been cast away and there was a beautiful, dark, fearsome dragon in the place of my pig.

But why fall in love with a dragon? Because I had loved the pig and the dragon wasn't a dragon all the time. And that was my fault. Three times I had kissed the pig, out of affection and gratitude, and because he was a dragon inside that pig skin I had broken a law of the equilibrium of the universe, and for each kiss the dragon was forced to spend a month a year in human form.

That's how he had explained it to me as he kissed me, made love to me as Jasper the man, just before he changed back into what he called his true self and flew away to the east, where all dragons come from, leaving me sick at heart beside the Place of Stones.

The blind knight had offered me love of a sort, Matthew Spicer had proposed marriage, but it had only been in the arms of Jasper, the Master of Many Treasures, that I had found that overwhelming joy that true love brings.

And that was why I was here, in this strange town many hundreds—nay, thousands—of miles from my home. I would find him, I had sworn I would. I would sacrifice anything for just one more embrace—

"Your turn."

"I beg your pardon?"

"Wake up, Summer!" said Dickon. "I said it was your turn to pay."

I fished among the small change I kept in my pouch (the greater coins I kept next to my skin) and all of a sudden I drew out an extraneous object and placed it on the table.

"What the hell's that?"

"The old man had it on his tray. . . . Quick, I must take it back," and I picked up the ivory figure and hurried out, leaving Dickon to settle up. Search as I would, however, there was no sign of the old man. Even the street seemed different, better lighted, less twisty, and when I found a stall holder I thought I recognized he said he had seen me standing in a corner talking to myself. Which was ridiculous!

In the end we returned to our lodgings, though I promised myself I would go back the next day and try and find the old man. In the meantime I put the figurine on the chest at the foot of my bed and curled up in bed seeking a sleep that seemed strangely elusive. I tossed and turned, flickered in and out of brightly colored dreams I could not recall, but was at last sinking into deeper slumber when all at once there was a voice in my ears, a tiny, shrill voice that snapped me back into consciousness at once.

"Stop thief! Stop thief!"

CHAPTER EIGHT

I sat up at once, my sleepy eyes just making out a shadowy form slipping through the open doorway into the near darkness outside. Stumbling off the bed I made my way over to the door, shut and bolted it. Normally I didn't bother with the bolt, as Dickon and I were the only occupants of the verandah at the moment. Feeling my way back to the chest, I discovered that the lid was open, meaning flint, tinder and candle stub must be on the floor somewhere. I found the first two and was fumbling for the third when that squeaky voice came again.

"To your right a little . . . That's it!"

Needless to say I nearly dropped the lot.

"Who's there?"

Nothing, save Tug's soft breathing and a snore from Growch. Fingers trembling, I at last managed a light and held the candle high. Plenty of shadows but no intruder. Tug rolled up on the floor in his blanket—he still wouldn't use the bed—and Growch curled up at the foot of mine. No one else—

"I'm here. On the floor by your feet. Please don't tread on me. . . ."

I stared down at the ivory figure. Surely not! I must be dreaming.

"Yes, it's me. You can pick me up, if you don't mind. Quite uncomfortable standing on one's head. Thanks."

I found I had picked it—him—up and put him on the

chest, right way up. I stared down; no damage from his tumble as far as I could see. But the voice! Surely that would have woken the others, or one of them would have heard the intruder. If there was one. Suddenly I wasn't sure of anything anymore.

"If you could just touch me with your ring for a moment—that's it—then I shall find the transition much easier. . . ."

I did as he said: my ring thrummed with energy for a moment, but there was nothing but good here.

"Dearie, dearie me!" said the squeaky voice. "It's been such a long time! Ivory is pretty to look at but it hasn't the warmth of amber or the manipulation of wood. But with wood there's always the threat of woodworm of course. . . ."

I sank to my knees in front of the chest; this wasn't happening! That little figure wasn't talking to me, it wasn't, it couldn't!

"Oh, yes I am! I suppose it must be rather disconcerting for you, but if you will bear with me I'll try and make the change to living as quickly as I can. . . ." He thought for a moment. "If you could just hold me in your hands for a moment, warm me up. That's fine. Don't worry about your friends: they can't hear us."

I put him down on the chest again and sat back on my heels to watch one of the most amazing things I had ever seen. It was almost like a chicken breaking from an egg, a crumpled poppy unfurling its petals from the bud; you wondered how on earth it ever fitted inside. Of course this creature's task was different: it had to turn from inanimate to living, but the process seemed about the same.

First I saw the nostrils dilate as the first breaths of air were inhaled, then the nostrils became pinkish and the antennae at the side of his mouth flexed back and forth. Like a chick's feathers, dry little hairs released themselves from the ivory and fluffed up around his face; dark brown eyes blinked and moistened. Then came the ears and throat, the former twitching back and forth till they were set as he wanted. A forked tongue tested the air.

"A little rest: this is tougher than I thought. It's been a long time. Please excuse the delay. . . ."

He curled back his lips, panting a little, and I could see a tiny row of chewing teeth. Now the process speeded up; tiny hooves stamped, ribs expanded, a rump gave an experimental wiggle and lastly a short tail with an outsized plume gave an exultant wave.

"There! That's better. How do I look?"

"Er . . . very impressive." I didn't really know what to say. The whole process was mind-bending, but as I didn't know what he was supposed to look like, I couldn't really qualify my statement.

He seemed to be reading my mind. "You're quite right! I've forgotten the colors, haven't I? Just watch. . . ."

In a way this was the most impressive of all his tricks. From being a dullish creamy yellow, he rapidly developed a uniquely tinted body that glowed like a jewel on the lid of the chest. First came a bright yellow belly, then the fur on his back developed shades of blue, purple, violet, brown and rose, his legs and tail darkened to gray and lastly the plume on his tail fanned out into crimson, gold and green. For a brief moment it seemed that his whole body was lapped by flame, but then he was as before.

"Not bad, not bad at all. I'm particularly proud of the tail: not exactly conventional, but we are allowed a certain latitude. . . . Just a moment. I'd feel more comfortable with a bit more space."

And something that had been beetle-sized rapidly expanded to the dimensions of a mouse.

"Er . . . are you going to get any bigger?" I asked nervously, as the growth seemed to be accelerating.

"Sorry! Not for the moment. Would you like to see just how big I can grow?"

"Not at the moment," I said hastily. "Some other time."

"Very well. I suppose it has taken it out of me a little. . . . Let me introduce myself. My name is Ky-Lin." His voice was less squeaky.

"Ky-Lin," I repeated like a dummy. I found it difficult to cope with what was happening.

"Yes, and you?"

"My name is Summer. Pleased to make your acquaintance."

"A mutual honor."

A little silence, then I plucked up courage. "I'm sorry, but I'm afraid I'm not quite sure to what I owe the pleasure of your company? I found you in my pouch last night, and I was going to try and find the old man tomorrow to return you—"

"Didn't he say that I went where I wanted? Where I thought I was needed?"

"Yes, but—"

"So, I am here. You need me, I think. You have a long journey ahead of you and I believe I might prove useful. The trip sounds interesting and if I comport myself well I shall have earned myself more points."

"Points? For what?" This conversation was very confusing.

"For my Master."

"The old man?"

"No, no!" He looked scandalized. "He is one of the Old Ones, a Master of Illusion, but quite earthbound I assure you. No, I speak of my Lord." He settled back on his haunches. "A long, long time ago there lived a great and good man called Siddhartha, later known as the Buddha. He was so wise and so loving that he gave up all worldly distractions. He had to walk about the world in poverty, preaching of the Divine Way to Eternal Life. He saw life as a great wheel that eventually led to Paradise, which is a way of becoming part of the Eternal. But this way can only be realized by living a perfect life, and as man is not perfect he is given many chances. These take the form of various animal lives or incarnations, accompanied by rewards and punishments—points, if you like. You may be a good horse in one incarnation, and be rewarded by being a man in the next. Or you may be a bad man, and find yourself a lowly insect in another. Do you see?"

I thought so, though it was a novel idea, these many chances to be good. Like all people in my country I had been brought up a Catholic, but since then on my travels had come across many other religions: Judaism, Hinduism, Mohammedanism. It seemed there was more than one road to God. A clever God would understand that just as different countries, different climates, different cultures produced different ideas, so He could tailor these to men's beliefs so that their worship was comfortable to them.

"You are partly following my Lord's teachings," he continued, "because you care about animals. We are taught to go even further; we believe that we must not damage any living thing, because we might be hurting one of our fellows, temporarily on a lower path or incarnation."

"But you—you are not like any creature I have ever seen."

"Because I, and my many companions, were created especially by my Lord Himself to epitomize how many creatures may be one, an harmonious whole. We traveled with Him, as His guards and friends."

"Your Lord, whom you said lived many years ago, has presumably found His Eternal Life: why are you still here, and not with Him?"

There was a longer silence. "I hoped you wouldn't ask. . . ."

"Sorry, I didn't mean—"

"It's all right. You should know." Another silence. "The fact is, I should be perfect, and I'm not. Wasn't."

"Wasn't?"

The words came out in a rush. "I-was-careless-and-trod-on-the-grass. I-was-also-greedy-and-lazy-and-rebellious."

He paused. "But the worst was—I-said-I-didn't-want-Eternity. . . . I thought it would be boring. There! Now you know. That's why I'm here. I can't change my shape, but I have to work off my badnesses by helping others, until my Lord Buddha decides I am fit to join Him."

It seemed so unfair to me. Poor little creature! How on earth could you remember not to tread on grass? I reached out a finger without thought and stroked his head, and there was a little grumbling purr, like a cat, but suddenly he twitched his head aside.

"You mustn't indulge me; that is pure pleasure, and I am forbidden anything like that. I've lost a point already, being proud of my plumed tail a moment ago."

"All right." I had made a mistake with my pig-dragon. "And how many points have you got now?"

"I don't know. The trouble is, my last choice was purely selfish, and my Lord recognized it as such. I came across an old man—he was nearly eighty—who wanted help translating Greek and Roman texts. I reckoned he might last another five years or so, but my Lord saw through my deception, and the old man lived to a hundred and ten. It was hard work, too," he added, and sighed.

I found myself trying not to smile. The idea of this vibrant little creature being tied to dusty scrolls for thirty years . . . I had another idea.

"You speak, or understand, other languages, too?"

"Most. My Lord arranged it so we have an inbuilt translator in our heads."

An extra bonus: perhaps he would be able to make sense of Tug's click-clicks, and find out where he came from.

Ky-Lin yawned, his forked tongue curling back on itself till I could see the ridged roof of his mouth. "And now, it is time for sleep. I shall, with your permission, curl up inside the chest, if you would open it up? Thanks."

A last wave of his tail and I found I couldn't keep my

eyes open nor my brain fit to think over what I had just seen and heard. As I pulled the blanket up round my ears, I realized that I hadn't asked him who had been the potential thief he had disturbed.

And in the morning there wasn't time.

Karim Bey sent for both Dickon and I shortly after dawn. He had found a caravan that had come in the previous day and intended to leave at midday for points further east, with a special order of furs, perfume and German glass. When Karim told Dickon I had asked to accompany it, he at once volunteered to go too. "Just to keep an eye on a trainee," as he put it.

I was surprised: I thought the distractions of the town would have been more enticing. I wasn't sure whether to be glad or sorry; Dickon was a passable lad, a good linguist, knew far more than I did about merchandising and had always been helpful. But there was something, just something I couldn't put a name to, that made me uneasy in his company. It wasn't his womanizing, though that was annoying enough, nor was it his vanity—how many lads of seventeen or so wouldn't take advantage of good wages to dress well? If I were back in my girl's guise wouldn't I want ribbons and fal-lals? No, there was something else, something *sneaky* about him.

We were hurriedly introduced to the caravan owner, a small and undistinguished character called Ali Qased, then Karim paid out moneys for our food and lodgings and the hire of a couple of mules, making sure we realized that the latter would be deducted from our commissions.

I hurried back to our lodgings for a quick breakfast, an even quicker packing—a sleepy Ky-Lin tucked surreptitiously in the lining of my jacket—and a prolonged and formal farewell to Chippi and his wife, with much head bobbing and wringing of hands from them both.

The sun was high in the sky when we set off, winding away from the city and up again into the hills, this time to the east. Tug was beside himself with happiness that we were at last on the move, and sang tunelessly as he trotted along beside us, disdaining the offer of a ride.

I didn't find things so easy. For some reason I felt out of sorts, with a grumbling stomach, a sort of warning that things might get worse. I was snappy with the others, critical of the journey, couldn't sleep—in fact it reminded me of nothing so much as those times before my monthly loss. It was a shock to realize too that these had not manifested themselves for nearly a year, a fact I had initially put down to the terrible journey I undertook to return to Matthew, after my dragon had flown away and left me.

The lack of a monthly flow had been a boon in my travels as a boy, and I had completely forgotten about it until now. Perhaps I should be worried, I thought; perhaps there was something permanently wrong. Surreptitiously I felt my stomach: a little swollen, but nothing else. If it was pregnancy I was worried about, then there was nothing to fear, of course, for Jasper was the only man to touch me in that way and the nine months needed to make a baby had long gone. Just in case I checked my pack to make sure the cloths I had packed were still there if needed.

It grew rapidly much colder the farther east and north we travelled, with an intermittent icy wind sliding down the ever-nearing mountains, and it was with relief that we mostly found small villages in which to spend the lengthening nights; tents in the open were no substitute for four walls and a roof, however basic. Tug was the only one who didn't feel the cold, merely wrapping himself up tighter in his blanket.

I kept Ky-Lin hidden, as we mostly shared quarters with Dickon, and for some reason I was reluctant to share him. I fed him scraps of rice or dried fruit, because of his taboo on eating or killing anything live.

One night we were on our own, Dickon and Tug foraging for wood for the communal fire and Growch off on an expedition of his own. I set out some raisins and a few nuts in front of Ky-Lin, watching his pleasure as he nibbled at the latter.

"You like them?"

"Mmm. One of my favorites. You know what I like best of all?"

"No."

"Flaked almonds coated with honey, or a nice pod or two of carob. Very bad for the teeth, but quite delicious."

I made a mental note to seek out either or both as soon as I could.

As I watched him I suddenly remembered something I had meant to ask a long time ago.

"Ky-Lin, that first night you came to us . . ."

"Mmm?"

"You woke me up calling out 'Stop thief!' "

He nodded.

"Did you see him?"

He nodded again, mouth full of nut.

"Did you see who it was?"

Another nod.

"Who?"

It seemed ages before he answered. "Got sticky fingers that one."

"Who has?"

"Your friend Dickon, of course! Who did you think it would be?"

CHAPTER NINE

"I don't believe it!" I shook my head. "There's nothing there he would want."

"Have you anything in your baggage he desires?"

I thought through all my belongings: clothes, writing materials and journal, now written in a form of shortened hand and difficult to decipher; tally sticks, a few herbs and simples, my forged papers from Matthew, Suleiman's letter—had Dickon made something that wasn't out of that?—mug, bowl and spoon, plus the lump of glass the captain's wife had given me. This had proved rather disappointing: beautifully shaped and cut, it nevertheless had looked nothing other than dull when I had looked at it one gray evening when we had been on our way to the tent city of Küm. My other treasure from that city, the Waystone, I kept in a pouch about my neck, together with some little scraps of discarded skin that had come from a certain little pig; just a keepsake, I kept telling myself.

But there must be something. Think ... I went through the list again in my mind. No, there was nothing else—nothing except the maps I had copied, and the one Suleiman had enclosed with his letter. Could it be these he had been looking for?

Ky-Lin was reading my mind. "Could be," he said. "Especially if he has the sort of suspicious mind that believes you are doing something other than just being an apprentice."

I remembered Dickon's accusations of being a spy, or on a secret mission for Matthew. "Let's take a look," I said. I peeked past the hanging leather that served as a door in this poor place; Tug was squatting by the fire, Dickon was talking to one of the village girls.

"All clear." I pulled out the two maps I had duplicated at Matthew's and spread them out on the dirt floor using elbows and knees to keep them flat. Ky-Lin trotted over to sit on the fourth corner.

I pointed to the first, larger map. "Here's where I come from, and that's the route, marked out, that we took to Venice. . . . Here's the sea we crossed to the Golden Horn, and this could be the way we took to Küm. But there are lots of trails leading from there, so we must have used the most easterly. I suppose we could be just about here, now. . . ."

Ky-Lin squinted horribly and shook his head from side to side which he explained helped him concentrate. "The trouble with maps is that they are never used by people who know the routes and know the terrain, so there is no one to update them. Most of them are hopelessly inaccurate, and at best are mostly guesswork. Distances, too, can be very misleading, for who counts his paces or even his days to mark his passage? Ask one caravan master how long it takes from this city to that and he will tell you ten, twenty days, depending on the weather. Another will take a different trail over easier ground and shorten the time by half, yet as the bird flies the mileage would be the same."

"It's marked with mountains and things," I said defensively. An erupting volcano graced part of Italia, a couple of small ships on the seas; there was what looked like a lion and a triangular temple on the coast of Africa, and Cathay was shown with snaky rivers and high mountains. In the corner where Ky-Lin was sitting was a great empty space and the legend: "Here be Dragons." That was one of the reasons I had been keen to have a copy.

"Pictures of them, yes, but are they where it shows them? I think you have a clue here," and he tapped his hoof right in front of where he was sitting. "To the ignorant layman, when you see the word 'dragons,' what would you immediately think of? Yes," he added, crossing my thoughts. "Treasure. Maybe your young friend believes you are on a treasure hunt, with or without Master Spicer's assistance or knowledge. Let me see the others. . . ."

The second of Matthew's maps he pronounced as better, but not much. I produced the one Suleiman had sent.

"Ah, this is more like it. The man who made this actually travelled these routes. I recognize this, and this, and this. . . ." He shook his head, crossed his eyes alarmingly, waved his plumed tail.

"But I can't read these squiggles. . . ."

"Those 'squiggles' are in Cantonese, but even without them I can see places I have visited. See, the Land of the Lotus, the Singing Gardens, the Desert of Death, the City of Golden Towers (not true, they are only gilded), and there are others I have heard of. The country of Snakes, the town of the Three-legged Men (named after an annual race they hold), the Blue Mountain, the—"

"Did you—did you say the Blue Mountain?"

"Yes. Here it is, just beyond the Three Fangs of the Mighty One. This means something special to you?"

All at once all I could think about was the vision the old man had shown me in that magical bowl of colored water, where I had been for a brief moment or two a dragon, steering my way through the Fangs and down to the valley beneath and the Blue Mountain with the hidden cave.

I jabbed my finger down on the map. "It's there, it's true, it's real! *That's* where I must go!" I was almost shouting with joy.

There was a sudden silence. The ivory figurine that had been holding down the map rolled off into the shadows. I looked up, and there was Dickon framed in the doorway.

I don't know how much he had heard or seen, but of course he pretended there was nothing amiss, merely saying that he had come to ask whether I would prefer rice or pancakes for our evening meal, but all the time he was speaking his eyes were darting suspiciously around the hut, glancing at the map I had immediately released so that it had scrolled itself and rolled into a corner.

Poor Ky-Lin, I thought: he will have to start all over again. Even while I was thinking this I was gathering up the maps and stuffing them back in my pack, and all the while chattering away like a demented monkey.

"Hello, Dickon, I didn't see you there! How nice of you to come and ask what I wanted. . . . Let me see, now. We had pancakes yesterday, didn't we? Or was it beans . . . On the other hand I'm a bit tired of rice. My stomach hasn't been all that good, as you know, so perhaps it had better be pancakes. Or do you think they will be too greasy? What do you suggest?"

I continued to rummage around for my writing things.

"I thought I would catch up with my diary of our travels, so I checked the maps to make sure I have the route all planned out correctly. They're not very accurate, though; what's this place called, do you know? Never mind, I'll just mark it as a village. . . ."

And so on, trying to cover my confusion and making it worse.

But he couldn't contain his curiosity for long. "I heard—I thought you were talking to someone . . . ?"

"Me? Now who could I be talking to: there's no one else here. The place is empty. . . ." *Think* of something quick, Summer! "Oh that! You heard me talking to myself, I suppose. Haven't you ever done that? It always helps if you're trying to work something out in your mind, makes it all much clearer. . . ."

I could see he wasn't satisfied, kept looking around the room, but there was nothing to see. "I'll order you rice then. It'll be ready soon."

As soon as he was gone, I rushed over to Ky-Lin and picked him up.

"I'm terribly sorry. I hope it isn't too difficult to come alive again?"

Almost at once out popped a living nose and mouth. "Easier each time. Give me a few minutes. Go and get your food; if you wouldn't mind bringing me a few grains of rice? I always get particularly hungry after a change. . . ."

The meal was an uneasy one. Dickon put himself out to be charming and entertaining, but I still worried about what he might have seen and overheard. Besides which, my stomach had started aching again and I definitely felt queasy. I couldn't finish all the rice and vegetables and excused myself before the others had finished, longing to just wrap myself in a blanket, lie down on my pallet and try to forget the pain in my guts in sleep. It wasn't particularly cold, but I was shivering.

"Did you remember . . . ? It doesn't matter. You look ill. . . ."

"Oh, hell! Sorry Ky-Lin. Yes. It does matter." I went to the door and called Tug over and explained what I wanted. He had been playing five-stones with the village boys, but he was always cheerful and willing these days. Two minutes later he was back with some rice and vegetables wrapped in a vine leaf.

"You still hungry, Summa?"

I made up my mind. "Tug come with me. New friend to meet."

Tug's eyes were as wide as I had ever seen them as Ky-Lin fluffed out his tail in welcome. But instead of dropping the rice or running off in horror, he instead gave a stiff little bow, then walked over to the creature and placed the food in front of him, standing back to watch him eat.

"Tug, this is a—"

"Ch'i-Lin," said Tug, and gave that jerky little bow again. "*Very* good. Go with Lord Buddha."

"He knows. . . ."

"My Lord's wisdom has travelled to many places, like the wind," said Ky-Lin, chasing the last pieces of rice with his forked tongue. "If I am not mistaken, this child comes from the Northern Plains."

"Can you speak his tongue?" Perhaps at last we should be better able to help him.

"I will try. . . ." And for the next few moments there was an incomprehensible (to me) series and exchange of clicks and hisses, at the end of which Ky-Lin's eyes were crossed and Tug had a broad grin on his face.

"I was right," said Ky-Lin. "The boy is one of the Plainsmen, the great Horsemen. They are nomadic herdsmen, live in tents, and travel many hundreds of miles in a year."

"And how far away is his homeland?" I asked, my heart already sinking in anticipation of his reply.

"Perhaps a thousand miles to the north, perhaps a little more."

It was as I had feared. I had promised Tug, in sign language if not in words, that I would take him back to his homeland, and I couldn't break a promise, even if it meant I went hundreds of miles out of my way. I looked at the hope in his face, and knew I couldn't let him down. How should I have felt if I had been snatched away from home and family at ten or eleven years old, transported hundreds of miles, only to be sold like an animal to the highest bidder? After all, my dragon would wait, wouldn't he?

"Do you know the way there, Ky-Lin?"

"I can guide you in the right direction, if that is what you wish; the way is quite clearly shown on that last map of yours. But I warn you that the country itself, besides being many miles away, is also far vaster than anything you have come across so far. Another thing; it will take many months to reach, and this caravan we travel with is taking us too far to the east."

Which meant we should have to abandon the safety of the caravan and strike out on our own. For a terrible moment I thought I hadn't got the courage; feeling as I did now, I would have been thankful to have just curled up for the winter and hibernated like the red-leaf squirrels near my old home. My ring gave a little throb, and I remembered we had Ky-Lin with us, and we hadn't failed up to now, had we? And we wouldn't: not with the help of God's good grace—and a little luck.

But we should have to be careful not to rouse Dickon's suspicions. He was the last person I wanted to accompany us, but if he got the slightest hint we were to be away on our own he would be sure to follow, especially if, as Ky-Lin had suggested, he believed we were after treasure. And, knowing Dickon, he would stick like a leech.

The following morning I made enquiries that all could hear as to when we would reach the next town, explaining that I needed the services of a competent purveyor of pills for my stomach pains. The answer was three days; once there I would plead indisposition and stay behind. Of course once I announced my indisposition, it miraculously cured itself, as an aching tooth will while queuing for the tooth puller, but I still pretended it was worsening, and this was aided by the fact that apparently I still looked pale and drawn.

In the meantime I introduced Growch to Ky-Lin, only to be informed that he had "known all the time, and just how many more spare parts was I going to invite along on what was, after all, supposed to be a special journey just for the two of us . . ." etc.

I realized that he was jealous, only had been too caught up in my own plans to recognize it, so from then on I made a special fuss over him, even going to the extreme of treating him to a bath and comb. He whined like hell, of course, but secretly I believe he thought any attention was better than none, and we were soon back to our old footing.

The journey that should have taken three days took five, due to torrential rains, but this worked to my advantage in the end, because Ali Qased, the caravan master, was eager to press on immediately before any more autumnal downpours held him up, and as far as he was concerned one sick apprentice more or less would only hold him up.

Using Dickon as my interpreter, he was quite willing I should stay behind until he returned—a guess of a month or more—but he also insisted that I consult the local apothecary, a shabby little man with an obsequious manner and a satchel full of phials of crushed insects, dried bats' wings, unidentified blood, powder of tiger claw, bitter herbs and pellets of opium. He prodded my stomach, shook his head, and went away to make up some pills.

To add color to my "illness," I took to my bed in the small attic room Dickon had found for me. He returned with powder in a twist of rice paper and half a dozen pills, insisting that I take them at once.

"You owe me two silver coins—"

"He's expensive!"

"Yes, but if you take these at once you may be better in the morning and ready to continue the journey. We don't leave till ten."

I fished out the money, then groaned. "I don't think I shall. . . . Now, leave me alone to get some rest."

"When you've taken your medicine. The powder is to be dissolved in water and the—"

"I haven't got any."

"What?"

"Water."

He nodded at Tug, who was arranging some stones on the floor in a complicated game. "Send your slave boy."

I was tired of his attitude towards Tug.

"Once and for all, he's not a slave. I bought him and gave him his freedom. And no, I'm not sending him: he couldn't make himself understood. Go yourself."

"He's a cretin. . . ."

"He's not that either. You just don't understand him."

I might add that Tug was perfectly well aware of Dickon's dislike and played up to it, acting like a village idiot when he was near, so Dickon's remark wasn't entirely unjustified. Now the boy stuck out his tongue and waggled his fingers in his ears.

"Tug . . ." I said reprovingly, wanting to giggle.

"Told you," said Dickon. "All right, I'll fetch you some water. Just stay here till I get back."

What did he think I was going to do? Fly out the window?

As soon as he had gone I scooped Ky-Lin out of my sleeve.

"Quick!" I said. "The medicines. Are they fit to take?"

He sniffed delicately at the twists of paper.

"Mmmm . . . the powder is harmless. Crushed pearl, a pinch of gentian for color, cinnamon for taste. The pills? Sweetener for coating, a little clay for setting; inside rat's blood, burnt feathers and a good dose of opium."

"Yeeuk!"

"You've eaten worse, certainly from my point of view! At least there is nothing to harm you permanently. Try and get away with just drinking the powder: the opium in a pill will make you sleep heavily, and if you want to be away tomorrow as soon as they leave . . . spit it out as soon as he's gone."

But the trouble was he wouldn't go. He watched me tip some of the powder into my mug and add water, stirring it with my finger till it was purple. I drank it down with an expression of disgust, though the taste was not unpleasant.

"I think I'll take a rest now. . . ."

"Pills first."

"In a minute! I'll just see if the drink will—"

"The pills are to be taken at the same time. Go on. Two."

"I am *not* taking two! Suppose they don't agree with me? Do you want to spend the night nursing me?"

"One, then. Now!"

I put it in my mouth, and tucked it quickly under my tongue, making exaggerated swallowing motions. "There! Now you can go and leave me alone."

He still wouldn't leave; instead he paced the floor, small though the room was: three steps one way, two back.

"How can I leave you on your own? Master Spicer would never forgive me if you worsened. . . . You said yourself that heathen boy can't make himself understood. No, my duty is to stay here with you. The caravan can manage without me."

The pill was gradually melting in my mouth. I could taste the bitterness through the coating.

"And Matthew would never forgive me if you broke your apprenticeship just to look after me! I'll be fine in a couple of days. I've enough money to stay here until you come back, and I can spend the time bringing my journal up to date and learning a bit more of the language. I wouldn't dream of you staying behind!"

"Don't tell me what I ought or ought not to do!" Then in a gentler tone: "I consider it my duty to look after you. Don't forget I am the only one who knows you are a girl . . ."

Was this an implied threat?

". . . and you wouldn't want anyone else to find out, would you?"

Yes, it was.

"What harm can it do for me to stay and—you to go?" The pill must be taking effect. I mustn't go to sleep, I mustn't! "After all, I can't go anywhere, can I? Ali Qased said his was the last caravan expected this year. . . ." I yawned uncontrollably.

At last he left, promising to look in again, and the next thing was Ky-Lin hissing in my ear: "Spit it out! Spit it out!"

The pill, what little was left of it, dropped to the floor. I struggled up on my elbow. "Mustn't sleep ... lots to do. Got to find out—find out—how to get away. Transport ... food. Can't ... can't sleep."

"Do-not-worry," said Ky-Lin, close to my ear. "We-will-see-to-it. Leave-it-to-us. Sleep-in-peace. ..."

I didn't hear or see them leave, knew nothing else in fact until a bright light flashed across my eyelids. I tried to open my mouth, my eyes, but nothing happened. It was as if I was frozen to my bed. The light flashed again.

"Perhaps you were telling the truth after all, little witch," said a voice I should recognize. Then more sharply: "Wake up, Summer! Time to get up," and someone shook me, none too gently. I moaned and rolled over, but could respond no further, slipping back down into a velvety darkness.

Then something triggered a thought. Of course I recognized the voice: it had to be Dickon. With a supreme effort I opened my eyes. There was a lantern on the floor, and by its light I could see Dickon going through my papers, my pack open at his side. He held up first one map and then another, frowning and muttering to himself. "Can't see much there. ... Possible, possible. We're way off track, though. ..."

He rolled the maps, turned his attention to my journal but, as I had anticipated, he could make little of my scrawl, especially as it had been only recently that the former stable lad had learned to know his letters. "Still, I heard her say there was somewhere she had to go ... but where, *where*?"

He glanced across at me, but luckily my face was in shadow and I closed my eyes quickly.

"Still, there's nowhere to go from here. Safe enough, I reckon."

At that moment there was a bark on the stone steps that led up to my room; the others were back.

With a speed that obviously owed much to practice, maps and papers were stuffed back in my pack and it was rapidly refastened. A moment later and he was standing over the bed, lantern held high.

Growch rushed in growling, closely followed by Tug. Dickon straightened up.

"Just checking on the patient, for the benefit of a cretin and a scruffy hound," said Dickon. "I know you can't understand, stupid bastards both, but I'll be back to check in the morning."

I heard his steps on the stair and tried to keep awake long enough to tell Ky-Lin, emerging from Tug's jacket, just what had happened, but he shushed me.

"Go to sleep. Don't worry about a thing. We have got it all organized. By this time tomorrow we shall be spending our first night afloat. . . ."

I could have sworn he said "afloat." But we weren't anywhere near the sea. I must have been dreaming.

And two minutes later I really was.

INTERLUDE

He was bored. Restless. Unhappy.

He told himself not to be stupid, that he had everything he needed, that dragons did not admit to boredom, or restlessness. And, most of all, not to unhappiness. Yet how else could he explain why he felt as he did? Dragons usually were only affected by purely physical things: heat and cold, hunger and thirst; and by the pure pleasure, endless delight, of jewels and gems, and the retelling of tales of travel.

But then he wasn't a dragon all the time, was he? Like now. Now he was a man sitting on a deserted beach somewhere, chucking stones into the sea and suffering from indigestion.

And that was another thing: a man ate what a man ate, dragons were different. If one had a fire in one's belly, used regularly or not, one could digest anything, bones and all, but a man's stomach churned on the remains of a dragon dinner.

He gave a snort of disgust. This just shouldn't be happening to him. He had reported back, been welcomed and initiated into the proper rituals, then allowed the treat of inspecting the Hoard. He had been obliged, however, to disclose his Affliction, as he termed it, and been rewarded with consternation and disbelief. Spells had been cast, charms used, lore memory consulted, but all to no avail. Nothing like this had ever happened before;

of course it was known that it could, but what mortal maid in her right mind had ever kissed a dragon?

At first, of course, they hadn't believed him, until he had done an involuntary change and back right there in front of them. It was the most exciting thing that had happened to the community since the Blue Dragon had returned hundreds of years back with his jewels and the tales of the witch who had stolen them, and the knight and the girl and the animals who had returned them.

His Affliction had had a mixed reception. Some of them thought it added to his powers, others that it must inevitably detract from the purity of line they had preserved.

Five minutes, ten, of thought, and he was still bored, restless and unhappy, and the sea a hundred stones fuller. He might as well admit it; he still hankered after that lass with the long legs who had rescued him from death in his first incarnation as a pig, cared for him, loved him and finally—irony of ironies!—given him the three kisses he would remember forever. That, and the moment of passion when he was caught between man and dragon— Aiyee! That experience had been enough to make anyone's toes curl!

Fire and ice! He must see her again—if only to convince himself that he didn't need to. . . .

It was late spring when he started his journey. Back first to the Place of Stones, where his transformation had taken place, then retracing her route back to that fat merchant she would probably marry. As a man he came down to earth to ask questions, see if she had passed that way, but to no avail. By midsummer he had even dared the servants at the merchant's house, only to find she had disappeared a few weeks before with her dog to parts unknown, and that the merchant, heartbroken, had gone on pilgrimage to Spain.

So, where was she, the girl whose memory still tormented him? North, south, east, west? He tried haphazardly: northern fjords, southern deserts, western isles, *eastern mountains—but surely even she wouldn't travel that far. Why run away from a perfectly good marriage anyway? What was she looking for now? What worm was eating her brain this time, silly girl?*

He grew crosser and crosser; what right had she to haunt him so? Time he pulled himself together; what he needed was a break, a few months, a year perhaps; time, anyway, that he sought some gifts for the Hoard, part of his dragon duty. Perhaps by then he would be free of what was rapidly becoming an obsession.

So, which way? Somewhere warm for the winter. Africa, India, the isles of the Southern Seas? It didn't really matter. . . .

PART TWO

PART TWO

CHAPTER TEN

I had never thought it would be so wonderful to be one's own mistress again, to be free of caravans, merchants, warehouses, tally sticks, accounts, invoices, bales and bargaining. Most of all it was wonderful to be rid of Dickon. More and more he had constricted my every move and his suspicions had haunted me so much I found myself glancing over my shoulder even now to make sure he wasn't following.

Of course being free was a comparative term. I had the others to think about and care for, Tug to return to his people and my own journey to complete, but at least we could proceed at our own pace.

It was bliss to just lie back against the thwarts of the boat, even hemmed in as we were by peasants, farmers, children, sacks of grain, rolls of cloth, strings of dried fish and crates of chickens. Above us was a cloudless sky, rice fields and stands of bamboo slid past with a lazy regularity, and the smooth water of the Yellow Snake River gurgled and slapped against the hull, accompanied by the flap of sail and creak of rudder.

Ky-Lin, Tug and Growch had done well while I lay deadened by the opium. Ky-Lin had remembered from the map that the river looped briefly towards the town some five miles away and had ascertained that boats travelled regularly both north and south, and in fact we had picked up one this midafternoon. The river eventually

129

turned to the east and Cathay, but by this way, though slower, we should be some two hundred miles farther towards our goal, with little effort on our part. Just as long as the money held out: we should have to be careful and economize where we could. Luckily nobody would charge for Growch, and Ky-Lin was tucked up in the hood of my cloak, both for safety and so he could whisper translations if necessary.

I patted Tug's knee. "Not bad, eh?" He shivered and snuggled nearer, his eyes rolling in fright. "It's all right," I said slowly, hoping he would understand. "Ky-Lin: tell him there's nothing to be afraid of."

But though the magic creature did his best Tug refused to be comforted, and I recalled my own experience with water. The first time I had been in a frail rowing boat carrying me away from marauding soldiers; the second I had nearly been drowned when I was cut off by an incoming tide and the third had been that dreadful storm when we had left Venice, so perhaps Tug was to be pitied. I stretched out my hand but he had bolted to the side and heaved up into the river.

I moved over to rub his back, a thing my mother had done when I was a child in some sick situation, and I had always found it comforting. Remembering my ring had many powers, I drew that gently down his spine too, and wasn't surprised when he turned to me with a weak smile and announced he was: "Better with no tum!" He added: "Like ride horse. Fall off two three time. Learn quick." And after that he was all right.

We travelled from one stopover to another, at each one discharging cargo and passengers and taking on others. I had no word of the native tongue, even having to bargain for our fare with sign language and Ky-Lin's whispers, but the people were kind and cheerful, inviting us to share their meagre provisions. These were usually cooked on a brazier in the well of the boat, although occasionally we tied up for the night by some village or other and dined there in one of the tiny eating houses.

In this way we travelled some seventy or eighty miles north, then the boat in which we were travelling turned back and we took another, smaller, which tied up every night. In order to eat I had to buy a small cooking pot, food on the way and have Tug forage for the wood for a fire. This took us another fifty miles, and then we swapped to a string of barges carrying cattle—not an experience to be repeated.

The weather gradually changed as autumn and the approaching north brought colder winds, rain, falling leaves, and cranes winging south. By now we were some hundred and fifty miles further on, but the river narrowed into a series of gorges through which water raced in a torrent, and only the hardiest and most reckless boatman would venture the rapids. It seemed this terrain was unchanged for fifty miles or so, and we decided to finally leave the river and start walking.

We hadn't gone more than a couple of miles or so when I, at least, was regretting it. I had gone soft, what with mule and river travel, and although Tug carried his fair share of the baggage, mine felt to weigh a ton, and we were all hot, sticky, and tired by the time we had walked ten miles that first day. A village gave us shelter for the night, we had a lift on a bullock cart the following day, which was a bit like travelling snail-back, but at least it gave my feet a rest. My stomach, too, had begun to play up again, but only intermittently. For the next three days it rained continuously and we were holed up in a miserable hovel with a dripping roof and I began to wonder if we had offended some local god.

On the fifth day our luck changed for the better. The sun shone warm, we dried out, and I reckoned we could risk a night in the open if we could find some bushes or convenient trees. During the day we had managed to gather some nuts and berries to supplement our diet, and as we were now in sight of a good-sized village, I decided to go in and buy rice or beans. Travelling on the river, the money had trickled away as fast as the

water ran, and I had no idea how much farther we had
to go.

We had just found a likely camping spot and set down
our baggage, dusk was falling and Tug was about to forage for wood, when we heard the sound of pipes and
firecrackers from the village. I never got used to the half
and quarter tones of eastern music and firecrackers
always made me jump, but Tug loved both, so we picked
up our packs again and set off towards the celebrations.
At the very worst there would be some scraps of food
dropping from the tables for Growch to scrounge, and
at best we might be invited to share with some hospitable villager.

Although the outer streets were deserted there had
obviously been a procession of sorts earlier, for the
ground was littered with scraps of colored paper and
burned-out firecrackers, but the noise now came from
the center of the village, as did a healthy smell of cooking
meat and rice. We followed our ears and our noses and
found ourselves in the village square.

In one corner a couple of spits were turning vigorously
and large pans were simmering over a trench fire; while
they waited for the food, the villagers were clapping an
entertainment. As usual at these functions, like any other
village in the world, certain unwritten rules for social
behavior were observed. The elderly were comfortably
seated around the perimeter, some with smaller children
and babies on their laps, the young men congregated in
one corner, the girls in the opposite, parents and middle-
aged bustled from one group to another exchanging gossip, and the older children played tag and got under
everyone's feet.

But for now all was relatively quiet as they watched
the performers. A trio of children, some younger even
than Tug, were working acrobatic tricks with a man who
was obviously their father, while an older boy twisted
himself into knots and did cartwheels round them; in
another space a pair of jugglers tossed balls, rings and

torches into the air and at each other, while on the fringes waited a great brown bear with a ring through its nose, shifting restlessly from paw to paw. Its owner, a thickset man with a pipe in his hand ready to play the music for the creature to dance to, suddenly jerked at the chain that ran through the ring in the bear's nose, which bit into the soft part of the nostril and made the poor thing squeal with pain. Simultaneously, it seemed, my heart jumped in sympathy and the ring on my finger gave a sudden stab.

The ring stabbed again, and all at once I had a brilliant idea. In what seemed another life my beautiful blind knight with his clear singing voice and the animals with me then had given performances such as these to pay our way. Why not try it again? True, the only original members of our troupe were Growch and myself, and all he had ever done was beg, turn somersaults, and lie down and "die," but surely we could concoct something between us. I asked Tug if he knew any tricks, through Ky-Lin.

"He says," translated the latter, "give him a horse and he is the best in the world. He also says he can turn cartwheels, do leaping somersaults and walk on his hands as well as the children over there. Oh, and he says he dances and plays the pipe also."

I had left my old pipe and tabor behind at Matthew's, but I supposed one could be bought somewhere here. In the meantime . . .

"Growch darling, come over here." But he had found some scraps under a table and was discussing their ownership vigorously with a couple of village curs. I dragged him away.

"What d'yer wanna do that for? Got 'em on the run, I 'ad—"

"Listen to me a moment! I'll buy you all the supper you want if you'll do me a small favor. Do you remember . . ." and I reminded him of our past performances, and tried to get him interested in some more immediate ones.

"Not on yer life! Right twit I used ter look, all ponced up in ribbons an' fings! Said then 'never again' I said. . . ."

"You never did!"

"Said it to meself. Never break a promise to yerself." And he scratched until the fur flew.

"Right. Have it your own way. But the only way we can buy supper—slices of juicy meat with lots of crackly skin, nice crunchy bones filled with marrow—is by earning some money performing here and now."

He hoofed out his left ear, looked at his paw and licked it. "Well, what you goin' ter do, then?"

What indeed. I didn't sing or play their music and couldn't stand on my head.

Ky-Lin spoke softly in my ear. "How about a little magic?"

"Real magic? How?"

"What they will believe is magic. How about a talking dog?"

"Growch?"

"Who else? Listen . . ." and he outlined a scheme so beautiful in its simplicity that I felt at once optimistic. We crept around a corner to rehearse.

I thought I foresaw a difficulty.

"How can I announce us and also name the objects when I don't speak a word of their language?"

"Simple!" said Ky-Lin. "Mime. I'll speak the words and you just open and shut your mouth and wave your arms about. Listen!" and all at once in my ear came my own voice, echoing my persuasions to Growch awhile back. This was followed by a rapid speech in the language of the country. As he was sitting on my shoulder it was like having an echo to the earlier part. "Convinced?"

With a little more practice it might just work. After all, they could only boo and jeer and turn us out of the village if they didn't like us, and we'd be no worse off. . . .

"Well," I said, patting my stomach, "I haven't eaten so well for weeks!"

"Very palatable," said Ky-Lin, licking the remains of the honey from his antennae.

"Good, good, good!" grinned a greasy-faced Tug, and belched—a habit which seemed to be the polite way to express appreciation in his country. "Do again, more money, more food . . ." He belched again.

"Growch? Are you satisfied?"

But a snore was the only answer. His stomach was so distended with rice, pork, beans and pancakes that it shone like a pink-gray bladder through the thinner hair of his belly. A couple of fleas scurried through the curls quite clearly. Oh, Growch! Still he had done a great job this evening: so had they all.

I curled up on my pallet in the small back room we had hired for the night and let the images of our performance dance behind my closed eyelids, secure in the comfortable discomfort of a just-too-full stomach and the consciousness of a pouch full of small coins . . .

"Illustrious villagers, fathers of industry, mothers of many, older folk with the wisdom of the years, youngsters who will grow strong and tall as their ancestors . . ."

"Move your mouth a bit more," whispered Ky-Lin. "It looks more authentic."

We should have to practice this more; still in the torch-light it probably didn't look too bad.

"Tonight we bring you, from the far corners of the world, an entertainment to delight and mystify. You will see marvels of agility from a prince of his people, feats of intelligence from a dog who learnt his wisdom from the Great Masters of the East, and finally an act so mind-bending that you will be telling your children's children of it for years to come. . . ."

It was strange to hear my voice ringing strong and confident, translating the words I gave Ky-Lin in a whisper into the local language. It was the showman's spiel, of course, used throughout the world with only local variations. Grab the attention of your audience, flatter them, then give them an inflated idea of the acts they were about to see, and provide the performers with exotic backgrounds for greater wonder and appreciation.

Puff the acts as they appear and keep the best till last, for that is how your audience will remember you when the bowl comes round for the coins. In this way Tug did his acrobatics, Growch his tricks. Then came the part I was dreading: if it failed we would be laughed out of town.

But it hadn't, the dear Lord be praised! In fact it had gone better than expected. After an introduction, explaining what we intended to do, Tug had moved among the audience borrowing an object here, another there. These he showed to Growch one by one, and the dog had then trotted over to where I sat with my back turned and "told" me what each object was with barks and yips, Ky-Lin, tucked up in my hood, correctly identifying the objects as Tug showed them to Growch. I then made a great thing of rising to my feet and pretending to consider what the dog had "told" me, Ky-Lin eventually announcing it in my voice. To add verisimilitude I had once or twice pretended that I hadn't understood, and made Growch repeat his noises with a little variation, till he had informed me he was giving himself a headache. . . .

Sleepily I began to plan ahead. If we could polish up the act a little, were sure of finding enough audiences, then we should not only not have to worry about money, but could afford some costumes: the more profitable you looked, the more likely you were to attract more money and greater respect.

It may have been the unaccustomed feast that lay uneasy on my stomach, but when I finally did fall asleep it wasn't of our better fortunes that I dreamt: it was of a poor tormented bear, dancing an eternal jig to a screech of pipes, his nose bleeding and his feet sore. . . .

From then on the travelling, though not perfect, became more tolerable. Our first "take" lasted until our next, more polished performance in a larger village. That one not only filled my pouch, but provided a bright costume

for Tug (he wanted to wear it all the time) and ribbons
for Growch (who never wanted them at all). Now we
could afford a lift to the next villages and if, when we
got there, they were too poor to pay us in anything except
a bowl of rice and a room for the night, then that was
all right too. We were moving in the right direction as
Suleiman's map showed and my Waystone confirmed.

The only drawback was that the weather was worsening; it was now late fall and we were travelling towards
the northerly cold as well. Every now and again a flurry
of sleet bore down on the winds, and a chill breath lay
over the early mornings. In the countryside the harvests
of rice and grain were safely gathered, fodder for the
wintering beasts stacked and fruits dried, cheeses stored.
The peasants knew that their food had to last until spring
so there was little enough to spare for travellers, even if
they could pay. One could not eat coin, but two handfuls
of rice saved meant another day's bellyful.

As we travelled farther, rumors began to trickle back
about a great celebration to be held in one of the princi-
pal cities of the province. Ky-Lin (who listened to everything about him) reported that the second and favorite
son of the ruler was to be married amid great pomp
and ceremony.

"They say it will be a sight no man should miss. There
will be enough food and drink to feed the whole city
free for a week, and entertainments are to be held day
and night. It is also said that those who have such entertainments to offer will be doubly welcome and paid
accordingly."

"It might be just a rumor. You know how these things
get exaggerated by hearsay."

He waved his plumed tail. "True, but judging by the
consistency of the tales, I think we can safely say that
there is to be a marriage, there will be celebrations and
possibly entertainers would find it worth their while to
attend."

"Is it far out of our way?"

"A little perhaps, but that should be outweighed by the fact that as we go towards the city more lifts will be available. The same after the celebrations, for everyone will disperse to their homes again, and that will include those who travel our way. It should bring us nearer Tug's people."

"Can we wait for a day or so more? Just in case . . ."

But it seemed that Ky-Lin was right. The roads became suddenly more crowded; not only with the usual traffic but with other entertainers and even a more prosperous traveller or two, able to afford his own transport, and they were all moving in the same direction. Now we were joined by caravans carrying goods and provisions, and it became more difficult to find food along the way, so we took to carrying and cooking our own, it having been tacitly decided that we would take our chances with the rest travelling to the celebrations.

Along the way we met other entertainers we had come across before—the father with his acrobatic children, two or three jugglers, a sword swallower. Also on the road were cages of exotic animals: I saw two lions, large apes, a striped horse and huge, comatose snakes. And then, in a largish village some seventy miles short of our destination, we came across the dancing bear again.

For once I had managed to secure a room for us in a ramshackle house on the edge of town, but at least it was shelter from the cold. The proprietor had also provided a reasonable meal of rice and vegetables, with even a bit of meat thrown in. It had been a miserably wet, windy day's travelling, but the rain let up in the evening, and we decided to take a stroll, having no intention of wasting a show on such an inclement night, but wanting to see if anyone else was desperate enough to try it.

As I thought, most houses were already tight-shuttered for the night, just a chink of light from their lamp wicks floating in saucers of oil to show they were occupied, and even these would soon be dowsed to save the precious fuel. It wasn't till we came to the ubiquitous square that we saw others had braved the weather. This village boasted the equivalent of a town hall, and on its steps lounged a couple of the village law enforcers, stout cudgels in their hands. In the square itself were half a dozen men, two women and about twenty children, watching the antics of a second-class juggler and a magician whose tricks were of the simplest. The juggler, a thin man with long, yellowed teeth, dropped his last few sticks, grimaced, and, picking up the single coin that had been dropped, disappeared down a side street. The magician continued to pull his colored scarves, open and shut his "magic" boxes, but now all eyes went to another attraction: the bear had emerged with his keeper, the latter obviously well away on rice wine.

The creature looked worse for wear than ever; he was shabbier and thinner than when I had seen him last, and his fur now stuck up in spikes from the soaking he must have got earlier that day. His owner was in a foul mood as well as being too drunk even to play his pipes properly. The worse he played, the more he jerked on the chain that ended at the bear's nose as it refused to respond, even kicking it with his heavy boots till it grunted in pain. A couple of the village curs decided to join in, nipping at the bear's heels till it roared in pain; the owner struck it on the nose with his pipe, the crowd jeered and the bewildered creature dropped to all fours.

The ring on my finger was throbbing, and I could bear the cruelty no longer. I started forward, but Ky-Lin hissed in my ear: "Wait! oh impatient one, wait a little longer."

"We must *do* something!"

"We will. Just be still. . . ."

Eventually the torture stopped. No coins were forthcoming, the dogs found something else to distract them and the bear owner gave a last cruel twist to the chain and led the beast off.

"Now we follow," said Ky-Lin, "if you still wish to help."

"Of course!" But how, I wondered.

We followed them at a discreet distance right to the outskirts of the village, where there was fifty yards or so of open land till thick wood crowded in. The bear and his keeper disappeared into the trees. With open ground to cover we were threatened with discovery.

"I'll go," said Growch. "See what 'e's up to. You wait 'ere."

Five minutes later he was back. "Anchored the bear to a rock in a clearin'," he reported. " 'E's on 'is way back. Better clear out."

We made our way back to our lodgings, but I couldn't settle.

"Can't we take him some food or something? The poor thing was starving." In a corner of our room, also used as a storeroom, there was a pile of root vegetables. I picked out two or three. "These'd do; I'll pay for them in the morning."

Ky-Lin thought for a moment. "We need a clear field," he said at last. "No interruptions. I think I can arrange that. Follow me...."

At a little smoky eating house we found the bear keeper, seated on a stool, arguing with the two law keepers we had seen earlier. They were not inclined to argue back, I could see that, but Ky-Lin had a little magic at his disposal. I heard him chuntering away to himself, and a moment later the stool on which the bear keeper sat collapsed under him, he grabbed at one of the law keepers for support and the pair of them crashed to the floor, fists flying. In a moment the other man had joined in, and the upshot of it all was one rebellious bear keeper dragged away to the village's small lockup to spend the night.

"How did you do that?" I asked Ky-Lin, as we hurried off to feed the bear.

"All matter has its own composition; it just needed

disarranging a little," he said, which I didn't understand at all.

Growch led us across the waste ground, littered with rubbish and odds and ends, and through the scrub to a path between the trees, now faintly illuminated by a quarter moon.

"Down 'ere a bit. You'll 'ear 'im afore you sees 'im, more'n like."

I had thought it was the moaning of the wind in the trees, but it was a voice, made clear and stark by the ring on my finger, throbbing once more in time with my heart.

"Oh me, oh my, how miserable I be! How I hurts, how I stings! How dark is the world, how drear . . . I be hungry, I be wet, I be cold! I long to be dead, dead or back in the land that gave me birth. My hills and forests, they call out to me. . . ."

"E's mad!" breathed Growch. "Stark, starin' . . . Don' go too near 'im, girl!"

In the clearing, chained to a rock, the bear was weaving his own kind of dance. Moonlight dappled his shabby fur as he swayed from front to back, his paws leaving the ground one after the other and back again, his head swinging from side to side, his eyes crazed and red.

Strangely I felt no fear, and my ring was comforting. I stepped forward and placed the roots on the ground in front of him, then stepped back again. "Food for you, Bear," I said slowly and clearly.

But the animal still swung back and forth, his eyes glazed, his jaw dripping spittle. I went forward again, and this time, in spite of an anguished squeal from Growch, I gripped the dripping muzzle firmly in my hands. "Stop it! We are friends. We have come to free you. . . ."

Gradually he stilled, and a pair of small black eyes looked straight up at me.

"Who are you?"

"A friend." I brought the ring close to his eyes. "We have come to help you."

"How? But how?" The head started swinging again. "I am chained, chained forever! Nose hurts, but keeps me chained . . ."

I hadn't thought about the chain. "Ky-Lin?"

A tiny sigh. "If I thought what I thought just then it would put me back another twenty points. . . . But I'm not going to think it. I am here to help. Now, listen: it is time for a little more magic. This time both yours and mine."

"How? I have no magic. . . ."

A patient sigh. "Of a sort. Just do as I say." He leaned over my shoulder and a tiny puff of smoke escaped his nostrils and drifted towards the bear. A moment later the beast's eyes closed, its head drooped. "He's asleep. Take out your Waystone and stroke it round and round the nose ring—no questions, just do as I ask. That's it: one hundred times, no more, no less. Are you counting?"

A minute, two, three. "Ninety-nine, one hundred. Now what?"

"Hold me close to the nose ring. . . ." There was a *ting* of metal and the ring snapped. "Twist it out of his nose." The chain fell to the ground, the bear opened his eyes and blinked. "Alteration of matter twice in one night: amazing! Just pass your Unicorn's ring across his nose: it'll ease the pain."

The bear was free: groggy, but free. I stepped back and breathed more easily. "Eat the food and then get yourself back to your hills or forests," I said. "Good luck, Bear!"

I was just going to ask Ky-Lin how on earth the Waystone had anything to do with snapping the ring in the animal's nose when I tripped over Growch who had stopped suddenly on the path back to the village. He growled menacingly.

I gazed ahead: nothing unusual. "One of these days you'll give me heart failure," I said. "Move over—"

It was then I screamed. Without any warning a heavy

hand clamped down on my shoulder, a voice hissed in my ear.

"Got you! Thought you'd escaped me, didn't you? Well, you can think again. . . ."

CHAPTER ELEVEN

It was just as well I had no pressing need to relieve myself. I leapt away, Growch growling, Tug cursing, but it was a moment longer before I recognized the shabbily dressed figure.

"Dickon!"

"The same, my girl! I've had the devil's own job finding you, although at the end you left enough clues with your playacting—"

"But why? Why did you follow us? I told you—"

"A pack of lies! *I* know where you're bound, and why! I'm just not going to let you get away with it, that's all! I don't know whether you're in league with Matthew Spicer, or that darkie fellow Suleiman, or whether you're working on your own, but either way I'm going to be a part of it."

"Part of what? Oh Dickon! You're not thinking we're after treasure, are you? I tell you, there's no such thing!"

"You have maps. On it is the legend 'Here be Dragons.' And where there are dragons there is treasure. Everyone knows that!"

"Oh, you silly boy!" I said wearily. "If you could read a bit more you would know that all mapmakers put that when the terrain is unknown. It's their excuse, don't you see?"

"Then why are you headed that way? What's in it for

you? What would drag you halfway round the world unless it was a fabulous treasure?"

"That's my business," I said. "Now why don't you leave us all alone and go back where you came from?" I was so utterly fed up with his sudden appearance that had I had a magic wand I would have waved him away to perdition. "I'm leaving, and I don't ~~want~~ to see you again."

His hand snapped down on my wrist. "Not so fast! I'm not letting you— Ow! Let go! Summer . . ."

"You want me to kill?" asked the bear, whom I had completely forgotten. On his hind legs he was taller than any man I knew, and he held Dickon against his chest as easily as I would hug a doll. I thought he had eaten his roots and disappeared, but it seemed he was trying to repay me for his freedom.

"No, no!" I said hastily. "You can let him go. Thank you just the same. He is no threat, just a bloody nuisance."

"You sure?" He sounded disappointed.

"I'm sure." I went forward to help Dickon to his feet, for the bear had dropped him pretty hard on his rear. "Get up, Dickon, and be on your way."

He scrambled to his feet. "You can communicate with that—that beast? I realized when I saw you all that time ago that you had some sort of rapport with the other animals, especially that flying pig of yours, but I thought it was just good training. But that—that Thing," and he nodded in the direction of the bear, now busy polishing off the roots I had brought him, "He's new to you, surely?"

"Best I've ever tasted," mumbled the bear. "Best I've ever tasted. My, oh my, oh my!"

I suppose I hadn't thought about it. My ring could give me access to animal communication, but this time I had just "talked" to the creature without prior reasoning. Well, it had worked.

"Yes," I said. "We can understand one another."

"Well, tell him to disappear," said Dickon, brushing himself down. "You've set him free, I saw you unlock his chain, but that's that, isn't it? Come on, let's get back to that room you've hired. I've got to talk to you. It's important."

To whom? I wondered. It meant that I couldn't get rid of him immediately, not if he had been following us so close he even knew where we lodged. I supposed the least I could do was explain once more and give him a few coins to speed him on his way. The trouble was, he had a very persuasive tongue. . . .

"Very well. You go ahead, you obviously know where it is. I'll just see this creature on his way. Growch, you go with him." I didn't want him searching my baggage again.

I turned to the bear, now cleaning his mouth with his paw of any residue of root.

"All better now? Good. Now you are free, free to go wherever you please. Your master is locked up for the night, but you had better get going so he doesn't catch you again. Why don't you go back home?"

The bear turned puzzled eyes towards me. "Home? Home many, many, many treks away. Not sure where to find. You help."

"Oh dear!" said Ky-Lin. "I should have guessed as much. Sorry, girl."

"What that?" said Bear, his scarred nose questing the air. "Demon?"

Ky-Lin showed himself and Bear seemed suitably impressed. "Good demon."

"I'm afraid he is of limited intelligence," said Ky-Lin for my ears only. "Probably taken too soon from his parents, and the treatment he has suffered would make it worse."

I felt that at any moment I should have a headache.

"Don't you have any idea which way is home?" I asked wearily.

He settled down on his haunches, closed his eyes and began to recite.

"Long times ago, cub with sister. Hunters come, kill mother, take cubs." He stopped, and his head began to sway from side to side again. "First treat good, feed well. Then hot stones to burn feet, make dance. Tie up with chain to stand high. Pipe make squeak, dance, dance . . ." and now his whole body was swaying, his paws leaving the ground rhythmically, one after the other. "Ring through nose, much pain. Sister lie down, not get up any more. Aieee, aieee!" and he lifted his muzzle and roared in pain and anger.

"Hush, now!" I was scared we were making too much noise. "No more pain. You'll find home soon. . . ."

"How? Bears not see good longways. Know from that way," and he nodded west. "Mountains. Trees. Streams. Caves. Honey, roots, grubs. Mother, warm, milk, play, sister, love . . ."

That did it. Love is so many things.

"If we show you the way to go?"

"Lose way without help. You help, Bear help. Show you where is honey, roots." He smacked his lips. "Bear find caves to sleep. Bear protect. Bear come with you."

I saw it was hopeless. "Very well. Bear come with us. First we find home for boy—" I nodded at Tug, who was keeping his distance, "—then we find your home. But we have little . . ." I hesitated, then drew some coins from my pocket. "We have little of these. They buy us food and lodging. You will have to forage for food."

"Is same as man get for dance—you want more? I dance for you. All eat well."

It was an idea, but we should have to move fast if we were to get away from his former master. If he wasn't chained we couldn't be accused of stealing him, I reckoned. I led the way back to our lodgings without meeting anyone. Perhaps the better for Dickon's peace of mind, Bear elected to sleep outside by the woodpile. I warned him to keep out of sight.

"If Bear want no see, no see."

Inside, Dickon had made up the fire in the brazier

and was sitting on a stool nervously regarding Growch, who was perched like a hairy statue on top of the baggage. Part of his left lip was snagged back on a tooth, showing he had had occasion to snarl.

"Not very trusting, is he?" said Dickon, sucking the knuckles of his right hand.

"Depends. He takes his duties very seriously."

"I was just trying to be friendly. . . ." There were a couple of neat blue puncture marks on his hand.

"Friendly is as friendly does," said Growch. "Don' call it friendly when 'e puts 'is paw where 'e shouldn'."

I sat on the other stool, a sullen Tug crouched at my feet.

"Now, Dickon, what was it you wanted to say?"

He shifted uncomfortably. "It's a bit difficult. You see, when I left the caravan, I—I sort of resigned."

"You *what*?"

"Chucked it in, said I wasn't going back. You see, I thought that when I found you—"

"Not that stupid business of a treasure again! If I've told you once, I've—"

"I know you have! I just don't believe you. I thought it was worth the risk."

"Well it wasn't! It was just plain stupid of you to throw all that away. Just look at you: where are all your fine clothes, your fancy haircut?" There must be a way out of this. "If I give you some travelling money and a note to Matthew, I'm sure he'd take you back."

"Why? You two got something special going? He'll take me back just to keep my mouth shut? Is that it?"

"I assure you, once and for all," I said through gritted teeth, "what I'm doing here has absolutely nothing whatsoever to do with Matthew Spicer. Quite the reverse, in fact."

"Well, I can't afford to go back, not now. I used all the cash I had in tracing you." He gestured at his rags. "Even had to sell my clothes. Got anything to eat? I'm starving! I'm also broke, and cold. Didn't reckon you'd use the river: clever, that." He stood up. "Thanks for offering some travel money, but how far do you think I'd get before winter caught up?" His tone changed; now it held a wheedling note. "Look, I'll accept all you say about not going after treasure, but you must see that you need me. You're going somewhere, that's plain, and presumably also coming back. So why can't I go with you? If it's no secret, then how can you possibly object? After all, you're only a girl, and you need a man to look after you. . . ."

"I seem to have managed all right so far with Tug and Growch. And now the bear has volunteered to join us." I stood up. "Going somewhere? Yes. I'm taking Tug back to his people, then finding Bear his home; after that, who knows? So, there's nothing in it for you except a lot of travelling with companions you have already found— unfriendly. What's more, we just can't afford you. Back there you spoke the language, you had experience of the routes; here, you're less than we are. We have to work our passage and we have enough mouths to feed already."

"I can work!"

"Doing what? Standing on your head, walking on your hands, turning cartwheels? Or would you fancy a bit of mind reading? Oh, come on, Dickon!"

"No, no, no! Don't be silly, I've seen your act twice— just waiting a good moment to approach you—and I think you could do with someone more polished to choose the objects from the audience. We could establish a code, you and I; if I said 'what have we here?' it could mean a scarf; 'what is this?' a piece of jewelry—"

"Don't be silly! If you spoke in our language folk would believe you were telling me straight out what was in your hand, and you don't speak their tongue. Besides, I don't need your code; Growch manages quite well to tell me what Tug has in his hand. If you've seen us perform you'll know how it works."

"Stuff and nonsense! That cur wouldn't know how to

describe—a spectacle case, for instance, or an embroidered purse, whatever primitive language you have going between you. I've seen you identify things like that, so, how do you do it? Mirrors? And where did you learn the language? They seem to understand you."

So he didn't know our secrets, didn't know about Ky-Lin.

"I don't need mirrors; I am told exactly what Tug holds up—by magic."

"Rubbish! No such thing. You can't kid me. It's all a trick, albeit a damned clever one."

I shrugged. "Think what you like. . . . So, what else could you do?"

"Manage the bear. With a bit more training, it'd—"

"He."

"He, then. I'm not in the business of sexing bears. *He* could learn a few more tricks, and we'd—"

"He doesn't like you."

"A bear on a chain doesn't have to like you. . . ."

"He's not on a chain, and he's never going to wear one again."

"Then how are you going to control him? He's vicious, you know."

"He's as gentle as—a lamb. Just a bit bigger, that's all."

"And the rest! That creature isn't safe! You can't control it with—"

"Him!"

"—a softly, softly approach. Now if you'd just let me have a go—"

"No!"

"Why not? We'd increase our profits, buy new clothes, even could hire a wagon to travel in; you'd like that, wouldn't you?"

All of a sudden he had become a part of the "we". . . .

"Of course I would," I said. "But I've freed Bear and in return for trying to find his homeland, he has already agreed to work with us. I don't know yet just what form this will take, but no way will I have a chain put back on him, or try and coerce him into something he doesn't want to do. He's suffered enough."

He looked at me for a long moment, but I couldn't read his expression. Then he looked away and shrugged his shoulders.

"Have it your way. I still think I could be an asset. Let me travel with you for, say, a couple of days: after that, if I don't prove my worth, we'll say farewell. Fair enough?"

"And if I don't agree?"

"I'd follow you anyway. And you wouldn't like any disruption to your plans, would you?"

That sounded like a veiled threat. Welcome me into the bosom of your little family, otherwise I'll throw firecrackers at the bear, interrupt your mind-reading sessions and tell everyone you're a girl. . . .

If I'd had more time to think, had considered how Ky-Lin could perhaps have come up with a better solution, I probably wouldn't have caved in so easily. As it was I was too tired to argue.

"Two days, then. We're off at dawn. Walking—until of course your grandiose schemes come to pass," I added nastily.

He had never been one to recognize sarcasm. Instead he beamed, giving me a glimpse of the handsome lad he had become, in spite of the rags.

"Thanks. I sort of thought you might see it my way eventually. We'll make a great team, you and I, Summer. You want to get ahead in the world, make some money, then I'm your man. You're really quite an attractive girl in your own fashion and if you let your hair grow and—"

"Have you eaten?" I was furious at his condescension. "Here you are!" I flung a couple of coins in his direction. "Don't disturb us when you come back. I'm sorry there isn't another blanket, but you could always go outside to the woodpile and curl up with Bear!"

But as it happened he did wake us, and that long before dawn.

I heard someone stumbling around, knocking over a
stool, treading on my foot, groaning. It must have been
around four in the morning, and I reckoned he must
have spent most of his money on rice wine and was too
drunk to keep quiet. Sitting up, I unwrapped myself and
lit one of the oil lamps.

"Can't you keep quiet?" I hissed. "Some of us are—
why, whatever's the matter? Are you sick?"

Even by the scanty light I could see his face had a
greenish cast, and he was swaying from side to side,
wringing his hands.

He shook his head, less in negation than in what
seemed an effort to clear it of some awful memory.

"No, no, it's nothing like that. . . ." Even his voice was
different: he sounded like a child afraid of the dark.

"Then, what? Here, sit down before you fall down.
I've got some water—"

He waved it away. "No thanks. It's just that . . . I've
never seen . . . Oh, Summer, it was terrible! You wouldn't
believe—" and to my complete consternation he broke
down and wept noisily. "We must get away, now!"

All animosity forgotten, I went over and laid a hand
on his shoulder.

"Tell me. Take your time, but I want to know. . . ."

I held my lantern high over the form of the sleeping
bear, curled into a ball like any domestic cat, paws over
his nose and snoring a little.

"Wake up, Bear," I said. "Time to go."

He opened his small black eyes, blinked, yawned and
stretched. "Why go in dark? Wait till sun."

"No, Bear; we move now. Village not safe anymore.
There are—there are men who seek to hurt you. Come,
quick: we are ready."

"You say go, we go." He lumbered to his feet and had
a good scratch, his loose skin moving up and down as if
it were an extra coat. "Why men want to hurt Bear? Bear
not do wrong. . . ."

No, Bear, I thought: you wouldn't think it wrong. To you it was the law by which you had been taught to live.

Dickon had told me how a man had come stumbling into the eating house where he had been sitting, yelling and shouting, pointing down the street towards the thatched hut where the bear owner had been imprisoned overnight. The clientele had all streamed out and followed the man to a terrible sight. The flimsy thatch on the low roof had been torn away, and inside lay the prisoner, the skin flayed from his back, his throat chewed open.

No, Bear, I said to myself again, you didn't do wrong. But I watched with a squeeze of horror in my heart as the animal completed his toilet by licking the last of the dried blood from his claws.

CHAPTER TWELVE

We made the best speed we could that day and the next, but to my great relief no one seemed to have followed us. There was no reason why they should, of course; they would assume that the bear had killed his master and then fled into the wilderness. All the same, I didn't want anyone to see the animal until I had changed his appearance a little. To that end he had a thorough wash and brush and, at Ky-Lin's suggestion, I used some wood dye to darken his mask and paint a broad stripe down his back, like a badger's. In truth though, washing and brushing and good food made more alteration than anything else: after a few days I doubt anyone—even his old master—would have recognized him.

The thought of what he had done still gave me shivers, but once again it was Ky-Lin, the creature who could not even bend a blade of grass, who understood better than I.

"He is a child," he said. "In his last incarnation he was probably a neglected baby never taught right from wrong and died before he learnt. The Great-One-Who-Understands-All would not blame him. He has a chance now to learn from us that we all owe each other something and that includes living together in a social harmony. He was just removing something that had hurt him—like you humans think nothing of swatting a wasp."

155

I managed a weak smile. "Wasps don't sting you," I said. "They wouldn't dare!"

He fluffed out his plumed tail. "The colors put them off," he said, perfectly serious. "Besides," he added: "Like your Son-of-God, we are taught to turn the other cheek. One good thing has come out of this."

"What?"

"The bear's owner has been sent away before he can compound his crimes. Perhaps the Great One will bring him back as a bear, so that next time he will have learnt and will be redeemed to a higher plane."

I didn't feel I was competent to enter into a religious discussion with Ky-Lin; all I was grateful for was that Bear was gentle and sweet-tempered with us, and willingly cooperated in perfecting our act.

Tug did his acrobatics first, then Bear ambled in, wearing a soft red collar I had made for him, decorated with little bells. Tug coaxed a weird tune or two out of the pipe I had bought for him, the bear danced and when he had finished dropped to all fours. Tug climbed on his back with a shivering, eyes-tight-shut-all-the-time Growch in his arms. Bear rose to his hind legs as Tug climbed up his back and, having perfect balance, the boy stood on the bear's shoulders, holding Growch aloft as Bear slowly clapped his paws together. Needless to say, the only one who needed persuasion, bribes and petting, was Growch.

"S'not dignified," he said, "for the star performer, the talkin' dog, to be 'ung up in the air like so much washin'. 'Sides, makes me all dizzy!"

"But just listen to the applause," I said slyly. "How many of your kind do you know that could be as brave? And just look at all the fine meals we're having, and all because of you. . . ."

After that he didn't grumble as much, but he still kept his eyes tightly shut.

I kept Ky-Lin a secret from Dickon still, and although the latter now took over the job of selecting trinkets from the audience for me, dressed in a multicolored costume I had sewn from scraps of colored silks and cottons I had bargained for, he was still mystified at my "guesses," as he called them.

For the most part Ky-Lin lived either in the lining of my jacket or in the hood of my cloak, though if we had a room to ourselves at night, he would come out and prance around like a tiny pony, all fluffed up and full of energy. Separate rooms were becoming an increasing problem, though, as we neared the city. At most, with the increasing traffic, we were making only a few miles a day, and accommodation in the villages we rested at was becoming difficult to find, bespoke by those who came first. Sometimes we were lucky, sometimes not.

On one of the luckier occasions we were only twenty miles short of the city: we tried the houses on the edges of the village first and, just as it started to rain—a rain that would last for two, soaking days—we found a widow woman willing to rent us her house.

Through Ky-Lin I learned that her daughter-in-law was expecting her first and had taken to her bed, so the woman was going to keep house for her son till the baby appeared. It was less costly to hire than I thought, and I asked Ky-Lin (who had done the bargaining in my voice) just why.

"I told her that on the third day from now she would be nursing a fine, healthy grandson on her knee."

"Wasn't that chancing it a bit? Supposing it arrives tomorrow and it's a girl?"

"It won't and it won't be."

I opened my mouth and shut it again. By now I was learning not to question Ky-Lin: he was always right.

We spent a restful night. The house, if you could call it that, had a largish room, partitioned off by a screen to make a living and sleeping area. Outside was a woodshed, where Bear was comfortable enough. I lit the small brazier and cooked a meal I had sent Dickon out for: ubiquitous rice, beans, and some vegetables. Out of respect for

Ky-Lin I kept our consumption of meat to a minimum (except for Growch). Him I kept content with a huge ham bone I had been saving, and Bear was perfectly happy with beans and some pancakes I made.

In the morning it was still raining, so I decided to do some sewing. I thought that my cloak, warm and comfortable as it was, needed tarting up a little for our performances, so had sketched a design of a blue dragon I had seen on a broken-down temple, brought a piece of sky-blue silk and now settled down to cut it out.

Suddenly I felt a cold breath touch my cheek, as though sleet had been chucked in my face. At the same time my ring stabbed like a pinprick and my stomach throbbed in sympathy. I had a vision of great mountains, like those that marched alongside our daily travels, but these were much nearer, rearing up until they filled the sky, the snow glittering on their sides, their tops clouded by the spinning of wind-driven flakes like a permanent veil. I saw a blue dragon, I saw a black dragon—

"Whassa matter?" said Growch. "Look like you seen a ghost. . . . Hey, you all right? That ol' stummick again? Too many of those black beans; been fartin' meself all mornin'."

"Nothing to do with the beans," I said, by now doubled over in pain, "I'll be better in a moment. . . ."

But I wasn't. It was worse by the minute, like I used to get with my monthly show, only sharper.

Ky-Lin whispered urgently in my ear. "Send Dickon out for a drink. Tell him you have woman's trouble and wish to be alone for a while. He'll go if you give him some coin: the rain's eased off a bit."

I gave him enough to get drunk twice over, and dragged myself off to my pallet in the partitioned part of the room. I heard Ky-Lin speak to Tug, and a moment later the boy had brought in both the little oil lamp and our own stronger lantern.

"Lie down," said Ky-Lin. "Take your clothes off and lie under the blanket—"

"Tug?"

"He has known all along you were a girl. You washed him once in a river, so he says, and you all got so wet your outline was unmistakable. He's never questioned it: I need him now to help me. Don't worry: it means nothing to him at his age."

"It hurts," I whimpered like a child.

"Not for long," and he spoke to Tug, and a moment or two later one of the opium pills I had kept in my pouch, just in case, was pushed into my mouth, followed by a draught of cool water.

I undressed with difficulty and lay on my back, as instructed by Ky-Lin. Then I was told to rub my ring in a circular movement round my navel, and whether it was the pill or that, or both, the pain diminished and I felt sleepy and relaxed. I began to fantasize. I saw again the cottage where I was born, the forest and river where I played as a child; I could taste the honey cakes my mother gave me, remembered the little church where the mural of the Last Judgment faded gently on either side of the altar. A knight rode by, a handsome knight; a white horse gambolled in surf no whiter than she; I heard a tortoise rustle away into the undergrowth and the clap of a pigeon's wings; I was flying, and then suddenly the dream changed. A castle whose stones were stained with the sins before committed, a thin, wheedling voice: "Tell me a story. . . ."

"Gently, gently," said a voice in my ear. "Nearly over . . ."

I dreamt again. A dog was barking, his voice ringing through woodland; I flew once more, then crashed to the ground, bruised and breathless; waves dragged at my clothes, I was so cold, so cold—

No, it was only my stomach that was cold, numbing the pain. . . .

"Rest, rest, lie still. Remember the Place of Stones and what happened there a year ago today?"

Yes, yes, of course I remembered! I was looking for a

pig, a large pig, who had disappeared. It was All Hallows'
Eve, exactly a year since I had left home, and the air
about crackled with mystery and magic. And then I had
found my pig, my dearest pig, and had kissed him and
suddenly there was a stranger in his place, a dark
stranger—but no! it was a dragon, a black dragon with
claws that could rend me in twain—

"Just a minute more . . ."

And the dragon was the stranger, no stranger, again.
And he had enfolded me in his arms. He had kissed me,
lain with me, and a hot flood of feeling had filled me
like an empty skin waiting to be filled and the pain had
been so exquisite that I had cried out—

"Aaahhh . . ."

But when I opened my eyes he was a dragon again
and had flown away into the east, his shadow passing
across the moon, and I was alone. . . .

A warm tongue caressed my cheek and my nose was
filled with the smell of warm, hacky breath. "Better,
Summer dear?"

But I wasn't Summer: I was Talitha. *He* had called
me Talitha, and he was . . . he was Jasper, Master of
Many Treasures.

"Wake up!" barked Growch.

"All over," said Ky-Lin. "No more pain."

I tried to sit up, but there was a sort of stitchy feeling
in my stomach. Tug's hands raised my head, propped
something behind it and fed me some welcome, warming
broth. Then I was lying down again, a blanket tucked
under my chin.

"You can sleep now," said Ky-Lin. "No more pain."

"But I don't want—"

"Yes, you do. In the morning you will feel wonderful.
Just breathe deeply and I will give you some Sleepy
Dust. . . ."

My mouth and nose were filled with the scent and
taste of fresh spring flowers, summer leaves, autumn
fires, winter snow. . . . I breathed it all in greedily until

I was floating way up, up, up till I could touch the damp edges of the clouds and twist and turn with the screaming swifts. Ghostlike, I flew on silent wings with the owls, hung on the tip of a crescent moon, fell back into a bed of thistledown, a nest lined with the bellyfur of rabbit, a bed with down pillows—a hard pallet with a couple of blankets and someone shaking me awake.

"Hey! You going to sleep all day as well?"

"Oh, piss off, Dickon!" I said irritably. "I was having a wonderful dream. . . ."

"Well, you can't sleep all day! We're all hungry, and you've got the money. . . ."

And will have to cook it too, I thought. "How long have I slept?"

"You were asleep when I came back yesterday, you've snored all night, and it's around noon now."

Nearly twenty-four hours! Still, it was as Ky-Lin had promised: I felt wonderful, relaxed, happy—and now I came to think about it: very hungry.

"Is it still raining?" A nod. "Well give me a few minutes to get dressed and we'll go to the eating house. My treat."

It was while I was dressing that I discovered something wrong.

"Ky-Lin," I hissed. "What's this around my waist?"

"Just something to keep you warm," came the small voice from under my pillow. "Leave it there for the time being, there's a good girl." He must have sensed my indecision. "Have I ever given you bad advice?"

So I left it where it was. It didn't discommode me at all, but I was a little disconcerted to find out I had started my monthly flow again, which was annoying after so long without.

It stopped raining on the afternoon of the third day, and with the weak sun came the widow woman, almost crying with joy, the rent money held out for me to take.

"It is as I said," whispered Ky-Lin. "Now, open and

shut your mouth as you do in our performances. I have something to tell her. . . ."

And to the openmouthed astonishment of Dickon, out came a soft stream of words from my lips and, for a moment hidden from all but the woman, Ky-Lin showed himself.

She fell to the floor and gabbled, the tears of joy streaming down her face, then bowed her way out of the door. Dickon picked the coins up and tucked them in his pouch.

"What was all that gibberish about?"

Luckily Ky-Lin had briefed me.

"It was a prophesy; her grandson will become one of the great sages of the country."

"Still don't know how you do it," he muttered. "However, a nice way of conning her out of the rent."

I bit back an angry retort. Ky-Lin whispered in my ear.

"Right, everyone," I said. "Time to go. We'll steal a march on the rest who have stopped over. With the roads empty we can make good time. Oh, Dickon: leave that money on the stool. Call it a present for the baby. . . ."

We made reasonable progress during the next couple of days, and on the second night, Dickon having gone out scouting the prospects for a performance, Ky-Lin made me lie down on the bed.

"I want to take the bandage off." He seemed uncharacteristically nervous; he had gone a shaky sort of blue color all over. "Let's have a look. . . ."

He spoke to Tug, who slowly and carefully unwound the cloth.

"Mmmm . . ."

"What's the matter?" I tried to sit up; my stomach felt cold.

"Nothing. Nothing at all." His color had returned to normal. "Take a look. . . ."

Sitting up, I gazed down at my stomach; at first I could see nothing and then—

"Hey, Summer! We've got a performance!"

Damn and blast and perdition! Hastily pulling my shirt down and my breeches up, I staggered over to the bolted door. Dickon burst in.

"There's a rich caravan just pulled in and they were enquiring about entertainment; Arabs and Greeks mostly, so you'll have to 'Magic' some of their language...." He sniggered. Little did he know Ky-Lin!

"But it's full dark; must be near nine at night."

"They're camping in the square, 'cos there's no other accommodation. Plenty of light, torches, lanterns. They're being fed now, so we'd better hurry before they decide to kip down for the night."

It was past midnight before we returned to our quarters, but my pouch was full of coins. It had been a treat to have a relatively sophisticated audience, for it was a rich caravan, and they had insisted on us performing twice over. They had travelled from the south, with a special order for the wedding: gold and silver platters, silver-handled daggers and filigree jewelry, and were near two weeks late. Tonight would be their last stop, for with horses and camels they could make the city easily by the next day.

So they were relaxed and generous, and Ky-Lin's Arabic, Greek and a little Persian was impeccable. When we packed up Dickon obviously had a yen to go farther afield, so I gave him a generous advance, knowing full well he had also gathered tips on the way from the audience, and he disappeared for a while in search of his own entertainment.

Growch was on a high; one of the objects held up for my "discovery" had been one of his "fluffy bum" pups, and he had nearly let us all down at this point, completely forgetting to concentrate, even running over to the puppy and investigating.

"Keep your mind on the job!" I hissed at him when at last he reached me.

"Thought I 'ad—*my* job. Why I came, an' all. Boy pup: pity."

I was so tired when we returned that all I wanted to do was flop down on my pallet and sleep, but there was one other thing to do: look once more at my stomach. I thought I had seen—but no, it couldn't be. I lay down, lifted my shirt and peered down, aware out of the corner of my eye that Ky-Lin was watching anxiously. At first nothing, then—

What looked like a pearl nestled in my belly button. I touched it gingerly: it gave a little to my touch. I tried to prize it out—

"No! Don't touch it yet; it hasn't quite hardened." Ky-Lin had gone quite pale again, and was peering anxiously over my shoulder. "Give it a day or two more. . . ."

"But what *is* it?" It resembled nothing so much as a jewel one might stick in a belly dancer's navel. "And how in heaven's name did it get there?"

"Er . . . I put it there. For safekeeping. Nicely insulated. Warm . . ."

"*What is it?*"

"Actually—well, it's quite simple really. It's a dragon's egg."

CHAPTER THIRTEEN

"A . . . what?" I was already asleep; I must be.

"Egg. Dragon's. Not yet set," said Growch succinctly. "Leastways, that's what I thought 'e said." He didn't seem the least surprised or alarmed—but then it wasn't happening to him.

I attempted to laugh it off, all the time nursing a horrible feeling it wasn't a laughing matter. "If this is all a joke, it's not in very good taste. Now be a good creature and take it away, Ky-Lin, and I'll forget all about it."

"I can't 'take it away,' just like that," said Ky-Lin unhappily. "It's yours. Yours and—*his*."

I knew immediately who he meant, but wasn't going to accept what he said. It was impossible! That sort of thing just didn't happen; it couldn't.

"That was what was hurting you, giving you the stomachache. It was ready to come out for the second stage of its development," said Ky-Lin. "Don't ask me how, or why; I'm no expert in this sort of thing, and indeed I doubt it has ever happened before just like this. Humans don't mate with dragons. Normally dragons are bisexual: they can reproduce themselves. Theoretically so can Ky-Lins; that's what my name means: male/female. We never have, though."

I remembered the pain of that embrace by the Place of Stones: the pain and the ecstasy. Had we bypassed the natural laws, my man-dragon and I? Was this, this tiny pearl, still semisoft and shining, a product of a love that had never been seen before, just because I had kissed a creature and made him man, however temporarily?

I gazed down at my navel and, gently, so gently touched the shining pearl. Just in case . . .

"But it's so tiny!"

"Oh, it grows. A fully developed egg, ready to hatch, will be at least as big as a human baby. But, I warn you, this one could take many, many years—longer than you have—to grow and mature. You will never see what it contains. You are just its guardian, for a little while. So, don't get fond of it. Your job is to keep it warm, give it its first few weeks of incubation." He sighed. "You are very privileged."

I didn't feel the least bit "privileged": quite the reverse, in fact. I felt confused, hurt, bewildered, used, somehow *dirty*.

Ky-Lin read part of what I was thinking. "You truly are privileged, dear girl. You may not realize it now but that egg, however it got there, has been a part of you for a year, you nourished it in your body, and whatever happens to it in the future, you will always be a part of it. Also remember, it was created in love."

I looked down again; right now it was tiny, soft, vulnerable. Anyone could squash it, crush it, snuff the little life that lay inside. . . . Without conscious thought my hands curled protectively over my navel, and emotion took over from instinct, realizing ruefully that once more I had conned myself into caring for yet one more burden. Once before they had all been maimed in their separate ways; this time they were all more or less normal, even if they still had their particular needs—except Ky-Lin, of course, though even he was trying to gain extra points towards his redemption.

"And so we are lucky seven," said Ky-Lin happily. "You and I, Growch and Tug, Dickon, Bear and the Egg. Just as the Old One foretold."

I shivered and crossed myself; the Good Lord protect us all and bring us to a safe haven. . . .

Two days later we topped a rise and there lay the Golden City beneath us. They called it golden because the stone used was a warm, yellow sandstone, quarried from goodness knew where, because the surrounding hills and mountains were dark and forbidding. Right now, at midday, the sun made the whole place glow, picking out the various towers and steeples that were gilded with real gold, till the whole scene shimmered with warmth and welcome.

We had a steep descent, but beneath us a wide river curled around the east of the city, a river so wide I could see the boats, like beetles at this distance, scurrying about on the water. To the south the plain widened out, and I could see a wide field, with men drilling and horses being exercised.

It looked like a place full of promise, but it took all of three hours to reach the city gates, the road ahead being crowded to suffocation with caravans, carts, wagons, cattle, horses and travellers on foot like ourselves. Past experience made us head for the side streets once we had passed through the west gate; the city would be crowded already, and the best chance of accommodation was out of the mainstream. We were lucky; entertainers were at a premium, and although I had to pay more than I had reckoned, we found two ground-floor rooms with accommodation in a shed for Bear, breakfast and midday meal included.

After a plain but satisfying meal of rice, chicken, and fruit, we left Bear behind and decided to explore the city. By now it was dusk, and evening fires hazed the rooftops. There was already a chill to the air but it made no difference to those who, like us, were determined to make the most of all the city had to offer. The main streets were paved and bordered with fine buildings, but the streets radiating from the main square were full of bustle, crowd, and character.

The stalls were crammed with all the goods in the world, or so it seemed. Over glowing braziers meat, fish, glazed chicken wings, and nuts sizzled and popped and every available space was filled with beggars, jugglers, fortune-tellers (bones, water, sand, and stones), and pretty ladies plying their charms, which is how we lost Dickon.

The rest of us found ourselves in the huge main square, deserted now except for a few gawpers like us. Ahead of us lay the palace, a heterogenous mass of gilded roofs, towers, tilted eaves, and balconies, approached by wide steps guarded by soldiers in green and gold. Flares, torches and lanterns kept the whole facade brightly lit, and through the screened and fretted windows could be glimpsed figures scurrying to and fro.

"This square is where the main celebrations for the wedding will take place," said Ky-Lin, who as usual had been listening to everything going on around him. "During the next few days, palace scouts will seek out the best entertainers and they will be invited to perform here in front of the prince and his prospective bride."

" 'Ow they goin' to choose us, then?" asked Growch.

"They go around the streets and smaller squares, list those they prefer, then send others for a second opinion."

We had already come across some half-dozen of these smaller squares.

"Do we keep to one or try as many as we can?" I wondered.

"More the better," said Ky-Lin. "That way we reach a wider audience and have a better chance of being noticed. Even if we aren't picked, we can at least earn some money. There are many very good acts here already, so we need to polish up our performances, make some new costumes, and I will provide some powders to burn that will give you a better light, sprinkled on torches. Can you walk on your hind legs, dog?"

" 'Course I can! Well, sometimes. A bit. I could try. . . ."

His legs were so short and his body so long, I sometimes wondered how his messages got from one end to the other. "That would be very nice," I said enthusiastically. "Worth an extra bone or two."

And he tried, he really did; at the end of two days he could stagger at least two yards. . . .

We made—I made—new costumes, we played the small squares and larger side streets from one end of the city to the other, and at the end of four days both Dickon and Ky-Lin recognized the same nonpaying faces at our performances.

Ky-Lin nodded his head in satisfaction. "Definitely scouts," he said.

In the meantime we had been making more money than in all our journey so far and I was perplexed as to where to keep it—by now a small sackful—safe. I daren't leave it in our rooms: quite apart from thieves I couldn't trust Dickon's sticky fingers, and it was Growch who suggested the solution. " 'Oo's the one they're all scared of? That great bear. 'E can guard it daytimes, and when we give performances, 'e can 'ave it tucked under 'is arm or sumfin'."

Which solved the problem.

With only twenty-four hours to go before the grand entertainment we were visited in our lodgings by two palace officials, smartly dressed in gold jackets and green trews, who informed me (through Ky-Lin) that we had been picked to perform in the Palace Square the following evening. It was a great honor, as the acts were limited to thirteen, the Moons of the Year. We were allowed a half-hour only, to give time for all the other acts, so we practiced curtailing Tug and Bear and it made for a crisper performance, which we took round the streets that night, able to boast that we were one of the chosen ones for the following night. Our purse was heavier than ever that day.

Our actual performance seemed to be over before it began. We had to wait through performing ponies, acrobats, contortionists, a magician, and a woman who climbed a ladder of swords and lay on a bed of nails with a man standing on her chest, but eventually the large hourglass was set down again in the sand and it was our turn. By now I had worked myself into such a lather of expectation that I was trembling in every limb, my mouth was as dry as the sands of the desert and I desperately needed to relieve myself.

Once we started, however, I was as cool as a draught of cold water, even remembering to direct our act towards the balcony where the prince had his seat. They said afterwards that the prince, a sophisticated man, was bored by much he saw, but that his prospective bride, an ingenuous girl, clapped enthusiastically the whole way through. Be that as it may, each performance was rewarded by a bag of silver coins, good, bad or indifferent, and was cheered impartially by the large crowd penned behind rope barriers at the perimeter of the square.

There were many acts after ours, but I fell asleep through exhaustion, tucked up against Bear, and only woke when Dickon nudged me. The square was emptying, torches guttering and a chill wind blew away the detritus of the evening.

"Bed," said Dickon. "There are three days till the wedding and after tonight the audiences will pay even better. . . ."

But the morning was to bring a further surprise. Before the first cock had even cleared his throat, another official from the palace, this one with gold braid and tassels, presented us with an invitation to perform that evening within the palace confines themselves. Apparently the prince and his bride-to-be wished a closer look at some of the acts they had enjoyed the night before.

"We've cracked it!" exulted Dickon. "Can't you just see it? We can advertise ourselves as by royal command!"

It was an attractive idea, but I could see it would only complicate matters. As far as I was concerned I had places to go, people and animals to answer to, and that was enough. I didn't want more than would carry us to our next destination, but Dickon wanted it all: gold, prestige, fame.

"Are you coming, then?" asked Dickon.

"Coming? Where?"

"I've just been telling you. Outside the city, on the parade ground, they're having races, entertainments, wild animals. It's a day out. It's a *free* day out. All you want is money for some food. Or, take our own. Hurry up, or all the best vantage points will be taken."

We left Bear in the shed; as the winter advanced, although he had never been allowed his natural hibernation since he was a cub, he nevertheless became more lethargic, and was quite happy to be left guarding the money and snoozing the day away. I hoped that when, and if, we ever found his homeland, he would find a convenient cave in which to sleep every winter till spring.

The races and entertainment were held in the amphitheater to the south I had noticed on first looking down on the city. Cordoned off and edged with a low wall of stones, it was an oval, sandy space perhaps three-quarters of a mile in length and half that distance wide. Roughly marked out were four staggered lanes for foot or horse racing, and in the center a raised circle for wrestling. Seats there were none, but plenty of boulders and banked sand, so we made ourselves comfortable behind the ropes, knotted with colored cloths, that kept us from the tracks.

Heats of the footraces had already been run, and the finalists rested while the children of the city had their turn. All kinds were represented, from the silk-kilted privileged to the half-naked urchins, and it was one of the latter I was glad to see that won the junior race, two laps of the track, to bear a purse back to his delighted parents.

I could see that Tug, too, would have liked to participate, but we didn't know the rules, so I consoled him with sticky sweetmeats from a peddler's tray. There was plenty to eat—if you could afford it—for behind the crowd there were braziers frying and roasting all sorts of delights, and trays of cheeses, cakes, boiled rice, and fruit. The poorer people had brought their own food, but we were in a festive mood and nibbled away all afternoon, fortified by drinks of water, wine, or goat's milk from the skins of the sellers.

The day wore on. We watched the wrestling—which seemed to be a near-killing exercise of arms, feet, hands, teeth and nails—and applauded the finals of the footraces. Then came the chariot races; light, wicker-framed two-wheeled carts with two horses. There were plenty of thrills and spills, and special applause when the prince's charioteer won the top prize. Next was an exhibition of kite flying, great monsters of birds, flowers, giants, and dragons, but there was little or no wind, so these were a disappointment. We were about to pack up and go back to our lodgings to ready ourselves for tonight's performance, when there was a clamor from far across the field.

A distant thunder of hooves, a murmur from the crowd: "The Riders of the Plains!" and into the arena galloped a troop of wild-looking horsemen, riding even wilder horses. They circled the arena at an even faster pace, churning the sand into swirls of smoke, manes and tails flying, the horsemen uttering wild yells of encouragement until suddenly, with no apparent signal, they crashed to a rearing halt in the center, shouting what sounded like a battle cry to my untrained ears.

There was an eruption at my side and Tug sprang to his feet, his face alight with joy, his fists raised over his head in salute.

"My people, my people! They come. . . ." and he was gone, scrambling over rocks and people with abandon, to disappear into the amphitheater amid the melee of men, horses, sand and dust.

I called after him, but it was no use: he couldn't, or wouldn't, hear.

"Leave him be," whispered Ky-Lin. "He will be back. Just watch."

And watch we did, an unparalleled exhibition of horse-manship. Horses raced, apparently riderless, till their rid-ers twisted up from under their bellies; one horseman balanced on the backs of two, three, four mounts at a gallop; they threw spears at targets as they raced past, hitting them every time; they leapt to the ground first one side, then the other, rode with their heads towards the horse's tail; they fought mock battles; they jumped— one, two, three men—onto the back of a galloping horse until we were exhausted just watching.

The crowd was as stupified as we were, then on their feet yelling for more.

And Tug? He was in the midst of it all. Running, riding, vaulting, balancing; handstands, yells, two hands, one hand, no hands ... On the ground he was a rather awkward boy with bandy legs and a usually sullen expres-sion; put him on a horse and he was transformed. I could see now that those bandy legs had been used to riding from the time he could toddle and saw from his face how much being back with his own kind meant to him. I didn't need the confirmation of his words when he finally climbed back to us, tattered, sweaty, and utterly happy.

"Found them! They mine ... Go home!" He started to speak in the few words of my tongue I had taught him, but soon lapsed into his own language, and I was glad to have Ky-Lin's whispered translation. Dickon stood by, his face a picture of bewilderment, but Growch's tail was wagging furiously: he at least under-stood what was going on.

"My people come for prince's wedding: special invita-tion. Prince rides with us, in disguise...." He pointed to a taller man, dressed as the rest, who was sneaking off the field. "His treat . . ." He waved his hand at the rest of the horsemen. "They are of my people, but not of my tribe, although they know of my father. He is chieftain. They return to our lands tomorrow, next day, before snows come and I will travel with them."

"If your father is chieftain, then you . . . ?" I asked through Ky-Lin.

"I am my father's first son, and will be chieftain when he dies."

So, I had rescued a prince among his people, this shabby boy who now squatted before me, took one of my hands in his and pressed it to his forehead.

"I shall always be in your debt," he said simply. "You bought my freedom, fed me and clothed me, treated me with kindness. I shall never forget you. And you, Great One," and he bowed in the hidden direction of Ky-Lin.

"Rubbish!" I said gruffly, conscious that I had difficulty in speaking. I ruffled his hair, just as if he were the young boy who had already shared our adventures, and not a young prince.

Dickon had finally picked up the drift of what was happening. "He's not going, is he? Not before the performance tonight, surely! In the palace, by special request, remember? You don't turn up only with half your act!" He looked scandalized. "Out here they could cut your head off for a thing like that—or at least chuck you in a dungeon and throw away the key. . . . Besides, just think of the money!"

In the excitement I had completely forgotten; although I did not believe we should be punished for turning up without Tug, it would certainly mean a revision of our act. I asked Ky-Lin to explain as best he could.

As we had been talking, we had gradually become surrounded by Tug's fellow countrymen, smelling strongly of horses and sweat. Smaller in stature than most, they were still a fearsome-looking lot, with their yellowish faces, high cheekbones, long hair, fierce eyebrows and drooping moustaches. Like Tug, they had black eyes and bandy legs. They shuffled closer, and I had the distinct impression that they were quite ready to kidnap Tug and carry him away if we had any intention of trying to keep him.

But Tug listened to what Ky-Lin had to say, shrugged his shoulders and nodded. Turning to his people he made a little speech, indicating us, then bowed quite regally in dismissal. The men glanced at each other, then, thankfully, bowed also and moved away.

"I have told them," said Tug formally, "that I have an obligation to fulfill, but shall join them later tonight. All right, Summer-Lady-Boy?" And he grinned, once more the boy I would always remember.

Returning to our lodgings, we washed and dressed in our costumes and made our way as previously directed to the side door of the palace, giving onto the kitchens, armory, stores, laundries, etc. We crossed the large, cobblestoned courtyard and were shown into an anteroom. Like the largest houses I had seen, this part of the building was strictly utilitarian. No fancy clothes, no elaborate decoration, everything meant for use. In the anteroom the other three acts were already waiting, obviously as nervous as we were ourselves. They became positively agitated when they saw Bear, however, and that coupled with the thought of bear droppings on the carpets, made me ask through Ky-Lin if we might wait in the courtyard.

It was chilly out there, so I walked over to one of the braziers to warm myself up. There were some half-dozen of these, crowded by off-duty soldiers, kitchen porters, and itinerants waiting for the scraps of the feast now taking place. Obviously they were still eating, for enticing smells were coming from the kitchens: behind the bland scents of rice and vegetables came the aromas of fish and meat, sharpened to a fine edge by the pungency of spices such as ginger and coriander. My stomach started to rumble, although we had all eaten before we came

out. A couple of trays of saffron-colored rice full of
niblets of dried fish were thrust out into the courtyard;
you ate, if you were lucky, with your fingers: the beggars
had brought their own bowls.

I managed a handful for Bear and Growch; one of the
better-dressed beggars shouted at me, gesticulating to
his friends.

"What does he say?" I asked Ky-Lin, passing him a
grain or two of rice.

"Not to waste good food on animals. Just ignore him."

"It's just that—I'm sure I've seen him somewhere
before. . . ."

"Where?"

I racked my brains, but came up with nothing; here,
there, somewhere, I was sure of it. "I don't know. . . ."

"Well, don't worry about it: it's our turn next."

It must have been near midnight when we came out
into the courtyard again, still dazed by the lights, music,
dancing, gold, embroideries, costumes, decorations, plate,
jewelry, and sheer opulence of all we had seen, touched,
heard, smelled, in the last couple of hours. The inner
reality of the palace was like something from a legend;
pointless to wonder where the money had come from to
create such luxury: to marvel and enjoy was enough.

In the vast banqueting hall in which we had been
called upon to perform there were patterned marble
floors, thick colored rugs, gilded pillars, painted walls and
ceilings, embroidered cushions, long carved tables, a silver throne, and men and women guests wearing robes
of silk and fine wools, heavily sewn with gold and silver
thread and studded with jewels. The whole area was
lighted to brilliance with oil lamps, torches and flares,
the light reflected from vast sheets of brass, placed the
best for catching the flames.

Behind painted screens musicians sighed and wailed
on strings and woodwind, with the insistent drubbing of
a tabor; there was a heavy scent of incense, sweet oils,

of opium and hashish, both cloying and exciting at the
same time.

The prince, on a silver throne, had been gracious
enough to lead the applause for our act, but as an audience the rich guests could not have been more different
from our credulous village spectators. There was a back-
ground murmur of conversation all the while, the
applause was polite and it seemed there was more attention paid to eating and drinking than to the performance.
It was not just us though: all the other acts were received
in the same way, a restrained appreciation for something
far beneath such a sophisticated guest list.

Still, the coins we were paid with this time were of
gold. . . .

As we came out into the courtyard we all breathed in
the clean, cold night air with relief. All but a couple
of the braziers had been extinguished and someone was
unfastening the heavy gates for us, just as a shout came
from away to our left, and a figure ran at us, followed
by a half-dozen others. I stopped, bewildered; it was the
man I thought I had seen somewhere before, but now he
was yelling out something over and over again. Ky-Lin hissed
urgently in my ear: "Run, girl, run! Tell them all to run
and hide. . . ."

"But why? What's he saying?"

"That's the man you thought you recognized; he comes
from the village where Bear's former master was found
dead. They are going to arrest you and Dickon on a
charge of murder!"

CHAPTER FOURTEEN

I opened my eyes: nothing.

I shut them tight again, screwed them up, rubbed them with my knuckles, opened them again.

Nothing. Black as pitch.

If I wasn't so cold and it didn't hurt when I pinched myself, I might have thought I was still asleep and dreaming, or in that muddled half-awake situation children find themselves in sometimes when nothing makes sense. Once—I think I was six or seven at the time—I found myself trying to pull up the earthen floor of the hut in which my mother and I lived, in the mistaken belief that it was a blanket. I had fallen out of bed but the fall had only half woken me, so I thought I was still there. I remembered crying with the cold and frustration, then Mama had leaned over and plucked me to her side again, scolding me heartily for waking her. . . .

I wanted my Mama again, right now, scolding or no. I wouldn't have cared if she had thrashed me—the physical blows wouldn't have counted against the warmth of contact with another human—but she was long dead and I was alone, totally alone, in a mind-numbing darkness that froze my mind and made icicles round my heart.

I hadn't even got the comforting presence of Ky-Lin: he had disappeared together with the others.

In the confusion of that sudden attack in the courtyard we had all become separated. The gate was half-open, I had shouted a warning, and a white-faced Dickon had been first away, followed by a bewildered Bear. I felt Ky-Lin leap from my shoulder, heard Growch growling and barking at my feet and was conscious of Tug trying to fend off my attackers. Somebody had grabbed the boy by his jacket, but he twisted free and punched someone else on the nose. Growch had another aggressor by the ankle and was being shaken like a rat, and a guard tried to catch me by the hair.

"Run, you idiots, run!" I yelled. "Watch the gate!" Which was already being closed again. I started off for the narrow gap that remained; ten feet, five, four. My hands touched the thick oak, I pushed with all my might, Growch squeezed through, then suddenly I tripped, fell flat on my face and was immediately pinned to the ground by half a dozen men. Fighting to keep my head clear, I saw the gate clang to, followed by a flying leap from Tug, who seemed to run up the ten feet or so like a cat scaling a wall, to disappear over the top.

So at least Tug, Growch, Bear and Dickon had a chance of escape, although I had no idea of Ky-Lin's whereabouts. Knowing how violence of any kind was anathema to him, I wondered if he had hidden himself away somewhere; wherever he was, I could certainly have done with his help during the next hour or so.

I had been hauled into the palace again, but this time to a small windowless antechamber, in which I was ruthlessly questioned, my accuser and his friends pointing the finger of guilt; a senior palace official tried to get a statement out of me. Impossible, of course: without a translator we couldn't understand each other at all. In any case I was so bruised, battered and confused by now, that I doubt I could have said anything sensible in any language.

My brain seemed to have gone to sleep, and after three hours we had gotten nowhere. For the moment it seemed it was one person's accusation against my silence, for my accuser was treated no better than I; finally we were both marched along endless corridors, down steps, across a winding walkway and finally into what could only be the dungeons. Then we were separated: my accuser went one way, I went the other, to end up in front of a low, barred door. The bolts were drawn, the door creaked open and I was flung headlong onto a pile of filthy straw; the door clanged shut and the bolts were drawn with a dull finality. Something was shouted from outside, and the footsteps marched away, their sound to be smothered all too soon in the darkness of the thick walls.

The stench of the cell was terrible. At first after I got to my feet I wasted my breath calling and shouting, but the air was so thick my voice lost itself in the gloom, and there was no answer. Next I felt my way all around the cell—with, strangely enough, my eyes shut: it seemed easier that way—only to find it was empty of all but a rusty ring on one wall with a chain dangling from it and a small drain in the floor, presumably for excreta. I must have spent an hour trying to find a way out, but in the end had sunk to my knees in the filth, as miserable as I had ever been in my life.

And what of the others? Dickon had got away and was capable of looking after himself, but Bear was too large and clumsy to hide. Tug and Growch would probably come looking for me, but what could a boy and a dog do on their own? And what had happened to Ky-Lin? I had not seen him at all and he was so small that someone might have trodden on him—But I could not bear to think of that.

I had no idea of time, for in that fetid darkness my inside body-clock seemed to have stopped; I found I could no more judge either time or distance.

My ears caught a sound: a tiny, scratching, rustling noise. My God—rats! No, I couldn't stand rats, I couldn't! There it was again. . . .

Rising to my feet I shuffled backwards until my trembling hands touched the damp wall. I listened: nothing, except a distant irregular drip of water. I must have imagined it. I took a deep breath, tried to relax. I counted to a hundred slowly under my breath. No sound—Scratch, scritch . . . thump!

I screamed: I couldn't help it. The sound bounced back off the walls in a dead, muffled tone. No one could hear me—I opened my mouth again—

"Steady there, girl," came a small voice. "It's only me. Quite a jump down—"

"Ky-Lin!"

"The same. Now, stand still, and I'll find you. . . ."

There were further rustlings and a moment later something touched my ankle. I bent down and found a plumed tail.

"You've grown!"

He was now puppy-sized.

"It seemed like a good idea. Better for getting around. There was a lot to do before we could get to you."

"We?"

"Tug, Growch, and myself. Bear was willing to help, but we left him guarding the money and baggage. All safe. Now, just listen; in another hour or so—"

"How did you get in?" I interrupted. The door was solid and I hadn't found the smallest space anything could crawl through. "How did you find the others? Where are they? Where's Dickon?"

"In what order am I supposed to answer these questions? Perhaps in reverse. The young man has disappeared: I smelled his fright as he ran—"

Typical Dickon, I thought. Keen for gold, coward for danger.

"The bear went back to your lodgings. I had climbed onto the boy's shoulder when I left you; we had to persuade the dog to follow us: he was all for staying by the gate."

Typical of Growch too: loyal and devoted, whatever the danger.

"We packed your belongings and moved them to a

safe place. The boy went away to arrange certain matters and is less than two hundred yards away with the dog. As to how I got in? Through the window."

"What window?" I stared around once more. "I can't see any window!"

"Perhaps because you are not looking in the right place. Besides, there is no moon."

"Where?"

"Look to your right . . . no, much higher, to twice your height. Keep looking; let your eyes get accustomed to the dark. There now: do you see it?"

Yes, now I did. A grayish sort of oblong. Like all things, obvious once you knew where they were, I wondered how I could have missed it earlier. I stared and stared, with growing hope, until I got dancing specks in front of my eyes. Specks . . . and lines.

"But—there are bars across! You might be able to squeeze through those, but I couldn't. Besides, it's miles too high to reach!"

"Don't exaggerate! We've thought about all that."

"You're sure?"

"Sure." He hesitated. "At least . . ."

"At least—what?" Hope received a dent.

"If everything goes according to plan. Don't *worry*! If plan alpha doesn't work, we can always go to plan beta."

"If I don't get away from here before morning they'll probably haul me up for questioning again, and I'll need you to translate. And you can't hide in my cloak if you're as big as—"

"There is another hour until the false dawn, and now is the time when everyone sleeps deepest. That's why we chose it." He interrupted. "And now, if you will excuse me?"

"Don't go!" I was going to panic again, I knew it.

"Courage, girl! We have things to do. Firstly, put the Waystone in my mouth—that's it. Now lift me to your shoulders and bring me under the window. . . ."

He was much heavier now, and the spring he took

from my shoulder nearly knocked me to the floor. I
stared upwards, and could make out a darker shape
against the outline of the window. He appeared to be
doing the same he did with the bear's nose ring: stroking
the iron bars in one direction. It seemed to take an age.

"Ky-Lin?"

"Shhh . . ."

I shushed, for what seemed a lifetime. At last the
scraping noise stopped. "That should do it: catch!" The
Waystone dropped into my cupped hands. "Can you
climb a rope?"

"I don't know. . . ." I never had.

"Well, now's the time to find out!"

Something touched my face and reaching out a hand
I found I was clutching a knotted rope. Looking up, I
thought I detected movement, a muffled whisper, but
still eight bars stood between me and freedom. It must
be getting lighter, because now I could make them out
quite clearly.

"Wait for a moment," breathed Ky-Lin. "But when I
say 'move!' you move!"

A moment's pause, a straining noise, a muffled thud
of hooves, and the first bar snapped cleanly away from
the window. Two minutes later another, then a third.
The fourth broke only at the top.

"Now!" said Ky-Lin urgently. I grabbed the rope tight,
wrapped my legs around it and tried to pull myself up.
The rope swung wildly, I made perhaps a couple of feet,
banged hard against the wall, let go and dropped heavily
to the floor of the cell. I didn't even manage a foot of
climbing before banging my knuckles against the slime
of the walls and falling down again.

"It won't work. . . ." I was desperate.

"Wait. . . ."

What seemed like a muttered conversation took place
above, then Ky-Lin called down: "Wrap the rope around
your waist, hold it tight in your hands, and hang on!"

I swung out and in against the wall, almost fainting at

one stage from the pain of a bruised elbow, but gradually I was being hauled higher and higher. At last, when I thought the strain was too great and I would have to let go, a pair of hands gripped my wrists and pulled me up the last few inches till my shoulders were level with the window.

"Tug . . . !"

With his hands to help me I tried to wriggle through the space left by the missing bars. At first it was easy, and I was halfway through and could just make out, in the grayness that preceded the false dawn, a courtyard and a couple of the Plainsmen's small horses, ropes around their necks. At last I was breathing fresh air again, and Growch's eager tongue lapped at my cheek. Another pull, I was nearly there—and then I stuck.

That last bar, the one that had only broken halfway, was lodged against my hip, and I couldn't move. Tug tried to maneuver me past it, but it was hopeless. At last Ky-Lin slipped in beside me and pushed sideways as Tug pulled, and with a final jerk I was free, minus some trouser cloth and skin.

But there was no time to feel sorry for myself. I was shoved onto one of the horses. Tug led both out of the gates, then went back to bolt the gates on the inside, climbing back out when he had finished.

"That courtyard is where prisoners' friends are allowed to bring the food," explained Ky-Lin. "They are fed through the bars. For most that is all they get. The boy has bolted the gates so they will think you escaped by magic—or flew away with the dragons—and nothing will be traced back to his people."

The sky was lightening perceptibly as we moved silently through the deserted streets, the horses' hooves muffled with straw, to one of the smaller gates in the city wall. A few early fires smudged the clear, predawn air, a child whimpered somewhere, a dog howled, but that was all.

A smaller gate it might be, but it was still some twenty

feet high, bolted, barred and with an enormous keyhole that could only encompass an equally enormous key. I knew these gates were not opened until the dawn call from the muezzin, and feared that if we lingered here my escape might be discovered. Besides which, we were a motley enough collection that any guards would remember, for at that moment two of Tug's people came to join us on horseback, Bear ambling amiably behind. Our packs were fastened on the horses.

I gazed fearfully at the gate house, expecting the guards to emerge any moment and tell us to be about our business; instead, Tug dismounted, went over, opened the door and a minute later reappeared with a key almost half his size. Over his shoulder I could see the two guards lying in a huddle on the floor.

"Sleepy Dust," said Ky-Lin, his tail fluffed out. "Good for another hour at least. . . ."

With a struggle Tug and his fellows managed to slide back the bolts and bars and manipulate the key; we slipped through the gate and there was a straight road leading north. Tug stayed behind to close up again and return the key, before scaling the gate and rejoining us on the road.

"Right!" said Tug, in my tongue. "Now ride. Slow first, then faster."

Once the city was out of sight behind a curve in the dusty road we quickened our pace; as we rode we shared rice cakes and a flask of water but there was no slackening until the sun was at its zenith, when Tug led us off the road into a stand of trees.

Behind the trees was a tumbledown, deserted hut, and Bear collapsed into the shade, closely followed by Growch. Tug dismounted and helped me down, bumped and bruised from the ride, my hip aching from the scrape against the broken bar in the cell. Tug's friends dismounted, took the muffles from all four horses' hooves and led them over to a nearby stream to drink. Our baggage they put in the shade. I drank deep of the clear,

cold water then lay down in the winter sun, glad of the
transient warmth. I felt I could sleep for a week. . . .

"Anyfin' to eat?"

I don't think I could have roused myself even for
Growch's plaintive plea, but luckily Tug and his friends
had lit a discreet fire and we were soon eating cheese,
strips of dried meat and pancakes.

Tug pointed to the road ahead. "Bear's way," he said.
"Keep to trail during day, not roads. Bear will soon sniff
way. We go now." He bent and put his forehead to my
hands. "My freedom—your freedom. It is right. When I
man, I travel much. Good for learn better things my
people."

I didn't kiss him good-bye, although I wanted to; I just
ruffled his hair, waved, and listened to the sound of
hooves as he and his followers rode away out of my life.

Just before I fell asleep, Growch already snoring at my
side, Ky-Lin at my feet, I asked the latter a question that
had been bothering me.

"Ky-Lin . . . if plan alpha had failed, what was plan
beta?"

"Plan what?"

"Beta. You told me—"

"Oh that. I haven't the faintest idea, but we would have
thought of something. Alpha, beta, gamma, delta . . . Now
that really would have been a test. . . ."

CHAPTER FIFTEEN

As far as I knew, we were never followed. It would have been difficult for the townspeople to trace our route, even if they had bothered. Probably it was as Ky-Lin had surmised: they would think I had had magic to help me escape, and you can't chase magic.

I slept—we all slept—for the rest of the day and the ensuing night, waking cold, hungry, but thoroughly rested. Tug had left us provisions, so we broke our fast with gruel and honey, cheese and dried fruit.

Bear was eager to be away, declaring in his slow way that we were on the right road for his homeland. He sniffed the air, sneezed, then shook himself like a dog just out of water, his pelt rippling like a loose furry robe.

"Not far," he said, and sneezed again. "Air smells good. Woods, rivers, mountains."

Fine. The sooner the better as far as I was concerned, then we could take the more northern route to where I hoped I would find the Blue Mountain. Right at this moment, though, I couldn't see how we were going to move an inch further. I had repacked our baggage and rescued our money—including the gold from the palace performance—from Bear and tucked it away. I thought I could just about manage my pack, though how far I could carry it in one day was doubtful, but there was another problem. Tug had left us provisions, obviously believing we would find villages few and far between the farther we travelled, but now I looked with dismay at the sack of rice, the smaller ones of beans and oats, the pack of dried fruit, another of dried meat, a half of cheese and the three jars of salt, oil and honey.

Now there was no Tug or Dickon to share the burdens. I thought of Bear: he was big enough and strong enough to carry the burdens, but he was too unpredictable in his mode of travel. Sometimes he was content to lope along by my side, but he would often go off on his own for long periods of time, searching for grubs, roots, and honey. During one of these foragings he would be quite capable of forgetting his burdens, or dropping them, or just leaving them behind.

I scratched my nose; perhaps I could fashion a litter, or a form of sleigh, but they would have to be pretty tough to withstand the terrain. Perhaps Ky-Lin could think of something constructive.

But once again, he had read my mind and was now shaking his head from side to side in self-reproach. "Aieee! What a fool I am! If only we could all exist on fresh air . . ." He pulled himself together. "But we don't and can't, so there is the little matter of carrying the provisions is there not?"

"Not exactly a 'little' matter," I said. "There's enough there for a small pony!"

"Of course! Exactly what I had calculated. And I must now work twice as hard for not having anticipated all this, otherwise my Lord will be displeased. . . . You will excuse me for ten minutes, please?" and he disappeared into the undergrowth. Perhaps he had gone to look for some wood to build a litter, I thought; in any case, he had no need to reproach himself for anything; he had organized our escape, designed our performances and been a cheerful companion in all our journeying. And even now, running off like that, he had moved from stone to rock, in order not to even bend a blade of grass. His Lord was surely a hard taskmaster. On the other hand, the idea of not harming anything living if one could help it appealed to my soft heart. I should—

" 'Elp! 'Elp! Go 'way! Geroff!" and Growch burst into the clearing, barking wildly, closely pursued by what looked like a running rainbow, about four times his size.

I leapt to my feet and snatched up the cooking pot, now fortunately attached to the other implements, but at least it made a satisfactory clanging noise. Both Growch and the apparition stopped dead. Pulling out my little knife and wondering where the hell Bear had disappeared to, I walked slowly nearer.

"Now then, what do you—my God! Ky-Lin!—but you've *grown* . . . ! Growch, it's all right: just turn around and look!"

Instead of the puppy-sized Ky-Lin, there stood a creature the size of a small pony, perhaps as high at the withers as my waist. He looked extremely diffident, in spite of his new size, for parts of him hadn't grown as quickly as the others. No longer neat and petite, he was now large and untidy. The only completely perfect part of him was his plumed tail, with a spread now like that of a peacock.

He looked down and around at himself.

"It's a long time since I did this," he said apologetically. "Unfortunately it would seem that not everything changes at the same rate. Perhaps a grain or two of rice, or a little dried fruit . . . Thank you."

Almost immediately the shortest leg at the back grew to the right size.

"A little more?" I asked.

Ten minutes later and he was more or less all of a piece, except for a smaller left ear, a bare patch on his chest and extremely small antennae.

"A couple of days and everything will be as it should," he said. "I hope. . . ." He glanced at the packs of food. "And now, if you would load me up please? If you would put the spare blanket on first, I would find it more comfortable, and I could manage the cooking things as well."

I tried to balance the load as evenly as I could.

"Have you . . . ? Can you . . . ? Do you do this often?"

"Bigger and smaller? Let me think. . . ." I could almost hear the sound of the mental tally sticks flying. "This will be the seventy-ninth time bigger. Three times with you: figurine to mouse-size, then puppy-size and now what you want, pony-size. Smaller? Fifty-three times. I think that's right."

"Try notchin' yer 'ooves," said Growch. He was still behaving in a surly way, just because he'd allowed himself to be panicked, and had let me see it.

"I couldn't do that," said Ky-Lin seriously. "They are living tissue and I mustn't harm anything living, you know that."

"Funny way o' thinkin' . . ."

"Well then, what is your philosophy of life, dog?"

"Filly—what? Oh, you means what life is? Life is livin' the best way you can for the longest time you can manage. Grab what you can while you can, is me motto. An' that includes nosh. Catch me eatin' rice an' leaves when there's rats and rabbits! Anyways, it don' make no difference when you're gone."

What a contrast! One striving for (to me) an impossible state of perfection, the other living only for the day. And I suppose I was somewhere in between. But even I was having rebellious thoughts about what I had been taught. After all I had experienced I couldn't imagine a happy Heaven without my animal friends somewhere around. And think how sterile it would be without trees and flowers, streams and lakes, sun and rain? Hold it, I told myself, crossing myself guiltily. God knows what He's doing. Would the Jesus who considered the beauty of the lilies, who knew where to cast a fisherman's net and admired the whiteness of a dog's teeth expect us to live without natural beauty in our final reward?

Bear made no comment when he saw Ky-Lin's change of size. As I said, he was a very phlegmatic bear.

We set off west by north, using the Waystone and a

fixed point every morning. We used mostly trails, but also the occasional road, though these were few and far between, only existing between villages, which also became scarcer. Money meant little out here in the wilds, so if we came to a village Bear danced for our supper, Ky-Lin keeping well out of sight to save scaring the children.

It was Bear also who was adept at finding shelter for our nights in the open: a cave, an overhang of rock, a deserted hut—we usually stayed warm and dry. Without realizing it, the turning of the year passed us by, and it grew imperceptibly lighter each day.

Careful as I was with our food, our stores diminished rapidly, for the villagers had little to spare and had no use for our money, relying on the barter system. Hens don't lay in winter, and their stores of grain, beans, cheeses, and fruit were all calculated to a nicety for their own needs. Now of course, Ky-Lin was eating as befitted his size and work load, so I sent Bear foraging. He seemed to find a sufficiency for himself, so I hoped for something to supplement our diet. Nine times out of ten I was disappointed because he either hadn't found anything extra, or had eaten it or just plain forgotten, but occasionally he returned with a slice of old honeycomb, a pawful of withered berries or some succulent roots which I baked or boiled.

There was one thing he was excellent at, however, and which helped our diet considerably, but we only found that out by accident.

One morning we came to a small river swollen by melted snows. It wasn't deep, perhaps three or four feet at most, but it was wide, probably a hundred feet across, rushing busily over stones around rocks, forming swirling pools and mini-rapids. I turned downstream to find an easier place to cross; no point in getting the baggage wet.

" 'Ey-oop! Just look at that!" Growch's voice was full of genuine wonder. I turned, just in time to see Bear flipping a fat fish from the shallows and swallowing it whole. "That's the second one. . . ." He was salivating.

I ran back along the bank, just in time to see Bear miss number three. He growled with disappointment and turned away.

"Can you do that again?"

He stared at me, his little eyes bright as sloe berries. "If I want fish."

"Well, want!" I said. "Did it never occur to you that we should like some, too?"

He stared at me. "You not like grubs and beetles I bring. Should ask."

"You eat our gruel and rice: we like fish. I ask now, to try."

He caught two more and I cleaned and grilled them over a small fire for our midday meal. They were delicious. After that, whenever we came across a stretch of water we encouraged him to go fishing. All he caught didn't look edible to me, but he wasn't fussy and ate the rejections as well. A couple of times we even had enough to barter for salted meat or beans, and we ate tolerably well.

The mountains came nearer to the north and west of us, the terrain was rougher and the air colder. Growch and I tired more easily, though Ky-Lin seemed unaffected, and Bear was positively rejuvenated. He bounced ahead of us most days, sniffing, grubbing, rolling in the undergrowth, snatching at leaves like an errant cub, splashing noisily through any water we came across, eating like a pig and snoring like one at night, too.

I reckoned we must have covered near three hundred miles since we left the Golden City when we stood on a wide ridge and looked down on a limitless land of forests, rivers, lakes and crags. Not a village or hamlet to be seen, no sign of human habitation for miles.

Bear sniffed deep, then reared up on his hind legs, to tower over all of us.

"My land," he said. "Start here, go on forever."

I smiled at his enthusiastic certainty. "Then we can leave you here?"

He sank down on his haunches. "Be with me until I find cave to sleep for rest of the cold, and I find you food to take with you. My country; I find fish and honey."

Near though the woodland had seemed, it took us two days to reach the forest proper, and as we came to the more thickly carpeted ground it was a difficult time for poor Ky-Lin, sworn as he was not to tread on anything living. Once under the trees it was easier for him; they were mostly pine and fir, and the dead needles made a nice carpet for his hooves.

Three days later Bear found his cave. Entered through a narrow cleft that widened out into a cozy chamber behind, it had not been occupied for years, judging by the thick drift of leaves that had piled up. The cave was situated at the foot of a bluff; in front the land stretched down to a thick stand of conifers and a stream trickled away to the right. An ideal hibernation place for a winter-weary bear.

He grunted with satisfaction. "Stay here till spring. You need fish. Go get, you light fire. Stay here tonight."

And off he trotted. True to his earlier word he had found us honeycombs and half a sack of nuts. He had obviously spied or smelled some water, so we could stock up with fish as well, God willing.

I dithered over lighting a fire inside the cave or out, but decided on the latter, reckoning that lingering smoke might disturb our night's sleep. There was plenty of wood and I filled the cooking pot from the stream and set it on to boil with salt, herbs, and some wild garlic I found growing nearby. It all depended on what Bear brought back, but if the worst came to the worst I could chuck in some rice and dried meat.

Just as I sat back on my heels, enjoying the warmth of the fire, and Growch had come to lean against me, there came a noise, and simultaneously my ring gave a sharp stab. Growch stiffened, Ky-Lin's antennae shot out in the direction of the forest and I sprang to my feet. It wasn't Bear, it was men's voices I had heard.

There it was again: voices, crackle of twigs, a laugh.

"Quick! Back in the cave, Ky-Lin. Growch, stay with me." There was no point in us all retreating to the cave; the fire was sending up a thin plume of smoke and whoever was out there would soon be coming to investigate. I didn't fancy being trapped in a confined space, but they might miss Ky-Lin if we hid him away. If we were lucky it might just be a couple of hunters, but my ring was still sending out warning signs and the hair had risen on Growch's back.

He growled. "There they are. . . ."

There was a shout, another, and three figures stood at the edge of the pine trees and gazed up the short slope towards us. I ignored them, putting more kindling on the fire and stirring the pot, although my hands were trembling.

"They look bad 'uns to me," muttered Growch. "Rough. Got weapons, too. Better run . . ."

Where to? The bluff was too steep to climb, the cave a trap.

"Just don't get into trouble," I urged. "Low profile . . ."

The strangers moved up the slope towards us, and now I could see them more closely my heart sank. They were ragged, dirty and unshaven with straggling moustaches and their hair tied up in bandannas. As Growch had said, they were armed; a rusty, curved sword, a couple of daggers, a club spiked with nails. They were used to this: as they moved up the slope they spread out, so they were approaching me from three sides, their dark eyes darting from side to side in case of ambush.

They came to a halt some ten yards away and I could smell the rank stench of sweat, excitement and fear. The one in the middle stepped forward. He spoke, but my heart was hammering so hard I couldn't hear him, even if I had been able to understand. Perhaps Ky-Lin was sending a translation from his hiding place in the cave, but I couldn't hear that, either. I could feel my knees knocking together.

"What—what do you want?" I asked in my own tongue, but my voice came out high and very unladlike. They glanced at each other, and the one in the middle muttered out of the corner of his mouth. He addressed me again. This time I heard Ky-Lin's translation.

"They are asking if you are alone."

I nodded my head foolishly, then could have kicked myself. Why, oh why couldn't I have indicated four, five others in the forest?

They grinned, shuffled closer, their hands resting on their weapons. The middle one squatted down in front of the fire, warmed his hands, pointed at the pot and asked a question.

"He asks if there is enough for all, and where is the meat," translated Ky-Lin.

I tried to smile, but my face seemed frozen. I shrugged my shoulders and waved at the pot, then at them. If you want meat, then go get it yourselves. . . . The leader leered at me, plucked a dagger from his belt and made slicing motions in the direction of Growch, who was growling valiantly. The man's meaning was plain: no ready meat, then the dog would do.

I backed away, pushing Growch behind me, still trying to smile as though it was all some huge joke—but I knew it wasn't. I thought even I might not be safe if they were especially hungry; I knew that in certain parts of the world human flesh was considered a delicacy.

"No," I said. "Please no! Let us alone. . . ." and I could hear myself whimpering like a child as I retreated with Growch until my shoulders were hard against the bluff behind me.

The bandits were laughing as they closed in for the kill, but suddenly there was a call from the forest behind, then another and another, as if the forest were suddenly full of strangers. My attackers drew back uncertainly, and at that moment Ky-Lin leapt from the cave, his tail seeming aflame with color. I snatched my knife from my belt and Growch attacked the legs of the man on the right. For a moment I hoped we could scare them away, but then I realized that Ky-Lin couldn't attack any of them: he could only frighten. Growch's teeth were sharp but not killers, and I had never used a knife on anyone in my life.

I saw Ky-Lin dodge a sword thrust and then be clubbed over the head and crumple into a heap and lie still; Growch was still snarling and growling and snapping and had done some bloody damage to one of our attackers; then a boot caught him on the side of the jaw, he shrieked with pain and somersaulted through the air, to land with a sickening crack against one of the rocks. At the same time I was caught from behind, my arm was twisted behind my back and the knife clattered harmlessly from my grasp to the ground. I screamed, but the sound was choked off by the hand at my throat.

I could feel the blood thumping in my ears as the hand squeezed tighter. I couldn't draw breath, felt consciousness slipping away—

So this was what it was like to die, I thought: strange but it doesn't hurt that much, it's just uncomfortable. I was already rushing away down a dark tunnel, a long tube with a tiny light at the other end, when suddenly everything changed.

The pressure went from my throat, my breathing eased, but I could feel cold air on my body. As conscious thought returned I realized they must have been searching me for hidden moneys, but their rough handling had torn my clothes and revealed my true sex. Now their handling of me changed in character; they were eager for something other than my immediate death, they wanted to enjoy my body first.

I struggled now, really struggled, for the threat of rape seemed far more terrible than the certainty of death. I could feel the obscenity of their hands on my private parts, their hot breath on my face, something hard and thrusting against my thigh, and the more I fought them,

the more they liked it. Despairingly I clenched my free
hand, the right, and aimed for one of the faces above
me. I missed, but felt another stab from my ring, my
magic ring.

"Help me," I breathed, "please help me. . . ."

The hands still probed, my back was naked to the
sharp stones on the ground, a mouth reached for mine,
excited voices were laughing and urging each other on,
then the whole world seemed to erupt in a world-shaking
sound: an ear-splitting roar like a volcano.

Suddenly I was free. My attackers no longer threatened. The air was cold on my bruised flesh as I staggered
to my feet, striving to cover my nakedness with the torn
remnants of my clothes.

That dreadful roar came again, loud enough to make
me cover my ears. I looked down towards the forest and
there, coming up the slope towards us, was Bear!

But it was a Bear I had never seen before. . . .

CHAPTER SIXTEEN

Even I was frightened.

Bear stood on his hind legs, his great arms spread wide, the five oval pads set in a row on his front paws each sprouting a wickedly curved claw. The mane on his shoulders stood up like an extra fur cape, but the greatest change was in his head. Usually the fur framed his face rather like the feathers on an owl, his round ears pricked forward: now his ears were slicked back to his head, the ruff of fur was gone and instead there was a pointed snout with lips curled back in a snarl over a double row of pointed teeth. Saliva dripped down onto his chest and the little eyes were red with anger.

He roared again, and the sound seemed to reverberate from the rocks of the bluff behind me, then he dropped to all fours and bounded up the slope towards us.

Suddenly I was alone. The bandits were running helter-skelter towards the trees, their weapons scattered, the air full of their cries of terror. As one passed too close to the bear I saw a paw flash out and ribbons of cloth and skin flew from the gashed shoulder of one of my attackers. He shrieked and clasped his arm, blood dripping through his fingers, but he didn't stop running, though he stumbled now and again in his flight.

Bear reached me and reared up, his snakelike head twisting down till he nearly touched me. He sniffed, and almost too late I remembered how shortsighted he was.

"It's me, Bear. . . ."

He sniffed again. "So it is. Smell of them. Heard you call. All right? The others, then," and he whipped round and shambled off towards the forest, where the crashing sounds of the escaping bandits were growing fainter.

I pulled my clothes together as best I could, though needle and thread were urgently needed, found the pouch that had been ripped from my neck lying close by, then hurried over to where Growch lay, moaning a little. He wagged his tail however as I lifed his head to my lap.

"You all right?" As I spoke I was feeling him all over for breaks or wounds, but although he winced now and again there didn't seem to be anything broken, until—

"Ouch! Them's me ribs!"

"Do they hurt?"

"Reckon I cracked a couple." He struggled to his feet, shook himself, groaned, and spat out a couple of teeth, luckily not essential ones. "You all right? What about 'im?" He nodded towards the motionless figure of Ky-Lin.

He lay where he had fallen, utterly still. My heart kicked against my breastbone. No, not dear Ky-Lin! Not after all he had done for us. He had existed for so many hundreds of years, he couldn't suddenly end like this. I bent over him, the tears dripping off the end of my nose.

"You're wetting my fur," came a muffled voice.

"Ky-Lin! You're alive!"

"Of course I'm alive! Take more than a knock on the head to finish me off!" and a moment or two later he was up on his hooves again, shaking out his crumpled tail and straightening his twisted antennae.

"You all right? I heard your ring call the bear, and I presume he has chased them off. Oh dear . . ." and he sat down suddenly on his haunches, looking puzzled.

"What's the matter?" I asked anxiously, for his colors had also faded.

"Long years; lots of changes; body material not what

it was ... Would you be kind enough to examine the dent in my head? It feels quite deep."

It was, a cleft running from where his left eyebrow would have been to the opening of his right ear. The skin, or hide, didn't appear to be broken, but I wasn't happy about the bone beneath. Recalling the healing properties of the ring I drew it slowly and gently along the indentation.

"That's better; a Unicorn has great healing powers. Dog would benefit too, I believe."

And so he did. I found some Self-Heal growing nearby, mashed it into a paste, bound up Growch's ribs and Ky-Lin's head, and they both declared themselves much recovered, though Growch said the healing process would be accelerated by a spot of something to eat. . . .

I remade the fire, got the pot boiling again, and threw in rice and some rather dessicated vegetables in deference to Ky-Lin's tastes, Growch getting a strip of dried meat to chew.

Where was Bear? There was neither sight nor sound of him, and the sky was darkening into twilight.

"He'll be all right," said Ky-Lin. "Why not get out your needle and thread while you wait? Your clothes are falling to pieces!"

By the flicker of the flames I was able to cobble together my jerkin, rebind my breasts and renew the laces in my trews; my shirt was in ribbons, and I used it for binding up the animals, but I had one more in my pack. First, however, I scrubbed myself with cold water, determined to rid myself of any lingering taint from my attackers.

It was now full dark, and the dancing flames threw our shadows on the rocks behind, making them prance like demons. A larger shadow overtopped us all: Bear was back.

I hadn't heard him approach, but suddenly there he was, fur smooth once more, his face round and innocent, in his jaws a couple of trout.

He dropped them at my feet. "Took long time to catch."

I looked at him. He seemed as unconcerned as if he had been out for a stroll. Skewering the trout I laid them across the fire to broil.

"Have you eaten?"

"Trout. Roots. Full."

I turned the trout. "What happened?" I was dying to know how far he had chased them, but knew I would have to be patient.

"Long walk to lake. Take time to catch."

"No, not that! The men—the bad ones. Did they all go away?"

He looked puzzled, licked his paw.

"I called you: you chased them. . . ."

"Oh, them. Yes."

"They won't come back?"

"Not ever. Gone."

I breathed more easily. He seemed very sure.

"All dead. Lives for life. You help me, I help you. Will have some honey. . . ."

I carved him off a chunk, although I thought he had said he was full.

"But how . . . ?" I didn't know how to put it, was afraid of the answer.

"Men?" He thought for a moment. "In ravine. Long way down to rocks. All still." He turned to the pot. "Smells good. Small portion . . ."

And that was all I, or anyone else for that matter, ever got out of him, for the following morning he was so deep in his hibernating sleep that we couldn't rouse him even to say good-bye.

His deep, rumbling snores kept me awake that night— that and the various aches and bruises I nursed. I kept thinking about the complexity of the creature, if one could call one so simple complicated. The problem lay in me, I finally decided; I just couldn't comprehend a mind that thought in such straight lines. All that concerned him was food, sleep, and play. Like all simple souls he could only hold one thought at a time: once fixed, though, the idea was carried out ruthlessly, whether it was to catch a fish, scoop out grubs from a dead log, sniff out a honeycomb, chase a butterfly—or kill a man. And someone as simple as that would have no conscience, wouldn't know what one meant.

When we stepped out of the cave the following morning, we realized that Bear had the best of it, snoring away the winter in his drift of leaves, because the weather had changed for the worse. A nasty, nippy wind churned the ashes of last night's fire, whipping the tall grass into a frenzy and driving the tops of the distant pines into uneasy circles. The sky was gray, flat and oppressive, and looked as though it might hold snow.

We packed up quickly, then had to decide in which direction to go. I pulled out Suleiman's map and unscrolled it on a rock. Ky-Lin bent over it, doing his disconcerting bit of shaking his head from side to side with his eyes crossed.

"We are too far west," he said finally. "If we could all fly over the mountains for a thousand miles, it would be easy. But not even a dragon would go that way in this weather." His sensitive antennae traced a line to the northeast. "We need to turn east and find the Silk River, then follow it north to the headwaters. Then when the weather is better we find the Desert of Death, cross that, and we are within a few miles—say, a hundred— of our destination."

"Yes," I said. It sounded simple, and also rather daunting. I didn't like the sound of that desert, and a thousand miles in a straight line meant many more afoot.

Ky-Lin glanced at me. "Don't be disheartened; think how far we've come already! The next few days, till we reach the river, will be tough; but once we get there, there will be plenty of villages."

He was right: it was tough. It took over a week of hard slog to reach any sort of civilization, and by that

time we had run out of provisions and were footsore and
cold and weary to the bone. The snow held off, but the
winds were fierce and biting, shelter hard to find and
our faces burned from several sharp showers of sleet. It
might be February, but the winter's hold was tightening
rather than otherwise. Once we came to the river it
was easier.

Apparently it connected farther south with another,
larger, which in its turn coincided with the caravan
routes, so the boatmen were used enough to taking paying passengers up to the headwaters, especially with the
rivers being so low at this time of year.

The town at the head of the river was one that concerned itself with the weaving of plain silks, ready for
transport in great flat barges to the caravan routes. During the winter months the river was too low for large-
scale transport, so the townspeople used this time to spin
the silks, dye some of the hanks and bale eveything up
for the first barges to come through once the melting
snows made the river navigable. We made our way to
this town by leisurely stages from village to village, with
a lift here, a boat trip there. Everywhere there were
mulberry trees, the harsh winter making the icicles that
hung from their branches tinkle like wind chimes.

The headwaters of the river were a disappointment.
No waters gushing from a spring, rather a seeping from
a huge bog that stretched for miles to the north. This
was a smelly place, and I was not surprised to learn
that it had been the custom, years back, to execute their
criminals by tying them up with a hood over their faces
and chucking them into the marsh. But the bog got its
own back. Eventually the bodies were spewed forth again
in the spring rains, to float away down the river, provid-
ing their own curiosity, for their long immersion in the
bog had preserved their bodies like tanned leather. I saw
one once; the clothes were stiff and shrunken, but the
whole effect was rather that of an amateur wood carving.
This practice of execution had been discontinued some

fifty years back, but the odd corpse resurfaced now and again.

The town itself was a prosperous one with everyone, from children to grandparents, all engaged in work connected with the silk trade. At one end were the weaving sheds, at another the huge barns where the silkworms were reared, in artificial heat if necessary. In between were the huge vats for the dyes, the boiling rooms, and the sheds of drying racks. Nearer the docks were the baling sheds.

We rented one of the ubiquitous summer workers' houses; it was like a thatched clay beehive, one large room with shelves built into the walls for food and utensils, a sleeping platform, a central brazier and smoke hole, and niches in the walls for lamps. The floor was covered with rush matting and there were a couple of functional stools and a low table. Clothes were hung from a pole above the sleeping platform. No windows, and the door was like a heavy sheep hurdle, to be placed as one desired.

Once we reached civilization again Ky-Lin had decided to revert to a smaller size to avoid embarrassing questions, and now he travelled once more on my shoulder, ready to interpret if necessary. Coin was acceptable once more so there was no problem with food, nor with the warmer padded clothing I bought, the kind the locals wore. My hair had grown quite long, too, as it hadn't been trimmed since we were in the Golden City, and I adopted the local custom, used by men and women alike, of plaiting it into a pigtail.

For six weeks the weather pressed in on us; rain, sleet, snow, gales, frost and ice. The little house however was warm and dry, raised as they all were from the streets to prevent flooding, and there was plenty to keep me busy. Mending and repairing, bringing my journal up to date, going to the market, cooking and cleaning, buying off-cuts of silk for underwear—luxury!—and yet I yearned for action. To be so near and yet still so far from my objective kept me in a permanent fret for the better weather.

Growch, however, was in his element.

Fortunately for him, unfortunately for me, he had at last found his "fluffy bums." The town was full of them. It seemed that every family had one as a pet, and at the rate Growch was carrying on, there would soon be the same amount of half-breeds.

After the first complaint from an irate owner Ky-Lin and I put our heads together and decided Growch was one of the rarest dogs in the world: "He-whose-stomach-is-of-two-dogs-and-whose-legs-are-the-shortest-in-the-world." With a title like that, who could resist seeing what the puppies would be like? The bitches were soon literally queuing up and Growch was totally exhausted.

He came in one day, even filthier than usual, his fur matted and muddy, his stomach dragging on the ground, his tail and ears at half-mast, his eyes—what you could see of them—half-closed and his tongue hanging out like a forgotten piece of washing.

"Serves you right," I said unsympathetically. "It's what you wanted, isn't it? The reason you came all this way with me?" I jabbed my needle into the sandal I was finishing off, trying hard not to laugh. "Unlimited sex, that's what you wanted, isn't it? Well now you've got it, so don't complain!"

" 'Oose complainin'? I ain't. It's just—just I think I've gorra cold or somefin'. . . ."

"Dogs don't catch colds."

"Well, a chill, then. Think I'll stay in fer a coupla days. Have a rest."

"All right," I said placatingly. "I'll give you a dose of herbs, and if you have a fever we'll have to cut down on meat. Slops and gruel for you, my boy," and I bent over my sewing again and coughed to hide my giggles.

The transition from winter to spring, when it finally came, seemed to take place over a couple of days only.

One moment a grim wind blew from the north and the ground was hard with frost, the next the sun shone, the ice melted and caged canaries were singing outside every door. It seemed thousands of little streams from the bog emptied into the river, which awoke from its sluggish sleep and ran merrily between its banks once more. Bales of silk were loaded onto flat-bottomed boats and set off southward, but the first trading boats didn't come upriver until the end of April, struggling against the swollen waters.

The whole town turned out to welcome the first string of barges, bearing long-needed supplies and the first of the seasonal workers, many of whom had relatives in the town. Ky-Lin and I had decided to start our journey north again within the week, so it was with holiday mood on me that I joined the rest of the town to watch the boats come in. I noted with satisfaction that the cargoes included dried fruits, grain, strips of meat and fish and cheeses, all goods that had been in short supply for the last month and that we would need for our journey.

Goods hauled ashore, passengers politely clapped and welcomed, bales of silk waiting to be loaded, we turned for our lodgings, content that the world had started awake again. In a few days we should be on our way.

"Got you!"

A hooded stranger, one of the passengers, had stepped from behind one of the warehouses and grabbed me by the wrist, so tightly I fancied I could hear the crunch of bone.

"Let me go! You're hurting me!" With my free hand I attempted to strike out at him, but he dodged the blow, holding me even tighter.

Growch growled warningly, and the stranger kicked out at him.

"You want to keep that cur of yours under control, Summer," came the voice again, but this time I recognized it, and my heart sank.

Dickon had found us again.

CHAPTER SEVENTEEN

His explanation of what had happened to him since he ran away when I was arrested was very plausible; I think that after all the rehearsal it must have gone through he even believed it himself.

After I had fed him—and I admit he needed food; he looked half-starved—and had gone out for a jar of heady rice wine to loosen his tongue, he settled down on a stool by the brazier, a second mug of wine in his hand.

"I just didn't know what way to turn," he confessed. "I went chasing the bear, but he escaped me—where did he go, by the way? Never saw him again. Good riddance, I say. If it hadn't been for him murdering his master you would never have been arrested in the first place."

As I remember it, he had been running in a different direction from the animal; as for the reason for my arrest, how could I blame Bear? I had never had my feet scorched to make me dance. I didn't think it necessary to explain we had returned him to his own land.

"I couldn't find your dog, either, but I see you got him back. I saw that heathen boy and his friends carrying off your baggage, but there were too many for me to tackle. Once a thief always a thief, I say; I never trusted him."

He took another swig of the wine.

"After that I went back to the palace and demanded an interview, late though it was." Unlikely even a minor palace official would have bothered to get out of bed; besides, they were looking for him, too. "I begged, I pleaded to be allowed to see you; I even offered a bribe"—as far as I knew he had no money at all—"but they said I would have to wait until morning.

"I walked the streets all night, my mind in turmoil, turning over in my mind the options open to us. I had little money, no influence, and my command of the language was not as good as it should be. I thought of you, all alone and helpless in some underground dungeon—" he leant forward and patted my knee "—and I wept to think of your suffering."

I'll bet: he probably spent the night in a brothel. But now he was getting into his stride, aided by the wine.

"I went back to the palace at crack of dawn, to find everything in complete turmoil! I found that you had disappeared into thin air—'flown up into the clouds' was the way they put it—but of course I knew that was rubbish, even with your magic bits and pieces and talking animals, so I reckoned that you'd had some kind of help. I thought, too, that they might recognize me as having been with you, so I decided to lie low for a while till things settled down; found a nice young lady who let me stay rent free for a while. . . ." His face grew dreamy, and he finished the mug of wine. "That's why I didn't immediately come looking for you. How did you escape, by the way? Bribe the guards? Pick the lock?"

"As a matter of fact," I said stiffly, "that 'little thief' as you called him, and his friends, pulled the bars from my cell and saw me safe on the road, together with my baggage, money, and extra provisions. He called it an exchange for the slavery I rescued him from."

"Oh . . . well, you never can tell, I suppose. Any more of that wine?"

"It's quite strong," I said, refilling his mug for the third time.

"I've got a strong enough head to take piss water like this. . . . Now, where was I?"

"Hiding," I said.

"Not for long, my dear, not for long! I found it very difficult to pick up your trail, though; no one had seen you go, though I realized you must have used one of the gates. After having questioned everyone I knew, and some I didn't, I remembered those maps of yours. You know the ones: 'Here be Dragons'?" I wondered whether he realized he had given himself away by confirming he had seen them. "I recalled the direction was north, but where? Here I was lucky." He tapped his nose. "I came across a mapmaker and—for a consideration—was allowed to take a peek and managed to copy a couple. Here!" He reached into his tattered clothes and brought out a couple of pieces of rice paper, the folds marked with the sweat from his body.

Gingerly I unfolded the scraps, still warm from his body. The first one was very like the ones I had copied at Matthew's house although with more detail: a couple more rivers and towns, more routes. The other was far more precise and Ky-Lin, viewing them from his hiding place on my shoulder, gave a little hiss when he saw it. I looked more closely. The Silk River was marked quite clearly, although in the unintelligible (to me) picture scribble they used. Here was our town, mountains to the north and west, and what looked like a plateau to the northwest.

Dickon was now nodding, his eyes closed, his body swaying on the stool.

"Keep that one," whispered Ky-Lin. "That is one we could use. If he won't part with it, we'll copy it while he sleeps."

But even as I prepared to tuck it away in my jerkin the mug fell from his lax fingers, his eyes snapped open and he reached and took the map from my hand.

"Oh, no you don't! I'm not having you running off on your own again. I have the maps, and we go for the treasure together!"

"There isn't any treasure! There never was!"

"Rubbish! What kept you going all this long time? We've been all through this before, and I know you're lying."

There was no point in arguing.

"If you really believe that, then go and look for it on your own. As for me, I am on a private pilgrimage to find a friend and there is no, repeat no, money at the end of it." I rose to my feet. "There is a spare blanket over there but you'll have to sleep on the floor. If you wish to relieve yourself there is a communal latrine at the end of the street."

Later I peered down from the sleeping platform; he was muffled up in the blanket on one of the grass mats, snoring gently. Slipping to the floor I made up the brazier and brewed myself a mug of camomile tea, an excuse in case he woke, though I usually had one before I went to bed anyway.

"What's so special about the map?" I whispered to Ky-Lin.

He sipped at the tea. "Nice ... The map shows that we are on the right track. It also indicates the way we must take once we cross the Desert of Death."

I shivered. "We must go that way?"

He nodded. "If you can study that map you will see it is the most direct route. The only other way lies through the mountains, which are notorious bandit country."

I had had enough of bandits.

"Then we had better pinch the map and copy it. Is he fast enough asleep, do you think?"

"I shall make sure. . . ." He trotted across the floor. I saw him touch Dickon's face with one of his hooves, there was a tiny puff of what looked like pinkish smoke, and he trotted back, nodding his head. "You can take it now; I gave him a little Sleepy Dust."

Together we studied the map. He pointed to where the town was marked: "We are here." With his delicate antennae he traced a way around the bog, shook his head and marked a path across the middle. "Quicker; as I remember there are markers."

I didn't ask how long it was since he had been this way. "What if they are no longer there?"

"We'll check first. After the bog the trail winds along that valley bottom to the desert. The Desert of Death," he repeated.

"Is it—is it that bad?"

He hesitated. "I have only been there once, and I was with my master and the others of my kind. Then it was not too bad, but you must realize that my brethren can manage on little water and food if necessary, and my Lord had reached such an exalted plane of consciousness that he could, I believe, have existed on air alone." He was perfectly serious. "Besides which, there was a town and temple halfway across."

"Isn't it very hot?"

"Yes, during the day. At night it can be equally cold. The terrain is difficult too. It is a bare, arid place, littered with small stones and rocks. It is necessary to carry all one's food and water; it is not called the Desert of Death for nothing. However if we take care and prepare ourselves properly it shouldn't be too difficult. I am sure I can find the temple again, and there we can stay for a while and stock up with fresh provisions; it is on the only oasis we shall come across."

He paused and his antennae flicked across the map.

"Once across the mountains we are in the foothills of the final range of mountains. Over them, just there, marked by a circle, is a Buddhist monastery. It looks over a deep valley, and in the center of that valley there is a conical hill—they say it could be the core of a long-extinct volcano—and because of the way the light falls and its distance, they call it the Blue Mountain. In the margin of the map is written: 'This is believed to be the home of Dragons.' This, by the way, and whatever your friend says, is an original map, not a copy."

"Then he must have stolen it. . . ." But I was not really

concerned with that; all I could do was concentrate on that little hill on the map. It looked so near, but also, if the truth were told, so insignificant a thing to hold all my dreams.

"I saw it once in the distance," said Ky-Lin, "and it did look blue, but I did not know then that it was rumored a dragon lair. Come, you should make a copy before he wakes."

My hands were shaking so much both with anticipation and the discovery that my mountain did exist, that it took me longer than I had anticipated to complete the copy, but we managed to get the original back in Dickon's clothing without him waking.

"Ky-Lin," I whispered. "How soon can we go?"

He considered. "The weather is set fair, new provisions have come into the town, we have the confirmation of the map . . . two days, perhaps."

"Why not tomorrow?" I couldn't wait to leave.

"Provisions to buy and pack for a start; you need to make a proper list. Then we shall need a half-dozen water skins, more blankets, a length of rope and you could do with a new pair of strong boots. In order to carry all the baggage, I shall have to grow again, and you will have to alert your friend to my existence."

I glanced over at Dickon. "But he's not coming!"

"You don't want him to accompany us?"

"Certainly not! We've managed fine without him so far."

"He could be useful carrying the baggage. . . ."

"I—I just don't want him along, that's all." I couldn't explain it. It wasn't the sort of thing you could put into words. I could quote his cowardice, his obsession with the thought of treasure, his searching of my belongings, the way he literally seemed to haunt my every move, but it wasn't just that; it was something deeper and more frightening. Inside of me there was an unspoken dread of him: not what he was but what he might become. He posed a threat to my future happiness, of that I was sure, but how or why I had no idea. It was like waking to a day of brilliant sunshine and being convinced that it would rain before nightfall, but far more sinister than that. All I was sure of was that I couldn't explain it.

"Very well; if you can manage the purchasing tomorrow, and the packing, then we'll make it the day after. I'll tell you again what we need in the morning."

"Can you give him some more Sleepy Dust?"

Ky-Lin hesitated. "It is not good for humans to give them too much. Ideally there should be a twelve-month between each dose. But he did not take much tonight; perhaps a small dose will do no harm."

From the moment he awoke in the morning Dickon did his unintentional best to hamper all my attempts to organize our departure; he was a positive pain, following me round the town as I made my purchases.

"Why are you buying that? We've got a couple already. What do we need those for? When are we setting out? Where are you supposed to be going on your pilgrimage? How are we getting there? I hope you don't think I'm going to carry that. Are we going to hire some sort of transport? How much money have you left? Are we going to do another performance?" Etc., etc., etc., till I could have screamed.

But I knew I had to behave in a calm and rational manner, as if the last thought on my mind was to escape from him that very night, so I made up answers to those questions I couldn't answer truthfully, telling a heap of lies with a smile on my face and my fingers mentally crossed. Fifteen Hail Marys later . . .

By late afternoon I think I had persuaded him we would not be leaving for a few days' time, and I tried to make my frantic packing that evening look like routine tidying up. He eyed the sacks, packs and panniers with distrust.

"We'll never carry all that!"

"It's not more than we can manage; you carry your share, I'll carry mine."

"I shall just look like a donkey. . . ."

"No more than usual," I said briskly. "Now, what would you like for supper?"

We dined well, as Growch and I would be snacking until we had crossed the bog, and we didn't know how long that would take, so it was chicken soup with chopped hard-boiled eggs, fried pastry rolls filled with bean shoots and herbs, and chopped chicken livers in a bean and lentil pudding. I had camomile tea, Dickon had rice wine. I thought to allay further suspicion by begging for a further look at his maps, knowing what his reponse would be.

"Oh, no you don't! I'm not having you learn them by heart and then steal a march on me! Once we're on the road together you can take another look."

I yawned. "Have it your own way. There's no hurry. I'm for bed. The clearing-up can wait till the morning. Blow out the lamp before you go to bed, please. . . ."

I watched Ky-Lin scuttle out of the door to effect his "change," and lay down, convinced that I wouldn't sleep a wink, but my eyes kept closing in spite of it: must have been that heavy meal. Still, Ky-Lin would wake me as soon as he returned. . . .

I woke to broad daylight, Growch still snoring at my side and Dickon returning with a pitcher of water for washing.

"Wake up, sleepyheads!" he called out cheerily.

What in the world . . . Where was Ky-Lin?

The answer came from beneath my blanket. "I spend all evening changing to a suitable size, then find when I return that your ridiculous friend has so jammed the door tight shut that I can't gain entrance! So, I have to spend more time changing to be small enough to get back in again!" He wasn't at all happy.

"Sorry," I whispered. "We'll manage it better tonight, I promise."

But the matter was taken out of my hands by Dickon himself. That evening I left a stew of vegetables simmering on the brazier, and suggested we take a walk. I was hoping this would give Ky-Lin the chance for his change, since we had discovered that the house next door was empty, and he could hide in there while I ate less and didn't fall asleep before Dickon, so I could ensure the door was left open.

Dickon, however, had other ideas. We were wandering through the bazaar examining the goods without any intention of buying, when I straightened up in front of a stall selling slippers and found he had disappeared.

Not into thin air and not forever. On the other side of the road was a lighted doorway, screened by a beaded curtain still gently swaying as though someone had just entered. I crossed over and peeped inside. A waft of perfume, smoke from incense sticks, rustle of silks, a mutter of feminine voices. It was obvious what sort of place it was. I knew Dickon had no money, so wandered slowly off towards our lodgings, fairly sure he would seek me out. I was right; I had only gone a hundred yards when he caught me up.

"I say, Summer: got a bit of change on you?"

"No. It's suppertime. Come on, before it spoils."

"It's just that—that I saw there was to be an entertainment tonight and I thought I might take a look. . . . There's an entrance fee, of course, and I'd need a few coins for drinks. Come on, Summer! Life's short enough without missing out on all the fun! You're a real sobersides, you know: getting just like an old maid!"

Old maid, indeed! I should like to see anyone of that ilk who had travelled as far as I had, faced as many dangers, had two proposals of marriage and a dragon-lover! But I mustn't lose my temper.

I thought quickly. If he went to a brothel—place of entertainment as he preferred me to think of it—then he would roll home hungry at midnight and keep us all awake. On the other hand, if I could drag out supper till around nine, then give him extra moneys, he might well stay out all night, which would be perfect for our plans.

"Supper first," I said. "Then I'll see if I have a few coins to spare. Er . . . do you think it's the sort of entertainment I should enjoy?"

"Certainly not!" he said, and added hurriedly: "You might attract unwelcome attentions. It would be a shame if I had to escort you back just when it started to get interesting. . . ."

I made sure he had extra helpings of the meal, much to Growch's disgust, watched him finish off the rice wine and gave him more than enough coin to buy his choice for the night.

"Don't wake us when you return. . . ."

I waited until he had turned the corner, then went to the empty house next door to see how Ky-Lin was managing. Very well, he informed me, but was there a bowl of rice to spare? It helped the changeover.

I was too nervous to go to bed; I reckoned if Dickon was going to roll home before dawn it would be around two o'clock. At three he still hadn't arrived, so I went for Ky-Lin.

"Any reason why we can't leave right now?"

"We should wait for a little more light, but I expect we can manage. Light a lantern, and load me up."

Less than ten minutes later we were creeping through the deserted streets and, following Ky-Lin's lead, found ourselves in the poorer section of town. I kept the lantern as well shaded as I could, but in this part of town the streets were ill-kept, and we stumbled over rubbish and filth, so we needed the lantern on full beam. Ky-Lin was uneasy that someone would see us, but to me the streets were as quiet as the grave.

The ground beneath our feet became soft and spongy as we left the last straggle behind, and I was glad that my new boots had been thoroughly oiled.

"How much further?" We were splashing through

pools of water now, and in the east the first graying of the sky announced the false dawn.

"Nearly at the causeway," said Ky-Lin, a large shadow ahead of me. "From there, about a mile to the first of the markers."

"Can't come too soon for me," grumbled Growch. "Me stummick is wet as a duck's arse and me paws full of gunge. When do we eat?"

Some time later we stood on a relatively dry pebbled causeway. Ahead of us lay a flat, steamy expanse of what looked like a vast, waterlogged plain, tinged pink by the just-rising sun. Tufts of grasses, the odd bush, a stunted tree or two, a couple of hummocks were all that interrupted the horizon, fringed in the distance by the ever-present and distant mountains.

Ky-Lin was concentrating: eyes crossed, head weaving from side to side.

"Well, this is it. I can see the first marker. Shall we go?"

CHAPTER EIGHTEEN

I was soaked to the skin. No, I hadn't fallen in the water, nor had it been raining; it was just the all-pervading miasma of damp that rose from the bog that drenched us all as thoroughly as if we had jumped in. Ky-Lin's coat shone with droplets of moisture, like a spider's web heavy with dew, and poor Growch's hair was plastered down to his body as if had been soaked in oil. I was not only wet, I was cold. Although there was a sun of sorts, it had to fight its way through the steamy mists it sucked up from the stagnant pools all around us.

The ground beneath our feet was solid enough, thanks to Ky-Lin's instinct; how he did it I couldn't even guess, for I had seen nothing to guide us. Around us the bog bubbled, seethed, slurped, belched and burped, an ever-present reminder of the dangers we faced if we stepped off the invisible path we followed.

No animals, no birds. Plenty of insects, though; whining mosquitoes, huge flies, buzzing gnats, all of whom welcomed the chance to land on my face and hands, and Growch's nose, eyes and bum. Ky-Lin they left alone, as if he were composed of other than flesh and blood.

We seemed to have been walking all day but the sun was at less than its zenith when Ky-Lin called a halt. There was a small, knee-high cairn to our left, and we shed our loads, sat down and I unpacked some cheese and dried fruit. Growch had a knuckle of ham which he chewed on disconsolately, deliberately dropping it into the muck every now and again to emphasize how hardly used he was.

Ky-Lin insisted we continue our journey as soon as we had eaten.

"To the next marker, and then perhaps another rest," he explained.

I sighed as I packed up again. "I haven't *seen* a marker yet! How do you know where they are?"

"You're sitting on one," he said. "Or were. The last one we passed was that pile of peeled sticks, and the first was that moss-covered rock."

"And the next?"

"The skeleton of a bird with one wing missing."

"But how can you see from all that way off?"

"Because my antennae give me enhanced sensibilities—like extra eyes, noses and ears; two are arranged so they see further ahead; two tell me what goes on at the side; two what happens behind."

I was busy counting. "You've got four pairs. . . ."

"The last ones are for seeing beneath the ground for a few inches, so I don't damage anything growing out of sight; a germinating seed, a worm, an incubating chrysalis: my master thought of everything."

"Then you could see where a squirrel hoarded its nuts?"

"Or a dog a bone," said Groweh, interested in spite of himself in what he had considered up to now to be a very boring conversation. "Or a burrow of nice, fat little rabbits?"

"If I could, I shouldn't tell you," said Ky-Lin. "The eating of flesh—"

"All right, you two," I said soothingly. There could never be true accord between one who believed all killing was wrong, and another whose greatest pleasure was eating red meat.

We had walked perhaps a half hour more when we came to a division of the ways. To our left the track had obviously been repaired, and was neatly outlined with stones; the track we had been following continued ahead, but was now rutted and pocked, with pools of standing water as far as one could see. Ky-Lin was plodding along the old path, head down, so I stepped onto the new one and called him back.

"Hey! You're going the wrong way!"

He turned his head. "No. I'm not. That way may look to be the right road but it is a deception. Especially constructed to trap the unwary. Go down that road and you step straight into a quagmire which will suck you down into an underground river that would carry you to a subterranean tomb."

But I was tired of him always being right, tired of the seemingly endless bog, tired of playing follow-my-leader! "I don't believe you! The road you are taking is the one that looks like it ends in disaster; why, even now you are nearly hock-deep in water!"

He splashed back to my side. "Very well, have it your own way. We will take this road. But I warn you, you are wasting our time."

I felt exuberant, glad that I had shown an obviously tiring creature the correct route, and for a while, as the ground beneath us remained firm and dry, my spirits rose still further, especially as it seemed a more direct route to the mountains ahead, and although my ring had started to itch intolerably, I ignored it, telling myself it was just another mosquito bite.

I turned to Ky-Lin who was some ten yards behind. "I told you this was the right— Ow!" Walking backwards, my feet suddenly found the path had disappeared and, scrabbling at the air for balance, I toppled back into the slimy, sucking mess, dragged down still further by the weight of my pack.

A moment later I felt Ky-Lin's teeth in my jerkin and I was dragged back onto the path, a sticky mess smelling like a midden.

I looked back: the open maw I had so nearly been

sucked down into was closing up again, and in less than a minute the path gave the illusion of being as it was before.

"Better get cleaned up," said Ky-Lin. "There's a small spring a little way back. . . . You're not crying, are you? Anyone can make a mistake."

"But you *knew* I was wrong: why didn't you shout at me?"

"Ky-Lins don't shout."

"Well they should!" I sniffed and wiped my eyes with my filthy hand. "We're friends aren't we? Well then: don't be sweet and gentle and kind and forgiving all the time. Next time I do or say or suggest something stupid or silly, say so! Loudly . . ."

"You shouts at me—" grumbled Growch.

"If I shout at you, then you deserve it!"

"Not always! I remember—"

"All right, you two," said Ky-Lin, in such a perfect mimicry of my earlier attempts to soothe him and Growch, that I couldn't help laughing.

"Sorry, Ky-Lin! And thanks for pulling me out. From now on you lead the way." And next time I would heed the ring, I promised myself.

After that interruption it was a real slog to reach the spot Ky-Lin had decided would be our night stop. Several times, when we reached a comparatively dry spot, I begged him to stop, but he was adamant.

"There we will be safe. The ground is dry, but more important is our safety."

"But there's nothing to threaten us—except mosquitoes," I added, slapping at my face and neck. "You're not going to tell me there are monsters down there!"

"I do not know precisely what is down there. But I do know that the place I seek will keep us safe from whatever could threaten."

So we trudged on. The sun sank below the horizon, the mist thickened and it grew more chill. All at once the air above us was darkened by clouds of great bats, obviously seeking the insects who had so plagued us during the day. They weaved and ducked and swerved only inches above my head, and I found myself wrapping my hands about my head, uneasy at their proximity.

"They will neither touch you nor bite you," said Ky-Lin peaceably. "Those are not the bloodsuckers."

Then as quickly as they had come, they were gone.

Everything was quiet; now the whine of insects was gone there was nothing to break the silence except the sound of our steps and an occasional suck or blow from the bog itself. It was eerie.

"You'd better light the lantern," said Ky-Lin, his voice loud in the gloom. "It's getting dark, and we still have a couple of miles to go."

Easier said than done. The air was damp, so was I, and when I opened my tinderbox I couldn't raise a spark. More and more frantic, my fingers now bruised, my breath dampening the dried moss, I was ready to cry with frustration.

"Here," said Ky-Lin. "Let me try." He breathed over the box, and miraculously everything was suddenly dry, and my lantern lighted us over the last stretch.

When we reached the marker it was not in the least what I had expected, although it was a place that was recognizable. There was the skeleton of a bird, hanging upside down on a roughly fashioned wooden cross, and the whole area, a paved rough circle some eight feet across, was surrounded by a raised rim of stones a couple of inches high. Within the circle were a couple of stunted shrubs, one with sharp, prickly leaves like holly, the other bearing hairy leaves with a sharp, bitter smell. In the middle was a symbol picked out in white stones, but I couldn't make out exactly what it was meant to represent.

"Right," said Ky-Lin. "We can have a fire now, dry ourselves out. The dry kindling and charcoal are in the left-hand pannier."

In a few minutes the fire shut out the dark, creating a cozy circle like a room. I reheated some rice left over from the day before, adding herbs, and also ate some cheese and a couple of sweet cakes. The food, though dull, put new heart into me. I was warm for the first time that day, and we were drying out nicely. Even Growch had stopped grumbling.

"How much further?" I asked Ky-Lin.

"If we make good progress tomorrow, then we should be across by nightfall."

"Can't be soon enough," said Growch. "Never bin so cold or wet in me life, I ain't. 'Cept for now," he added, stretching his speckled stomach to the glow of the fire.

"Throw on the last of the charcoal," said Ky-Lin. "And sleep. If you wake, or think you do, pay no attention to what you see, or think you see."

"Why?" How could you see something that wasn't there?

"This is a Place of Power," he said. "And as such attracts both good and evil. But we are safe as long as we stay within the circle." Searching the ground he found a couple of discarded leaves from the bushes and threw them on the fire, where they blazed brightly for a moment then smoldered, giving off an unpleasant smell. "Lie down, close your eyes. . . ."

I scarcely had time to wrap myself in my blanket before I was asleep and slipping from one fragment of dream to another. I played in the dirt in front of my mother's house, drawing pictures on the ground with a stick; I struggled through a storm to reach shelter; once, for a startling moment I saw the father who was dead before I was born: I knew the tall smiling stranger was my father because I could see him from where I lay in my mother's womb. He had stretched out his hand to rest it on her belly and through his fingers I heard the resonance of the name he then gave me, that my mother later denied me: Talitha, the graceful one. My dragon had known that name. . . .

Another dream—no, this time a nightmare. I was shut in, enclosed, chained up in the dark, and something was there beside me, something with scrabbly sounding claws like a crab, something with fetid breath, something that was crawling nearer and nearer, something that had grabbed at my arm and was drawing me into its mouth— I screamed.

And woke.

And it was real, not a nightmare. Something had gripped my arm, something I couldn't see, and it was dragging me over the edge of the rim of stones, down into the stinking depths of the bog. I screamed again, Growch barked wildly and suddenly there was light, a flashing light, my jerkin was gripped in strong teeth and I was dragged back to safety beside a fire blazing up a shower of colored sparks, nursing a bruised arm.

"What—what happened?"

"You tossed about in your sleep and your arm went over the edge," said Ky-Lin. "Whatever you dreamt about awakened one of the creatures in the bog."

"But—what was it?"

"Look." And there, in the extended light thrown by the still-sparking fire, I saw the waters of the mere surrounding us stir and shift as strange creatures broke the surface. Just a claw, a spiny back, an evil eye, the glimpse of a whiplike tail, then they disappeared again in bubbles of foul-smelling gas.

"Some of these creatures are blind, some deaf, but all are hungry. They are not necessarily evil—evil needs an active determination—and that is a concept alien to them. They will eat you or their fellow creatures, even each other, but they lack discrimination. You should be afraid of them, but also feel pity. Human beings have choice, most animals too. They have none."

I shivered. They were foul, distorted creatures and they made me feel sick. If I had been dragged a little further I should now be beneath that slime with mud in my lungs, being chewed into fragments. How could I possibly show pity for such? I wasn't a saint like Ky-Lin, full of his Master's all-forgiveness, I was just a frightened human being.

The rest of the night Growch and I huddled together, both for warmth and for company. I slept but little, for the creature who had grabbed me seemed to have woken all the rest, and the waters around us seethed and gurgled, every now and again throwing up a great gout of water. I heard the wicked snapping of teeth, splash of tails, queer gruntings and groans. Even worse were the lights. Livid yellow, sickly green, lurid purple, they shone both above and below the surface. I couldn't tell whether they were animal or plant or some other manifestation, all I knew was some of them hovered, some zipped through the air, others hopped in and out of water like frogs, with a strange whistling sound.

I must have dozed off eventually, because when Ky-Lin woke me it was light again and, apart from the mist, insects and unhealthy-looking surroundings, all was as it had been the day before.

"Let's get going," I said. I couldn't stand the thought of another moment in that place. We ate breakfast as we walked, stale pancakes and dried fruit, and made good progress, although the path, if you could call it that, was almost covered with water most of the way. At noon we halted briefly at the last of the markers, so Ky-Lin told us, though to me it looked just like a bundle of dried rushes. There was little left that didn't need cooking, but even Growch didn't grumble at the rice cakes and cheese.

But Ky-Lin ate very sparingly, and kept glancing back the way he had come.

"What is it?"

"Not sure. We were followed earlier—men and horses, but they have gone back. But there is still someone back there, I am sure."

"Can't you see anything?"

"No. The land where we rested last night is on a sort of hummock, and that is between me and our pursuer, if there is one. No one from the village comes further than the circle, where they used to hold sacrifices and ritual executions—"

"You never told me that!"

"Would you have felt any easier?"

"Worse!"

"So all I can think is—"

He was interrupted by a scream, a howl of pure terror. In that misty desolation it was difficult to tell what direction it came from, but as it was repeated Ky-Lin's antennae got busy, swivelling this way and that and finally pointing firmly back the way he had come.

There was a further shriek: "Help me! Oh God, help me. . . ."

"It's Dickon!"

I felt a sudden violent jolt of revolt. If he were in trouble, then let him get out of it himself. I didn't want him with us, he had no right to follow, and more and more I felt he was a threat to us all. I wanted to run away, put my hands over my ears and escape as fast as I could, leave him to die, but even as I wished it my reluctant feet were carrying me back along the path we had come.

He was sinking fast. He had obviously stepped off the path, tried to cut a corner where the trail twisted back on itself after a half mile and had been caught in a morass. Already the green slime was bubbling up around his hips, and the more he struggled, the faster he sank.

He was crying, tears of pure terror, choking on my name.

I pulled the rope from Ky-Lin's pack, put one end between his teeth and threw the other towards Dickon; it fell short, and I drew it back, already slick with green slime. He started to flail his arms, and sank down further still.

"Stay still, you fool!"

This time he caught the end of the rope and Ky-Lin and I started to drag him out, but it was hard work, as at least half his body was now out of sight. We at last were making headway when the rope suddenly refused to move; we tugged again with all our strength and found we were not hauling at one body, but two: tangled up with Dickon was a corpse, one of the criminals executed ages ago. The face had been eaten away, and as Dickon caught sight of the grinning skeleton skull he gave another scream and let go the rope.

I threw it again and this time we managed to pull him free, the corpse releasing its hold and sinking back beneath the slime, throwing up its arms as it disappeared in an obscene gesture of farewell.

Dickon at last lay on the path, gasping and groaning, covered in stinking mud and slime. He staggered to his feet, attempted to thank me, but I had had enough.

I walked away from him and didn't look back.

CHAPTER NINETEEN

And what is more I didn't even speak to him until we
had finally crossed the bog by last light and reached firm
ground. I let Ky-Lin lead the way and followed close
behind with Growch, paying no attention to the plodding
footsteps behind, the whimpers and groans.

The bog finally petered out into a series of dank pools,
bulrushes, bog grass and squelchy mud. The land then
rose sharply into a stand of conifers and we moved thankfully into the shelter of the trees and were immediately
enclosed in an entirely different atmosphere. The needles
underfoot cushioned our tread, the air was soft and full
of the clean smell of resin, and the evening breeze
soughed gently in the branches above.

I could hear a stream off to our right, so, after
unloading Ky-Lin, I brushed aside the needles till I
found some stones, then built a fire from pine cones and
dead wood, before unpacking the cooking pot and going
in search of the water.

The stream dropped into a series of little pools and,
after filling the pot, I stripped off and stepped into the
largest one, enjoying the shock of cold water, and
scrubbed myself as best I could with my shirt and drawers, which I washed as well. Ky-Lin had followed me and
drank deep, then stepped into the water and managed to
surround himself with a fine cloud of spray, coming out
as clean and fresh as ever.

I was about to don my clothes again, wet as they were, when he remarked: "The egg is ready to find another resting place: put it in your pouch for safety. Wrap it in a little moss."

I glanced down: it had certainly grown, and looked ready to pop out of my belly button any minute. I picked it up between finger and thumb expecting it to still give a little, but no. It was set hard and came away easily. I wrapped it in some dry moss, promising myself to make a proper purse for it as soon as I could. The pearly sheen had gone, and it now held a sort of stony sparkle, like granite in the sunshine.

A nose nudged my knee. "Where's the dinner then? Fire's goin' a treat, and all it wants is—"

"Clean diners," I said, picking him up and dropping him into the pool, leaving him scrabbling to get out and cursing me fluently.

Back at the fire, which I noticed had been replenished by a cowed Dickon, I put the pot on to boil, added dried vegetables, salt, herbs, dried fish and rice, and mixed some rice flour to make pancakes on a heated stone. A livid Growch came back in the midst of all this preparation and shook himself all over everything and everyone, so that the fire spat and sizzled and God knows what ended up in the cooking pot.

Dickon still cowered on the other side of the fire, a truly sorry sight, his clothes tattered and torn and covered with drying mud and slime, his face greenish under all the muck. I enjoyed my first words to him.

"You'd better go over to the stream and wash yourself. You stink! Wash your clothes out as well: you're not sitting down to eat like that. They'll soon dry out by the fire." Then, as he hesitated, glancing nervously at Ky-Lin, who was resting a little way away: "Go on; he won't bite you!"

"What . . . what is it?" he whispered.

" 'It' is a mythical creature called Ky-Lin. He and his

brethren were guardians of the Lord Buddha. He is
my friend."

His lip curled in a familiar sneer, obvious even through
the layer of dirt on his face. "Oh, another of your only-
talks-to-me creatures is he? Like the cur, the mad bear
and the flying pig you once had—"

"Not at all!" I said sharply. "He understands you perfectly and talks as well as anyone. He's worth his weight
in gold, and has been a perfect guide. If it hadn't been
for him I could never have pulled you out of that morass,
so mind your manners. Now, go wash!"

He told me later that the reason he had been able to
find us was that someone from the seedy edge of town
had seen us go, and he had persuaded a couple of
horsemen to follow us as far as the Place of Power. But
no further.

"I should have thought that by now you would have
got the message," I said. "We don't need you; we can
manage without your ceaseless suspicions and innuendos.
The only reason you followed this time is because of
your obsession with treasure, a treasure I have told you
again and again doesn't exist. I am on a private pilgrimage to find a friend of mine and Growch has come along
to keep me company."

"And—him?" He jerked his head in Ky-Lin's direction.

"I've told you that too. He is my guide and my friend,
and I am his mission, if you like."

"Mission, suspicion . . . All a load of shit if you ask
me. Anyway, who's this 'friend' you're looking for?"

"None of your business. And there is no place for you
where I must go. I have a little money saved: I shan't
need it where I am going, and I'm willing that you should
have it if you will go back." I realized as soon as I opened
my mouth that it was the wrong thing to say. By implying
that I was unlikely to need money, it would only make
him more convinced than ever that I was in expectation
of finding more. I think my next remark made it worse,
if possible. "I can give you ten gold pieces."

I still had the money Suleiman gave me, together with the coins my father had left me—but he wasn't having those.

I saw his eyebrows raise, but he was still staring into the fire, avoiding my eyes. The other two were already asleep, but I had stayed awake in order to have it out with him.

"If it is as you say," he said slowly, "then it matters little to either of us whether I go now or stay and see you safe. If I do the latter, then at least I can bear a message back to Matthew Spicer that I have left you safe and well. I can still be useful in fetching and carrying and I wouldn't feel I was doing my duty after all we've been through together if I didn't offer you my protection while I could."

Oh, very clever! I thought. Showing merely friendship and concern for my safety, but ensuring he kept his eye on me—and my money—right to the end. If I hadn't still had this indefinable feeling that only harm could come from his accompanying us, then I probably wouldn't have hesitated—but if I didn't know exactly what I was afraid of, how could I insist on leaving him behind?

"Very well," I said. "But I expect you to share all the chores and portage. And don't," I added, "grumble. Wherever you find yourself, or however tough it gets. I still think you're wasting your time."

"We'll see," he said, and by the next morning he was almost his usual cocky, arrogant self, just as if he had donned a new suit of clothes.

In fact more clothes were the first things we bought when we came across a decent-sized village. Our winter things had suffered badly in the bog, and besides the warmer weather was here and we needed thinner coverings. I bought us both loose cotton jackets and short breeches, reaching to the knees, and on Ky-Lin's recommendation, straw hats against the sun. I was going to buy sandals as well, but he advised me to keep my boots until we had crossed the desert.

As the villages we passed through were scattered, it didn't seem worthwhile Ky-Lin changing his shape or trying to hide, so we met a great deal of superstitious terror, but were better able to bargain: in many cases I believe they were only too glad to get rid of us!

As we worked our way through the foothills of the mountains towards our next objective, the Desert of Death, my spirits rose with each day that dawned, each mile we walked, each hour that passed. This was the last barrier to surmount, the last real test of our endurance. And with Ky-Lin to lead the way, what could possibly go wrong?

Suddenly, one day, there it was, stretching to the horizon as far as the eye could see. Even the mountains to the north seemed farther away than ever, misty blue in the haze that hung over the sand. There was no gradual approach; it seemed that one stepped off civilization into the wilderness like crossing a threshold. One pace and there you were.

We spent the night at the last village marked on the map, a tiny place squashed between two rearing crags, like a piece of stringy meat caught between two teeth. We were curiosities; very few travellers came their way, but even their awe at seeing Ky-Lin could not overcome their horror at the realization that we were intending to cross the desert.

At first Ky-Lin was reluctant to translate what they said, seated with us in the headman's hut that night, privileged guests, but I insisted, and he was honest enough to interpret literally.

Did we understand that it was called the Desert of Death?

Yes, we did.

Did we understand why it was called thus?

We thought so.

Did we know that no one returned from such a journey?

There was no call to, if they were travelling further on.

Then it was our turn to ask some questions.

Did the villagers ever venture out there?

Sometimes.

Why did they go?

To hunt desert foxes and hares.

Then there must be food for them, and water?

A shrug was the only answer.

How far did the hunters go into the desert?

Well provisioned they could last for a week, over a twenty-five-mile radius. After that there are no more animals to hunt.

What about other settlements?

Another shrug, then someone ventured that there were legends of a fabulous city, a great temple, but . . .

But what?

More shrugs. A long time ago, many lifetimes. No one came back to tell. Maybe it got lost under the Sand Mountains.

What are those?

Great hills of sand that march across the desert, eating everything they come across.

"Are you sure we're going in the right direction?" muttered Dickon.

"You can always turn around and go back," I whispered in return.

All the village turned out the next morning to see us off, and it didn't help one bit that they were burning incense, chanting prayers, and already looked at us as if we were ghosts.

"Don't worry too much," said Ky-Lin. "I assure you that out there, there is a huge temple and a thriving town: I've been there. It's situated on an underground river, but there is plenty of water. It was a while ago since I was there, but bricks and mortar and bronze and gold don't just disappear."

Comforted by his assurance we made our way to a line of scrub that, the villagers had informed us, marked the course of a now dried-up riverbed. Ky-Lin frowned a little as he gazed down at the river pebbles that lined the bottom.

"I remember a river running here. . . . Perhaps I was mistaken. Still it goes the way we want to, so let's follow it."

As the sun got higher in the sky the sweat started to trickle down my face, back and from under my arms. Five minutes later I saw Dickon drop behind and take a surreptitious swig from one of the water bottles he was carrying. He and I both carried four, and Ky-Lin another two, and these were meant to last us until we reached the temple: Ky-Lin's were for cooking and washing, ours for drinking. I was sorely tempted to copy him but decided to wait until Ky-Lin called a halt.

By my reckoning this must have been near noon, and we were now in a shimmering landscape, strewn with rocks under a baking sun. I blinked gritty eyes, but the shimmering persisted, like some curtain of gauze billowing out over a scene at best only guessed at.

"Right," said Ky-Lin. "Unload me, please, and then start digging."

I had wondered why we bought two mattocks some days past: now it seemed I was to find out.

"Digging?" Dickon and I queried in unison.

"Digging," said Ky-Lin firmly. "Every midmorning and every night you will dig a hole, or a trench, or whatever you prefer, to hide us from the worst heat of the day, and the extremes of cold at night. During the journey we will travel till noon, then rest until sunset. Then we shall march again till it gets too cold, and rest till dawn. That way we shall escape the worst extremes of temperature. First, a drink for everyone—only a mugful—and after the hole is dug we can eat."

Growch was so exhausted he just lay on his side, panting, his tongue flapping in and out like a snake tasting

the air, so I served him first, letting him lap the luke-
warm water from the cooking pot. He was so grateful
that he showed us the best place to dig, and even helped
for a while, the sand flying out between his hind legs far
faster than we could dig. Once we had dug a reasonable
trench we settled down in it and shared out the rice
cakes, dried fruit, and cheese that was to be our midday
meal from now on. At night we should have something
cooked, and I would make enough rice cakes to eat cold
at the next meal.

Propping a blanket across the trench, supported on
the upended mattocks, I settled back to sleep for a while
in sticky shade, but saw Dickon once again helping himself from one of his water skins, and was alarmed to see
that he had almost finished one. Well, he'd get none of
mine: I had to share with Growch.

I noticed that Ky-Lin had eaten but little and drank
less; when the same thing happened that evening, I questioned him.

"I can manage for a few days; then I shall need rice,
water, and salt in quantity."

"Salt? In this heat? It will only make you thirstier!"

"Not at all. Everyone needs salt, and you humans
sweat it away in the hot sun. Without it you will become
weak and dizzy, and your arms and legs will ache. That
is why I insisted you bring salted meat with you: at least
you will receive some that way."

We moved on again as the sun sank, a red ball, into
the western sky, and kept the same routine day by night
by day. It was very hard to reconcile the great extremes
of temperature; at midday I would have given anything
to be naked and blanketless, at night I could have welcomed two layers of everything. Once the shimmer of
heat left the land at night, the stars were incredible; they
seemed to be so much nearer, as if one could reach up
and snatch them from the sky. It seemed some little
compensation for the sting of sweat in one's eyes at midday, and the chattering of one's teeth twelve hours later.

Have you ever heard a dog's teeth chatter?

By the third day the mountains we had left had disappeared into haze, those we were moving towards seemed no nearer, those to the west invisible. The desert makes you feel very small: there is too much sky. There is nothing to mark your progress, no trees or bushes or other landmarks, so you might just as well be standing still, or be an ant endlessly circling a huge bowl.

When I woke on the fourth morning and reached for the last of my water flasks, I found it was missing. I had been careful to follow Ky-Lin's instructions; it would be on the fifth day that we would reach the temple, and the water must last that long. There was a full day to go, and there wasn't a drop left! Frantically I shook the other skins: all empty. I couldn't have dropped the full one, surely! No, I remembered clearly the night before shaking it to make sure none had evaporated.

Springing to my feet I was just in time to see Dickon emptying the last of the water down his throat and sprinkling a few drops over his head and face. He started guiltily as he saw me.

"Sorry! I was just so thirsty.... Anyway, it's not far now. We can manage for a day...."

I struck him hard across the mouth. "You selfish bastard! You had four skins all to yourself, and Growch and I had to share! I wish you had never come, I wish you were dead!"

"Hush, child!" said Ky-Lin. "Bring Dog over to me and close your eyes. I will give you some of myself...." and he breathed gently down his nostrils onto our faces. "There! You will not feel thirsty for a while."

And it was true. Both Growch and I managed that day without needing water; somehow Ky-Lin had transferred liquid, precious water from his body to ours: I only hoped that it would not hurt him. Magic only goes so far.

That day we travelled faster and further than any day before, and the following morning Ky-Lin woke us early.

"By midday we should be there," said Ky-Lin

encouragingly. "Just over that little ridge ahead and you will see the temple. And then water, food, rest, shelter . . ."

The struggle up that ridge was a nightmare. The sweat near blinded me, I ached, my limbs wouldn't obey me, my throat hurt, I was too dry to swallow. At last we topped the incline and, full of anticipation, gazed down on Ky-Lin's fabled city.

Only it wasn't there.

Nothing, except a heap of tumbled stones.

CHAPTER TWENTY

I gazed around wildly, thinking for one stupid moment that we were in the wrong place, but one look at Ky-Lin's stricken face told me the truth.

It was Dickon who voiced all our thoughts.

"Well, where is it then? Where's your town, temple, water, food, shelter, and rest?"

I had never seen Ky-Lin look so dejected. For an eye-deceiving moment he lost all color and almost appeared transparent, his beautiful plumed tail dragging in the dust. But even as I blinked he regained his color, and his tail its optimism. The only sign of disquiet was a furrowing of his silky brow.

"Well?" Dickon was panicking, his voice hysterical. "What do we do now?"

"What happened, Ky-Lin? There was something here once. . . ."

He turned to me. "I don't know. I wish I did. I told you it was a long time since I was here. Let's go down and see. There must be something we can salvage from all this."

At my feet Growch was whimpering. "Sod me if I can go no further. Me bleedin' paws hurt, me legs is sawn off, me stummick tells me me throat's cut and I could murder a straight bowl of water. . . ."

I picked him up, though my body told me I ached as much and was twice as thirsty, and we all stumbled like drunkards down the slope to the first of the tumbled wrecks of stones. When we reached them we found they were not stones but mud bricks, and as I looked around I could see this was the remains of what had once been a street of shops or small dwelling places, and as they fell they had crumbled and broken.

Ky-Lin prowled down the street, looking here, there, everywhere. "No sign of war or pestilence. This place has been empty for many, many years, but it looks as if they went peaceably. Everything has been cleared away, no artifacts left about, no evidence of fire. . . . Let's take a look at the temple, or what's left of it."

Not much. We threaded our way through other deserted, tumbledown streets until we reached what must have been a courtyard. It surrounded a partly stone-walled temple, with now-roofless cells behind, which would have housed the monks. Sand had drifted deep on the temple floor, the roof had fallen in and the stone altar was empty. No idols, no incense, no prayer wheels, no bells. Only the wind, shush-shushing the sand back and forth across the stone floor in little patterns. On either side of the altar were a couple of stone lumps, now so eroded by sand, sun and wind that they were unrecognizable.

Unrecognizable to all but Ky-Lin, that was.

"Here, girl: come see what is left of my brothers. . . ."

Nearer I could see what must have once been their heads, their tails.

"Were they Ky-Lins too?"

He nuzzled the stones lovingly. "Once. But these two attained Paradise a long time ago, and the monks carved them to remind them of my Master's visit." He sighed. "At least it shows one thing, all this: the soul outlasts the strongest stone."

"How about getting your priorities right?" came Dickon's voice over my shoulder. "Souls belong to the dead: we're living. But we won't be much longer unless you find us something to eat and drink."

Without cooking I had a couple of rice cakes, some dried fruit, a little cheese.

"If you will unload me please," said Ky-Lin, "you will find one small water skin under the blankets. One mug of water each, no more; the rice cakes and cheese will be enough for now."

Strange: I had never noticed that particular water skin before, but then he was Magic. . . .

I shared my cheese and water with Growch, and although his share of the liquid was gone in half a dozen quick laps, I sipped mine as slowly as I could, running it over my parched tongue before swallowing, to get the maximum benefit; behind me I heard Dickon's water gone in a couple of quick gulps. I went over to Ky-Lin with some dried raisins and apricots.

"Come, you must eat something too; we depend on you to keep us going."

His forked tongue, ever so soft, lapped the fruit from my palm. "Now get some rest. Go into the shade of that wall. I am going to reconnoiter. I shall return as soon as I can."

I settled back with my back against the stone. Just five minutes' nap, and then . . .

And then it was dawn. Someone had tucked a blanket round Growch and me, and further away Dickon was snoring softly. I was neither hot nor cold, hungry nor thirsty, and I felt rested and refreshed. Beside me was a heap of wood, smooth, bleached wood that had obviously been around for a while. Beyond, Ky-Lin was curled around, fast asleep, only the rise and fall of his chest showing that he was still alive.

A surprisingly wet and cold nose was shoved in my face. "What's for breakfast, then?"

I used half the water that was left to boil up rice, beans, dried vegetables and herbs, on Ky-Lin's advice adding the rest of the salted meat, and some rather dessicated roots he had found. They smelt oniony, and looked like water lily suckers. The wood burned brightly and too fast, with a sort of bluish flame, and I kept it down as much as I could, for now the sun was high and extra heat was unwelcome. Just before it was cooked I took the pot off the fire and clamped on the lid tight, then buried it in the sand so it would retain heat and absorb the last of the liquid, as I had seen it done in this country to ensure both tenderness and conservation of fuel.

"And now," said Ky-Lin, "we must find somewhere to shelter. I can smell wind, and that here will mean a sandstorm." He led us through the remains of a small archway to the left of the altar. Behind was part of a wall and domed roof, and a set of steps leading down into the darkness. There was remarkably little of the ubiquitous drifted sand.

"The way the wind blows here," explained Ky-Lin, "the sand merely piles up on the other side of the wall. Now, we shall go down the steps to better shelter. Once at the bottom, if we spread out the blankets, we shall be snug enough."

Something scuttled past my feet and I gave a stifled scream.

"Scorpion," said Dickon. "I'm not going down there, and that's flat!"

He kicked out at the creature, who raised its stinging tail threateningly and disappeared through a crack in the wall.

"The ultimate survivors," said Ky-Lin. "When everything else has disappeared from the earth, the ants, the scorpions, and the cockroaches will have it all to themselves. Don't worry," he added. "There are no more down there. Follow me," and he disappeared down the flight of stone steps.

"You're on your own," said Dickon, as I prepared to follow. "I'm not going down."

I fumbled my way down steps worn smooth by generations of monks. Once at the bottom the air was pleasantly cool, with only a fine layer of sand underfoot. The light from above was enough for me to see that this was a little cul-de-sac, but large enough to hold us all comfortably.

"Come on down!"

"Not on your life," came Dickon's voice, oddly distorted by the turn in the stairs, although Growch had already joined me quite happily.

"In that case," I yelled back, "you can go out and fetch in all the baggage. And the cooking pot," I added.

I knew he wouldn't, and it took the three of us to transfer everything to safety, Dickon grumbling all the while. By the time all was stowed away safely the wind had risen enough for us to hear even at the bottom of the stairs, and when I went out to retrieve the cooking pot it was really nasty up top. The wind was whining like a caged dog, gusting every now and again into a shriek, and with it the sand was spiralling as tall as a man, blasting into any unprotected skin like the rasp of a file. The very heaps of sand in the courtyard had changed position so much that it took me several minutes to locate where I had buried the cooking pot; it was still hot, and I had to take off my shirt and wrap it in that to carry it safely, the driving sand stinging my bare skin unmercifully.

I served out half the contents of the pot; a bowl each, my meat ration for Growch, and half a mug of water, and as I scoured out the bowls with the ubiquitous sand I wondered which of us was still the hungriest and thirstiest. Settling down on my blanket, I asked the questions that would probably mean the difference between life and death to us. Somebody had to ask; I didn't want to, but it was obvious Dickon wanted to hear the answers even less than I did.

"What did you find out, Ky-Lin?"

"I searched the whole of the ruins while you were asleep. I gave you all a little Sleepy Dust to ensure you slept for a day and a half—" He raised his left front hoof as we protested. "Yes, yes, I know; but you needed the rest, and I wanted time without your worries burdening me. I needed to let my senses roam free.

"This place was abandoned some eighty years ago. What drove them out was probably the threat of famine. From what I could determine, the wells on which the town depended for its water started to dry up, due to the river deep beneath the desert floor changing course. There may still have been enough for drinking, but certainly not enough for irrigating their crops.

"Added to this, there was the unprecedented advance of the Sand Mountains, a phenomenon peculiar to this desert. The villagers mentioned them, remember? They are formed by a combination of wind and sand, and move to any place they are driven. They may not be seen for a hundred years, but given special conditions they can build up within days, and overwhelm anything in their path. Such a disaster overtook this town. They had enough notice to move out in an orderly fashion, so everything portable was taken with them. The monks were the last to leave."

"And where are the Sand Mountains now?"

He shrugged. "Who knows? They were not here long, but time enough to destroy the fabric of the buildings, as you saw."

"Where did the people go?"

He shrugged again. "Probably west and north. The way we go. . . ."

Here it was, the question I had so been dreading. "Any—any sign of water?"

He looked at me with compassion, then shook his head. "No, I found no trace of water. Not yet, anyway. That doesn't mean there isn't any."

Dickon leapt to his feet. "No water, no food—what the hell do we do now?"

"We would do well to pray. Now, together. Each to our own God or gods." He bowed his head. "In any case it will concentrate our minds if we are quiet for a few minutes. Prayer always helps. Focus on our predicament and ask for guidance. . . ."

I wanted to pray as my mother had taught me: speak

to God direct, she had always said. But she had sent me
to the priest to learn my letters and the Catechism, and
it was these familiar formulas, as comforting as a child's
rhymes, that I now found filled my mind; the priest had
taught me that God could only be approached through
His intermediaries, those like Himself. My mother, on
the other hand, had never been afraid to speak her mind,
and she told me God was there to be talked to, just like
anyone else, person to person.

I don't know whether she believed in Him; I think she
only believed in herself. I recited three rapid Ave's under
my breath, not thinking of anything really, except the
comfort of the formula. I glanced at the others; Ky-Lin
was obviously in communication with his Lord, but Dickon's hands were twisting as if he was wringing out a cloth,
his eyelids flickering. No point in looking at Growch; his
god, Pan, was a heathen.

But it was Growch who saved us.

I was in the middle of my third Paternoster when a
sacrilegious interruption destroyed all thought of prayer.

"Bloody 'ell! Effin' little bastards!"

"Growch!"

"Sorree! But what d'you say if'n you'd just been bit on
yer privates by a bunch o' ravenin' ants?"

"Ants? But—"

Ky-Lin and I had the same thought at the same time.
Ants in a town deserted for many years and surrounded
by an arid desert could mean only thing: ants, to exist,
need both food and water, however minimal. So, somewhere there was water!

"Move, dog!" said Ky-Lin. "Slowly and carefully. The
lantern, girl!"

At first the flames flickered wildly all over the stone
floor because my hand was shaking so much, but as it
steadied we all saw what had so rudely interrupted whatever Growch had been thinking about. A double line
of ants, both coming and going, the ones advancing
towards us laden with what looked like grains, the others

empty-legged. I swung the lantern to the left; the laden ants were disappearing into a large crack in the masonry, obviously behind which they had their nest. The outgoing ones, where did they go?

I swung the light the other way, but obviously too far: no ants.

"Gently does it," breathed Ky-Lin. "Back a little . . ."

And there it was. There was a long, straight crack in the floor, and down this the ants were appearing and disappearing without hindrance. I brushed away some of the sand, and there was another crack in the stone, this one at right angles to the first. Ky-Lin used his tail on the sand as well, and between us we uncovered a full square, some two and a half feet along each side. It was obviously an entrance of some sort to an underground storage area, but how did it work? I scraped away at the center: nothing! I blew at the sand, I scrabbled with my fingers, still nothing.

Ky-Lin's delicate antennae were probing the surface. "Try here," he said, indicating the corner farthest away. I brushed away the sand and there, recessed into the stone, was a rusty iron ring.

"That's it! That's it!" I was now in a fever of excitement. "There must be something down there, there must!" and bending down I tugged at the ring, but all I got was red, flaky dust on my fingers; the square had not budged.

Dickon had finally worked out what all the fuss was about, and exercised all his strength, again to no purpose except for rusty fingers.

"Let's try this scientifically," said Ky-Lin. "Neither of you is powerful enough to shift the trapdoor on your own and I cannot get a grip. Think, my children; how can we raise it?"

I knew he had something in mind, but Dickon and I could only gaze at each other in perplexity. It was Growch, puffed up with his success in finding the stone trapdoor, who provided us with the simple answer.

"Well, you are a coupla dummies! Rope, that's what you want: rope."

Of course! And while the increasing wind raged outside and the sand trickled its way in little drifts down the steps, we found the rope in the baggage, looped it through the ring in the floor and, one end tied round Ky-Lin's neck, the other held by Dickon and myself, we tried once more to heave the square of stone from its bed.

"One, two, three, heave! One, two, three, heave!" We heaved, we pulled, we jerked, we struggled, but the damned thing wouldn't shift. We tried again and again, and finally there was a faint grating noise and it seemed the trapdoor shifted just a fraction.

"We've got it!" yelled Dickon. "Just one more heave. All together now—heave!"

Another minuscule shift in the stone, then it settled back into its square with a little puff of dust. The ants had disappeared, not surprisingly.

"Once more," exhorted Dickon. "Pull up and back this time. Now!"

We heaved as hard as we could, there was a sudden snap and we all three landed in a tangled bruised heap in the corner, the rope coiling itself round our legs. I pulled the length through my fingers, conscious of a bruised shoulder. "But it hasn't broken. . . ."

"No," said Ky-Lin. "It was the ring that snapped; it had rusted right through."

I burst into tears: I couldn't help it. "It's not fair! I'm so thirsty. . . ."

Ky-Lin nuzzled my neck comfortingly. "Courage. We haven't lost yet." He inspected the broken ring. "It was weak at this one point. Perhaps it could be repaired. Remember the bars in your prison, girl? Well this time we shall have to try the process in reverse. Give me some space; I shall have to think about this."

Obediently we moved back, and one look at Dickon's stricken face told me what I must be looking like too.

True, we didn't know what we would find down there, but hope had been rekindled, only to be dashed again by a few flakes of rust. I had never felt so thirsty in all my life, not even as a child in a high fever when I had cried and begged my mother for the cool spring water she had trickled down my throat from a wet cloth.

"Shut your eyes, children, you too, dog!"

Suddenly I fet the hair curl on my head, and even behind closed eyelids I was near blinded by a brilliant light. There was a smell of ozone, of snow, of wet iron. I opened my eyes to see Ky-Lin momentarily surrounded by a haze of colorless flame. I shut my eyes again, and when I opened them the ring was whole again, though considerably smaller.

I stretched forward to touch it, but Ky-Lin stopped me. "Not yet; it is not yet cool enough. . . ." He looked tired, diminished.

I put my arms about his neck. "Rest awhile; we can wait."

But it seemed an age before the ring cooled enough to try; up above it was full dark, and the wind still howled.

At last Ky-Lin nodded his head. "This time just keep pulling: no sudden jerks."

Once more I looped the rope around his neck, once more Dickon and I took up the slack at the other end. This was it.

"Now," said Ky-Lin softly. "Pull as hard as you can— and pray. . . ."

CHAPTER TWENTY-ONE

This time I didn't pray; I swore.

It made me feel better as I once more took the strain of the rope, endured the aches in my shoulders and arms, the rasp in my throat, the grit between my teeth—oh yes, I really enjoyed that swear, and I used all the bad words I had ever heard, whether I knew their meaning or not, and included the sort of things one sees written on walls. In fact I was concentrating so hard on remembering all the words, with my eyes shut, that I didn't see the stone begin to shift.

The first I knew was Dickon's mutter: "It's coming, it's coming. . . ."

There was a sudden slither, a grinding of stone against sand, and the rope burnt through my fingers. I collided once again with the other two, but this time it didn't hurt, and I found I was staring down at a black hole in the floor, revealing a triangular gap and the glimpse of more stone steps leading downward.

With the opening came a sudden breath of stale air, thick with the stink of rancid oil, dust, decaying meal—

"I can smell water," said Growch. "There's some down there somewheres. Faint, but it's there. Shall we go?"

A gap that would admit a dog wasn't large enough for two adults and a pony-sized mythical creature, so we had to push the stone trapdoor right away to one side before we could descend, Ky-Lin in the lead and Dickon and I

with the two lanterns. Growch in his eagerness near
tripped me up. I sat down hurriedly on one of the steps,
noticing that even here the sand had penetrated, the only
clear spaces being the lines where the ants had trailed
up and back over the years. I had a sudden idea, which
got shoved to the back of my mind immediately I
reached the chamber.

It was a huge cellar in which we found ourselves, the
stone roof supported by a row of pillars marching away
into dark corners our lanterns didn't reach. The floor was
flagged, and on either side stone shelves lined the walls.
Empty shelves, no sign of containers to hold the water
Growch still insisted he could smell. Slowly we walked
the full length of the cellar, the lantern light sending our
shadows into black giants that climbed startled pillars,
crept along stone walls, trailed our footsteps like
devoted pets.

To the left and right of us there were only empty
shelves, dust and ancient cobwebs like dirty, disinteg-
rating lace. The atmosphere was dry and choking and I
sneezed involuntarily, expecting the noise to echo and
reverberate, but the cellar had a peculiar deadening
effect and the sneeze seemed to die at my feet. It was
like being stuck behind the heavy curtains of a four-
poster.

We reached the far end and there, ranged against the
walls, were several tall clay pots, seemingly sealed with
wax stoppers. My heart gave a bound of anticipation and
I rushed forward, lantern bobbing wildly, my knife cut-
ting hastily through the seals. I stepped backward, cov-
ering my nostrils as a dreadful stench seeped out.

"It's fermenting grain," said Ky-Lin. "Not fit to touch.
Except for the ants," he added. "This is what has kept
them going over the years. With luck it will last for many
years more. They are sensible creatures and will not
overbreed, so perhaps—"

"But where is the water?" shouted Dickon, coughing
and choking, all control gone. "Don't you realize, you

stupid creature, that we will die without it? Who cares about bloody ants? Fuck the ants!"

"I care about them," said Ky-Lin severely. "And so should you. I care for all living creatures, and if you would just realize that those little creatures can point the way to your salvation—"

"Fuck salvation!" yelled Dickon. "And fuck you too!" and flung his lantern full into Ky-Lin's face.

There was a burst of colored light—red, green, purple, orange, blue, yellow—then nothing.

Darkness. Even my lantern had gone out.

A brief moment of panic, angry sobs from Dickon, then a comforting nudge at my ankle.

"You stay 'ere, nice an' quiet, an' I'll nip up top an' get your lightin' things. Don' move now," and Growch's claws click-clacked away over the stone floor. A faint light came from the opening above, and I saw him disappear over the last step. A moment or two later he was back, and thrust the box into my free hand with his muzzle.

"Nice bit o' light, an' things'll look different . . ."

My hands were shaking so much it took two or three goes before I could light my lantern. I swung it over my head and saw Dickon, his face all blubbery with angry tears, the other lantern shattered at his feet.

"I didn't mean to hurt him," he whined. "It wasn't my fault! He shouldn't have riled me! Where's he gone, anyway?"

Where indeed? I rushed from one end of the cellar to the other, my lantern swinging wildly, but there was no sign of Ky-Lin. Perhaps he had gone up the steps?

Growch shook his head. " 'E's not up there. 'E ain't nowhere as I can see. Can't smell 'im neither."

I stumbled and fell to my knees, the lantern nearly slipping from my fingers. I had fallen over something, a stone, a pebble—

No, not a stone, not a pebble. A tiny little image, looking as old as the stone from which it had been fashioned.

Tears stung my eyes as I recognized the pudgy little features, the plumed tail.

"He's here," I said. "What's left of him."

The stone was cold in my hand. There was no life here, no flicker of movement. Just the small shell of what had been a vibrant, loving, colorful creature. Even my ring was cold and dead, like Ky-Lin.

I felt anger rising in me inescapably, like the sudden jet of blue flame from a burning, sappy log. I thrust the stone figure under Dickon's nose.

"You killed him! You destroyed him with your evil temper! I hate you! I hate you! I *hate* you!" I sobbed, and swung my lantern at his head as he ducked.

"Steady on there," said Growch mildly. " 'E wouldn't 'ave wanted no 'istrionics. What's done is done. Nuffin's ever truly lost. 'E may be just a bit of stone in yer 'and right now, but what 'e was is still 'ere. What 'e taught you. Well then, try and think like 'e would 'ave wanted you to. Pretend 'e's still 'ere. If you concentrate 'ard enough it'll be like 'e's still speakin' to us."

I could feel my ring warming up again; looking down it had a pearly glow. Growch was right, wherever his doggy wisdom had suddenly come from. My anger evaporated. I kissed the little stone figure and tucked it in my pouch, promising it a better resting place when I found one.

What would he have done now? I shut my eyes and concentrated. Looked for water, of course. Just before we came down here, when I was sitting on the step, I had had an idea, a good one, I was sure. But what was it? Something to do with . . . Stone? Tracks? Ants? Yes, that was it. But how could it help? Think, girl, think! Ants, sand-covered stone, tracks, Ky-Lin saying they had to have water—That was it!

Rushing back to the steps I held the lantern high, searching for ant trails, but our comings and goings had made a complete mess of anything I was looking for, and the ants themselves were milling around in aimless circles. Half-shuttering the lantern, I settled down to wait.

"What the hell are you doing?" asked Dickon irritably. "We're wasting time. We should be searching for water."

"I am."

"What? Sitting on your arse?"

"Just shut up, keep still, and be patient."

"I know, I know, I know!" said Growch triumphantly. "Clever lady."

Which left Dickon in the dark, especially as he couldn't understand Growch, but seeing us both concentrating he lapsed into silence. The ants settled down and began their marching from the nest above. Down the steps in a double line, then—yes, my theory was correct. The line split into two, one set of ants going off to the darkness at the rear end for food, the other half turning left, and—

"Under the steps!" I called out. "We never looked there!"

Behind the steps was a man-sized space and three shallow steps leading down to a small cistern and—a thousand candles to Saint Whoever when I could afford them!—it was still a third full.

The water was clear, but littered with unwary ant bodies and with a layer of silt beneath, but nothing had ever tasted so good. We scooped it with our mugs into the cooking pot, then all of us drank till we were full and I for one felt slightly sick.

Growch rolled over with a grunt and a distended belly. "Near as good as a beef bone . . ."

A drink seemed to bring Dickon back to sense once more and cooled his temper for days to come. "We mustn't stir up the water too much," he said. "We need to fill the water skins with clean."

Looking at the cistern more carefully, wondering how the water hadn't dried up long since, I noticed a darker patch at the back which felt damp to the touch, so there was obviously seepage from some long-forgotten spring or rivulet behind. Not enough to keep the temple in water, just enough for the ants—and us. Praise be!

By now it was full dark above and the wind still whined and shrieked unabated, so we moved everything down into the cellar and I used what fuel we had left to cook up enough rice to keep us going that night and the following morning.

We fell asleep over the meal, but I had had sense enough to remove everything eatable from the ants though, remembering Ky-Lin, I sprinkled a few grains on the floor near their trail. Ky-Lin would have done the same if he had been with us, of that I was sure, making some gentle remark about it being a "change of diet" for the insects. Anyway, they deserved it: they had shown the way to the water.

The following morning the wind was gone as though it had never been and the sun shone brilliantly from a clear sky. We all wanted to get going as soon as possible, but now there was no Ky-Lin to help with advice and porterage, we were faced with real problems. The mythical creature had told us that the temple was "halfway," which meant there were at least five more days of travel to endure. He had consulted the maps and shown me the route we should follow, and with my Waystone I thought I could manage that. Burdened as we were, though, we should probably have to expect at least one more day's travel, bringing it to six, which would be over the limit for even the stretching of what food we had.

Well, we could go hungry, but not thirsty. I spread out everything from our baggage, hoping we could leave at least half behind to lighten our load, while Dickon carefully filled the ten water skins. I knew how heavy these were from bitter experience, but they were essential. But what to leave behind? The remaining food, blankets against the cold, and mattocks, these must come as well. Money in a belt around my waist, personal possessions (and the egg) in a pouch at my neck. Cooking pot, spoons and mugs (I had dismissed the idea of boiling everything up before we went: in the desert heat it would be uneatable in twenty-four hours); honey and salt were heavy to carry, but both were necessary. Likewise my few packs of herbs, the maps, sewing kit and oil: all had their uses.

In the end all we could reasonably do without was everything we were not actually wearing, the broken lantern, one blanket out of three, my writing things and my journal. This last went with me, I was determined on that; at worst if our skeletons were found in the desert, it would explain everything. I hefted the bundle we could leave: I could lift it on one finger. Well, two. So that wasn't going to make much difference.

"Dickon," I called out. "We'll never carry all this!"

He emerged with the last two water skins. "I've been thinking about that. The water is covered with a small grid the monks must have stood on to bucket up the water, and if you recall, there was a metal cover lying to one side. We could use both as sledges; why carry if you can pull? Both are metal, so they shouldn't wear away. The grid is no problem, and the metal cover has holes where it fitted over the cistern, so if we cut the rope in half you can pull the grid as it's smaller, and I'll take the cover. Right?"

So it was decided. We then ate, packed up and waited for the worst of the day's heat to dissipate, deciding to keep to Ky-Lin's order of march: early evening and dawn. While we were waiting I soaked some beans and dried vegetables for the following day, ready to cook. Fuel was going to be a problem, but I persuaded Growch to pick up everything we could burn during the march. Before we left we drank as much as we could take from the cistern, and I even took the luxury of a quick wash, soaking my clothes as well for a cool start to the trek. The water was all cloudy by the time I had finished, but it would soon settle back for the ants and I left them a few more grains and a dollop of honey as compensation.

We left the trapdoor open, in case other travellers

came that way, and I took a soft stone and drew the universally recognized symbol of an arrow on the cellar floor to indicate the position of the cistern.

And so we left the temple to the ants and set off across the desert towards the dying sun.

At first our progress was slow but steady. The management of the improvised sledges was difficult to master. The metal cover travelled easier, but was more unstable. As we travelled the sledges became lighter each day, and now we took turns with each. The weather stayed clear, my directions appeared to be correct, for each day we persuaded ourselves the mountains we were headed for came fractionally nearer.

Then on the fourth day we ran into trouble.

The night had been overcast, for once, and we had overslept after a hard day's trek the previous day. When we awoke the eastern sky was bright and we cast long shadows ahead of us. We ate a hurried breakfast—not as much as any of us wanted, but rations were short by now—and set off at a good pace for a steep rise just ahead. We hauled the sledges up the rise, looking forward to the incline beyond and—

"What the hell . . . !" If he hadn't said it, I would. Ahead of us, about a mile distant, reared a sudden and unexpected range of mountains.

Sand Mountains.

These were the ones Ky-Lin and the villagers had warned us about, the giants who could stay in one place for years and then, given the right conditions, move across the desert floor at a terrifying speed, destroying everything in their path. And here they were, straight across our path, barring our way to the mountains. At the moment they were quiet, a range of sandhills some fifty to a hundred feet high at their lowest. And they stretched for miles. As we moved close an errant wind agitated sand on the tops into whirls and curls like smoke, and every now and again miniavalanches of sand fell down the steeper slopes.

For the rest of the morning we tried to climb those restless, shifting mountains, but for every stride up, we tumbled back two. The sledges became bogged down in the sand and we sank to our knees in it, like falling into quicksand, and twice we nearly lost Growch. Eventually we tried to find a way between, but the sand blew in our faces and filled our footsteps within seconds.

There was only one thing for it: we should have to take the long trek round them; the worst of that was we had no idea whether the way east or west was shorter, as they stretched as far as the eye could see in both directions.

Three days later we struggled round the western end and tried to pick up our bearings. We had wasted three days to find ourselves in virtually the same spot we had started out from and the real mountains seemed as far away as ever. On we tramped, our travelling time curtailed by our increasing weariness from lack of proper nourishment. Two days later the last of our food and water was gone and we piled all our goods onto the smoother sledge, pulling it in tandem to conserve our strength.

I began to see things that weren't there—houses, lakes, trees, camels, people—shimmering in the distance some feet above the desert floor, and beside me Dickon was hallucinating too. On the tenth day we put Growch on the sledge because he could move no further and lay there with his tongue hanging out like one dead.

Dickon and I now fell every dozen yards or so and our throats were so parched we couldn't even curse each other. At last we both tripped and fell together and I just wanted to lie there forever and forget everything. I was conscious it was high noon already and I knew if we didn't get up and seek shelter we should surely be dead before nightfall.

I rose to my knees and peered ahead, but all I could

see was one of those fevered images again: a train of camels seeming to stride six feet above the sand and some half mile away. I collapsed, without even the energy to rouse Dickon, to offer a last prayer, and drifted off into unconsciousness.

But somewhere, somehow, I could swear I heard a dog barking. . . .

CHAPTER TWENTY-TWO

... a dog barking. Cautiously I opened my eyes. Normally in the desert Dickon and I slept within feet of each other, but now all my hands encountered was a blanket. There was a dim light over to my right, it must be the moon. No stars. And where was Growch? I was sure I had heard him a moment ago. I struggled to sit up, and there was a cold, wet nose against my cheek.

" 'Ad a nice kip, then? Thought we'd lost you at one stage. Feel a bit better?"

"I don't understand. . . . What's happened? I—" And then, suddenly, it all came back to me. The desert, the vast, terrible, unforgiving desert. Sun, heat, thirst, hunger, hallucinations, death already rattling in my throat, the last thing a dog barking . . .

I sat up slowly, stretched, wiggled my fingers and toes. I seemed to be all in one piece, but I was dreadfully stiff, my throat was sore and my head ached.

"Wanna drink? On yer right. On the table. That's it. Careful now, don' spill it."

Blessed, beautiful, clear cold water. The most wonderful liquid in the world. I drank it all, then burped luxuriously. I looked around me. I was obviously inside a house or hut, and the light I had thought the moon was a saucer oil lamp. I was on a pallet of sorts and it must be sometime at night. So, we had been rescued, but how and when? Where were we? And where was Dickon?

263

More than one question at a time flummoxed Growch. "I'll tell yer, I'll tell yer, but one at a time! Dickon? 'Is lordship is around and about in the town somewheres, and—"

"Which town? What's it called? Where is it?"

" 'Ow the 'ell do I know? A town's a town ain't it? Same as all towns. 'Ouses, streets, people, dogs, food . . . We're still in the desert, but they got plenty o' water. Goats, chickens, camels. It was their camels as brought us in. I barked till I was 'oarse, managed to get over to the caravan, and they came back and picked you up."

"Oh, Growch! You saved our lives!" and I hugged him till he swore he couldn't breathe and why did I have to be so soppy? All the while his tail was wagging like mad, so I knew he was secretly as pleased as could be.

"An' afore you ask, all yer belongings is snug as well." I felt for my money belt and neck pouch: all safe.

"Short and long of it is, they brought us in—gave you camel's milk out there, they did, an' you sicked it all up—" I was not surprised: the very thought of camel's milk made me ill again. "—then they gave you water an' things an' brought us 'ere. Got two rooms, an' I kep' 'is lordship away from all what is ours."

I stretched again, felt my headache lessening. "What time is it?"

"Middle evenin'. Sun down, moon not yet up."

"I must have been asleep for—nine or ten hours, then?"

"An' the rest! Four days ago it was when they brought us in. There's a woman been feedin' you slops an' things with a spoon."

"Four days!" I swung my legs over the edge of the bed, tried to stand up and fell back again. "By our Lady! I feel so weak!"

"Not surprised. Slops never did no one no good. Yer wants some good red meat inside of yer, like what I have." He smacked his chops. "Nuffin' like it. Treated me real well they 'as. Called me a 'ero . . ."

"And so you are," I said, giving him another hug. "Be a dear and go and find Dickon for me?"

Two days later I was up and about again, with an urge to get going as soon as we could. It was now well past Middle Year, we had been travelling for over fifteen months, and now I had recovered from my ordeal I felt a renewal of hope and energy. But it seemed we should have to wait a little longer. The nearest town, at the foothills of the mountains we were seeking, was a good four-day journey away by camel train—the same one that had rescued us—and they were not due to leave for another two and a half weeks, and strongly advised us not to try it on our own.

They were a hospitable people, and their town was clean and prosperous. Everywhere we went we were greeted with bows and smiles and clapping of hands, and though we couldn't speak a word of their language, we managed very well with sign language and the occasional drawing. As they existed solely on the barter system, our money meant nothing to them, and they insisted on treating us as honored guests. Which was lucky, seeing we had nothing to barter with.

Under the town was a river system that kept their cisterns full, with enough also for their crops of fruit and vegetables and the watering of their stock: goats, chickens, ducks, camels. They even kept ponds stocked with fish that looked rather like carp. The only goods they needed from outside were rice, clay for pots, and cotton cloth, and these they traded for with their own produce, which included pickled eggs, a special spiced pancake and other delicacies, desert fox furs, and exquisite carvings fashioned from the soft stone they found round-abouts. Once a month they journeyed to do their bargaining, and we agreed to await the next caravan.

There was plenty for us to do, however—for me at least, that is. Our clothes, what was left of them, were a disgrace, and I had spent four or five days doing the best

I could with my sewing kit, when we had an unexpected
bonus. Growch, investigating a tempting little bitch—
what else?—had chased her into a store where cotton
cloth awaited making up into the loose clothes the inhabitants preferred, and had been diverted by finding a huge
nest of rats. He had set about them in true Growch
fashion, and the grateful owner of the store had come to
me, counting out at least twenty on his fingers, bearing
also a roll of cloth sufficient to clothe both Dickon and
myself.

Only when all my tasks were done, which included
tedious things like washing blankets and mending panniers, did I keep a promise I had made to myself some
weeks past. We had found out that the monks who had
fled the destruction of the temple in the desert had
found this town in time for survival, and had built a small
temple to give thanks for their deliverance. This temple
was now in the custody of one of the original monks,
then a boy, now a blind old man of near a hundred. One
of the village boys was his apprentice, and led him about
the village with their begging bowls—always full—and
assisted in leading the prayers.

One evening, when I knew the old monk and his aco-
lyte would be dining, the sun tipping over the rim of the
world had led to the lighting of the dried camel-dung
fires for cooking and the last of the workers and herd's
boys came tramping home, I made my way down the
deserted streets towards the temple, the sad stone rem-
nant of what had been Ky-Lin clutched in my hands.

It was only a small edifice, this temple, built from
desert stone and mud bricks, but inside the floor was
flagged, the air smelt of incense and oil saucers burned
in front of the stone altar. Someone had left a garland
of wildflowers by the crossed knees of the little smiling
Buddha.

I had thought I would feel like an interloper, not
knowing the language either, but it felt entirely natural
to stand in front of the idol and speak in my own tongue.

I looked up at the statue, who stared above my head the while with empty, slanted eyes and an eternal smile, then I knelt down, as I would in one of my own churches, shut my eyes, and folded my hands around the remains of Ky-Lin.

"Please forgive me for not knowing your customs and language, Sir, but I have a special request. In my hands are the remains of a true friend, counsellor and guide, whom You lent to us to help us on our journey. He no longer has life, as You can see, but his death was a tragic accident, and he would have been the first to forgive.

"He was one of Yours, a Ky-Lin, who was left on earth to work off some trifling sins he had committed. Well I thought they were trifling. . . . Whatever they were, I assure You they must have been more than cancelled out by his care of us. So, will You please take him back? He spoke of a place where all was perfect and at peace: we would call it Heaven. Please allow him in Yours. Amen. Oh, and thanks for lending him to us. Amen again."

The Buddha had one gilded hand on his knee; the other was cupped on his chest. Reaching up as far as I could, I kissed the tiny stone that had been Ky-Lin and placed him gently in the cupped hand.

There: it was done. Ky-Lin could rest in peace.

I rose to my feet, bowed to the Buddha and backed out of the little temple. The idol seemed to be smiling more broadly than ever.

I had never ridden a camel before. It was extremely difficult to adjust to the rocking, swaying movement so far above the ground, and there was more than one moment when I definitely felt camel-sick. However, even the lap-held Growch agreed that it was better than walking, and in four days we were in a village in the foothills of the mountains where we said good-bye to our kind hosts, replenished our stores and set off in a direction of north by west.

At first we had an easy time of it; the tracks we followed

led to other villages and small towns, where our money
was accepted. We travelled easily into autumn, through
reddening leaves, ripening fruit and the migration of
small animals and birds: pint-size deer, foxes, squirrels;
duck, swallows, swifts; the large butterflies flirting their
just-before-hibernating wings on clumps of pink and
purple fleshy-leaved plants. Peasants brought in the
last of their harvest, stored their fruits, pickled and
salted their meats, and the bats were coming out earlier
and earlier to catch the last of the midges that stung us
so heartily during the day. So, were the bats eating us,
I wondered?

As we climbed higher the air became more exhilarat-
ing, and the streams were ice cold from the snowy
heights above. All this, and the plain but adequate fare
we ate satisfied me well enough, but Dickon was always
grumbling, comparing our food with the comparative luxury he had enjoyed on the caravan routes.

"Nobody asked you to come," I said crossly one day,
when he had been whining all day about not being
allowed extra money to buy some more rice wine.
"You're here because you wanted to be, remember?"

"And you're not being reasonable," he said, dodging
the issue. "A man needs a bit of relaxation now and
again, a sip or two of wine."

"You've already had a sip or four," I said. "And you
said not yesterday that it was piss water, rotgut."

"Depends on the vintage . . ."

"This stuff doesn't have any vintage. They make it all
the year round."

"I only want a nip. Set me up for the evening."

I flung him a coin. "Buy yourself a measure then. But
only a small one, otherwise you won't be fit to go on."

I was right. That afternoon's trek was a complete waste
of time. He swayed from side to side of the road, fell
over twice, and when I went to help him up he made a
grab at me.

"C'mon Summer: gi'e us a kiss!"

I kicked him where it hurt, and when he doubled up pushed him into a ditch and marched on for a half mile without him. By then, as I could see he wasn't following, I retrieved my steps, my temper near at boiling point, especially when I found him still in the ditch, snoring his head off. I was strongly tempted to leave him where he was and travel on alone, but common sense told me I couldn't manage the baggage on my own.

We climbed higher and higher, but the mountains we were aiming for, our last barrier, called on the maps Ky-Lin had explained to me the "Sleeping Giants," still seemed many miles away. Travelling during the day was still pleasant, but the nights were increasingly chill and we needed extra clothes plus the blankets to keep warm, especially if we spent nights in the open. A couple of times we slept under both blankets together, Dickon and I, but his behavior on these occasions worried and annoyed me. On both these times after I had dozed off, I awoke to find his hands where they shouldn't be.

At first I thought he was searching my person for money, but the intimate movement of his hands on my breasts and thighs persuaded me otherwise. I could not believe it was a personal thing, rather that he had been robbed of his usual visits to houses of pleasure, but in any case I found it highly embarrassing.

After all we had travelled together in enforced intimacy for many months, and in all that time, especially with all our differences, there had never been any hint of sexual familiarity. As it was, on both occasions I had turned away as if in my sleep, wrapping myself up tight so there was no way he could attempt anything further.

I tried to enlist Growch's help, but his views on sex being what they were—the more the merrier, whoever or whatever it was—I received little encouragement, until I slanted my argument towards the money I was carrying.

"I don't like him searching me like that when I'm asleep. Just think what would happen if he ran off with all our money!"

Growch knew what money meant: it meant food.

"Right, then. I'll see 'e don' touch you nowheres from now on. Sleep between you both, I will."

Which worked much better, especially as my dog by now smelt so high that Dickon and I slept back-to-back by choice. It was either that or holding our noses all night.

We came to the last village before the snow line of the mountains we planned to cross to our goal. I consulted the best of the maps. It showed a route that wandered away in the lee of the mountains to the east for what looked like a week's journey, before finding a gap into the valley beyond. There was another trail, however. This led almost due north from where we were now and, looking up, I could see, or believed I could see, past a thick stand of coniferous forest, the gap I was seeking, the first in the three-peaked range. This reminded me of the illusion/dream the old man in the market had engendered in me, when I had imagined I was a dragon flying through that very gap.

But when the villagers realized our intent there was an indrawing of breath, a lowering of lids, a shaking of heads.

"What's the matter with them? There's a trail that starts off that way. I can see it leading up to the forest."

Dickon shook his head. "They seem to be afraid of something up there."

"What?"

"How the hell do I know? Look at that old fool in the corner: he's been jabbering away for five minutes now, but I can't understand a word he's saying. Can you?"

"N . . . no. Not exactly. But he's making signs as well." I felt uneasy, not least because the ring on my finger felt uncomfortable, as if it was too tight. I went over to the villager and squatted in front of him watching his dirt-ingrained hands expressing alarm and dismay. Making signs that I didn't understand—oh, what I wouldn't have done for Ky-Lin's comforting presence!—I motioned him to slow down, hoping this would make him more intelligible. It didn't, but one of the brighter of his friends understood what I wanted and came to join us.

It went something like this—all in sign language, whether with hands, eyes, expression, body language, or sheer acting and mime.

Why can't we go that way?

Huge men up there. Giants.

No giants now.

Yes. They also eat people.

Cannibals?

They eat anything. Prefer meat.

Have you seen them?

Heard them howling.

Wolves?

No. Human voice.

How do you know they are human?

When they howl we leave them food at the edge of the forest.

How do you know they aren't animals?

Footprints.

What sort of print?

In snow.

Show me.

And that was the most puzzling of all. They drew in the dirt the outline of a foot, but it was no ordinary one. In general it followed the shape of a human foot, but it was two or three times as large. I drew one smaller, but they rubbed that out and drew an even larger one. What was worse, this foot had eight toes, with sharp long nails, if their drawings were to be believed.

I looked at Dickon. "Superstition?"

"Could be. They've never seen one of these creatures."

"Exactly. And if they've seen some prints in the snow—well, when snow melts so do the prints. Outwards. So a small print would look bigger after an hour or so. Right?"

"Could well be wolves, as you suggested."

"Wrong time of the year for them to be hungry. Shall we chance it? It'd save three or four days' travel. . . ."

"Why not? I'm game if you are."

"Of course!" At least I would have if my ring hadn't kept on insisting that somewhere ahead lay the possibility of danger. But this way would save so many days, and if we were careful . . .

In order to try and reach the gap before nightfall, we set off before dawn. None of the villagers came to see us off. At first it was easy, a clear track leading up towards the forest, which we hoped to skirt to the east. On the fringes we could see where the villagers below had started to clear the wood for fuel, for we came across chippings, a discarded and broken axe, a couple of sleds they used for transporting the wood.

Dickon pointed to one of these. "Why shouldn't we borrow one? It would make carrying all this stuff much easier. Quicker, too. The runners on the underside are obviously meant for snow."

Growch cocked his leg, then thought better of it. "Good for a lift, too, for those poor critturs as 'as short legs . . ."

"We can't just steal it. . . ."

"I said 'borrow,' " said Dickon quickly. "Once we get to the top we can send it back down. The slope'll carry it back."

"All right, we'll haul it unladen till we get to the snow line, to preserve the runners, then we'll load it up."

When we stopped to eat the sun was already high in the sky, and I reckoned we were nearly halfway to the summit. For some reason, although nothing stirred except a couple of eagles taking advantage of the thermals high above, we all felt irritable and uneasy. Dickon kept glancing over his shoulder in the direction of the forest we were skirting, my ring was getting more uncomfortable by the minute, although I reckoned any threat would come from the trees and we were giving them a wide berth. Growch said his mind felt "itchy." I knew exactly what he meant.

We carried on climbing. The forest thinned out to the left of us, and we came across the first patches of snow as the air grew colder. To our left the sun began its western descent and I realized it would be a race for the gap between us and the dark. We stopped briefly for food again, and this time we loaded the sled with everything portable, including Growch.

I looked up. Another couple of hours should do it, and there would be the valley I had dreamed of for so long, the valley that cushioned the fabled Blue Mountain. "Here be Dragons. . . ."

"Let's go," I said. "Let's go!"

Now we were crunching our way through real snow, unmelted all the way through summer, not the slush we had encountered on the lower slopes. The sled slid easily in our wake; we had attached the rope so that we could both pull it. The slope however grew steeper, and now we were bending forward, me at least wishing I had stouter boots: the cold was already striking through the soles and I had hardly any grip, but at least we were nearly there. The thinning forest was behind us and the gap was only some half mile away. The last bit looked the worst; the incline became so steep that it looked as though we should have to crawl on hands and knees.

We took a final breather; less than a half hour should do it. The breath plumed from our nostrils like smoke. Growch's eyebrows, such as they were, were rimed with frost. The sun was near gone, a red ball waiting to slide down the western mountains.

"Right," I said. "One more push should do it. . . . What's the matter?" Dickon was staring at something in the snow just ahead of us. With a sudden look of horror he backed away, his hands held out in front as though he was pushing the sight away from him.

"Look, Summer," he said. "Look there! It was true what they said!"

And there, clear as crystal in hitherto untrodden snow, was the print of an enormous eight-toed foot.

CHAPTER TWENTY-THREE

I clapped my hands to my mouth and stepped back in unconscious repudiation, but there was no denying what I had seen. It was as clear as the ice that lined it, reflecting the last of the red sun so it looked as though the giant that made the print had bled into the snow. Dickon pointed out another print, another and another. They came from just above us and then went away down towards the forest.

I swallowed, hard. Those footprints were just as large and terrifying as the villagers had indicated, and I couldn't begin to imagine the height and breadth of a creature who boasted feet that big. And eight toes . . .

Suddenly the sun was gone, like blowing out half the candles in a room at once, and a cold chill of terror gripped us all. Without realizing it Dickon and I were holding hands and a trembling Growch was actually sitting on my feet, his hackles raised, moaning softly.

"We—we'd better get going." I found I was whispering, although there seemed to be nothing moving in the snow. "It's clear straight up to the gap, and if we . . ."

My voice died away as a hideous ululating howl split the quiet around us, followed by another and another. With one accord we ran, sled forgotten, scrambling on all fours to find a grip. I could feel the hairs rising at the back of my neck and my heart was bounding like a March hare.

The howl came again, and this time it was answered by another—from ahead of us.

We came to a sudden, skidding halt.

"What the devil—!"

And Dickon's prophetic exclamation was answered by a horrific apparition that rose from behind a huge rock to our right. Nearly twice the size of a man, it was covered in fur—brown, black, gray—and its face was a twisted mask of hate, with huge fangs sprouting from its jaw. Slowly, lumberingly, it left the shelter of the rock and, with arms raised, came down the slope towards us, uttering that hideous howl we had heard before.

As one we fled down the slope towards the shelter of the forest, slipping, stumbling, falling, rolling, all thought gone save the urgency of escape, although something deep inside seemed to tell me to stop, not to run, but it was such a tiny voice that my fear drowned it.

Not looking where I was going I crashed into the trunk of a tree, knocking all the breath from my body, and I whooped and coughed with the effort to draw air into my lungs. I was aware of Growch gasping and panting beside me, and the inert form of Dickon a few yards away.

I struggled to my feet to see what had happened to him.

"Come on, Growch, we must get—"

"Too late!" he whimpered. "Look behind you!"

I turned, and found we were surrounded. Not by giants, but by strange, hairy humans holding stone axes and primitive spears. They were no taller than I, slightly hunched, and the hair on their bodies, thick on back and arms, was a reddish-black. Prominent brows and jaws, small eyes and noses, wide mouths with yellow teeth and long, tangled hair were common to all and they were mostly naked, though some of the women had bound their babies to their backs with strips of fur.

These creatures looked at us and chattered to themselves in a series of grunts, sibilants and clicks, and a moment later a couple of them dragged the half-conscious body of Dickon forward and dumped him without ceremony at my feet. He had a bruise the size of an egg on his temple. As I looked down he stirred, put his hand to his head and sat up, opening his eyes.

"Holy Mary, Mother of God!"

But he wasn't looking at the strange creatures who now crowded closer till I could smell the rank odor of their bodies; he was staring back up the hill the way we had come. I followed his pointing finger and gasped. Down the hill came striding the giant we had fled from, swaying from side to side, arms spread—Arms? What beast had four arms? I sank to my knees despairingly, clutching Growch for comfort, for surely the hairy people would have no defense against this hideous apparition.

From the giant came that dreadful wolflike howl again, and to my amazement it was answered with like from the hairy people around us, waving their weapons in the air in greeting with what could only be described as grins on their faces.

I scrambled to my feet, pulled Dickon to his. What the hell was happening? Surely the giant and the hairy people weren't in league with one another? Why didn't they—

Dickon and I gasped together. The giant careening down the hill towards us had been gathering speed in a more and more wild manner and now, suddenly, it broke in two! No, no, all in bits. Two pieces came rolling towards us, another sheared off to the left, one slithered to a stop against a tree—

And the hairy people were laughing, dancing, waving their spears!

"Laugh too," came a tiny voice from somewhere. "It's all a big joke to them. You've been had."

And I only realized just how much when two of the "pieces" came to a stop, unrolled, and became two more of the hairy people, one of them still wearing the misshapen boots that had made such a convincing giant's footstep. The other man went back and retrieved the mask that had so horrified us, plus the long cloak that had so convincingly covered one man riding on another's shoulders.

My heart sank even further as our captors, as they must be thought of now, closed in, pointing at the boots, the mask, the cloak, laughing and jeering and miming our terror, confusion and fear when faced with the "giant."

"Laugh with them," came that tiny voice again. "It's your only chance to get away. . . ."

But I couldn't. I tried; I forced the muscles of my face into what I knew was a hideous rictus, but I knew it only looked threatening, like that of a chattering monkey. I nudged Dickon, tried to make him smile, laugh, speak, do anything, but it was hopeless: he was almost rigid with fear.

One by one our captors fell silent, glanced at each other, at us, scowled: we weren't enjoying their joke. They muttered again, then gestured that we should follow them into the forest. Dickon fell to his knees again. Growch whimpered in my arms, and my ring felt as cold as ice.

"Do as they want," said the little voice in my head. "Don't despair!"

So on top of everything else, I was hearing voices. It must be all my terrified imagination, but the voice sounded so much like my dead-and-gone Ky-Lin that I could have cried. Perhaps it *was* his voice, perhaps his ghost had come back to comfort me. I could feel the tears, warm on my frozen cheeks.

"Help us," I whispered. "Wherever you are . . ."

Our captors hauled Dickon roughly to his feet and jostled us both along a narrow track through the trees. Too soon the last of the light was gone, forest gloom descended, and I had to hold one hand in front of my face to push aside the whippy branches I could hardly see. It was less cold under the trees, and the only sounds were the shush-shush of pine needles under our feet and an occasional grunt or snort from our captors, just like a sounder of swine.

After what seemed like hours, but can only have been minutes, we stumbled into a clearing. Other hairy people came out from the trees: the old ones and young children. About fifty or sixty surrounded us now, pointing, grimacing and, what was much worse, touching us; pulling at our clothes and hair, pinching our cheeks and arms, treating us as though we were strange animals instead of human beings.

I wanted so much to hear that ghosty voice of Ky-Lin's again, but, try as I could, the noise around us drowned all else. The sound of wood being dragged to the glowing pit in the center of the clearing, the hissing of the logs, the snorting grunts of those around us—I should have liked to cover my ears, but daren't put Growch down.

The women arranged a framework of sticks across the fire, and on these were spitted several small animals: squirrels, what looked like rats, a small snake. In baskets at the side were pine nuts, roots, wild herbs and a fungus of some sort. The smell of the cooking meat was hardly appetizing, nor was the sight of the filthy fingers that turned the sticks, poking the flesh now and again to see if it was cooked through.

Hands on our shoulders forced us down to sit a little away from the fire while the men went into a huddle, glancing over at us every now and again and then having some sort of discussion.

I poked Dickon, a rigid figure of fear. "It doesn't look too good, does it? Got any ideas?"

He shook his head, probably not trusting himself to speak, and I remembered what the villagers had intimated: these people were cannibals. I shivered, in spite of the heat from the fire, but the ring on my finger, though cold, didn't convey any threat of imminent danger; for the moment we were safe.

By my side lay one of the "giant's" boots; shifting Growch a little, I picked it up to have a closer look. It

really was rather ingenious. The sole was made of two
bear pads, sewn together, just four claws on each, making
eight in all; the top was ordinary leather, the whole sewn
over a wickerwork frame and padded, so there was just
enough room for a human foot: it must have taken some
practice to walk properly, especially with someone else
perched on one's back.

One of the hairy ones saw me examining the boot,
scowled for a moment, then nudged his fellows and
brought over the other with a grin, miming their walk.
He also brought over the mask for me to examine as well.

Near to it was quite crudely carved, I guessed from
the hollowed stump of a tree, so that it fitted loosely
over the head. The nose was a natural hooked beak of
wood, stained red by some sort of dye, the eyes had been
burnt out and were outlined in yellow. The top of the
mask was covered with hair, real hair, and with a shock
I realized it was human. Of course it could have been
cut from someone's hair within the tribe but I had the
terrible feeling that it came from some more reluctant
source. They showed me the robe as well, and my suspicions were proved right: these were human scalps sewn
together.

I pushed everything away with a sudden surge of revul-
sion, and they laughed as if it were the best joke in the
world. Seeing them then one would have thought them
a happy and harmless people, until one realized that their
secrets would not have been shared if they had any intention of letting us go.

There was a diversion: apparently the meal was ready.
Flat pieces of bark and large leaves were produced and
filled with nuts, roots and fungi. Sticks were snatched
from the fire and fought over, the meat on them charred
on one side, raw on the other.

No one offered us anything.

They ate noisily, licking their fingers before wiping
them on their stomachs, hair, each other, and the women
spat out half-chewed bits to feed to the smallest of their

scrawny brats. Too soon for us the meal was ended; they finished with the last of the unwashed pine nuts, crammed into their mouths so that the black, powdery stain covered their faces and hair, the grease on their skins spreading it still further.

Now they were looking for entertainment—or was it more food? Several of the women were rubbing their stomachs, looking at the men, looking at us. My ring was throbbing again, so cold it felt as though it would burn straight through my finger. I looked around desperately, but we were ringed in on all sides. Suddenly two of the men separated from the rest and came towards us; Dickon and I scrambled to our feet and backed away, a trembling Growch hugged close to my chest.

Dickon was pushed unceremoniously aside and they approached me, great grins on their faces; in the sudden clarity that terror can bring, I noticed how stained their teeth were: fangs for tearing at the front, grinding molars at the back—

One of the men leaned forward, jabbering excitedly—and tried to pluck the terrified Growch from my arms. I had thought they came for me, and was quite prepared to take out my knife and hurt them as much as I could before I was overpowered. But Growch? No, never! Not my little dog spitted over a fire till his hair singed and the blood and fat ran spattering into the fire! I had rather slit his throat myself to spare him the pain and betrayal.

"Get away! Get your filthy hands off!" I was shouting hysterically. "Dickon, for God's sake *do* something! Help me. . . ." Now my knife was in my right hand, Growch still held with my left, and as one man advanced still further I connected with a lucky slash across his arm and he retreated with a grunt, sucking at the blood.

Dickon's voice came to me. "Give them the wretched animal, for Christ's sake! It's him they want. Give us time to escape. . . ."

I couldn't believe my ears! Give up Growch! In sudden anger I turned on Dickon and slashed out at him also, and saw the bright beads of blood spring from a cut across his cheek. Turning, I hit out again at my two attackers, and had the satisfaction of seeing them spring back from the arc of my knife. But now the others behind were closing in and I couldn't deal with them all—

"Help me! Help me!" I didn't realize I was screaming, or to whom, but all of a sudden everything changed.

"Leave this to me!" boomed a voice, and with a burst of firecrackers that would have done justice to a town celebration, into the clearing came bounding a huge creature, an apparition surrounded with light and noise and color and fire.

The hairy tribe scattered in all directions, sparks from the unguarded fire catching at their hair and stinging their bodies. For a moment I thought we had exchanged one horror for another, then I suddenly recognized the creature for who he was, larger now than I had ever seen him—

"Ky-Lin! But how ... What did—"

"Follow me! No questions, just hurry!"

I can't remember much of that frantic dash through the trees, out into the snow and up towards the gap. I do remember finding the sled, Ky-Lin taking the rope between his teeth and dragging us all as hard as he could towards safety. I remember, too, the chill of terror when we heard the howls of pursuit behind us, as the tribe realized Ky-Lin provided no threat and they were losing a source of easy food. Their noise came nearer and nearer, a couple of ill-thrown spears skimmed past our heads, and we were there!

A gap as wide as a door, no more, a glimpse of a valley, more hills and we were through. Ky-Lin loosed the rope and the sled careened faster and faster down a slope of snow towards the valley below.

Now the moon was up, and through the tears of cold in my eyes and the wind whipping my cheeks a scene of beauty spread itself beneath, and there in the midst of it all was a coldly blue shape on the horizon.

"Look, look!" I cried out to Ky-Lin who had been left behind. "It's there, we've found the Blue Mountain—"

The sled veered, skidded, struck something hard and I was lifted into the air. Suddenly everything was upside down, and then my head hit something, lights buzzed through my brain, and everything went black.

PART THREE

CHAPTER TWENTY-FOUR

The first thing I was conscious of was a pleasant smell: sandalwood, beeswax, pine, cedarwood. It reminded me of Ky-Lin. Then, what must have woken me, a dissonance, not unpleasant, of tinkling bells, and a faraway chanting, a deep resonance of a gong. For a moment longer I savored the light warmth of blankets tucked under my chin, then I became aware of a dull throbbing in my head and an unpleasant taste in my mouth.

I opened my eyes and sat up, immediately wishing I hadn't done either.

I closed my eyes and lay down again, but must have groaned, because at once there was a rustle of clothing and a woman was chattering away quietly by my side. Her hands were cool on my forehead; my head was raised and a feeding cup pressed to my lips. The drink was warm and fragrant, tasted of mint and honey and camomile and took away the nasty taste in my mouth. I wasn't about to open my eyes or sit up again, but there was a sort of puzzle that wouldn't go away: where was I, and indeed *who* was I? I couldn't remember a thing, so decided to think about it later. . . .

When I opened my eyes again the room was full of soft lamplight and shadows and I remembered who and what I was, what had happened before, but I had no idea where I lay. My head still hurt, but the pain was lessening. Putting up a languid hand I found a cloth wound tight about my forehead, the rag cool and damp to my touch. The last thing I recalled was riding at a giddy speed on the sled down the mountain, of hitting some obstruction and flying through the air to hit my head on something—it must have been quite a bump for me to feel like this.

Something moved up from the foot of the bed, and a sloppy tongue and hacky breath announced the arrival of my dog.

"Feelin' better? Thought we'd lost you again we did; glad we didn'. Gawd, what a place this is! All corridors, steps, passages . . . 'Nuff to turn a dog dizzy! Don't think much of the nosh, neither. All pap, no gristle, nuffin' to get yer teeth into. Still, most 'portant thing is you're back with us. I said to meself yesterday, I said, if'n she don' wake up soon, I'm—"

"Growch!"

"Yes?"

"Can I speak? Can I ask you a couple of questions?"

" 'Course. Ain't stoppin' you am I? Now then, what d'you wanna know? Don' tell me, let me guess. . . . Where is we? Well, I ain't ezackly sure. It's a sort o' temple, high up in the mountains. Took us near a week to get 'ere, what with you bein' unconscious an' all, but that big beast, 'e pulled the sled wiv you on it all the way. 'Is lordship fancy pants weren't much use, 'e was all for stayin' in the first village we come to but Ky-Lin 'e said no, you needed special treatment and the best nursin'. Must say, though—"

"Growch?"

"Yes?"

"Where are Ky-Lin and Dickon?"

"Well, 'is lordship's next door, snorin' 'is 'ead orf, an' the lady what was tendin' you 'as gone fer a nap. Ain't seen much o' Ky-Lin, seein' 'e's special 'ere. 'E comes an' checks on you, then back 'e goes to them monks. They seem to think a lot o' 'im. 'E's the only one allowed inside their temple." He settled down on the pillow next to me, had a good scratch, licked my ear and continued.

"This place, bein' 'arfway up a 'ill, is sorta built in layers. The temple and the monks' part, they's at the top. This bit, the guests', is next down, then at the bottom is a 'uge courtyard, with goats 'n chickens 'n bees 'n things. All around is workshops—they weave these blankets down there; must say they're the softest I ever come acrost. Come from a goat wiv long hair what they combs. Cooking is done down there, too, an' the washin'. . . . Well, then: look 'oose 'ere!" and he jumped off the bed to greet Ky-Lin.

He seemed to have grown larger and more splendid than ever. His hide and hooves shone with health, his eyes were bright, his colors clear and vibrant. His plumed tail was truly magnificent and his antennae curled and waved like weeds in a stream. Bending over the bed he touched these latter to my head and immediately the dull ache lessened. I flung my arms about his neck in greeting.

"I thought it was you out there in the forest speaking to me—but then I believed I must have been hearing things! How did you come back to us? When I left you on that altar I was convinced you were—you were dead. Are you sure you are real?"

"Of course I'm real, silly one! I never really went away. I was hurt, yes, but we soon heal. A little rest, a word or two from my Master, and I was well enough to follow you. I was sitting in the lining of your jacket most of the time, staying quiet until you needed me."

I hugged him again. "Thank you a million, million times! Thank you for saving us, for bringing me here, for everything. Without you . . ." Words failed me. "But there is just one thing I don't understand."

"And that is?"

"When—when I thought you were dead . . ." I hesitated.

"Yes?" he prompted.

"I said a prayer for you. I said to the Buddha that I thought you had already done enough to go to your Heaven. Why didn't he listen?"

For the first time he looked embarrassed. He looked away, he looked back, his eyes crossed, he shook his head from side to side. Finally he mumbled something I couldn't catch.

"What did you say?"

"I said ... said I was given a choice. My Lord was willing for me to go to rest with Him, or—go back and see it through. I'm afraid that for me there was little choice."

"How wonderful of you to choose the hard way!"

He raised a hoof, looked even more abashed. "No, no, no praise! It was partly selfish. I told you once before that I didn't think I would enjoy eternal peace and rest. Besides, I have grown used to this whole big, imperfect world. I actually enjoy being in it. I shouldn't, you know; it should be renounced, like anything imperfect." His head bobbed again. "My Lord said I was a child still, putting off the moment to go to bed."

The awkward silence was luckily broken by the entrance of Dickon, rubbing sleep from his eyes.

"What's all the noise about? Oh, you're awake at last, Summer. Feeling better? What's the matter? Why are you laughing?"

"What in the world are you wearing?"

"A nightshirt. What's so funny? You're wearing one too. . . ."

I had never seen him look so ridiculous. The high-necked gray garment had short sleeves and was slit down the sides, to end just below his knees, so that his thin, hairy shanks poked out below it, and if he moved incautiously, one caught a glimpse of dimpled backside.

Before I disgraced myself by laughing too much and gave myself a second headache the nursing woman bustled in, dismissing everyone except Growch—who retreated growling under the bed—gave me a bitter draught, blew out all the lamps bar one, tucked me up tight, and I had no alternative but to sink back again into a drugged sleep.

Three days later I was well on the road to recovery. My headache was gone, the cloth on my head had been removed, no more bitter draughts, and I was allowed out of bed to sit by the fire. There was a washroom down the corridor and at last I could have a tub of hot water to bathe in, although I had been sponged down while I was in bed.

Without asking, both Dickon and I had been provided with new clothes, the sort the peasants wore: padded jackets and trousers, with cotton drawers and undershirt and felt slippers.

The first thing I did, after a really good wash, was to check that all my belongings were safe, although Growch assured me that he had "guarded 'em with me life!" All was as he said, though I was surprised to see how much the egg had grown. One evening when Ky-Lin paid a visit, I asked about this.

"All the eggs I have ever seen stay their laying size: it's the chick inside that grows, not the shell. Why is this different?"

"The simple answer is that I don't know, but then I've never had to deal with a dragon's egg before. Obviously they don't behave like other eggs, but I can assure you that there are live cells in there and I can hear them growing."

It was exciting, awesome, and although I knew I should never see what was inside, I desperately wanted to. "Can your antennae see inside?"

"If they could—and I'm not going to try it—I wouldn't tell you. Some things are best left alone." And with that answer I had to be content.

However he did reveal something to me I hadn't suspected, perhaps to take my mind off the question of the egg.

"Have you looked at that piece of crystal lately?"

"The one the captain's wife gave me? No, not recently."

"Then perhaps you should take another look."

"Now?"

"Why not?"

I unwrapped it carefully and laid it on the bed. "There's nothing special about it—oh!" Ky-Lin had rolled it to the end where it caught the light, and now it was as though a rainbow had entered the room. The lamps caught the glass in a hundred, a thousand bands, strips and rays; red, crimson, scarlet, orange, yellow, green, viridian, pine, cobalt, ultramarine, mauve, purple, violet—and colors in between one could only guess at.

"Hold it up," said Ky-Lin. "Let it find the light it has been denied so long. . . ."

I was blinded by color; it was the most wonderful jewel I had ever seen in my life. As I swung it between my fingers the light flashed around the room ever faster, creating a gem within a gem, and we were all patterned with color like strange animals—even Ky-Lin's tail was dimmed.

"What *is* it?"

"Whatever it is, turn it orf!" said Growch. "You talk about *your* 'ead achin'. . . ."

"It is only a crystal," said Ky-Lin. "But beautifully cut. I've never seen a better. Anyone would be delighted to own that."

I was reluctant to put it away, like a child with a toy. I must try it again tomorrow. . . . Tomorrow? Why was I wasting time like this?

"Ky-Lin . . . are we in the right place? Is the Blue Mountain near? Is that really the place of dragons?"

"Legend has it that this is one of the few places on earth where dragons can still be found. The Blue Mountain is a half-day's journey away."

"Then I must go there. Now. Tomorrow." But if this was the place where my dragon-man had headed for, why was it I had no sense of him being near? Surely my love was strong enough to sense his presence, even over a half-day's journey. I couldn't come this far to find I was wasting my time! "Tomorrow," I repeated firmly.

"You may go," said Ky-Lin, "when you are completely recovered. Not before. A week or so."

"But—but I want to go now!"

"At the moment you couldn't walk up a flight of steps, let alone climb a mountain. Come now, be sensible! It has taken months to get so far: surely a few days more won't change the world!"

"I shall be perfectly recovered in far less time than that," I said firmly, although I was fighting a rearguard action, and knew it.

"We shall see," was all he said, but three days later he came for me. Not to climb any mountains, but to speak to one of the monks, the Chief Historian and Keeper of the Scrolls.

I followed him down a narrow, twisting corridor, following the curve of the hill on which the monastery was situated, narrow slit windows giving hair-raising glimpses of the sheer drop below. Once I thought I caught sight of the Blue Mountain itself, but couldn't be sure. Down some steps, up a lot more and then we found ourselves in a small chamber, scarce six feet by six.

Facing us was an intricately carved grille, decorated with red enamel and gold paint. Beside the grille was a small brass gong and a shallow wooden bowl with a red leather handle. The silence lay as thick as last year's dust.

"Strike the gong once," whispered Ky-Lin. (It was a room for whispering). "Wait a count of five and strike it twice, then once again."

"What is this—some sort of secret society?"

"Each monk has his own call; if you do it any differently you may get the Chief Architect, the Cloth Master, the Master of Intercession or even the Reader of the Weather. Every monk is trained to be an expert in one thing or another."

I wondered if there was a Master of Sewers and Latrines. . . ."

"Go on!"

I tiptoed to the gong—there was no need; the stone muffled even our whispers—struck it once, then stepped back hastily; it was far louder than I had expected.

"It won't bite," said Ky-Lin.

I struck the gong twice more, for a moment waited and struck it once again. As the last echoes died away, the silence seemed thicker than ever. Then came a faint creak, the distant sound of chanting, another creak, and the chant dying away. Another, more comforting sound; the flap, flap of sandals, a wheezy breath, a cough. Almost immediately a shadow formed behind the grille, a mere shift of light and shadow, and a thin high voice asked a question.

Ky-Lin answered, then turned to me. "If anyone knows of the dragons, he will. He has consented to speak to you through me. He is not allowed to speak to a woman directly. I will translate for you both. What is it you wish me to ask him?"

"Ask him how recently there were dragons here?"

Apparently the answer took some time, but eventually Ky-Lin translated. "He says it is unclear. There has been certain activity reported around the Blue Mountain during the last fifteen months, but these reports have not yet been substantiated."

"What sort of activity?"

"Strange lights, odd noises, a smell of cinders, an unexplained grass fire," he translated.

"And has it always been a tradition that dragons lived here?"

Apparently the records of the monastery only went back the three hundred years since its inception. At that time there was no direct mention of dragons, only a passing reference to the fact that the locals believed the Blue Mountain was "haunted." One hundred years later, when the monks had consolidated and had time on their hands, there were several references to a "Blue Monster," which had been reported many years back ravaging the crops in a particularly bad year for harvest. This particular monster apparently flew in the sky and breathed flame and smoke. There were no other sightings until another year of drought, when the creature was apparently spotted "drinking a river dry." Another time it was seen at night circling the valley, beating wings that "caused a great draught to blow the roofs off several houses, and the populace to take their children and hide them." Further sightings were reported over the years, but nothing recent.

"Is there nothing about dragons over the past two years?"

"He says not."

"Nothing at all out of the ordinary? However unlikely it might seem?"

"The Master has much patience, girl, but even I can see it is wearing a little thin. . . . However, I am sure he will give us a recital of every unusual or unexplained event that has come to his attention over the last couple of years, if I ask him."

Triplets, all of whom survived; a two-headed calf that didn't; a fish caught in the river with another fish in its belly; a plague of red ants; an albino child; another born with a full set of teeth; a rogue tiger carrying off villagers in the foothills to the north; rumors of a great battle to the east; the sudden appearance and disappearance of a stranger borne on a great wind; death of the oldest monk at the age on one hundred and twenty—

"Wait!" I said. "The stranger: does he know any more?"

Ky-Lin made his query, received his answer.

"Well?" I asked, for a tiny hope had started to flutter in my breast and Ky-Lin was looking puzzled.

"It seems . . ." He hesitated. "It seems all this happened in a village to the north of here, many miles away, and a report was brought in by visiting monks. There is doubt as to its authenticity as the only witnesses were children, yet there is no doubt that some unnatural phenomenon took place, for damage was done to buildings and many heard a strange noise. The children, a six-year-old boy and his three-year-old sister, went out early one morning to relieve themselves and suddenly there was a great wind and a man in a black cloak was standing by them. The children said he looked angry with himself, but then he laughed and spoke to them, but they don't remember what he said. They saw him run off down the street, then came the fierce wind again and they thought they saw a great bird in the sky."

I remembered a dark man in a black cloak, a man with a hawk nose, piercing yellow eyes and a mouth that could be either cruel or tender—

"That must have been Jasper!" I said excitedly. "He had to spend part of his life in human guise because I kissed him! Ask him—"

"Whoever—or whatever—it was, it won't be there now," said Ky-Lin firmly. "And you may have one more question and that's it. You are here on sufferance, remember? Now, what do you want to ask?"

I thought for a moment. "Ask him how long ago this took place."

"Do you have the coins I asked you to bring?" I nodded. "Then when we receive our answer, bow once, place the coins in that bowl and push it under the grille. Then step back and bow again. The monks need the money, you needed the information, and the bows are common courtesy here."

"What did he say?" I pestered Ky-Lin as we walked back down the winding passage.

"He said that all this took place sometime during the winter before last, but the exact month is not known."

"But that means it could have been my dragon-man! He left me at the Place of Stones at the beginning of November and 'during the winter' could be anytime in the next four months!"

"Patience! There is absolutely nothing to indicate that he is here."

"But I've got to find out! And if you won't take me to the Blue Mountain, I'll go alone!"

CHAPTER TWENTY-FIVE

"The one thing Ky-Lins can't do," said Ky-Lin firmly, "is fly. Ky-Lins can change their size, their substance, their colors. They can run like the wind, go without food and drink, speak any language. They can produce Sleepy Dust, firecrackers and colored smoke. They also possess certain healing properties, but fly they don't!"

We were standing at the foot of the so-called Blue Mountain. So-called because close to it didn't look blue at all. It was a sort of blackish cindery gray, rising steeply from the valley floor. Conical in shape, it was almost entirely bare of vegetation, and I was quite ready to believe it was the core of an extinct volcano. It smelled rather like the puff of air you sometimes get from a long-dead fireplace.

Ky-Lin had explained not once but twice why it looked blue at a distance, but I had become more than a little confused with the principles of distance, air, refraction (whatever that was), and vapor.

"Well," said Growch. "It's as plain as me nuts as we can't climb that. We ain't ruddy spiders."

Now Growch wasn't supposed to be here at all. Three days after Ky-Lin had questioned the monk, he had come to me suggesting we visit the Blue Mountain the very next day. "I can carry you," he had said, "but even with what speed I can make it will take several hours. I suggest, therefore, that we set off before light, in order to be back before nightfall. I shall wake you when I am ready, and shall ask one of the cooks to make you up a parcel of rice cakes and honey, and a skin of water."

"Don' eat 'unny," said Growch. "You knows I don'. Bit o' cheese'll do. An' a bone."

"You're not coming," I said firmly. "This is my journey. After all," I added placatingly, as his shaggy brows drew down in a dreadful frown, "this is only a reconnaissance. I just want to know what's there."

"Never!" he said. "Not never no-how. You ain't goin' nowhere without you take me. You'd never 'ave got this far without me, and you knows it. Why d'you think I left the comfort o' that merchant's 'ouse to go with you? Not to be left behin', and that's flat! I bin with you since the day after yer Ma died an' you left 'ome, ain't I? An' if'n you even tries to go without me I'll bark the place down, that I will!"

Blackmail, that was what it had come down to, so he had come too, and to my secret satisfaction had hated every moment of Ky-Lin's erratic bounding from stone to rock to pebble, as he had borne us on his back across the valley.

So had I, if it came to that, but there's nothing like sharing one's woes, is there?

We had left well before dawn, Dickon unaware and asleep, and were let out through the gates of the courtyard by a half-awake porter. We had followed the twisting track down to the village below, and once on level ground I had climbed on Ky-Lin's back, taken Growch up in front of me and started the long journey across the valley floor.

At first, along the level bare tracks, it was easy, Ky-Lin skimming smooth and steady with scarce a jolt to disturb us, but when the trail petered out we had a much more adventurous journey. At first I couldn't understand why Ky-Lin was bounding about like an overgrown and demented grasshopper, but then I remembered his devotion to not even spoiling a blade of grass or errant ant.

Obviously there must have been many such in our path, for we jigged and jagged our way across the plain till the breath was near knocked out of me.

"Sorry," said Ky-Lin at one point. "It's not all (bounce) that easy (leap) by the last light (swerve) of the (crunch) moon, but once the sun comes up (hop) it should be better." Bump.

I sure hoped so.

It was a relief to us all when we finally arrived at the foot of the mountain. Sliding off Ky-Lin's back I collapsed on the ground, dropping Growch as I did so, and we spent the next couple of minutes shaking ourselves together. We looked up at the mountain; smooth rock all the way to the top, no bushes, shrubs, trees, grass or foot- or hand-holds that I could see. Far, far above us was what could be a ledge of some sort and a hole in the rock, but it was too high up to see clearly.

"Now what?"

"Breakfast," said Ky-Lin, "and then I will scout around the base of the mountain."

He was gone about an hour, and appeared from the opposite direction.

"What did you find?"

"Better news, I think. Around the other side, to the south where the sun shines strong, there has been a certain amount of erosion over the years. The rocks are porous, and I think there is a way up, a narrow way that follows a crack in the rock. Up you get, and we'll take a look."

Perhaps because he had been this way before, our ride this time was easier, and the other side of the mountain provided a surprise. As Ky-Lin had said this side faced due south, and perhaps because of this the lower slopes were covered with vegetation—young pines and firs at the foot, and bushes, grass and scrub to about a third of the way up before it reverted back to bare rock. There were also numerous cracks, fissures and gullies worn away by rain, wind and sun.

I saw what I thought were several promising paths, but Ky-Lin ignored all these and led us about halfway round the southern side before stopping.

"Here we are: take a look."

I couldn't see anything, but Growch's eyes were sharper than mine.

"I sees it. Bit of a scramble, then there's a crack as goes roun' like a pig's tail an' outa sight roun' the other side."

"Does it go all the way up to that ledge we saw?"

"Seems to," said Ky-Lin. "We'll have to try it. It's the only way I can see to get us there."

After the first "scramble" as Growch had put it, which was a hands and knees job, the first part of the narrow path seemed easy enough. We were gradually working our way round to the westward, and when I looked down the first time the plain still looked only a jump away, but by the time we were facing northwest it looked a giddy mile away, although we could only have been a thousand feet up. Now the path became more difficult. It narrowed, and some of the footholds were crumbling away; at one point, when I paused for a moment's rest and gazed down again, I felt so dizzy I had to shut my eyes and cling to the rock, too paralyzed to move another step.

"C'mon, 'fraidy cat!" It was Growch's ultimate insult. "If'n I can do it, so can you!"

I chanced one open eye, and there he was, perched on a rock some three feet above me. As I watched he leapt down beside me and then up again.

"Up you comes!"

Then Ky-Lin was beside me. "I told you not to look down. Come on, I'll give you a lift up to the next bit. Don't let us down now, girl: there's only a short way to go."

And, incredibly, he was right. With a leap of anticipation I saw the ledge we were heading for not a hundred yards away, and five minutes later we were there.

It was obvious that the ledge was part natural, part

engineered. The natural rock jutted out like a platform, perhaps six feet, but its inner side had been painstakingly excavated to a depth of about ten feet further and smoothed down, making a natural stage some fifteen feet deep and the same wide. Stage? What about a landing strip for a dragon? Especially as, at the back, leading into the heart of the mountain was a dark, yawning passage.

Suddenly the strange, cindery smell was much stronger and I wanted to gag, so much so that I turned away and looked across the plain to where the faraway mountains raised their snowcapped heads. And with the sight came a scent from the distance, a hint of snow, thyme, ice, pine, a perfume to dispel the one that had so disturbed me.

Ky-Lin lay down with a sigh, hooves tucked under. "Well, we're here. Are you going in?"

I stared at him. "Aren't you coming?"

He shook his head. "Dragons are not—not within my commitments. It's like . . ." He struggled for an explanation. "It's like two different elements. The difference between a fish and a bird. Our boundaries just don't cross. I have my magic, they have theirs."

I thought of flying fish, of sea-diving eagles; for a moment at least they tried different elements. But Ky-Lin was adamant.

"This is your adventure, girl. I brought you here, I can take you back, but in there I cannot help you."

For a moment I hesitated. The passage looked dark and forbidding. I wished I had had the forethought to bring some form of illumination. I looked at Growch.

"You coming?"

His ears were down, his tail between his legs. " 'Course . . ." Not very convincing.

"Come on then: this is what I came for."

"What *you* came for! Orl right. Lead on. . . ."

But I didn't want to either. I closed my eyes, just to remind myself why I was here. The maps had shown a Blue Mountain, and I had no other lead to where my dragon-man had gone; he was the reason I had travelled so many miles, to try and find the one who had so roused my body and my heart to the realization that no one else but he would do. A dragon-kiss, that was why I was here.

I tried to recall the magic of that moment; the fear, the joy, the exhilaration of that moment nearly two years ago, when I had tasted what love really meant—but like all memories and the best dreams the edges were blunted by time, the sharpness rubbed off by recollection. However, this was why I was here, so how could I fail at the last moment, just because I was scared of a dark passage?

"You'll wait, Ky-Lin?"

"Of course. Just take it slow and easy. I don't believe there will be anything to fear except yourselves."

I peered down the tunnel. "It's very dark. . . ."

"You want a light? You should have reminded me humans cannot see in the dark like us. Here, pluck some hairs from the tip of my tail. Go on, it won't hurt you."

It might hurt him, though. I chose a small handful and gave a gentle tug; it stayed where it was.

"It won't hurt me either," said Ky-Lin. "As I say, I'm not a human."

I tugged harder and *pop!*—out they came, immediately fusing together into a minitorch that burned with a brilliant white light. I nearly dropped it.

"That won't hurt you either," said Ky-Lin. "You can even put your finger in the flame. It's really an illusion, like my firecrackers."

"How long will it last?"

"As long as you need it. Now, off you go: you're wasting time again."

Holding the torch high I stepped into the tunnel, Growch's wet nose nudging my ankles. Now that we had a light he didn't seem so reluctant. Step by step, my free hand against the tunnel wall to keep me steady, I stumbled along—stumbled because the way was littered with small stones, and even as we walked other stones and pebbles detached themselves from the roof and walls to complicate our passage.

At first the tunnel—some six feet wide—went straight, and if I glanced behind I could see the comforting daylight behind me. Then it kinked sharply to the left, to the right and to the left again, till the only light we had I held in my hand, except for a faint illumination I could not trace to its source. It was very still; the air smelled of rotten eggs and cinders, and it was strangely warm.

We seemed to have been travelling into the heart of the mountain for what seemed ages but could only have been a cautious five minutes, when suddenly the tunnel widened into a huge cavern. It was so wide and high that, even with the brilliance of Ky-Lin's torch, we couldn't see the roof or the far walls.

Two things I noticed at once: both the smell and the heat were suddenly increased, and as far as the latter was concerned it was like walking from winter into spring. The heat seemed to be coming from somewhere beneath our feet, as a hearthstone will keep the warmth long after the fire itself is out. It increased as we advanced further into the cavern, until we were halted by a great fissure that stretched from one side to the other, effectively blocking our way to the other side. It was from this great crack that the heat and the smell came.

Cautiously I peered over the edge, down into darkness so deep it was almost a color on its own. Up came a waft of hot air; Ky-Lin had said this was the cone of an extinct volcano, but there was certainly something down there still. No noise, however; no grumbling and bubbling, so perhaps I was mistaken.

I stepped back and held the torch as high as I could once more. It was like being in a huge cathedral, ribs and buttresses of rock rearing up into shadow. On the other side of the fissure, to add to the illusion, huge lumps of stone could well be mistaken for effigies of long-dead knights. But giant knights these, in fact the shadows thrown by the torch gave these effigies of stone less than human characteristics: heads and claws and scaly backs.

"There's a sorta bridge here," Growch grumbled. It wasn't the sort of place to be too audible.

A thin arch of stone spanned the chasm; perhaps a couple of feet wide, it looked both daunting and insubstantial, and the thought of what might lie below was more than enough to make me decide not to chance it. Besides, I persuaded myself, there was nothing over there to look at, only misshapen lumps of rock and, now I noticed for the first time, some irregularly spaced heaps of pebbles, the sort of heaps a child might make while playing.

I felt terribly let down. All that travelling, the building up of anticipation, the hard times, the dangerous ones: was it all to lead to an empty, hot cavern scattered with stones and smelling of cinders? And where, oh where was Jasper? Where was my wonderful man-dragon? How could the maps, the legends, my own intuition, all be so wrong?

In sudden frustration and anguish I called out his name. "Jasper! Jasper! Where are you?" but the echoes engendered by my voice magnified his name into a frightening "Boom! boom! boom!" that bounced off the rocks, hissing on the sibilant, popping on the plosive, till I felt as if I had been hurled headlong into a thunderstorm.

Terrified, I clapped my hands to my ears, dropping the torch, but to add to the din Growch started yelping in fear and the noise was so dreadful it almost seemed as if the stones themselves were adding to the clamor. To add to the confusion the fallen torch was now pointing directly across at the misshapen rocks and I definitely saw one move—

That did it. I snatched up the torch, and with one accord Growch and I headed for the tunnel and fled as if the Devil himself were after us, never mind stones and stumbles, emerging out onto the ledge again with a speed that nearly had us over the edge.

"Well," asked Ky-Lin, comfortingly matter-of-fact. "Was it worth the climb?"

Out it all came, my disappointment, the way we had almost scared ourselves to death, the sheer empty futility of it all.

"I had thought it would be so different," I finished miserably. "Just great big rocks and heaps of pebbles."

"What did you expect?" he asked mildly. "A welcoming committee? Besides, rocks are rocks are rocks, you know. . . ."

I could have done without his homespun philosophy right then, especially as I didn't understand what he was getting at, and nearly told him so. Instead we wended our way down the mountain again and endured another bumpy ride, and it was well past dark when we arrived back at the monastery.

And the last person in the world I wanted to face was Dickon, but there he was, near hysterical.

"Where the hell do you think you've been? You've been missing all day! What on earth time is this to return?"

"Oh shut up, Dickon," I said wearily. I was exhausted, bumped, bruised, fed up and near to tears. "I'm tired. I want a bath and I want to go to bed. I'll tell you all about it in the morning."

"I know what it is: you went off on your own to find the treasure!"

"How many times do I have to tell you?" I yelled back. "There is no bloody treasure! There never was!"

"Oh, yes?" he sneered. "That's what you keep on saying, isn't it? Well, let me tell you this; nothing you say will ever convince me that you dragged us all this way for nothing—"

"Us? You mean you! Who dragged you? You insisted on coming. Each time we tried to go on alone, you insisted on following. You left the caravan to follow us, *you* travelled up the Silk River to find us, *you* tracked us across the bog—"

He evaded that. "But where did you go today, then?"

"Look," I said. "If you will leave me in peace right now, I have already told you I'll explain it all in the morning."

"Promise?"

"I said so."

"I can trust you?"

"It's your only choice." I shrugged. "If you believe I am going to lie, I can do it as well now as tomorrow. Think about it. Goodnight."

But even after a welcome soak and a bowl of chicken and egg soup, and a bed that welcomed like coming home, I could not sleep. I nodded off for an hour or so, then woke to toss and turn. I was too hot, too cold, itchy, uncomfortable. The longer I tried to sleep, the worse it became. I dozed again, with dream-starts that melted one into another. One moment the once-fat Summer fled an imagined horror, the next a huge moon was shining too bright on my face; now great bats chased across the sky, their wings obscuring the same moon. I woke fretful and pushed a too-heavy Growch away. I rolled down a steep mountain to escape the pursuing flames, a sudden wind rattled the shutters and I opened my eyes to see the oil lamp guttering. It must have been about three in the morning.

Growch stretched and yawned. "You goin' ter tell 'im where we went?"

"What choice have I? And what does it matter anyway?"

And I burst into useless tears.

CHAPTER TWENTY-SIX

About two hours later I had had enough. Although it was still full dark I disturbed Growch again as I flung aside the blankets, donned my father's cloak and stepped outside onto the narrow balcony that served both my room and Dickon's.

Although it was October, the night was still comparatively warm and the stone of the balustrade under my fingers was no colder than the air. Below was a set of steps leading down to a small, ornamental garden, no bigger than ten feet by ten, facing south. I had sat there during the day a couple of times, on one of the two stone benches, amid pots of exotic plants, ivies, and those tiny stunted trees so beloved by the people of this land. Pines, firs, even cherry trees were bound and twisted into grotesque shapes no higher than my hand, yet it is said that they were as much as one hundred years old!

I wondered vaguely if it hurt them to be twisted so unnaturally, and whether it would be a kindness to dig them all up secretly and replant them in the freedom of unrestricted soil many miles away. Or were they so used to their pot-bound existence that they would perish without special nurturing?

The stars had nearly all gone to bed, those left pale with tiredness, but the waxing moon still held a sullen glow as it balanced on the tips of the faraway mountains. It was the color of watered blood, the warts and scars of its face showing up like plague spots. A faint breeze touched my cheek; false dawn would come with the going down of the moon. As I watched I could almost imagine it starting to slide down out of sight. My breathing slowed: I was in tune with the speed of the heavens.

Then, just as the jaws of the mountains gaped to swallow the moon, there came a lightening of the sky in the east. False dawn had turned everything dark gray, and somewhere a sleepy bird woke for an instant, tried a trill and fell silent once more.

And suddenly, like a stifling blanket being pulled off my head, came a lifting of both mind and spirit. I felt so different I could have cried out with the relief. But what had brought all this about? I gazed around at the fading stars, the sinking moon, a lightening in the sky to the east—no, it was none of these.

Then I looked back at the nearly gone moon and realized there was something different about the marks on its face. It was there, then it disappeared. I rubbed my eyes, but when I looked again the moon had slid away and so had the strange mark I thought—I imagined?—I had seen.

I wouldn't, couldn't allow hope to rise once more, only to be dashed. And yet . . .

I went back to bed and slept until midday.

And so, in the afternoon when Dickon again tried to question me about yesterday's activities I told him what we had done almost indifferently, as though it didn't really matter anymore. And at that moment it didn't.

"So you see we just went to look at the place the legends say the dragons live in, but after all that there was nothing there; nothing except an extinct volcano and heaps of rocks and stones, that is."

"Why didn't you let me come?"

"Ky-Lin carried us: he couldn't have managed you as well."

"I should like to have seen it. There might have been something you missed."

"Go see for yourself, then," I said recklessly, and described how he could climb up to the cavern. "But I tell you, it's a waste of time!"

"Then if there was nothing, and you didn't find this friend you told me about, why don't you just pack up now and go back to your tame merchant boyfriend?"

"Here's as good a place as any to overwinter."

"What about money?"

I shrugged. "I offered you some once. I still have it. I might even do a little trading myself. And you: what are you going to do with yourself now your journey is over?"

He looked aghast. "But—I understood we were together in this! I haven't come all this way just to be cast aside like an odd glove. I've got no capital! If you decide to trade, we trade together. What do you really know about buying and selling? Why, you can't even communicate with these people without that colored freak at your heels. . . ." He had always been jealous of Ky-Lin. "At least I have been learning the language in my spare time. You wouldn't last five minutes without me and you know it!"

"Well I shall have to try, shan't I? Don't worry, I shall manage. I shall stay around here for a while, and I shall stay alone. Apart from Growch, of course."

I felt mean, but somehow knew I had to shed him. I knew I had to be on my own, that whatever pass I had come to in my life, whatever awaited me, I had to meet it alone, free of the threat that someone like Dickon posed. No, not "someone like": it was the person himself I had to be free of. He had always made me feel uneasy, that was why I had tried so hard so many times to go ahead without him. And had failed. He was not evil, most people would just see him as a nuisance, and wonder why I had tried so hard to be rid of him. I couldn't explain it, even now: it was just something that was part of him that one day would do me great hurt, of that I was sure. It was nothing of which he was aware either, just as a straight man will not glance back to see he has a crooked shadow. . . .

I made one last try.

"My offer of the money still stands." I'd manage somehow.

"You can keep your ten pieces of gold—or were they thirty pieces of silver?" And he slammed out; as a parting shot it wasn't bad at all.

For the next hour I made a full inventory of my possessions. It was time I moved from the monastery, now I was fully recovered. I would try to rent a couple of rooms in the village below, rather than presume too much on the hospitality of the monks.

There wasn't much to take with me. A few well-worn clothes, sewing kit, leather for patching, monthly cloths, comb; my journal, writing materials and maps; a cooking pot, spoons, mug, and sharp knife; a bag or two of herbs. With a blanket to wrap it all in and my father's cloak, that was about it. Except, of course, for my money belt, in which I still had a little coinage from our performing days, Suleiman's gold, and the assorted coins from my father's dowry to me.

Lastly there were my special treasures: the Waystone, the beautiful crystal gem and, last but first as well, the dragon's egg. I took it out now and looked at it: even since the last time I had done this it seemed to have grown. I cradled it in my hands, marvelling at its perfect symmetry and the way the light caught the speckles that glinted like granite on its surface. I remembered what both my long-ago Wimperling and Ky-Lin had said about the hundred years or so of incubation it needed before hatching, and was sad I should never see what it contained; I should have to find a suitable place to leave it soon, for it needed quiet and rest, to develop as it should.

There were three or four hours to go until dark, so Growch and I hitched a ride taking woollen cloth from the monastery down to the village, but we hadn't gone far down the narrow, twisty track when Growch announced that we were being followed.

"Who is it?" I asked, peering back up the track. I could see nothing.

" 'Is lordship. 'Oo else?"

"Hell and damnation! Why can't he leave us alone?"

"Wanna lose 'im?"

"Of course."

"Then when we gets to the first 'ouses, jump off quick an' follow me, sharpish."

Once on foot, I realized just how well Growch had used his time when he was off "exploring," as he put it. No doubt he had been in search of his "fluffy bums," but he had learnt the village like a cartographer.

He led me a swift left turn down a side alley, turned right into a courtyard and straight out again through someone's (luckily unoccupied) kitchen, across another street, into a laundry and out again, ducking under wet clothes; two sharp lefts, three rights and then helter-skelter up some steps, down others and into a stuffy little room, greasy with the smell of frying pork and chicken.

Growch trotted up to the cook, who had obviously met him before, because he aimed a halfhearted blow with his skillet, then fished out a pig's foot.

"C'mon," said Growch through the gristle. "Out the back."

This led out onto a street where the unoccupied ladies of the town held their nightly "entertainments." Everything was now closed, shuttered and barred, and backed out onto some unattractive garbage heaps, but I could hear awakening chatter behind the closed doors. Growch went over to inspect the rubbish, but I called him sharply back.

"That's enough! You'll be sick. . . ."

" 'Ow often you seen me sick?" It was a rhetorical question, and he knew it.

"Where now?" I asked, changing the subject.

" 'E's a'ead o' us now. Let's see what 'es up to. I'll scout, you follow close."

So we crept along the irregular streets, stepping in and out of afternoon-going-on-evening shadows, passing the elderly taking patches of sun, children playing primitive games with colored squares of baked clay, or chasing each other in the eternal game of tag. I ducked under lines of washing, stepped around rubbish, avoided the throwing out of slops. There seemed no system or plan to the village; it had just grown. Every now and then we passed through little squares, apparently there just because the houses had been built facing one another. Several lanes led nowhere.

Suddenly I heard Dickon's voice. He seemed to be involved in some sort of altercation and, rounding a corner, there he was, arguing with a couple of villagers over a tatty-looking horse. From the look of it he wanted to "borrow" the horse against future payment, but they were having none of it.

I ducked back into the shadows, but he had seen me. All that rushing around with Growch for nothing, but perhaps after all it had only been an excuse on the dog's part to pick up a snack or two. He wouldn't admit it if it was.

"Hey, Summer! Come here a minute. . . ." Dickon led me aside. "Look here. I've been thinking about what you said earlier: the parting of the ways and all that stuff. Well, I've decided to do something about it." He stood back and folded his arms. "I think it would be best if I took off for a few days, before the winter sets in. I could travel between the villages, see what opportunities there are for trade, check on what goods they are short of, that sort of thing. What do they import now? Rice, salt, oil, metals; those are taken care of, but there must be other commodities they could do with. Why, if I sat down and worked it all out I bet I could do substantial undercutting of the other traders."

"Very commendable," I said. Why was it I didn't believe him?

"Well, what do you say? I was just bargaining with these fellows for the loan of their horse for a few days, but they obviously want cash down. Now, if you want me to make a life of my own—if you still insist you don't want to come in with me, which is the most sensible thing to do, let's face it—then you can't deny me this chance. I just need a few coins to hire the horse and kit myself out—"

"How much?" At least it meant he would be out from under my feet for a few days.

He named a sum, but I shook my head. "Too much. I'll talk to them, or try to. . . ."

"No, no, no. No need. I'll do my own bargaining. Probably bring them down by half . . ."

Which meant he had been trying to con me out of some extra for himself. Apparently the men were satisfied with his revised offer, and I paid out a few coins from my money belt after they had shown us where the horse was stabled and included the hire of saddle and bridle.

We started back up the steep track to the monastery together, hoping for a lift on the way, but quite prepared to walk, though Growch would grumble long before the top.

"I suppose you were in the village looking for lodgings," said Dickon carelessly, when we had walked for about five minutes. "Any luck?"

"Not yet," I answered, equally carelessly. "Plenty of time."

"Oh. Yes, of course. Well you might as well wait now until I get back and I can give you a hand shifting your gear."

"There's not much to carry. Anyway, Ky-Lin can help me."

"How?"

"He can do the bargaining. Don't worry, just take your time. I'll be fine."

He hesitated. "In that case—I'll need a bit more money. For provisions."

I gave him a couple of coins. "That should be enough for some cooked rice and dried fruit."

He inspected the coins. "Not very generous, are you?"

"We've managed on less."

Just then we heard the rattle of the little wagon that carried goat milk down from the monastery twice a day coming up behind us, so we rode the rest of the way.

That he was determined on going somewhere there was no doubt; that night he was packed up well before bedtime, and had already arranged a lift down to the village before cockcrow.

Once again I couldn't sleep. Once again I went out onto the balcony, once again gazed out at the waxing moon. Had it been just my imagination that had showed me a fleeting shadow across that glowing surface? Was my sudden change of spirits due to no more than an illusion? And then, just as the moon touched the tip of the mountains I saw it again! No bigger than a distant leaf in autumn, it drifted across the face of the moon. I was almost certain now. Almost . . .

My heart thudding, not even bothering to throw a cloak over the nightshirt I wore, I ran down to the little garden below, my hands grasping the balustrade so hard they hurt. But there was nothing there, nothing.

Nothing other than the whisper of air across my cheek as though great wings were beating far above.

I waited and waited, but it seemed that was that. Despondently I trailed back to bed, and was just dozing off when there came a sudden rattling crash. It seemed to come from the direction of Dickon's room. He wasn't sleepwalking, was he? Or perhaps he had decided to get up extra early so as not to miss his lift to the village. Once again I hurried out onto the balcony; now the noise appeared to be coming from the little garden. The stupid boy hadn't fallen down the steps, had he?

"What the devil do you think you are doing, Dickon?
Some of us are trying to sleep. . . ."

"Some of us can't sleep," came a voice from below.
"And who the hell is Dickon? Not that stupid boy who
stole your money all that long time ago, surely?"

CHAPTER TWENTY-SEVEN

"Wimperling!" I called out joyously.

But no, it wasn't my little winged pig, the one who had flown me to safety all that long time ago, because he wasn't a pig at all, was he? He had almost broken my heart when he had burst to smithereens at my third kiss and left only a tiny piece of shrivelled hide that even now I wore in the pouch around my neck.

"Summer? Somerdai ... my Talitha. Come here, my dear. Let me see you!"

A man, a tall man dressed in the colors of the night, was leaning on the balustrade in the little garden. I knew who it was although I couldn't see his face, of course I did, but was I still asleep and dreaming?

"Come on down! It's been a long time...."

And many, many wearisome miles. Heat, cold, exhaustion, near starvation, danger; and my imaginings of it had not been at all like this, a hidden-faced stranger who lolled against a balustrade and called my name as though we had only parted yesterday. The memory that had sustained me had been of a snatched embrace, a burning kiss, a wrenching away. Quick, violent, fraught with emotion for both of us.

"Do I have to come up there and fetch you?" It wasn't a soft, warm voice like my blind knight had used in his seducing mood, nor the comfortable town-burr of the merchant, Matthew Spicer; it had a harsh, nasal quality, a sort of scraping reluctance for the words to form. A disturbing voice, a compelling one, but not necessarily a very nice one.

"No," I said. "I'm coming down."

And slowly, almost reluctantly, I moved down the steps till I stood on the bottom one, clutching the neck of my nightshirt as if it could be the one gesture that kept me from being stripped naked.

"You're thinner," said the voice. "And your hair is shorter. But your eyes are just the same; great big wondering eyes, mirrors of your soul. Why don't you come nearer? Are you afraid?"

"I—I don't know. I don't remember . . . I didn't think—"

"If you don't know, remember, think—then why are you here?" The voice was gentler now, as if it was getting more used to human speech, and there was even a hint of amused tenderness. "And why don't you use my human name?"

Jasper. Master of Many Treasures. The dragon-man, man-dragon I had travelled half the known world to find. And yet I couldn't even use his name. Why? I was frightened, shy, now uncertain of those feelings I had been so certain of before. Or thought I had. Even while I cursed myself for my stupidity I could feel the tears welling up in my eyes, spilling down my cheeks, blurring my vision, till the figure before me wavered and dissolved.

Something touched my face, and the corner of a cloak caught the tears as they fell, absorbed them as they coursed down my cheeks, wiped my nose.

"Blow . . . That's better! Am I so terrifying? Why you're trembling. . . . Here, wrap my cloak around you. There, isn't that better?"

As he was still wearing the cloak himself—yes, it was. Suddenly, very much better. But he didn't press it; he had one arm round my shoulders now and with the other hand he lifted my chin, but we were still inches away from a proper embrace. Physically, that is; emotionally, as far as he was concerned, I could see it was miles.

"Open your eyes: look at me! I don't bite."

"Dragons do," I said, still feebly resisting the temptations of his sudden nearness.

"I'm not a dragon all the time. I've learnt a lot in the time we've been apart, including how to keep my two selves separate—usually. I make mistakes, of course—and I still find it difficult to land on narrow balconies at night, as no doubt you heard. . . ."

"Have you been a dragon all the time till now?"

"Mostly, but not all. So now I am owed a little mantime."

"Three months in every year," I said, remembering.

"And all because you kissed a rather ugly little pig three times—"

"You weren't ugly! I mean the Wimperling wasn't! You—he—wasn't exactly beautiful, I suppose, but very endearing."

"More than me, I suppose! Perhaps I'd better reverse the process."

"You can't, can you?" Forgetting to be shy I opened my eyes properly and looked up at him.

It wasn't fair: I had forgotten just how handsome he was. The dim light threw half his face into darkness, but the dark, frowning brows, yellow eyes set slightly aslant, strong, hooked nose and the wide mouth that could express both harshness or humor, strength or tenderness, they were quite clear. Tentatively I raised my fingers to the hand that cradled my chin; two years ago it had been cold, with the traces of scales still evident, but now it was warm and smooth.

"Remember me?" He was teasing.

"Of course I do, but—" I lifted a finger to trace the thin line of moustache, the short hairs along his jawline. "You're not quite the same."

"Neither are you, my dear. You've grown up." He tipped my chin higher. "There are great shadows under your eyes, your mouth is firmer, you are much slimmer. . . . Was it bad, your journey? No, don't tell me now," and his mouth brushed mine so gently it was come and gone like the touch of a moth's wing. "We have plenty of time to talk." His lips met mine again, lingering there longer, exerted a stronger pressure. "I can't tell you how nice it is to see you again. And what a surprise!" The next kiss still teased, though it was more like a proper one. "You know something, my little Talitha? You are practically irresistible! Tell me something; how did you manage to end up here, of all places in the world to choose from?"

For a moment the meaning of what he had said didn't sink in, but when it did I pushed away from him and stood there, bewildered. His question meant that he didn't realize that I had come all this way just to seek him out; he didn't know how much I loved him. How could I now betray my foolish hopes, my enduring love, to someone who obviously thought of me just as a temporary plaything?

The hot blood rushed to my cheeks and I was about to cover my shame and confusion by muttering something utterly inane like "looking for treasure," when I was saved from making a fool of myself by glimpsing a sudden flash of white on the balcony above.

I tugged at Jasper's sleeve. "Quick, you must go! Dickon—yes, the same one—is up there on the balcony, and he mustn't see you!"

"Then I shall come again tomorrow night. Earlier."

"He's away this morning for a few days—"

"Good." He leapt up on the balustrade. "Tomorrow. Midnight . . ." He paused for a moment, then plunged over the edge.

My genuine cry of fright was echoed by a yell from Dickon above. I rushed over to the void, terror-stricken, my heart in my mouth, then I heard the *crack*! of opening wings and saw my man-dragon soar away into the darkness.

Dickon, who had seen nothing of this, joined me at the balustrade. "Who was it? What happened? Where did he go?"

I was still trembling, though he didn't notice this, and I tried to keep the shakes from my voice as I answered.

"I've no idea. A thief, a voyeur? I heard a noise, got up and came down here. I tried to talk to him, find out what he was doing—" how long had he been listening? "—but when he saw you he jumped down to the rocks below." I leant over the edge. "There's no sign of him now."

"You must be more careful! Are you sure that money of yours is safe? Bar your door and your windows. Get that lazy dog of yours to stand guard out here at night." He seemed genuinely worried, though whether it was me or my money he was more bothered about it was difficult to say. "Promise me you won't do anything—foolish—while I am away?"

No, I wouldn't do anything foolish. I had done enough of that already, including coming here in the first place, following an impossible dream.

"I promise," I said. "I shall be here when you return, safe and sound. And—" the thought coming to me unbidden and forcing itself into speech "—and I may change my mind about staying here after all."

"You mean . . . go back to the merchant?" He sounded incredulous. Then, suddenly, suspicious. "You have found what you seek, then?" I could almost see the picture of a heap of treasure in his mind, followed by the thought: where has she hidden it?

"Why not? There I was safe and secure. A good marriage . . ." I shrugged. "Or I could still go into trade somewhere else. It's not entirely a man's world, you know; there are women physicians, builders, painters, herbalists, farmers, metal workers, writers. . . . And now I'm going back to bed. Have a good journey."

It was a relief to be rid of him, but unfortunately this also gave me too much time to think. Over and over again I reviewed in my mind Jasper's visit, what he had looked like, what he said, and, more important, what he didn't. I had been stupid, shy, tearful, but he had been— different. I suppose it was ridiculous of me to suppose we could pick up just where we had left off over two years ago, for that had been a moment of such high intensity it could not be repeated, but I had expected him to understand why I had travelled all this way to see him again.

Instead he was treating me with an amused tenderness, just as you would a particular pet, indulging my tears and stupid behavior. But hadn't he said I was now grown-up, too? And did he truly not know why I was here? Long, long ago he had warned me against loving him: was this because he knew he was incapable of such emotion? Or was it that he no longer found me attractive?

Had my journey been in vain, then?

I'd be damned if it had! My pride wouldn't let me just creep away without a fight. I hadn't come all this way to be brushed aside. As for being attractive—well, just let him wait and see!

Off I went down to the village and when I returned spent the rest of the day with scissors, needle and thread, warm water, the opening of this jar, that bottle.

Ky-Lin visited me at around six. I hadn't seen him for days, but it seemed he knew, somehow, of Jasper's visit.

"Was it how you imagined it, girl? Was it worth all the journeying?" He looked around at my preparations. "You know, I remember something my Master used to say to his disciples: 'Be careful on what you set your heart, for it may just be you achieve your desire.'"

I didn't understand; surely to get what you wanted was the ultimate goal.

He looked at me steadily, his plumed tail swishing gently from side to side. "You will understand someday, I think." I had never seen him look so sad. "Do not forget I am still here to help you, if you need me."

*   *   *

At last I heard the monks chanting their evening prayers, the dissonance of their softly struck bells. Soon it would be midnight. I slipped the green silk gown I had made that afternoon over my head. There was no mirror of course, but it felt good, the dress swirling round me in soft, loose folds, as it did so catching the perfume of sandalwood oil I had used in my bathing water. On my feet were a pair of green felt slippers I had hastily cobbled once the dress was finished, and I had a green ribbon in my hair.

I had told Growch whom I was expecting and asked him to please not interrupt our meeting.

"Din' last night, did I? You goin' to do naughties tonight, like the first time you met?"

Ridiculously I felt myself blushing: fancy being embarrassed by a dog! "None of your business what I'm going to do!"

"You looks nice," he said unexpectedly. "Quite the lady . . ."

Probably I was now wearing the most beautiful dress I had ever possessed, and after what Growch had said, I wished, I wished I had a mirror. It would be nice to see a beautiful Summer, just for once, especially as I had spent so much of my life as a plain, fat girl nobody looked at twice.

I left a lamp burning in my room, took the lantern from Dickon's room and set it on the balcony. Tonight was overcast, the moon hidden behind a scud of cloud. There was a sudden sound behind me: only a moth, banging helplessly against the oiled paper of the lantern. I brushed it aside, although the flame was well shielded.

Suddenly it was cold; a chill wind came rushing from the snowcapped mountains to the north and whirled around me: my skin shivered into goosebumps and the breeze lifted the hair on my head into tangles. Winter was giving its warning—or was it something else that made me think of a dying end?

The wind ceased as suddenly as it had risen, the clouds parted and the moon shone clear and bright. I twisted the ring on my finger—strange, it seemed much looser; perhaps I was losing too much weight—but it was warm and comforting, and I pushed any dark thoughts from my mind as a shadow flicked across the edge of my sight and swooped away beneath.

I ran down the steps to the little garden and there, just climbing over the edge, was my man-dragon, his cloak flapping behind him like wings. He stopped when he saw me, one foot still on the balustrade.

"My, what have we here, then? A strange fair lady!"

"Wha—what do you mean?"

"To what do I owe this honor, beauteous maid?" Stepping down, he gave me a bow, his hand on his heart. "I swear you are the very vision of loveliness. . . ."

For a moment I truly believed he didn't recognize me, then he laughed, came forward, and took my hands.

"You look absolutely wonderful, Talitha! I wouldn't have believed it possible!" Did it depend so much on the clothes I wore, I wondered? "Of course you are beautiful anyway, always were, but that dress frames your loveliness perfectly! Did you make it especially for me?"

"Of course not!" I lied too quickly. (Never let a man think you've tarted yourself up just for him, Mama used to say. They are big-headed enough as it is. A little disarray is perfectly acceptable.) "It's just something I had put by."

He turned over my right hand, brushing his thumb across my index finger. "With fresh needle marks? You're not a good liar, my dear—no, don't be angry. I am deeply honored, believe me," and he sang a little song I used to be familiar with in my own country.

"Silver ribbons in your hair, lady;

"Golden shoon upon your feet.

"Crimson silk to clothe you, lady:

"And a kiss your knight to greet!"

Only he changed all the colors to "green," and I got a kiss at the end of it, a proper one this time.

In an instant my arms went around his neck and my body curved into his, so you couldn't have passed a silken thread between us. I felt as though I was melting, fusing with him until we were metal of the same mold. I couldn't breathe or think, all I could do was feel.

Then at once everything changed. Suddenly I was standing alone, scarcely able to keep my feet for the trembling in my limbs, shaking with a frustration I had no words for, an ache that came from the deepest parts of my body.

All I could say was: "Why?" and I didn't even realize I had spoken out loud.

"No," he said. "No, my very dear one, no."

I didn't understand. "What's wrong? What have I done?"

"Done? Nothing, nothing at all. But we can't let this happen again. It was bad enough last time, against all the laws of nature, and I was the one who let it happen. No, now don't cry. . . ." He came forward and held my hands again. "Remember this: we are different, you and I. You are human, through and through, and nothing but. I am three-quarters, nay more, of a completely different creature. Normally I have a different form, different morals, different view of life, different future. There is no way, absolutely none, in which we could ever have a future together, even for a few days, and anything less wouldn't be fair to you. Don't you understand?"

"What about the quarter that isn't dragon? What about the times when you are 'He who Scrapes the Clouds' or whatever is your dragon name? What about the man who stands before me now? What happens to Jasper?"

"Jasper," he said, "may be the Master of Many Treasures, but not of his own soul—if he has one, that is. He is ruled by his larger part and that is dragon; he is subject to dragon rule and dragon law. He may make no important decisions contrary to those that are already laid down, unless it is first referred to the Council for consideration. And unless this Jasper is a Master Dragon, which he is not, then there is no hope of changing the laws or of making any appeal against them. . . ." He was speaking in a dull, monotonous way, like a priest bored with the service.

I tried to humor him. "What is the difference between an ordinary dragon and a master?"

"Treasure. The gathering of enough to satisfy the Council. The last master brought five great jewels, still much admired. An emerald from a rainforest on the other side of the world, a sapphire from an island in the warm seas, a diamond from the mines of the southern desert, a ruby from a temple of the infidel, and a priceless freshwater pearl from the Islands of Mist."

"How long ago was that?"

"Some five hundred years."

I gasped. So long ago! "Then how long can a dragon live? And what is the Council?"

"A fit dragon can live for a thousand years, perhaps more. Once there were hundreds, all over the world, together with other similar creatures of all sorts, shapes and sizes. Now their bones lie scattered, for our legends say that a disaster came from the sky, a great ball of fire that brought with it a breath of death that destroyed millions of creatures, the dragons among them. Some survived, but very few, and those only in the high mountains, where the contamination couldn't reach them. Other pockets of safety conserved other creatures, mainly small ones: lizards, tortoises, lemurs. Then the world gradually changed, mammals growing strong at the expense of the dragon." He glanced at my indignant face. "That is what our legends say; yours are probably rather different."

"God created the world," I said stiffly. "And Adam and Eve came before dragons. I think. If He ever created them; some say they come from the Devil."

"Who's he?"

He didn't know? "And in any case I don't think Noah would have been able to cope with a pair of dragons in his Ark. It must have been difficult enough putting lions and sheep with rats and camels. . . ."

He was laughing now. "Oh Summer-Talitha, you take things so seriously, so literally!"

I was so happy to see him back to normal, as it were, that I couldn't take offense. I knew what was right, so what the dragons believed in didn't matter. "And the Council?" I prompted.

"All the Master Dragons who survive, eleven in all."

"And where is the Council?"

"You've seen them."

"I have?"

"Of course!" He smiled again. "Let us say they saw you, and the dog. They told me so."

"The Blue Mountain?"

"Yes."

"But there was nothing there—except rocks and stones and pebbles and dust and a nasty smell."

"Rocks and pebbles? Are you sure?"

I remembered something Ky-Lin had said: "Rocks are rocks are rocks, you know. . . ."

"You mean—the cavern was full of dragons? The rocks . . ."

"Yes."

"And the pebbles?"

"Treasure. Heaps of it."

So Dickon had been right after all! There *had* been a fabulous treasure waiting at the end of our journey. . . .

I was silent for a moment. "How do they hide—look like rocks?"

"A mist of illusion. Easy stuff."

"But don't you think it's an awful waste having all that treasure just sitting there doing nothing?"

"It's very pretty. A delight to run between one's claws, to taste with one's tongue. Did you know all jewels taste different? Like bonbons do to humans . . . Myself, I prefer the tang of a fire opal."

I thought he might be joking, but a glance told me he wasn't.

"I still think it's a waste."

"Why? What about all those kings and princes, merchants and misers who do precisely the same thing? They have rooms full of treasure that never see the light of day. What about those who bury treasure so it is lost forever? What about those vandals that actually destroy what you would call treasure, just for the joy of it? Why should a few ageing dragons be denied their simple pleasures? Which is worse: to steal a jewel every now and again, or to take lives in the name of religion, or whatever?"

"But dragons eat people, too!" I remembered the tales of my childhood; beautiful damsels chained to rocks, children offered up, young men stripped naked to fight with a wooden sword a battle they could not hope to win.

"Perhaps some did, once. There were many more of us then. Now we eat seldom, and then only to fuel our fires, speed our wings. And there are not many of us left who undertake journeys of any distance."

"Why?"

"Most of them are too old, some well over the thousand-year norm. All they want is a little heat, a little sleep, and their memories. They are great tale-tellers. To them the puny adventures and battles and wars of humankind are like a breath, soon expended."

I wondered. Sometimes he spoke of "us," sometimes of "them." Was this because of the life he was forced to lead? A quarter man, three-quarters dragon? I must try and keep him thinking of dragons as "them," and concentrate on making him feel like a man.

"Well, waste or no, I didn't come all this way for treasure," I said, choosing my words carefully.

"Why, then?" He released my hands and slipped an arm about my waist. "Adventure? Curiosity?"

No, Love, you great idiot! I thought, but of course didn't say it. "A little of both, I suppose," I said. "All that travelling we did, while you were still the Wimperling, gave me a taste for it. Besides which, I have had a chance of earning my own living. Real money . . ."

"And where did you pick up that little thief, Dickon, again?"

I explained. "I kept trying to leave him behind, but he persisted in believing that I was after treasure, dragon treasure. Thank God he has given up that idea and gone off for a couple of days looking for trading opportunities."

"Oh, I don't think he has given up. Did you tell him about your visit to the Blue Mountain?"

"Yes, but—"

"I flew over his encampment earlier, frightened his horse off into the bush. Take him the best part of a day to catch up with it again."

"You don't mean . . ."

"I do mean. He's camped at the foot of the Blue Mountain, and tomorrow, if I'm not much mistaken, he'll be climbing the path you took, looking for the treasure!"

CHAPTER TWENTY-EIGHT

The crafty devil! Telling me he was looking for new opportunities, and making me pay for yet another treasure hunt! I should never have told him about the Blue Mountain; it was obvious he hadn't believed me.

"He won't find anything, will he?"

"No more than you did."

"Well, I hope he falls off the path!" I said crossly. "He's been nothing but trouble ever since we met up again."

"Tell me . . ." and he spread out his cloak on the stone flags of the little garden, sat cross-legged and pulled me down beside him. "I want to hear everything that's happened to you since the Place of Stones."

I glossed over that dreadful journey back to Matthew's, for after all it wasn't his fault I had near starved to death; I told him of my decision to turn down Matthew's offer (but not the real reason), made him smile over my forgeries of the merchant's signature and running off dressed as a boy to seek my fortune. I made my adventures as amusing as I could: storm at sea, ambush, imprisonment, the bog, bandits, the Desert of Death and the hairy people.

When I had finished he ruffled my hair, leant forward and kissed my cheek.

"I reckon it was a good job you had your friend Ky-Lin with you. I have heard of them, but never seen one. You could have easily died a dozen times without him. . . ." He frowned. "But all this doesn't explain why you left the caravan trails and came this way."

Ah, Jasper, my love, this was the difficult part. . . .

"I wanted to see you again," I said lightly. "Man-dragons are a little out of my experience, you see. Added to that, the coins my father left me led me all the way across every country to this one. And on Matthew's maps this part was marked: 'Here be Dragons.' Simple as that."

"Was it? Was it really?" He slipped his arm about my waist again. "You know something? I went back to look for you after I made my initial journey here. I worried that you would find it difficult to find your merchant's house again. But you had vanished from the face of the earth! Nice to know you were all right." He cuddled me closer. "Well, now that you've found your man-dragon again, what do you want of him?"

"A couple of kisses," I said promptly. "Proper ones. Not no-commitment-it's-dangerous-you-mustn't-get-entangled-with-a-dragon-man. Neither should it be let's-have-a-laugh-and-a-kiss-and-say-good-bye! I want you to pretend," I snuggled up closer, "just for a moment, that I am the most desirable woman in the world. . . ." My hand stroked his cheek. "I am a princess under a spell, and only you can break the ice about her heart." Had I gone too far? "It's not a lot to ask, it can't threaten your life! You're not going to change back into a pig, or anything like that—"

"I should hope not!"

He was chuckling; that was encouraging. At least there was no outright rejection.

"Well, then?" Now for it; my heart was beating uncomfortably fast and loud. "Or can't you pretend?"

"I don't need to pretend," he said, and gathered me in his arms.

At first he just held me close, his hands stroking my hair, my cheeks, my hands. Every time he touched me my inside tangled itself up into knots and I feared he would hear my heart, but he hummed a gentle little droning song, as soothing as the sound of a hive or the turning of a spinning wheel. Gradually the tune and his gentle touch calmed my mind, but not my body.

I was aware of my skin, my blood, my bones. I could see his shadowy face bent over mine; I could hear his soft voice, with the slight grating tone in the lower notes; in the air was the pungency of the rough-headed autumn plants in pots in the garden, the night-wind smell of Jasper's clothes, and a certain slightly musky scent that seemed to come from his skin. My whole body was stimulated to a point I had not thought possible, and now came the taste of his lips.

I thought of the tang of burnt sugar, the bitter black heart of an opium poppy, the smoke from autumn bonfires, the cold, iron smell of ice and snow, newly washed linen sun-dried, the sharp bite of a juicy apple, a snuffed candle—then I didn't think at all.

At first he was experimenting with my lips and tongue, but gradually as he pulled me closer I knew that at last it was me, me, me! that he wanted. I didn't care if it was lust without love, desire without commitment, I just kissed him back with all my heart. His hands found my breasts, his body was full of a hard urgency that found a response in my yielding form.

"Summer Talitha," he murmured. "My little love . . ."

For answer I pulled him down so we rested together on his cloak, our bodies inhibited only by the clothes we wore. For a brief instant it seemed he might think better of it, but then I took over the caressing, my fingers moving on his chest and stomach, untying the laces of his trews, my mouth thrust up hungrily to his. . . .

And then it was too late for either of us.

I remember the rip of silk as my dress parted company with its stitches; I remember the feel of his crisp, dark hair under my fingers, the rasp of his beard against my cheek; I remember stifling my cries in the soft skin where his neck met his shoulder; I remember, oh I remember the hard thrusts I welcomed with fierce ripostes of my own; I remember—but there are no words to describe the cascades of delight that followed, never will be. No words, no music, no painting: nothing can adequately portray raw emotion like that. Until you have felt it you will never know, and if you have you will realize it is beyond description.

Afterwards we lay in each other's arms. Only now did my cheeks sting where his beard had rubbed them; only now was I conscious of the uncomfortable rucks of the cloak beneath us; only now did my insides ache with an inward tension as though they pulled against a cat's cradle of tiny inside stitches. I was sticky and sweaty, but so was he, and it didn't matter.

He stirred, sighed, stroked my hair. "You are a witch, girl: you know that?" He leant up on one elbow and gazed down at me. "You realize I had no intention of that happening?"

"I know." I put up a finger and traced the line of his nose. "But I did." I sat up. "And you wanted it too."

"Maybe. But it was wrong, wrong! We shouldn't have done it."

"Why not? Who are we hurting?"

"Ourselves." His voice was bitter. "In time I could have forgotten you and, whatever you think now, you would have forgotten me too. But now I shall always want you. You will always want me. If we looked for love elsewhere, or tried to do without, we should both think only of each other. We have forged a link that can never be broken."

"But that was the way I wanted it—"

"You didn't understand what you were getting yourself into. We can never be together, don't you understand? And you will suffer more than I. In my dragon form I can forget you for three-quarters of the year, but you—you will never forget!"

"Then I shall wait for the quarter-year you are a man," I said obstinately. "Wherever it is. That will be enough for me. Three months with you is better than none at all."

He rose to his feet in one swift movement and crossed to the balustrade. His whole posture was stiff, his hands clenched on the stone, his shoulders raised, his head bent.

"It's impossible."

I went to stand at his side, clutching at my torn gown, aware all at once of a chill wind that blew from the north, making the stars shiver in sympathy. The moon was down, but a pale light had followed her descent, a trace of silver on the permanent snows.

"Why is it impossible? Don't you want to see me again?"

He glanced at me, but I couldn't see his expression. "Of course I want to be with you, as often as I can— but that is just the point. It's not possible!"

"But *why*, if you want to? What's to stop you?"

He turned, gripped my shoulders. "It's not as simple as you seem to think! If I could know for sure, say to you: all right, my dear, my love, I am yours from November until January. Find us a house where we can be one for those three months of the year. . . . Or if I could say: I can be with you in March, May and September, find me that house etc."

He released me, leant over the balustrade again. "But it doesn't work that way: I wish it did. I just don't have those certainties. These—" he gestured at himself "—these remissions, if you can call them that, give me very little warning. At first, they gave me none at all and it was dangerous. Then I had no idea how long they would last either: five minutes, five hours, five days. . . ."

He traced the line of my jaw with his finger. "That was one of the reasons I gave up looking for you; it was too unpredictable, the time I could spend asking questions, and twice I nearly got killed." He sighed. "It has become easier, like changing to come and see you. I can control it for a couple of hours or so, and if it is going to be longer, a week or so, I get a warning beforehand, a sort of painless headache. But I still don't know how long it will last."

I was devastated. "But—"

"No," he said firmly. "I couldn't live with you all the time. My dragon side is too unpredictable. Nor could you keep me in a shed at the bottom of the garden betweenwhiles, just waiting for my nicer side to come out. I think the neighbors might object," he added, with a smile. "Oh, come on darling: we'll think of something!"

"But what?" I was close to tears.

He shrugged. "Right now I have no idea. I shall consult the Council, though I warn you they are finding it difficult to accept that I am not completely dragon. No precedent, you see. Plenty of legends, but no firm records. At the moment I am something of a celebrity, but there are those who wish to cast me out." He shook his head. "I should have a better case to argue if I could bring them the jewels they so desire—my permit to become a Master Dragon. But that, of course, will take time."

"So it is just some jewels they need?"

"To become a Master Dragon and not a mere Apprentice—as I am now—I have to be able to perform the usual flying tricks: spirals, hovering, steep dives, flying backwards, backspins, and I also have to contribute something of value to the Hoard. It can be of gold or silver, but they prefer the easier-to-handle glitter of jewels, cut or uncut."

"Do there have to be a certain number of these?"

He shook his head. "Recently—within the last thousand years or so that is—it has become traditional to bring in a selection, but the foremost criterion is that of color. Sometimes one stone is enough; we possess, I believe, the largest uncut emerald the world has yet seen. As big as your fist, Talitha, but too fragile to cut."

An idea was forming in my mind. "Do they have light in that cave of theirs?"

"Of course. There are a number of small openings that let in both sun- and moonlight, and with a blast or two of fire they can light semipermanent torches. Why?"

"Just wait a moment. . . ." Running up the steps I found what I wanted in my room, disturbing a sleepy Growch, then went back out again, picking up the lantern as I rejoined Jasper in the garden. Setting the light on one of the benches I opened my fist and slowly twisted the crystal the captain's wife had given me in front of the flame. Even with that relatively dim illumination the crystal threw a thousand rainbow lights across the garden, the balcony, our faces and clothes, the wall above, the rocks beneath, and we were almost blinded by reds and greens, yellows and purples, blues and oranges.

Jasper took it from my fingers. "By the stars! This is the most beautiful . . . Where did you get it?"

I explained.

"Do you know what it is?" He sounded excited.

"A crystal. Nicely cut, but—"

"But nothing! This has been cut by a master! In fact—" He looked at it more closely. "In fact I believe this may be one of the thirteen lost many hundreds of years ago when pagan hordes overran the city of the Hundred Towers. . . . So far six have been traced of the thirteen that were made by the Master of Cut Glass—one for each lunar month, you see—and this might well be the seventh." He was handling it as reverently as I would a splinter of the True Cross. "We—the Council that is— already possess one of these, but to have a pair . . . Do you realize what this means? If you let me take it to them, that will mean automatic Dragon Mastership!" He wrapped his arms about me. "And that would mean I would be equal to any, and they would be bound to consider any request I made!"

"They could agree to—regularize your changes?"

"Yes! I can also ask to spend my man-time with you."

He was fairly dancing around the small space of the garden, holding me up high against his chest. "We can

find somewhere. . . . Why, I've just remembered the very
place! There is an island set in the bluest of seas, miles
away from the trade routes, where the sun shines warm
year round and the land is peopled by the gentlest of
natives, who would welcome us both. Everything you
planted would grow, and there are fish in the sea—"

"It sounds like Paradise," I said wistfully. I could see
it now. Yellow sands running up to the greenery of a
forest, cool streams running between moss-covered
stones, hills blue in the distance, huge butterflies feeding
from the trumpets of exotic lilies, trees alive with the
chatter of multicolored birds. A little hut set in a clearing,
not too far from the sea, lines set out for fish, a net
for the collection of shellfish; a patch of ground for the
vegetables, another for a few chickens and a goat; a hammock slung between the trees, and Growch for company
when Jasper had to be away . . .

His kiss prevented any further daydreaming.

"And now I must go, and quickly; I can feel a change
coming over me already. Forgive me, my dear: I shall
hope to see you tomorrow." He kissed me again. "And
I shall keep an eye on your Dickon. . . ."

"Not *my* Dickon!" I protested, but Jasper had disappeared. Instead a black dragon hung on to the balustrade:
scaly body, gaping jaws, huge leathery wings outspread,
yellow eyes burning in a bony skull. I was afraid, but not
so frightened as I would have been two hours or so
earlier if Jasper had suddenly appeared in his dragon
shape without warning.

The intelligence in those yellow eyes was benign, I
was sure of that, so I had no hesitation in picking up the
crystal and placing it in one outstretched claw.

"Godspeed, my love," I said, then stepped back hurriedly as the wind of his wings blew hair, dress, leaves,
petals around me like a whirlwind.

All that long day I was in a fever of impatience. I
mended my green silk dress, sorted out my belongings

for the umpteenth time, brought my journal up to date, couldn't eat; snapped at Growch, then hugged him; washed my hair and set it; didn't like the result and washed it again to hang loose, and sun-dried it.

Ky-Lin paid a visit around midmorning, looked at all my preparations, fluffed the tip of his tail up like a peacock and retired, remarking: "I hope you know what you are doing. . . ."

Of course I did! I was getting ready for my love, shedding what I did not need, preparing for the time when we would both be together forever, even if only for part of each year. Nothing was more important than this, yet the day seemed to crawl by, the sun standing still in the sky on purpose, the hours marked only by gongs, dissonant bells, and the soft, monotonous chant of the monks.

Several times I went out onto the balcony and looked in the direction of the Blue Mountain, wondering how Jasper was presenting his case to the Council; I wondered, too, if Dickon, that handsome treacherous boy, had reached the cave, only to be as disappointed as I had been.

At last the sun really did start to slide down the sky to the west. I supped some broth and bread, tasting nothing in my impatience, took a warm bath, slid into my mended dress, combed my hair until it sparked out from my head like a halo, then sat down by the door to the balcony to wait.

And wait.

The moon came up, near full now, and flooded the countryside with light, the stars pricked through their cover; at midnight a small wind blew up; at one it died down again, and I was yawning; by two I was half-asleep and must have drifted into a dream, because I thought I was talking to my old friends Basher, Traveler, Mistral, and the Wimperling, when suddenly the latter took wing, swung around in the sky and came back to land at my side, only this time he was a man.

"Jasper!" I started up, suddenly wide awake once more. "What did they say?"

"I am now a Master Dragon, thanks to your gift!" Glints like raindrops or tiny diamonds seemed to surround him. "But . ."

"But what? Will they let you go?" I ran into his arms.

He kissed me, but there was a constraint in his manner. "They are considering it, yes. But they want to see you: face-to-face."

CHAPTER TWENTY-NINE

I drew back, shocked and horrified. "B—but I can't! They might eat me!"

He drew me close again. "Nonsense! They are so pleased with the Dragon Stone that a whole village full of desirable maidens could parade in front of them and they would never notice! They were so euphoric they gave me the accolade of Master Dragon at once, without asking to assess my flying skills. Just as well: I think I would have failed on the backspins. . . ." He kissed my brow. "Then I asked for leave of absence from my dragon form for a fixed term each year. They wanted to know why, of course." He frowned. "It was very difficult for them to understand. To them, fair maidens were for dining on, not living with—in the legends, of course," he amended hastily.

"There must be lady dragons," I said. "Couldn't you have explained it that way?"

"There are no 'lady dragons' as you call them. There may have been once, I suppose, but now many of those left are bisexual. There are others, like myself, who are totally male, who can fertilize the bisexuals, though most of them manage on their own. It's a bit difficult to explain, because it just—just happens. You don't think about it."

He was right: I didn't understand at all. Except the bit about him being totally male. I wouldn't like to think

343

I had been making love with a bisexual. Then I suddenly remembered something so important I couldn't get the words out straight.

"Supposing . . . if it's as you say . . . the dragon's eggs . . . your being a male . . . it isn't possible, is it? I mean you and me . . . Ky-Lin was so sure!"

"What in the world are you talking about?"

But I had second thoughts; my ring had given a warning tingle. Don't tell him yet: wait and see.

"Nothing. When were you thinking of taking me to see them?"

"When? Right now."

"*Now?* But I'm not ready, I've nothing suitable to wear, how do we get there, I don't want to—"

"Now!" he said firmly. "The sooner the better. Trust me—you do trust me, don't you? You would have trusted the Wimperling, as you called him, with your life, wouldn't you? Good. Go get your cloak and wrap yourself up tight: you're going to be dragon-borne tonight!"

And it all happened so quickly I had no chance to argue. One moment I was standing there in my silken dress, terrified at the whole idea, the next I was back on the same spot, swathed and hooded in my father's cloak.

Jasper held me close.

"You are not used to riding on the back of a dragon, and now is not the time to teach you properly." I could feel him laughing a little. "So we'll do it the easy way. I shall carry you—no, don't panic! You won't know much about it. Close your eyes and relax. I am going to make you go to sleep for a little while, long enough to get you safe to the mountain. I don't want you struggling at the wrong moment."

His lips came down on mine and I surrendered to his embrace as his fingers came up to my neck. A little pressure—in my mind or my body I wasn't sure—and I slipped into a sort of waking unconsciousness. I didn't dream, or anything like that, but the sensation of flying

was curiously dimmed, though I could sense wind, the
clapping of wings, a cindery smell. . . .

My stomach gave a sudden jolt, like the leap of a
stranded fish.

"Sorry about that: I came down a bit sharply and
changed early. You can open your eyes now, my love."

It was lucky his arm was around my waist, otherwise
I might have tumbled to the ground. I was shaking and
cold and my hair, in spite of the hood of my cloak, felt
as though it had been attacked by a flying thornbush. I
thought my eyes were open, but everything seemed as
black as pitch. I blinked rapidly a couple of times and
tried again. Looking up now I could see the stars and
the moon illuminating the ledge on which we stood, but
I had been staring straight at the entrance to the passage-
way that led to the cavern, and this still remained omi-
nously dark. How could we possibly negotiate that
without a light?

"Come," said Jasper. "Take my hand."

I pulled back. "It's so dark. . . ."

"I know the way, just as easily as you would in the
dark of your own home without a candle. Besides, there
is some light. Wait and see."

I allowed him to draw me into the passage, but closed
my eyes like a child, only to be told to open them once
we had passed the first turning.

"If you don't I shall let go your hand!"

Promptly they were open, to be faced with a faint
silver glow from the rocks around us, like a seam of
precious metal running through the stones. It was not so
much a light as an emanation, and only extended a few
feet in front and, glancing back, the same behind. As we
paced it kept step with us.

"What is it? Dragon-magic?" I whispered.

He pressed my fingers. "No, it's a natural phenomenon; a kind of phosphorescence that is activated by the
heat of our bodies as we pass."

The ring on my finger was tingling gently; no immediate

harm, but a warning to go carefully; I wondered for the second or third time why it seemed to be getting so much looser.

The last time I had been in this passage I had cursed at the twists and turns, eager to reach the end; now I wished it would go on forever.

It didn't, of course. In less time than it takes to tell we had rounded the last corner and there was the cavern, lighted now by a broad spear of moonlight that shafted down from an opening in the roof of the cave and lit a pile of rocks—or were they? I gripped Jasper's hand more tightly.

Gently he loosed himself and stepped forward. "You are speaking with animals, so your ring will translate," he said to me. "Pay careful attention to what is said, and remember your manners. These are creatures as old and venerable as any in the land."

Then he spoke again, but this time it was in a series of creaks, groans, hisses, sighs, and rumbles.

"I have brought her. . . ."

I could understand what he said, the ring translating in my mind as he spoke. I had been staring straight ahead at the rocks, expecting some movement, but as he spoke I glanced to my side, and was horrified to see it was no man who stood at my side but a full-grown dragon! My heart gave a great jerk, then steadied. Didn't I say I would trust him? In spite of this I had backed away a little, but my ring, though still throbbing, had not increased its warnings.

The dragon at my side—black, with tiny pinpoints of light illuminating his wing tips—turned his bony face towards me, the yellow eyes still surprisingly kind. The rumble of dragon talk started again, but thanks to my ring, Jasper's own voice came through, warm and comforting.

"Don't be afraid: it's better that I appear to them this way. Come, stand by my side. And toss aside that cloak. I want them to see you as you really are."

I was quite glad to throw the cloak aside. It was very warm in the cavern. The fissure that divided us from the other side was throwing out a summer's night heat, and I found I was perspiring. I stepped to Jasper-dragon's side, aware once again of the cindery smell and the roughness of the stones beneath my feet. And now came a sound, a sort of stirring, slithery scrape—

"What is it?"

"Watch. . ."

Across the chasm something stirred, a general sort of shifting; rocks altered their shape—round, square, oblong, irregular, jagged—and also changed their position relative to each other. A few pebbles rattled against each other. I could feel the hair rising at the back of my neck, although Jasper-dragon stood calm and quiet beside me. My ring gave a warning twinge, but no more.

I thought I saw a claw, a bony head, a wing, decided I must be mistaken, then all at once everything seemed to shimmer, like the sun on a long road on a hot day. No, not quite like that; perhaps more like glancing down into a swift-flowing stream, trying to make out what lay on the bottom through the uncontrollable shift of the water.

"Here be Dragons," I thought stupidly, and suddenly they were there.

Still half-veiled, distorted, shimmery, around a dozen of the huge creatures bestirred themselves, yawning, stretching, unwinding long sinewy tails, opening dark eyes, extending claws and wings. With them came color and light; it seemed they emanated their own illumination, for now I saw gleams and sparkles at their feet. The piles of pebbles, so dull and uninteresting before, now started to glow and sparkle with an unquiet riot of colors as the dragons stirred them with their claws. Ruby, beryl, garnet, fire opal, coral, rose quartz, topaz, peridot, emerald, sapphire, amethyst, aquamarine, agate, jet, bloodstone, jasper, opal, pearl, diamond—they were all there, plus gold and silver. Then I saw that the light that shone

over all did not come from the heaps of gems, nor from
the dragons, but rather from the shaft of moonlight
catching the facets of a jewel that hung in the air above
all: the crystal I had given Jasper.

He stepped forward and then came that confusing
rumble of speech again that my ring sorted out for me.

"I have brought the girl, the giver of this gift that now
shines above us all." A soft hiss from across the chasm.

"Bring her forward."

I was nudged forward by one of his wings. "Don't
be afraid. . . ."

I went forward hesitatingly till I stood at the lip of the
chasm and felt as well as saw the flickers of light that
flashed across from the moonlit crystal; now everything
I looked at had a strange unreality.

"I'm here," I said unsteadily. "What do you want of
me?"

For a moment there was silence and I thought perhaps
they had not understood my human speech, although the
ring should be translating to them as well, but then came
a low, grumbling growl, like Growch magnified ten times.
I thought about turning and running, right away back
and out to safety, but in spite of an involuntary step
backwards, I otherwise stood firm.

The ring on my finger was still throbbing, but it was
an encouraging feeling rather than a warning. I repeated
my question.

"What do you want of me?"

When the answer came, it was not what I had
expected. "You gave this Dragon Stone as a gift to our
colleague. He-whose-wings-scrape-the-clouds?"

They must mean Jasper. "I did."

"And what do you hope for in exchange, daughter of
man?"

I squared my shoulders; all or nothing. "When your
new Master Dragon was in his first incarnation, I saved
his life; I ask you now for the price of that life. Let him

spend his man-life time with me, a quarter of each year that we may have together."

Another growling roar, louder this time. "You are impertinent!"

"I do not mean to be. If I had not been in that place, at that time, assuredly the growing creature that was to become your splendid He-whose-wings-scrape-the-clouds would never be standing here in front of you, an addition to your—your . . ." (what on earth was a collection of dragons? A flock? A gathering? The ring gave me the answer) ". . . your doom of dragons. I admit that I kissed the creature he was then three times, causing this—this, to you, malfunction in his makeup, but that was a human manifestation of what you would recognize as kinship. . . ." Where were the words coming from? This wasn't me talking! Thank you, ring! "As it is, if you agree to my proposal, for nine months of the year you will have his company and his services, those of a Master Dragon. Can you afford to lose these? If you refuse our request—and it is his as well as mine—he will merely be sulky and uncooperative and absent himself from your meetings.

"There are few enough of you left: your distinguished race has been declining noticeably during the last thousand years. Do you want this to go on happening? I rescued one for you: surely you can grant me a quarter of his time?"

There was silence. And silence. The air in front of me shimmered and the lights went out, one by one, as the moon passed beyond the opening high in the cavern. The dragons disappeared and so did their jewels till only the rocks and pebbles remained.

I blinked back the tears. "Why didn't they listen to me?"

"But they did." He looked across the chasm. "They just haven't made up their minds, that's all. You were magnificent, by the way. . . ." If he had been in his human form, I'm sure he would have been smiling. "What's a day or two to a dragon, who measures your years as ten to his one? Give them time, my love, give them time. . . . And now I must take you back. Put on your cloak and wrap it tight. Close your eyes. . . ."

Once again I felt the pressure on my neck, his breath on my face and then I was asleep with the wind on my face, the flap of wings in my ears, the smell of cinders in my nostrils, the dizzy descent—

I was lying in my own bed and a voice whispered in my ear: "See you tomorrow."

"You gonna sleep the 'ole day away?" said Growch peevishly. "S'long after my breakfast . . ."

I sat up, blinking, to find the sun fingering its way through the shutters and the sound of chanting.

"What time is it?"

"Dunno. Near enough noon, I reckons."

I looked down. I was still wearing my green silk dress, my father's cloak. I remembered what had happened during the night, and I sighed. There must be something I could do to persuade them. . . .

"Enjoy yer trip?"

So he had been watching. "What? Oh, yes. I suppose so . . . Sorry, Growch, I've been neglecting you, but I've got a lot on my mind."

"That wouldn' include food, would it?"

I sighed again, but I loved him, grotty foulmouth that he was, and his devotion deserved some reward.

"I think that would do us both good. Let's go down to the market in the village and see what they've got."

And over honeyed and spiced roast ribs, egg noodles and sweet-berry tart I made final plans for the strategy I had been planning for the last couple of days. As far as I could see there was only one sure way of granting that which I wished for both Jasper and myself.

Tonight I would tell him my plan.

First, though, there was plenty to do. Practical things like hanging my dress free of wrinkles, taking my sheets down to the laundry woman in the courtyard, washing my hair free of wind tangles, warm water for a bath, bringing my journal up to date with last night's happenings. Certain things to be specially packaged, two letters to write. The first, to Matthew Spicer, was finished quickly. The other, to his agent in Venice, Signor Falcone, took longer. And I must have a talk with Ky-Lin.

And what if it all went wrong? The letters were easily torn up, but the rest? I wouldn't think about that.

Something else had been niggling me for days: I had been neglecting my prayers. Of course there was no Christian church within a thousand miles but God was God, wherever worshipped, so at the next call to prayer in the monastery I knelt and closed my eyes, offering up my heartfelt thanks for all that had gone before, and my various deliverances from evil. I prayed for those dead, my mother and my father, and for those I hoped still lived: the no-longer blind knight, Matthew and Suleiman, Signor Falcone, the sea captain and his big wife, little prince Tug, even Dickon. Then there were the animals. Jesus had been a shepherd to his people, so surely He would understand the prayers to those creatures I had loved and lost to their new lives: Mistral, Traveler, Basher, Ky-lin, of course, even Bear, and my darling Growch. Last of all there was Jasper, my one and only love, Master of Many Treasures. Easy enough to pour out my prayers for the man, but how did one pray for a dragon? I suppose if one owned a lizard that grew out of all proportion, turned nasty, started to fly around all over the place and charred all it ate, then one could pray for a dragon.

I tried my best, but even the patience of God must have been tried by my ramblings.

I took out the egg. It had grown even larger. I placed it on the clothes chest against the wall and covered it with my shift. I looked around the room: all seemed ready. Bed freshly made with clean sheets, my dress free of creases, a skin of honeyed rice wine and two mugs on the side table—

" 'Spectin' 'im in 'ere, then? Where does you want me to go?"

Oh, poor Growch! But I had thought about him earlier. A large bone awaited him in Dickon's empty room next door.

"You goin' to do naughties again?"

I nearly cancelled the bone.

CHAPTER THIRTY

The rest of the day dragged by on leaden feet, and two or three times I found myself pacing restlessly around and around my room like a caged animal, chewing my nails, until Growch planted his tail under my foot and I had to spend a quarter-hour apologizing.

The sun went down and I tried to stay relaxed, knowing that Jasper would not come till moonrise, for dragons don't like flying in full dark, and the few stars were still lie-abeds, reluctant to leave their day's sleep.

The night was chill: no wind, no clouds. I took to twisting my ring about my finger; it was definitely looser today, and with a pang I thought I knew the reason why. This was one of my possessions I had not taken into account on settling my affairs. I must see Ky-Lin. There was also an addition I must make to Signor Falcone's letter.

I could leave it until tomorrow—no, I would do it right now. So it was with pen in hand, paper in front of me, legs curled up beneath, and my tongue between my teeth (normal position when I was writing) that Jasper found me. I had my back to the balcony door, which was open, in order to sit as near as I could to the candles, and the first I knew was when he dropped a light kiss on the nape of my neck.

I jumped up, scattering paper, pen and ink; there was

a huge blot on the paper which no amount of sand would soak up.

"Jasper! How did you manage to be so quiet?"

"You were busy!" He kissed me again, this time properly. "Catching up on your correspondence?" He was only joking, but it was too near the mark for me. I gathered up the papers, turned them facedown.

"Something like that . . . oh, I am glad to see you! I thought the moon would never rise."

He drew me out onto the balcony. "Well there she is, near full. Whatever they call the days and months here, do you realize that tomorrow night it will be two years since we returned to the place where I was hatched at that farm by the Place of Stones? All Hallows' Eve . . . Remember?"

As if I could ever forget. That was the night when my beloved Wimperling had turned into an even more beloved man-dragon. Fiercer, more unpredictable, someone to fear as well as love, an unknown quantity in many ways, he had still captured both my imagination and my heart. I had watched him fly away that night knowing he had taken part of me with him.

And that feeling of loss had never grown less. This was why I had travelled so far to find him, knowing that no other man would do for me. My thoughts scurried back to another All Hallows' Eve: the night I had found my mother dead and had left my home forever to seek my fortune. That had been three years ago, but it seemed more like ten. So much had happened to that naïve, ingenuous, then-plump girl who had believed that all she had to do was travel to the nearest town to find a husband! So proud I was then, I remembered, of my book learning and housekeeping skills. The ability to read, write and figure had been useful, especially when travelling as Matthew's apprentice, but as for my skills in cheese making, embroidery, rose-hip syrup, possets, headache pills, smocking, elderflower wine, besom making, green poultices, patchwork, face packs, spinning and weaving—none of these had ever been exercised.

The fine sewing had descended to plain sewing and mending, the cookery to tossing whatever there was into the pot on an outside fire, and the fat girl had slimmed down dramatically and was lithe as a boy.

So here came another All Hallows. I felt a tiny prick of foreboding—whether it came from the ring or not I wasn't sure—but after all, the saints had seen me through so far, and there was no need for the superstitions of a hag-ridden night to disturb me now.

"Yes, I remember," I said, in answer to his question. "I reckon they are lucky for me, those dates."

"Me too!" He hugged me tight. "Don't you want to know what the Council said?"

No, I had been too frightened to ask. "Yes, of course I do! Tell me?"

"Well it's not bad, and it's not good. They are still deliberating, but although it seems they will probably agree to my spending my man-time with you, they are still divided on whether I can have three months at a time. Most of them would prefer one, I think."

I pretended to consider, all the while knowing that I had something priceless with which to negotiate. "Yes, I suppose that would be better than nothing. April, August, December? Then I would have you for late spring, full summer and the snows of winter."

"Good." He was kissing my throat and shoulders now, and it was difficult to concentrate. "They want to see you again, tomorrow night, to hear their decision. That's good, because I don't think they would waste their time seeing you once more if they intended to refuse."

"Perhaps they mean to serve me up for supper," I said lightly.

My dress fell to my ankles; those shoulder ribbons were too easy.

"I told you, sweetheart, they don't eat damsels anymore—if they ever did."

"I believe you," I said obediently. My hands went to his head, feeling with pleasure the strong bones under my fingers as he bent to my breasts, the exquisite reactions this engendered almost unbearable. The rest of my body was shivering with anticipation—that or the night wind, I had no idea, nor did I care, for a moment later he had swept me up in his arms and carried me to the bed. As I felt his weight press down on me, his mouth on mine, his hands busy elsewhere, the rapture I felt surpassed anything I had ever known. But even as I lost myself in his embrace I thought I felt a faint tingle in my ring, and somewhere a dog barking—

But a moment later all was forgotten with his body in me, with me, by me, part of me. . . .

Later, much later, we lay in each other's arms, at peace. It must have been near dawn, for the last, low bars of moonlight lay aslant the floor and the candles were burning low. I snuggled closer, feeling his body stir in sympathy.

"Jasper?"

"Mmmmm?"

"Do you—do you . . ." But no, I couldn't ask him. Women always wanted the answer to "that" question, if it hadn't been volunteered before: men always tried to avoid committing themselves. That much my mother had taught me.

"Do I—do I . . ." he mimicked gently. "Of course I do! Why do you think I am here? But you want to hear me say it, don't you my love?"

"It doesn't matter, truly it doesn't—" Liar!

"It matters to both of us," he said gently. "You see when I saw you again and realized just how far you had travelled to see me—I know you pretended otherwise but it didn't work—I felt guilty. Then my conscience took over; my man-conscience, because dragons don't have one you would recognize. That conscience told me you would be far better off without me, so I tried to play it casual. I wanted you to think I no longer cared

for you, because I knew I could never give you the sort
of life you deserve—"

"But you have! I—"

"Hush! Let me finish. This sort of life we hope to
wrest from the Council isn't anywhere near perfect. You
could do much better: go back to your merchant. At least
there you will be safe, secure and loved for twelve
months of the year."

"I don't love him, I never did!"

"I know, I know! As the Wimperling I knew; as myself
I know. But my conscience—that damnable thing that a
certain young woman encouraged in a pig once upon a
time—won't let me capture and keep you without a struggle. Dragons are totally selfish: sometimes men are not.
I love you so much I want what is best for you."

There. He had said it. "And I love you, as you know.
All I want is to be with you, even if it's only for a day a
year, so don't let's have any more trouble from your
conscience. Go ahead: be selfish!"

He smiled wryly. "I knew it wouldn't work. . . ."

"But I have something that might. . . ." I slipped from
his side and, naked, crossed to the clothes chest, peeled
back my shift from the egg, picked it up as if it were
the finest porcelain and carried it back to the bed.
"There! What do you think of that?"

He sat up, slowly at first, then suddenly, as though he
had sat on a pin.

"What's this?" He answered his own question. "It's a
dragon's egg, or I'm—I'm a pig again! Where did you
find it? How long have you had it?"

"I've had it for about a year. But it was hidden for a
year before that, and it has grown a good deal since it
first saw the light. When I first saw it, it was about the
size and color of a freshwater pearl, but it was quite soft
to the touch. So I kept it safe and warm until it hardened.
Since then, until now, I have kept it in a pouch round
my neck. Pretty, isn't it? Somehow I never thought a
dragon's egg would look like this. . . ."

"Where did it come from?"

"Guess!"

He scowled. "I don't want to guess: I want to *know*! This is important, don't you realize that?"

"Of course I do! It is our bargaining power: it's the most valuable thing we have!"

He leant forward, took it in his hands. "This is incredible! The Council can surely refuse us nothing now. But I must know where you found it."

"Oh, it has an impeccable pedigree." I was enjoying this. "Like a mug of rice wine?" He shook his head impatiently. "It is a Master Dragon's egg, no less."

"How do you know that? How could you know . . ."

"Because it's yours, that's why!"

"Mine!" I watched the various expressions chase their way across his face: amazement, disbelief, doubt, hope, puzzlement and, finally, a sort of bewildered joy. "But—how do you know? How can it be?"

"That time at the Place of Stones. Remember? You held me in your arms, you kissed me, you changed back and forth from dragon to man, man to dragon, and all the while you were—you were . . . You made love to me."

"But—it couldn't happen that way! It's impossible!"

"You told me dragons could self-procreate and that's difficult for me to believe. If that can happen why couldn't you have produced a life of your own for me to hold?" I leant forward and kissed him. "All I am sure about is that it is yours, and that I held it within me for a year. I had no usual monthly flow during that time, and it was Ky-Lin, the creature I told you about, who helped me with the pain of producing it. Since then I have been normal. So, I truly believe we share it."

"Mine—and yours," he said wonderingly. "They say there is nothing new under the skies. . . . What do we do with it?"

"It belongs to those who are left: the Council, to guard and nurture until it is time for the hatching. Many years too late for me, my love . . . But surely, with a gift such as this, you can persuade them to give me your lifetime as a man to spend with me? Not a week, a year, our time as man and woman together. When I am—gone—then you can be theirs again. In return for the egg, another dragon for them."

He rose from the bed and took me in his arms.

"My dearest dear, my little love, there is nothing would please me more! I'm sure they will agree—and that island I promised you still waits for us!"

He drew me tight and showed me just exactly what I had to look forward to.

It was nearly dawn; the first flush of light was graying the outlines of the shutters as I opened my sleepy eyes. Jasper had left me as the last rays of the moon slanted across the valley, promising to put our request to the Council. He had left the egg with me.

"Tomorrow night we shall go together with the egg, and exchange it for our freedoms—don't worry: they will want our egg more than any jewel in the world: it is their promise of continued life. After tomorrow night, the world is ours! We can be an ordinary couple—even go to one of your churches and become man and wife. Would you like that?"

So, there were—how many hours? Perhaps sixteen. And everything to do. And nothing. I stretched luxuriously and turned over on my back. I would have just five minutes more, then get up and go down to the market and buy something special for Growch, to make up for sequestering him in Dickon's room all night.

It can only have been a couple of minutes' doze when I heard the door to the balcony creak open and soft footfalls on the matting. A moment later a hand stroked my shoulder. Jasper must have come back. I turned over to face him, my eyes still closed, my arms outstretched in welcome, disregarding the sudden prickle of my ring.

"Forgotten something, my love?"

A breath on my cheek, a fumbling hand and then a

weight, an alien weight on top of me, a strange mouth grinding down on mine and an insistent knee pushing my thighs apart. I struggled violently, but an arm was across my throat, a hand pinioning my hands above my head. His sweat was rank in my nostrils, his knee grinding my thighs, his mouth and tongue a-slobber all over my face. I jerked my head aside, took a gulp of air and yelled as loud as I could.

Instantly the arm across my throat pressed down harder and now I was choking. My ears were full of a roaring sound, my eyes felt as though they were popping out, I couldn't breathe, but I knew I couldn't resist much longer—

There was a yell of surprise, a frantic growling and all at once I was free, gasping for welcome breath, and my assailant was rolling in agony on the floor, flailing and kicking ineffectually at a small dog, whose sharp teeth were fastened firmly in his left buttock.

I couldn't believe my eyes. "Dickon!" I croaked. "How could you! What in the world were you thinking about?"

"Get the bugger off me, damn you, get him off!"

I took my time, pulling down my green dress, wiping my face with the hem, spitting his taste from my mouth. "All right, Growch, let him go. He doesn't deserve it, but thanks anyway. Where were you?"

"Shut me in 'is room. Came out through the winder. E's bin askin' for that 'e 'as! Pretty boy won' be able to sit down for a day or two. Let 'im try showin' that to the ladies! Now if'n I'd got 'im at the front—"

"That's enough, Growch," I said hastily. Standing up, hands on hips, I glared down at Dickon, who was trying to examine his bites, a near-impossible task without a mirror. I was glad to note that all other pretensions had withered into insignificance.

"Now then," I said. "Why? What have I ever said or done to make you think you would be welcome in my bed?"

Dickon rose to his feet, rather unsteadily, but his chin

was jutting out dangerously. "It's rather what you haven't
done! All the time we've been together you've been playing the little virgin, Mistress-Hard-to-Get, and at the
same time you've been giving me those come-hither
looks, little enticements, half-promises—"

I was astounded. After doing my utmost to discourage
anything like that! "You must be mad," I said finally.
"Utterly mad."

"Don't kid me! I've seen you—it's been all I could do
to keep my hands off you! Touching me, making sugges-
tive remarks, all but stripping off and asking for it . . ."
He ranted on, while I tried desperately to remember if
I had ever given him the slightest encouragement, knowing all the while I had not. But the more I heard him,
the more I realized that he truly believed what he was
saying. In some part of his twisted mind his sexual psyche
had convinced him that he was irresistible, so if I didn't
fling myself at him it was my fault, all my refusals merely
stimulating his desire still further.

"Why do you think I kept on going to those brothels?
Because if I hadn't I wouldn't have been able to keep
my hands off you!" His voice was rising, he was on the
verge of hysteria.

"Dickon, I never meant you to believe—"

But he was past listening to anything except his own
twisted logic.

"I worshipped you! I believed that one day, if I waited
long enough, you would come to me, say you loved me,
ask me to be with you while we worked together. That's
why I followed you! Not for any treasure that doesn't
exist: You were my treasure, my unspoilt, virgin bride!"
He was so far out of control by now that his hands were
tearing at the loose robe he wore.

"And then I come back unexpectedly and what do I
find? You in the arms of a stranger as soon as my back
is turned, all decency and decorum forgot! What do you
think I felt, seeing your abandoned behavior? You, whom
I thought above reproach behaving like a strumpet! Why,

you're nothing but a whore, a bloody whore!" Saliva was trickling from the right corner of his mouth, and his eyes were glazed.

It took only a couple of steps and I had slapped him hard on both cheeks.

"Don't you *dare* speak to me like that! You don't deserve an explanation, but I think you'd better know that the man you saw is my betrothed. He is the one I have been seeking all this long time, the 'friend' I told you I sought. My journeyings have all been towards this end and have never, ever, had anything to do with treasure! And now we have found each other again, we are going to spend the rest of our lives together." I paused. He had reeled back when I struck him, and now he was regarding me with a bemused expression on his face. But at least now he looked sane. "Now, isn't it time you apologized?"

"I—I—I . . ."

"I—I—I!" I mocked. "And you are supposed to have the gift of tongues! You'll have to do better than that."

He tried to pull himself together; it was a visible effort. "Of course, I didn't realize . . . but now you've explained . . ." He seemed to draw into himself; his eyes hooded any expression, his lips drew back into a thin line. "I am sorry," he said formally. "I was obviously mistaken. What are your plans now?"

I was surprised by how quickly he was back to normal. "I was going to see you later today if you were back," I said. "Or leave a message with Ky-Lin. But if you like we can talk now."

"Let's get on with it. Tell me." He sat down on the stool, drawing his confidence around him again, like his tattered clothes.

So I told him I was leaving that night with Jasper for another life in another place, where no one could follow us. I explained that I had not forgotten him. He was to have all the moneys I had left (excluding my father's coins, which were to go to the monks) on condition he took a package of letters and my journal and delivered them to Signor Falcone in Venice. This gentleman, I explained, would reward him handsomely for his efforts, but only if the packet was delivered intact.

"You will do as I ask?"

He stood up. "I have no alternative."

"Then I will leave it on my bed, together with my blanket, the cooking things and anything else I don't need. Do with them what you will." I held out my hand. "Thanks for your help. No bad feelings?"

Ignoring my hand he suddenly embraced and kissed me, then as quickly stepped back, so abruptly I nearly fell.

"No bad feelings," he said. "But you can't blame me for trying."

And that was the last I saw of him.

Ky-Lin visited me at midday. He knew without the telling what I was planning to do. He looked at me gravely, asked me once more if I truly knew what I was doing. Of course I reassured him, told him of my happiness, our hopes for the future. He looked so down, not like his usual ebullient self, that I feared he might be ill.

"Ky-Lins are never ill."

"Then what is it, my dear? You don't look at all happy."

"I cannot answer that. Ky-Lins are always supposed to be happy."

"I know—it's because your task is finished, isn't it? You've seen me through, done all you had to do—"

"No. I have not. But I am not allowed to interfere."

"I don't understand. . . ."

He must have seen my distress for he came forward and laid his head against me. I bent and kissed him, stroked his sleek hide.

"I wish you could come with us."

He drew back. "I told you: we do not deal with dragons.

There is a rule. It is like your Waystone; there are laws that repel, others that attract."

Although I didn't understand what he was saying, that reminded me to tell him what I had done with Dickon, and how I had enclosed the Waystone in my package to Signor Falcone, asking him to deliver it to the captain's wife, telling her that the crystal she had given me had been a gift to my betrothed's kin. "Rather neat that, don't you think? After all, it has gone to Jasper's dragon relatives!"

But he didn't smile.

Later he took the pouch into which I had placed my father's coins, promising to deliver the money to the monks. I asked him if he would give Growch a tiny pinch of Sleepy Dust later, to make his flight to the Blue Mountain easier, and this he promised to do around suppertime.

The cloak I shall leave behind. Its color, weave and texture are the same as the cloth of the monks' robes, and now I am sure that the father I never knew once lived here. He probably committed some sin and had to leave; this would explain why the Unicorn's ring would no longer fit him and also why the coins of my "dowry" led me across the world to this place. So it is fitting that it remain here with the coins.

This is the last I shall write. Half an hour ago Ky-Lin left me, having given Growch his "dose." My dear dog is fast asleep on the bed now, snoring gently. I have told him nothing except that we are going on a trip, but have fed him all the things he likes best, in case it is a long journey.

Myself, I cannot eat. Surprisingly, I feel depressed. Perhaps it is something to do with my ring. It had been a part of me for so long that I felt a real sense of loss when it just slipped from my finger when Ky-Lin was here.

At first I couldn't believe it. I just stared at it, then

picked it up between finger and thumb. It was so light, so thin, just a sliver of horn so delicate I could crush it between my fingers.... I tried to put it on again, but somehow it had curled around itself so that now it was too small.

"You have no need of it anymore," said Ky-Lin gently. "It cannot go where you go. Let me take care of it. I shall keep it safe until there is another who needs it."

"But aren't you due to go to your heaven?"

"My task is not finished. You have your future, but others ... There is another who will need me for a while. And afterwards?" He shrugged. "Time is a relative thing."

"Don't talk in riddles! So, where will you keep my— the ring?"

He bent his head. "It will have a home on the horn of my forehead. Like to like."

Again he was being abstruse, but I placed the ring as he had said, and it fitted at once as if it were a part of him.

"And now, good-bye. It has been an interesting time. I shall miss you, girl, but I shall pray for you. Now if you cry like that, you will get my hide all wet, and Ky-Lins don't like the damp...."

It is All Hallows' Eve, not far from midnight, and the moon, a bloodred full moon, has just risen. The piece of paper on which I am writing this I will tuck away into the package at the last moment.

It is strange, writing like this in the present; I have been used for so long to write in the past, catching up on my journal, which I hope will explain to Signor Falcone—and Matthew if he passes it on—exactly what has happened to me. I hope they will understand how all my life for the past two years has led to this moment, how this is the culmination of all my dreams.

How do I feel? Frightened a little, yes, but once Jasper is here all fear will go. The egg is by my side; I have sewn it into the scrap of skin that was once the Wimperling, the outer self of Jasper. Two years ago, to the day, we created this egg; a year earlier I started on this travelling, and now that I was about to lose it I had a sudden flood of maternal feeling for the egg and had to tell myself it was only a stone, even though within it lay hidden a tiny creature that was certainly a part of Jasper and perhaps of me too. But even if I kept it I would never see it hatch . . .

It has been a long, long journey. God keep all those I have loved.

Moonlight floods the room: out with the candle. The light that is the love of Jasper and myself will illuminate the rest of my life.

A last prayer . . .

Away with this. He is here!

EPILOGUE

To the illustrious Signor Falcone: greetings. This by the hand of Brother Boniface of the Abbey of the same name in Normandy.

Sir, I introduce myself as the Infirmar of the Abbey. Recently I took under my care a traveller by the name of Ricardus. When he was admitted to the Infirmary it was obvious he suffered from a low fever, with much coughing and spitting of blood. We kept him close, administered plasters to his chest, doses for the ill humors and bled him, but a practiced eye could see that the Good Lord was the only one who could intervene in a terminal illness.

Alas, this was not to be, our prayers being unavailing, and the Lord moving in mysterious ways.

Two days before the patient died, fortified by the rites of Holy Church, confessed and given the Last Rites, he asked to make a deposition that was to be forwarded to yourself. He had given us the last of his silver for Holy Church and was currently in a State of Grace, so I placed a young novice who writes in the shortened form by his bedside. He took down the words of Ricardus, later transcribing them into proper form, the result of which is here to your hand.

A great deal of what the patient said was not understood, and towards the end he rambled a great deal, but

*the words are his and will doubtless mean more to your-
self, illustrious Signor.*

I am dying: they told me so. They don't mince words,
these monks. All that chanting; reminds me of a monastery where—

To be fair, I asked them, but then I think I knew,
anyway.

I am accursed. . . .

At first, after I delivered Summer's package to you,
and went on with the letter to Master Spicer, everything
was fine. With the moneys you both gave me I set up in
business for myself. For the first ten years I travelled the
Western World and had ample compensation for my out-
lay. And yet . . .

Some years ago I caught a disease in a brothel in
Genoa—God curse it!—which no medicines, poultices or
prayers could assuage. Another infection caused my hair
to fall out and great boils appeared on my body. Then,
to add to all this, I contracted the Great Itch on my arms
and legs and great sores in my groin that caused me
much discomfort. Because of these afflictions I remain
covered at all times, and have had to confine my business
to the colder northern clime where such garb is accepted
all year round.

Yet still did I prosper, enough to buy me those pleasures not readily available to those in my unfortunate
condition, but during the last couple of years, due to
unwise investment in cargoes that foundered, all my fortune has dwindled away, and now I only possess the
silver in my pocket and a certain object which I shall ask
to be forwarded to you. Of that, more later.

I lied to you, you know. When I brought Summer's
journal, fifteen years ago, I made it sound so romantic,
didn't I? And you have probably believed all these years
that she flew off into the sunset with her man-dragon
and lived happily ever after.

But it wasn't like that. That night didn't go as any of

us expected, least of all her. Why didn't I tell you the truth? Because I thought you and Master Spicer would pay more for good news than for bad, that's why.

I fancied her myself, did you know that? When she turned up in that boy's gear, with those long legs and all . . . Respected her, too. All that reading and writing, the way she trained those animals of hers, the ladylike way she spoke. She never paid any attention to the men, either; always kept herself to herself, never flirted. She behaved like a virgin and I treated her like one. I mean, I never really tried it on. Not really. Not until the end, that is, when I saw her with that fellow of hers—

No more now, I'm tired. Leave me a candle. It'll be full dark ere long.

The patient worsened overnight, with much coughing up of blood and loss of breath, and was not well enough to dictate in the forenoon. In the afternoon we were afflicted with sudden gales, which stripped the last of the fruits in the orchard and loosened the roof on the guest house. These strong winds seemed to stimulate the patient, who indicated he wished to continue his deposition, albeit in a more disjointed and rambling way. . . .

Where was I? Oh, yes.

I fancied her, yes, but I doubt I would have left the caravans to follow her unless I was sure she was after treasure. There were the maps, you see—and who was right in the end?

She told me there was nothing, and I know now she believed that, but I thought she was trying to con me, wanted it all for herself. The thought of treasure can do strange things to your mind. . . . *Radix malorum est cupiditas* . . .

She talked your monk tongue, learnt it from an old priest. . . . But you met her, you know what she was like. No, not you, him . . .

God, I'm thirsty, give me wine! Gnat's piss . . .

Of course I didn't know about him then, her pig-man-dragon, did I? How could she prefer a man like that? All dark, with yellow eyes like a wolf! The girls have always said I was handsome, well endowed—still am, and know how to use it too—

Heard them that night, saw them as well. Disgusting, from one I had thought so pure! Tried it on after he'd gone, but she wasn't having any; set the dog on me, she did. Hated that dog!

But I knew what I knew then, didn't I? Knew that what I'd seen wasn't what it seemed. Heard enough to know where to go that night—

Moon was red as blood, bats flying like witches. Alone . . .

For Christ's sake, can't you stop that wind? I'm fucking dying, and I want some peace! Ahhh . . .

The patient being in obvious distress he was dosed heavily with poppy juice till he quieted and enjoyed an uneasy sleep. He continued late that night, when he awoke, although his testimony became increasingly disjointed.

I was there before them, knew where to hide, they didn't see my horse. They came down on the ledge and she had that blasted dog in her arms. One moment he was a dragon—near shit myself—then just the fellow she slept with. Followed 'em down the passage, not too close . . .

Got to the cavern. Hid in the entrance. They walked to the chasm, he said something and the whole place lighted up. Talk about fucking rainbows! There was this light. . . .

Thirsty: any more of that wine? God, how you drink it, I don't know! Now if you were me, travelled all over the world, tasted the wines of— What was that? Bells, bells, bells! Same in that monastery. Bloody monks . . .

The jewels! Never seen anything like those jewels!

Piled up like mountains they were. Forgot to be afraid of the dragons. Gold, too. Enough to buy you and your trading empire out a thousand times. Dazzled . . .

There was a lot of growling and hissing and roaring and from what I had heard last night they were going to try and exchange that obscene thing she called a dragon's egg for him, her fellow, to stay human. Well, she brought it out from behind her back, held it up for them to see, then laid it on the ground together with her sleeping dog. It all went quiet, I tell you!

Then Summer and her boyfriend walked over a kind of bridge and there was a sort of ceremony, lots of spitting and hissing and roaring, and then they started to walk back, with smiles on their faces like they got what they wanted. It was their own fault, I tell you! They stopped in the middle of the bridge and started kissing and cuddling and I couldn't stand it no more!

Couldn't get near the jewels, but if that egg thing was that important, why shouldn't I have a piece of the action? Never meant no real harm, just a bit of a threat; hold it over the chasm, they'd give me enough of the loot to keep me going.

Crept forward, had my hands on the thing, when that bloody dog woke up and started barking—

How was I to know they thought it was a plot? How was I to know they thought she and him was in it too? I didn't mean no harm, honest! No one can say I haven't suffered for it neither. He was trying to shout something and she was clinging to him like ivy when it happened—

Oh, God, Jesu, I can see it, hear it, smell it, now!

I swear I didn't mean to. . . . The fires of Hell, I can feel them now! I'm burning, burning! Christ Jesus, I never meant to hurt her! I loved her, God curse it, I loved her. All right, so I was jealous; that too. But you don't hurt those you love, do you?

What time is it? Time for me to go. Creep into a dark corner, like an animal. Like the bloody dog . . . The rainbow creature came for him afterwards, all bloody and

singed as he was, took him away and healed him. But
you can't heal a mind, can you? She loved them both,
more than she ever cared for me. . . . Hated them!

The fires, the fires! Have you ever smelled singeing
flesh? She screamed, so loud it burst something in my
heart. Couldn't feel anything for anyone after that.

It seemed the top of the world blew off. They were
in the middle of the bridge when it collapsed, he had
her in his arms and the flames came up and caught their
hair. I saw him change man-dragon, dragon-man, so
quick you couldn't blink and he wrapped his wings about
her and then they were gone as though they'd never
been!

That scream . . . she knew it was me. She looked at
me. Just once. Oh, Summer, it wasn't my fault, it wasn't,
I swear it!

Dark, it's dark; why don't you light the candles?

*The patient became delirious, then relapsed into a
coma; he awoke for the last time just before midnight.
He was given wine, but was unable to drink it. He asked
the time, day and date.*

All Hallows' Eve? I might have known it. She had her
revenge after all. Fifteen years . . . Oh, Lord: was it worth
it all?

*Ricardus lapsed again into a coma, the storm returned
to harass us, and then, just before midnight, he woke once
more, sat bolt upright in bed and uttered his last words.*

But I did get something out of it! And now those
dragons can search till Doomsday, God curse them and
curse you all! Do with it what you will—

*This is the testimony the man Ricardus asked us to
forward to you. If you feel so disposed, our messenger
will willingly bring moneys back to us for Masses to be*

said for the deceased's soul, for I fear he did not die in a State of Grace.

In fact any donation towards the upkeep of the Abbey would be most welcome. . . .

I also send with Brother Benedict whatever poor possessions Ricardus carried with him: his few clothes were distributed to the poor, as was his staff and mug and plate. There was, however, a certain object he referred to in his disposition and kept in a pouch around his neck; a round pebble wrapped in hide, and a scrap of paper. Although the object appears to be worthless, no doubt it will prove of sentimental interest to yourself. As you can see, the piece of paper bears the misspelt legend: "This be Dragonnes Eg."

POSTSCRIPT

In the Indian Ocean there is a small island, situated well off the trade routes. It was charted in the eighteen thirties by the Portuguese, who mapped it as Discovery Isle. Many years later the missionaries arrived and once they understood the native language, found that the inhabitants had always called it "Dragon Isle." When questioned, the islanders related the legend that accompanied the name.

There were two points of consistency, otherwise the tale had obviously changed with the years and recollection. The points of agreement were that one day in the distant past a great black dragon, sore wounded, had arrived in the skies from the northeast bearing a burden. It had circled the island three times before alighting somewhere in the hills to the north. The other point of agreement was that the creature eventually left in the same direction, after circling the island in the same fashion.

Between these two "facts," there were two different versions of events. The first had it that the dragon laid waste to the forests of the island till the air was black with the fires, then he buried whatever he carried in a cave high in the mountains before flying away again.

The other version had the dragon again alighting in the hills with his burden and three days later a man and a woman, both badly injured, coming down to dwell among the islanders. This story would have it that the pair recovered and lived for many years at peace, the woman communing with the beasts of the field, the man a master of weather. In the fullness of time the woman died, and the man bore her body up into the hills and buried it, then the great dragon appeared again and flew away, sorrowing. . . .